SHE'S NOT THERE

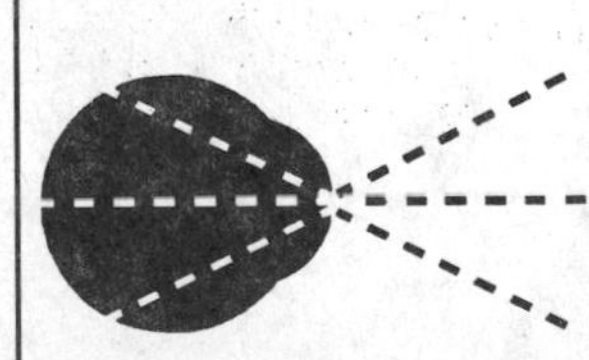

This Large Print Book carries the
Seal of Approval of N.A.V.H.

SHE'S NOT THERE

JOY FIELDING

THORNDIKE PRESS
A part of Gale, Cengage Learning

Farmington Hills, Mich • San Francisco • New York • Waterville, Maine
Meriden, Conn • Mason, Ohio • Chicago

Thorndike Press, a part of Gale, Cengage Learning.

Thorndike Press® Large Print Core
The text of this Large Print edition is unabridged.
Other aspects of the book may vary from the original edition.
Set in 16 pt. Plantin.

LIBRARY OF CONGRESS CATALOGING-IN-PUBLICATION DATA

Names: Fielding, Joy, author.
Title: She's not there / Joy Fielding.
Description: Large print edition. | Waterville, Maine : Thorndike Press, 2016. | © 2016 | Series: Thorndike Press large print Core
Identifiers: LCCN 2016000329 | ISBN 9781410486257 (hardback) | ISBN 1410486257 (hardcover)
Subjects: LCSH: African Americans—Fiction. | Large type books. | BISAC: FICTION / Thrillers. | GSAFD: Suspense fiction.
Classification: LCC PR9199.3.F518 S54 2016 | DDC 813/.54—dc23
LC record available at http://lccn.loc.gov/2016000329

Published in 2016 by arrangement with Ballantine Books, an imprint of Random House, a division of Penguin Random House LLC

Printed in the United States of America
1 2 3 4 5 6 7 20 19 18 17 16

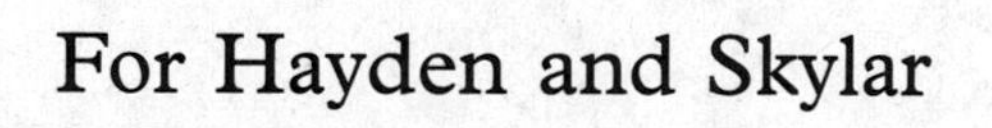
For Hayden and Skylar

ONE: THE PRESENT

It was barely eight A.M. and the phone was already ringing. Caroline could make out the distinctive three-ring chime that signaled a long-distance call even with the bathroom door closed and the shower running. She chose to ignore it, deciding it was probably a telemarketer or the press. Either alternative was odious, but given a choice between the two, Caroline would have opted for the telemarketer. Telemarketers were only after your money. The press wanted your blood.

Even after all this time.

Fifteen years tomorrow.

She buried her head under the shower's hot spray, the lather of her shampoo oozing across her closed eyes and down her cheeks. That couldn't be right. How could fifteen years of seemingly endless days and sleepless nights have passed by so quickly? At the very least, she would have thought public curiosity in her would have waned by now. But if anything, such interest had actually increased with each successive anniversary. Reporters had been calling for weeks, some from as far away as Australia and Japan: What was her life like now? Were there any new leads? Any new men? Another suicide, perhaps? Did she still harbor hopes of seeing her daughter again? Did the police still consider her a suspect in the child's disappearance?

Except Samantha would no longer be a child. Barely two when she'd vanished without a trace from her crib at an upscale Mexican resort while, according to the press, *her parents cavorted with friends at a nearby restaurant,* her daughter would be seventeen now.

Assuming she was still alive.

So, in answer to some of their questions: there were no new leads; she would never give up hope; she no longer gave a hoot what the police thought about her; and her life would be a lot better if the vultures of the press would leave her the hell alone.

Her head bowed, water dripping from her nose and chin, Caroline reached up to turn off the shower taps, satisfied that the phone's intrusive ringing had finally stopped. She understood it was just a temporary respite. Whoever had called would call again. They always did.

Stepping onto the heated white-and-gray marble floor of her bathroom, she wrapped herself in her white terry-cloth bathrobe and swiped at the layer of steam that coated the large mirror above the double sink with the palm of her hand. A forty-six-year-old woman with wet brown hair and tired green eyes stared back at her, a far cry from the "beautiful" and "reserved" young woman "with haunted eyes" that the newspapers had described at the time of Samantha's disappearance, somehow managing to make the words "beautiful" and "reserved" ugly and accusatory. Around the ten-year mark, "beautiful" became "striking" and "reserved" morphed into "remote." And last year, a reporter had demoted her further, referring to her as "a still attractive middle-aged woman." Damning her with faint praise, but damning her nonetheless.

Whatever. She was used to it.

Caroline rubbed her scalp vigorously with a thick white towel, watching her new haircut fall limply around her chin. The hairdresser had promised the bob would result in a more youthful appearance, but he hadn't reckoned on the stubborn fineness of Caroline's hair, which refused to do anything other than just lie there. Caroline took a deep breath, deciding that tomorrow's press clippings would probably describe her as "the *once* attractive mother of missing child Samantha Shipley."

Did it even matter what she looked like? Would she be any less guilty — of neglect, of bad parenting, of *murder* — in the court of public opinion because she was less attractive than she'd been at the time of her daughter's disappearance? Then, she'd been excoriated in the press for everything from the cut of her cheekbones to the shortness of her skirts, from the shine of her shoulder-length hair to the sheen of her lipstick. Even the sincerity of her tears had been called into question, one tabloid commenting that at one press conference, her mascara had remained "curiously undisturbed."

Her husband had received only a tiny fraction of the vitriol that had come Caroline's way. As handsome as Hunter was, there was a blandness about his good looks that made him less of a target. While Caroline's natural shyness had the unfortunate tendency to come across as aloof, Hunter's more outgoing personality had made him seem both accessible and open. He was portrayed as a father "barely holding himself together" while "clinging tight to his older daughter, Michelle, a cherub-cheeked child of five," his wife standing "ramrod straight beside them, separate and apart."

No mention of the fact that it had been at Hunter's insistence that they went out that night, even after the babysitter they'd hired failed to show. No mention of the fact that he'd left Mexico to return to his law practice in San Diego barely a week after Samantha's disappearance. No mention of the proverbial "straw that broke the camel's back," the final betrayal that had doomed their marriage once and for all.

Except that had been her fault, too.

"Everything, my fault," Caroline said to her reflection, withdrawing her hair dryer from the drawer underneath the sink and pointing it at her head like a gun. She flicked the "on" switch, shooting a blast of hot air directly into her ear.

The ringing started almost immediately. It took a second for Caroline to realize it was the phone. One long ring, followed by two shorter ones, indicating another long-distance call. "Go away," she shouted toward her bedroom. Then, "Oh, hell." She turned off the hair dryer and marched into the bedroom, grabbing the phone from the nightstand beside her king-size bed, careful not to so much as glance at the morning newspaper lying atop the crumpled sheets.

"Hello."

Silence, followed by a busy signal.

"Great." She returned the phone to its charger, her eyes pulled inexorably toward the newspaper's front page. There, next to the yearly rehashing of every awful fact and sordid innuendo that had been printed over the last fifteen years, the rewording of every salacious detail — "Adultery!" "Suicide!" "True Confessions!" — was a large photograph of two-year-old Samantha, smiling up at her from beside an artist's sketch of what her daughter might look like today. Similar sketches had been plastered all over the Internet for the past two weeks. Caroline sank to the bed, her legs too weak to sustain her. The phone rang again and she lunged for it, picking it up before it could complete its first ring. "Please. Just leave me alone," she said.

"I take it you've seen the morning paper," the familiar voice said. The voice belonged to Peggy Banack, director of the Marigold Hospice, a twelve-bed facility for the terminally ill in the heart of San Diego. Peggy had been Caroline's best friend for the last thirty years and her only friend for the last fifteen.

"Hard to miss." Again Caroline struggled not to look at the front page.

"Asshole writes the same thing every year. Are you all right?"

Caroline shrugged. "I guess. Where are you?"

"At work."

Of course, Caroline thought. *Where else would Peggy be at eight o'clock on a Monday morning?*

"Listen, I hate to bother you with this," Peggy said, "especially now . . ."

"What is it?"

"I was just wondering . . . Has Michelle left yet?"

"Michelle's at her father's. She's been staying there a lot since the baby . . ." Caroline took a deep breath to keep from gagging. "Was she supposed to work this morning?"

"She's probably on her way."

Caroline nodded, punching in the numbers for Michelle's cell as soon as she said goodbye to Peggy. Surely even someone as headstrong and self-destructive as her daughter wouldn't be foolish enough to skip out on her court-mandated community service.

"Hi, it's Micki," her daughter's voice announced in tones so breathy that Caroline barely recognized her. "Leave a message."

Not even a "please," Caroline thought,

bristling at the nickname "Micki" and wondering if that was the reason her daughter had taken to using it. "Michelle," she said pointedly, "Peggy just called. Apparently you're late for your shift. Where are you?" She hung up the phone, took a deep breath, then called Hunter's landline, determined not to be negative. Maybe her daughter's alarm clock had failed to go off. Maybe her bus was running late. Maybe she was, right this minute, walking through the doors of the hospice.

Or maybe she's sleeping off another late night of partying, intruded the uninvited voice of reality. Maybe she'd had another few too many before getting behind the wheel of her car, ignoring both her recent arrest for driving under the influence and the suspension of her license. Maybe the police had pulled her over, effectively scuttling the deal her father had worked out with the assistant district attorney, a deal that allowed her to avoid jail time in exchange for several hundred hours of community service. "Damn it, Michelle. Can you really be that irresponsible?" Caroline realized only as she spoke that someone was already on the other end of the line.

"Caroline?" her ex-husband asked.

"Hunter," Caroline said in return, his

name teetering uncomfortably on her tongue. "How are you?"

"Okay. You?"

"Hanging in."

"Have you seen the morning paper?"

"Yes."

"Not an easy time of year," he said, always good at stating the obvious.

"No." *Although you seem to be managing rather well,* she thought. A young wife, a two-year-old son, a new baby girl to replace the one he'd lost. "Is Michelle there?"

"I believe she's helping Diana with the baby."

As if on cue, an infant's frantic wails raced toward the receiver. Caroline closed her eyes, trying not to picture this latest addition to Hunter's family. "Peggy called. Michelle's supposed to be at the hospice."

"Really? I thought she was going in this afternoon. Hold on a minute. Micki," Hunter called loudly. "It's probably just a misunderstanding."

"Probably," Caroline repeated without conviction.

"What did you think of the sketch?" Hunter surprised her by asking.

Caroline felt her breath freeze in her lungs, amazed that her former husband could manage to sound so matter-of-fact, as if he was referring to an abstract work of art and not a picture of their missing child. "I — It's —" she stammered, her eyes darting between the photograph and the drawing. "They've given her your jaw."

Hunter made a sound halfway between a laugh and a sigh. "That's funny. Diana said the same thing."

Oh, God, Caroline thought.

"What's up?" Caroline heard Michelle ask her father.

"It's your mother," Hunter said, his voice retreating as he handed Michelle the phone. "Apparently you're supposed to be at the hospice."

"I'm going in this afternoon," Michelle told her mother, the breathy whisper of her voice mail nowhere in evidence.

"You can't just go in whenever you feel like it," Caroline said.

"Really? That's not how it works?"

"Michelle . . ."

"Relax, Mother. I switched shifts with another girl."

"Well, she hasn't shown up."

"She will. Don't worry. Anything else?"

"You should probably call Peggy, let her know . . ."

"Thanks. I'll do that."

"Michelle . . ."

"Yeah?"

"I was thinking, maybe we could go out for dinner tonight . . ."

"Can't. Have plans with my friend Emma."

"Emma?" Caroline repeated, trying to disguise her disappointment. "Have I met her?"

"Only half a dozen times."

"Really? I don't remember . . ."

"That's because you never remember any of my friends."

"That's not true."

"Sure it is. Anyway, gotta go. Talk to you later."

The line went dead in Caroline's hand. She dropped the phone to the bed, watching it disappear amid the rumpled white sheets. "Damn it." Was Michelle right? Her daughter had always had a lot of friends, although none of them seemed to stick around for very long, making it hard to keep track. Something else to feel guilty about.

She checked the clock, noting it was closing in on eight-thirty. She had to be in school in half an hour. She pushed herself to her feet, already exhausted by the thought of twenty-three less-than-eager students slouched behind their desks, glazed eyes staring up at her, their dislike for the subject obvious and unequivocal.

How could they not love math? she wondered. There was something so glorious, so pure, so true, about mathematics. Her father had been a math teacher and had passed his passion for it down to her. It was about more than just solving puzzles and finding solutions. In an irrational world so full of ambiguity, so fraught with happenstance, she'd basked in the absoluteness of it, taken comfort in the fact there was no room for either interpretation or equivocation, that there was always only *one* right answer and its rightness could be *proved.* Another sign, Michelle would undoubtedly argue, and had on more than one occasion, that mathematics bore absolutely no relationship to real life.

Caroline returned to the bathroom and finished drying her hair. Then she put on the navy skirt and white silk blouse she'd laid out the night before. "Don't you have anything else to wear?" Michelle had once asked.

"Don't you?" Caroline had countered, indicating her daughter's standard uniform of skinny jeans and oversized T-shirt. Like many young women of her generation, Michelle was an ardent follower of the latest trends in fashion, fad diets, and exercise regimens. “Everything in moderation” was a concept as foreign to her as algebra.

“Okay,” Caroline said to herself. “Time to get moving.” She was already running late. She said a silent prayer there’d still be a pot of coffee brewing in the staff room. She could tolerate a lot of things, but a day without coffee wasn’t one of them.

The phone started ringing just as she was heading out the door. The first ring was immediately followed by two shorter ones, indicating yet another long-distance call, likely the same person who’d phoned earlier. “Don’t answer it,” Caroline said, this time out loud. But she was already walking toward the kitchen, pulled toward the sound as if by a magnet. She picked the phone up in the middle of its fourth ring. “Hello?”

Silence.

“Hello?”

The sound of breathing.

Great, Caroline thought. *Just what I need — an obscene caller. Long distance, no less.* “I’m going to hang up now,” she announced, lowering the phone.

“Wait.”

She brought the phone back to her ear. “Did you say something?”

Silence.

“Okay. I’m hanging up now.”

"No. Please."

The voice belonged to a young girl, possibly a child. There was an urgency to her voice, something at once strange and familiar that made Caroline stay on the line. "Who is this?"

Another silence.

"Look. I really don't have time for this . . ."

"Is this the home of Caroline Shipley?" the girl asked.

"Yes."

"Are you Caroline Shipley?" she continued.

"Are you a reporter?"

"No."

"Who are you?"

"Are you Caroline Shipley?"

"Yes. Who is this?"

Yet another silence.

"Who is this?" Caroline repeated. "What do you want? I'm hanging up . . ."

"My name is Lili."

Caroline mentally raced through the class lists of all her students, past and present, trying to match a face to the name, but she came up empty. Could this be another one of Michelle's friends she didn't remember? "What can I do for you, Lili?"

"I probably shouldn't be calling . . ."

"What do you want?" Why was she still on the phone, for heaven's sake? Why didn't she just hang up?

"I think . . ."

"Yes?"

"I've been looking at the sketches on the Internet." Lili paused. "You know . . . of your daughter."

Caroline lowered her head. *Here it comes,* she thought. It happened every year at this time. Five years ago, a man had called from Florida, claiming his new neighbor's daughter bore a suspicious resemblance to recent sketches of Samantha. Caroline immediately took off for Miami, missing all three of Michelle's performances in her high school's production of *Oliver!,* only to have her hopes dashed when the man's suspicions proved groundless. The following year a woman reported seeing Samantha waiting in line at a Starbucks in Tacoma, Washington. Another wasted trip followed. And now, with the widespread release of the most recent sketches in the papers, on the Internet . . .

"Lili . . . ," she began.

"That's just it," the girl interrupted as once again Caroline felt her knees go weak and her breath turn to ice in her chest. "I don't think Lili is my name." Another silence. "I think my real name is Samantha. I think I'm your daughter."

Two: Fifteen Years Ago

"Are we there yet?" Michelle whined from the backseat of the late-model white Lexus. She tugged on her seat belt and kicked at Caroline's back.

"Please don't do that, sweetheart," Caroline said, swiveling around in the passenger seat to face her scowling five-year-old. Next to Michelle, Samantha slept peacefully in her toddler seat. And there in a nutshell, Caroline thought, eyes darting between her children, was the difference between her two girls: one daughter a fidgety little mouthful of childish clichés; the other a perfect little Sleeping Beauty. Caroline had always disdained parents who favored one child over another — her own mother being a prime example — but she had to admit that it was occasionally harder than she'd anticipated not to do just that.

"I'm tired of driving."

"I know, sweetheart. We'll be there soon."

"I want some juice."

Caroline glanced toward the driver's seat. Her husband shook his head without taking his eyes off the road. Caroline's shoulders slumped. She understood Hunter didn't want to risk getting juice all over the buttery leather seats of his new car, but she also knew it meant another twenty minutes of pleading and kicking. "We'll be there soon, sweetie. You can have some juice then."

"I want it now."

"Look at the ocean," Hunter said in an effort to distract her. "Look how beautiful —"

"I don't want to look at the ocean. I want some juice." Michelle's voice was getting louder. Caroline knew the child was working her way up to a full-blown tantrum, that it was only a matter of seconds before there would be an eruption of seismic proportions. Again she glanced at Hunter.

"If we give in now . . . ," he whispered.

Caroline let out a deep breath and stared out the side window, knowing he was right and deciding to concentrate on the spectacular, unblemished view of the ocean running alongside the well-maintained toll road. Perhaps Michelle would follow her example.

"I'm thirsty," Michelle said, quickly scuttling that hope. Then a full octave higher, her voice trembling with the threat of tears. "I'm thirsty."

"Hang on, sweetie," Hunter said. "We'll be there soon."

There was Rosarito Beach and the Grand Laguna Resort, a luxury hotel and spa complex that Hunter had selected as the perfect place to celebrate their tenth wedding anniversary. Located between the Pacific Ocean and the foothills of Baja's Gold Coast, Rosarito was only thirty miles south of San Diego, and its proximity to the U.S.-Mexican border made it a popular tourist spot for Southern Californians, providing them with the opportunity to visit a foreign country and experience a different culture without the inconvenience of having to travel very far.

Seventeen miles of stunning ocean road led into the main urban district of Rosarito, a four-mile stretch of beach consisting of condos, gift shops, restaurants, and fabulous resort hotels. They'd selected the Grand Laguna over the others because not only did its website promise romantic settings and breathtaking sunsets but it also boasted of a daily afternoon program for children under the age of ten. The hotel also provided an evening babysitting service, which meant that Caroline and Hunter could have some much-needed time for themselves. Her husband had been increasingly distracted of late, mainly because the law firm in which he'd been hoping to be named partner had recently merged with another firm, throwing his status into limbo. Caroline knew this was another reason that Hunter had been so keen on Rosarito. If work summoned, he could be back at his desk in a matter of hours.

The trip had started out well enough. Samantha had fallen asleep almost as soon as the car was out of the driveway, and Michelle had seemed content playing with her new Wonder Woman doll. Unfortunately, fifteen minutes into the drive, an ill-advised attempt to get the doll to fly had sent Wonder Woman crashing to the floor, where she disappeared under the front seat, unleashing Michelle's first flood of tears. Then heavy traffic along Interstate Highway 5 coupled with a delay at the San Ysidro border crossing at Tijuana had stretched the thirty-mile drive into a ninety-minute ordeal. Caroline wondered if she should have listened to Hunter when he'd suggested leaving the girls at home for the week. But that would have meant entrusting them to her mother, something Caroline would never do. Her mother had made enough of a mess with her own children.

Caroline pictured her brother, Steve, two years her junior, a handsome man with sandy brown hair, a killer smile, and gold-flecked hazel eyes. His easy charm had made him their mother's pride and joy. But what he had in charm, he lacked in ambition, and he'd spent most of his adult life shedding careers as regularly as a snake sheds its skin. A year ago he'd gone into real estate, and much to the surprise of everyone — except, of course, his mother, in whose eyes he could do no wrong — he seemed to be prospering. Maybe he'd finally found his niche.

"I'm thirrrrrsty," Michelle wailed, the word threatening to stretch into eternity.

"Sweetheart, please. You'll wake the baby."

"She's not a baby."

"She's asleep . . ."

"And I'm thirsty."

"Okay, that's enough," Hunter snapped, spinning around in his seat and waving his index finger in the air. "Listen to your mother and stop this nonsense right now."

Michelle's response was immediate and complete hysteria. Her shrieks filled the car, bouncing off the tinted windows and pummeling Samantha awake. Now two children were screaming.

"Still think kids were a good idea?" Hunter asked with a smile. "Maybe your brother is right after all."

Caroline said nothing. Hunter was well aware that her brother and his wife, Becky, had been trying unsuccessfully for years to have a family of their own. Their failure to do so was a constant source of tension between them, a situation Caroline's mother took great pains to exploit, chiding Becky regularly for not providing her with more grandchildren and causing unnecessary friction between her daughter and her daughter-in-law.

Divide and conquer, Caroline thought. Words her mother lived by. What else was new?

"How much longer?" Caroline asked.

"We should be there soon. Hang in there."

Caroline leaned her head against the side window and closed her eyes, her daughters' cries piercing her ears like overlapping sirens. Not exactly an auspicious start to their vacation. *Oh, well,* she decided. *It can only get better.*

They were there, waiting.

At first Caroline thought that she must

have fallen asleep in the few minutes between closing her eyes and their arrival at the magnificent Grand Laguna Resort Hotel, and that she had to be dreaming. But after sitting up straight and lowering her window she realized that what she was seeing was, in fact, very real, that there were indeed six people standing outside the main entrance of the hotel, waving in her direction and laughing, their familiar faces looking pleased and self-satisfied. "What's going on?" she asked Hunter as a valet in a crisp white-and-gold uniform stepped forward to open her car door.

"Welcome to the Grand Laguna," the valet said, his words all but disappearing into the chorus of "Surprise!" that was rushing toward her.

"Happy anniversary," said Hunter, the smile on his lips spreading to his soft brown eyes. He bent forward to kiss her.

"I don't understand."

He kissed her again. "I thought you might enjoy having some family and friends along to celebrate our anniversary."

"Hey, you two," Caroline's brother, Steve, called out. "Get a room, for God's sake."

"Good idea," Hunter said, laughing as he exited the car. He was quickly surrounded by the three waiting men.

"Isn't this the most absolutely beautiful place you've ever seen?" Steve's wife, Becky, asked, rushing forward.

Caroline pushed herself out of the car's front seat, taking a quick look at the ten-story coral-colored horseshoe-shaped building framed by blue skies and palm trees. She had to admit it was every bit as magnificent as she'd been led to expect.

"You're looking a little overwhelmed," her friend Peggy whispered, coming up beside her and drawing her into an embrace, her curly brown hair tickling the side of Caroline's nose. At approximately five feet six inches and one hundred and twenty-five pounds, the two women were almost the same height and weight and fit together comfortably.

"I'm flabbergasted." Caroline turned toward her husband. "How did you manage this?"

"Blame your brother. It was his idea."

"Couldn't very well let you celebrate ten years of wedded bliss without us," Steve said with a laugh.

Caroline looked from one smiling face to the next: her brother and his wife; old friends Peggy and Fletcher Banack; new friends Jerrod and Rain Bolton. The truth was she'd been looking forward to having her husband all to herself for the week. It had been a long time since they'd had the luxury of intimate dinners for two, time to kick back and relax, to reconnect with each other. But the welcoming committee's collective delight was as contagious as it was obvious, and Caroline's ambivalence quickly melted away.

"Mommy! Mommy! Get me out of here."

"Coming, sweetheart."

"Allow me." Peggy opened the back door and lifted Michelle out of the car. "Whoa. You're getting to be such a big girl."

"I want some juice," Michelle said.

Becky had already scooted around to the other side of the car and removed Samantha from her car seat, and was cradling the two-year-old in her arms while smothering the top of her head with kisses. "Hi, there, beautiful girl. How's my little angel?"

"She's not beautiful and she's not an angel," Michelle protested.

Samantha stretched her arms toward her mother.

"Oh, can't your auntie hold you for a few minutes?" Reluctantly, Becky handed Samantha over to her mother, then stepped back, tucking her short dark hair behind her ears. Caroline thought she looked tired behind her smile, and wondered if she and

Steve had been fighting again.

"What took you so long?" Rain asked as the valet removed the luggage from the trunk. "We've been waiting over an hour. I'm positively melting in this heat."

"Well, melting or not, you look great."

Rain smiled, a wide smile that revealed just the right number of perfect teeth, and tossed her wavy honey-blond hair over the left shoulder of her floral print caftan. Her eyes were blue, her lipstick red, her bare arms tanned and toned. A former model, she would have been beautiful even without the ton of makeup she always wore. Caroline marveled, not for the first time, that Rain had chosen a man as mousy as Jerrod for a mate. Shorter than his wife by several inches and looking a decade older than his forty years, Jerrod was as nondescript as Rain was striking. They made an interesting couple.

The group approached the tall glass doors that opened into the flower-filled, air-conditioned lobby. Samantha was happily ensconced in her mother's arms while Michelle was glued to her right thigh, pulling down so hard on her white blouse that Caroline feared she might rip it. "Did you all drive down together?" she asked.

"Steve and Becky came in their car,"

Peggy explained. "We drove down with Rain and Jerrod."

"Is your name Rain?" Michelle asked.

Rain laughed, shaking her blond mane. "It is. My mother was very dramatic. And probably more than a little depressed, if you think about it."

"I think it's a silly name," Michelle said.

"Michelle," Caroline cautioned as they approached the front desk. "Don't be rude."

"I have to pee," the child announced.

"Shit," said Hunter.

"Mommy," Michelle said, "Daddy said a bad word."

Caroline's eyes drifted across the lobby's Spanish-style decor toward the courtyard situated between the two huge wings of the hotel.

"Wait till you see this place. There's an enormous pool and the most gorgeous garden restaurant. Plus a kiddie pool, and of course, the ocean . . ." Becky waved her hands in its general direction.

"And the rooms are so beautiful," Peggy added.

"Are we all on the same floor?"

Rain scoffed. "Not even the same wing. You guys are on this side." She pointed to her right. "The rest of us are all the way over there." She spun to her left.

"Mommy, I have to pee."

"I know, sweetie. Can you hold it for a few more minutes?"

"Don't forget to sign Michelle up for the kids' club," Steve said pointedly.

"What's a kids' club?" Michelle asked.

"Oh, you're gonna have such a good time," Becky enthused. "Every afternoon you do arts and crafts or search for buried treasure or go hunting for crabs . . ."

"I don't want to hunt for crabs."

"Well, then, you can swim or build sand castles or play games with the other kids."

"I don't want to play with other kids. I want to play with Mommy."

"Don't worry, sweetheart," Caroline said. "We'll have lots of time to play."

"Is Samantha going to the kids' club?" Michelle asked.

"No, sweetheart. She's too little."

"She's not little. She's big."

"We'll talk about it later," Hunter said as the receptionist handed him the keycards to their room.

"Suite 612," the young woman said, dark eyes sparkling.

"Oh, you have a suite," Becky said, a hint of envy in her voice. "Can't wait to see it."

"Thanks for making the rest of us look bad," Fletcher joked to Hunter as everyone crowded into the waiting elevator.

"There's too many people in here," Michelle complained loudly.

Caroline couldn't help smiling. She'd been thinking the same thing.

The theme from *Star Wars* escaped from someone's pocket to fill the small space.

"You've got to be kidding me," Becky said, rolling her eyes toward the ceiling as Steve extricated his cell phone from his jeans. "Again?"

"Hello, Mother," Steve said, holding the phone to his ear with one hand while lifting his other hand into the air, as if to say, *What can I do?*

"She just called an hour ago," Becky announced to the group.

"Yes, they just got here. Did you want to speak to Caroline? No? Okay. Yeah, I'm sure she'll call you later." He looked to Caroline for confirmation. Caroline shot him a look that said, *Thanks a lot.* "What? Yes, I know it's dangerous. Believe me, I have no intention of parasailing."

"Bless her little black heart," Becky said. "The woman never stops."

"No. Not interested in horseback riding on the beach either. You never know what those horses have been drinking. No, I'm not making fun of you. I totally understand your concern. Yeah, okay. Talk to you later. Love you, too. Bye." Steve returned the phone to his pocket. "What can I tell you?" he said with a laugh. "She's just looking out for her little boy."

"Does Grandma Mary have a black heart?" Michelle asked.

"No, darling," Caroline said. "Of course not."

"We'll have to wait for the autopsy to find out for sure," Hunter said.

"You must be kidding," Becky scoffed. "She'll outlive us all."

"Nice talk, you guys," Steve said. "This is Caroline's and my mother you're talking about. Show a little respect."

Becky's snort of derision filled the small elevator.

"Not exactly what I had in mind," he said.

"Sixth floor," Fletcher announced, to Caroline's great relief. "Everybody out."

"So, what do you think?" Hunter asked Caroline after everyone had finally cleared out of their two-bedroom suite.

Holding Samantha in her arms, Caroline cut across the brightly furnished living room to the window overlooking the courtyard and stared down at the garden restaurant directly below. Bright red umbrellas shaded tables covered with white linen. Flowering coral and white shrubs grew at appropriate intervals. An enormous amoeba-shaped pool was situated off to one side, surrounded by red-and-white-striped lounge chairs. Everything was literally a stone's throw away. The world at her fingertips, Caroline thought, turning back toward her husband, taking in the room's bright yellow walls, the red velvet sofa and red-and-gold wing chair. "It's beautiful. Everything. You did good." She walked around the dark wood coffee table into his waiting embrace.

"Were you really surprised or were you just pretending?"

"Are you kidding? I was absolutely shocked."

"Yeah? Well, I just might have a few more surprises up my sleeve, Mrs. Shipley." He nibbled the side of her ear.

"Mommy," Michelle called from the bathroom. "Mommy, I'm finished. Come wipe me."

Caroline lowered her head to his shoulder.

"Isn't she old enough to do that herself?" Hunter asked as Caroline handed Samantha over to him and walked toward the bathroom.

"So, what do you think?" Caroline asked her daughter, repeating the question Hunter had asked her just minutes ago, as she led Michelle into the child's yellow-and-white bedroom. A twin-size bed, covered with a bright red, white, and gold print quilt, was positioned against one wall. A crib, covered with an identical but smaller quilt had been wedged against the opposite wall, a window between the two.

"I don't like it."

Why am I not surprised? Caroline wondered. "What don't you like, sweetie?"

"I want my own room."

"Come on. It'll be fun sharing a room with your sister."

"I want to sleep in your room."

The phone rang. *Thank God,* Caroline thought, grateful for the interruption. Even talking to her mother would be better than this.

"That was Rain," Hunter said, popping his head into the room seconds later. "She made reservations in the garden restaurant for eight o'clock tonight."

"Assuming we can get a sitter."

"Already taken care of."

Caroline looked from the smiling toddler in her husband's arms to the pouting youngster at her side, then back at Hunter. "My hero," she said.

THREE: THE PRESENT

I think my real name is Samantha. I think I'm your daughter.

The words slammed against the side of Caroline's head, like a hammer. She felt her brain wobble, warm syrupy fluid leaking into the space behind her eyes, the pressure building until it could no longer be contained and it spilled down her cheeks in the form of tears. "This isn't funny," she whispered into the phone, her whole body starting to shake. "You shouldn't do this."

"I'm really sorry," said the girl on the other end of the line. "I know how this must sound."

Caroline tightened her grip on the phone, as if by doing so she could keep from falling over. "You have no idea how this sounds."

"I guess it seems pretty crazy."

"It's far from pretty and far worse than crazy," said Caroline, amazed at the sound of her own voice, that she was able to form coherent sentences. "It's mean. And it's cruel."

"I'm sorry. That wasn't my intention."

"What *is* your intention?"

"I don't know. I'm not sure. I just thought . . ."

"You didn't think." Caroline was angry now. How dare this girl, this stranger, this *Lili,* lay claim to her daughter's name, to her identity?

"I saw the pictures. I wasn't sure what to do."

"Who the hell are you?"

"I told you."

"You're a reporter, aren't you?"

"No. I swear."

"Then why are you doing this?"

"Because I think . . ."

"You think you're my daughter?"

"Yes."

"Because you look like some sketches on the Internet," Caroline said, her voice flatlining, as if her vocal cords had been run over by an eighteen-wheeler.

"Partly."

"Partly?" Caroline repeated.

"It's more than that."

"What more?"

"Just . . . a whole bunch of things."

"What things?"

A slight pause. "Well, for starters, we're the same age."

A scoff of derision. "Lots of girls are seventeen. What's your birthday?"

"Supposedly August twelfth."

"Samantha was born in October."

"I know, but . . ."

"But what?"

"Can't birth certificates be faked?"

"You think someone faked your birth certificate?"

"Maybe. I mean, it's possible."

"Possible, but unlikely. What else have you got?"

Another pause, longer this time. "We moved around a lot, when I was little."

"So?"

"From one city to another, one country to another," the girl continued, despite Caroline's growing impatience. "We were always packing up and leaving. We never stayed in one place very long."

"Who's 'we'?"

"My parents and my brothers."

"So you have parents."

"My father died last year."

"But your mother is still alive?"

"Yes."

"Were you adopted?"

"She says I wasn't."

"You don't believe her?"
"No."
"Why not? Have you stumbled across some documents hidden in the attic? Has anyone else in the family ever hinted that you may have been adopted?"
"No."
"Then why do you think you were?" Caroline asked in an effort to avoid asking herself more pertinent questions, namely, Why was she still on the line? Why was she still talking to this girl, this *Lili,* who was delusional at best, deranged at worst. Why didn't she just hang up?
"I don't look anything like either my brothers or my parents."
"Lots of kids don't look like their parents or siblings."
"It's not just that."
"What else is it?"
"I was homeschooled, kept away from other kids."
"Lots of kids are homeschooled these days. It doesn't suggest anything sinister. And it makes sense in your case, if you moved as often as you claim."
"It's just that I'm so different from the rest of them. Not just how I look, but what I'm like, what I'm good at, how I feel about . . . I don't know . . . *everything.* It's

like they're on one planet and I'm on another. I've just never felt I belonged."

Caroline almost laughed. She leaned against the kitchen counter, rubbed the bridge of her nose with her free hand. "You *do* realize you're describing almost every teenager in America."

"I guess."

"What does your mother have to say?"

"About what?"

"About *what*?" Caroline repeated, incredulously. "About everything you've just told me." There was a moment's silence. It hovered, like an axe, above Caroline's head. "She doesn't know, does she?"

A long silence.

Of course the girl hadn't confronted her mother with her suspicions. Or her plans to call Caroline. The whole idea was so ill-conceived, so far-fetched, so ludicrous.

And yet, so appealing, so comforting, so wonderful.

Her daughter. Alive. On the phone. After all these years.

Was it possible? Could it be possible?

No, it couldn't. Even asking the question made her as delusional as the girl on the other end of the line.

"Look," Caroline said forcefully, "I have to go. I'm already late for work."

"No. Please don't hang up."

"Look, *Lili,*" she said, trying to keep her emotions in check, her voice as gentle as possible. "I'm going to give you the benefit of the doubt here. I'm going to assume you're just a very sensitive, lonely young lady who misses her father very much and is having trouble processing his death. Your imagination is in overdrive. But let's look at this realistically. Just because you look more like a few sketches on the Internet than you do your family doesn't mean . . ."

"We never had computers in the house," the girl interrupted.

"I don't understand. What's that got to do with anything?" Caroline asked, although she did find it strange. Who didn't have a computer in their home these days, especially if they were homeschooling their kids? "I'm sure your parents had their reasons . . ."

"They said they weren't going to be one of those families who let technology rule their lives, that kids spend too much time on Facebook and looking at pornography . . ."

"Well, there you go. Wait," Caroline said, pouncing on a perceived inconsistency as deftly as an early bird spearing a worm. "You told me before that you saw the sketches on the Internet. If you don't have a computer . . ."

"I was at the library," Lili explained easily. "This boy kept staring at me. He said I looked just like this girl who disappeared fifteen years ago. He's the one who showed me the pictures."

"They're artist's renderings, not photographs. They're just projections, based on things like bone structure and shape of the eyes. No one knows how accurate they actually are. Look. It doesn't matter. What matters is that you're not my daughter."

"How can you be sure?"

Caroline said nothing. *Hang up,* she told herself. *Hang up now.*

"What if I take a DNA test?" the girl asked.

"What?"

"What if I take a DNA test?" she asked again.

"A DNA test," Caroline repeated when she could think of nothing else to say.

"That way we'd know for certain one way or the other, wouldn't we?"

Caroline nodded, although she said nothing. In her fantasies, Samantha simply showed up on her doorstep and fell into her waiting arms. There was an instant, instinctive connection. None of her imaginings had ever involved anything as clinical as DNA testing.

"So how would I go about getting tested?"

"I have no idea." Caroline was reeling, her brain trapped inside a thick fog, unable to connect words or form cohesive thoughts. "I guess you'd have to contact the proper authorities," she was finally able to spit out.

"Who are they?"

"I'm not sure. Probably the San Diego Police Department would be a good place to start."

"I don't live in San Diego."

Caroline remembered the distinctive long-distance ring that had stopped her as she was heading for the front door. She should never have gone back, never have picked up the phone. "Where *do* you live?"

A sigh of hesitation. "I'd rather not say."

Another sigh, this one Caroline's. Of course the girl would rather not say. "Good-bye, Lili."

"I live in Calgary."

"Calgary?"

"Calgary, Alberta."

"You're Canadian?"

"No. I told you. We moved around a lot. We've been here for about two years. Before that, we lived in Seattle and before that, Madison, Wisconsin. I spent most of my childhood in Europe. We came here just before my father got sick."

"And you'd be willing to come to San Diego?"

"I would, but I can't. I don't have any money . . ."

"Uh-huh," Caroline said. The fog in her brain was starting to dissipate. "Now I understand. You want me to send you money . . ." *I'm such a fool,* she thought.

"No. No. I don't want your money."

"What *do* you want? Do you want me to send you a plane ticket? I can do that," Caroline pressed, feeling a sudden surge of control. She was calling the girl's bluff, what she should have done in the first place. "I'll just need to know your last name so I can make the reservation."

"I can't tell you that."

"Really? Why not?"

"Because it's not important. What difference does it make? I already told you I can't come there."

"I tell you what. I'll even get a ticket for your mom. She can come with you."

"No. My mom can't know about this."

"I thought you thought *I* was your mother."

"I did. I *do.* Oh, God, I don't know what to think anymore." A pause filled with the threat of tears. "Look. Even if she's not my real mother, she's the one who raised me. I don't want to hurt her, and I can't just take off without telling her. She'd go crazy with worry."

Caroline closed her eyes, remembering the panic of that awful night fifteen years ago when she peered into Samantha's crib and found it empty. Fresh horror pricked her skin like hundreds of tiny needles, poisoning her bloodstream and racing toward her heart. She felt dizzy, faint, as if she might throw up. "So, it would appear we're at an impasse," she said when she could find her voice.

"Maybe you could come here."

"What?"

"Come to Calgary. We could go to a hospital or a clinic, find someone to do the test. That way we'd know for sure."

"I know *now,*" Caroline said. Did she? If she was so damn sure this girl wasn't her daughter, why was she still on the line? "All right. Listen. You've given me a lot to digest. Let me think it over and get back to you."

"No."

"What?"

"I can't give you my phone number. You can't call me."

Caroline's anger resurfaced. What was the

matter with her? She'd been dealing with this kind of crap for fifteen years, some of it well-meaning and sincere, most of it mean-spirited or downright hateful. This was either a clever scam or a sick joke. A ploy for money or a plea for attention. Most likely just another bloodsucking journalist seeking to exploit her vulnerability, her gullibility, to put a fresh twist on an old tale, gather whatever new information might be available, perhaps even extract a confession. She'd probably read all about this phone call in tomorrow's papers. "Look, Lili, or whatever the hell your name really is . . ."

"Come to Calgary."

"No."

"Please. I've already checked and there's a flight that leaves San Diego for Calgary first thing tomorrow morning. You'd be here by noon. I could meet you at your hotel."

"What hotel?" Caroline asked. What was she saying? Was she crazy? How many times could she put herself through this? Hadn't she already made ill-advised trips to Miami and Washington, only to watch her hopes turn to disappointment and ultimately despair? Was she really prepared to go through it all again?

"The Fairfax. It's right downtown, and it's pretty nice."

"No, I can't. It's too ridiculous."

"It isn't."

"This whole conversation is ridiculous. You're ridiculous. *I'm* ridiculous for sitting here talking to some girl who's either a champion con artist or a total whack job. I'm sorry. I have to hang up."

"Please . . . you said you'd think about it."

Caroline stared at the wall of cupboards across from her, watching them blur together, separate, then come together again. She couldn't seriously be thinking of going to Calgary. Could she? "All right," she heard herself say.

"You'll come?"

"I'll think about it."

"I'll be waiting in the lobby," the girl said, and then the line went dead.

FOUR:
FIFTEEN YEARS AGO

"Well, look who's here," Rain said as Caroline maneuvered her way through the rows of chaise longues that twisted around the hotel's sprawling outdoor pool.

"You made it," Peggy said, patting the empty chair beside her.

Becky nodded in her direction but said nothing. Even though the floppy hat and oversized dark glasses hid most of her sister-in-law's face, Caroline could tell Becky had been crying. She'd seen enough of this face over the years to recognize the puffiness in her cheeks, the downward twist of her mouth that overrode her attempts to smile.

Clearly her brother and his wife had been fighting. Again. Caroline wondered what the fight was about this time, then pushed the thought out of her mind. Whatever it was, it was none of her business. And she was determined to enjoy her last day in paradise. Hunter had generously volunteered to look after Samantha so she could spend a few hours at the pool with her friends, unencumbered; Michelle had finally embraced kids' camp, or at least had gone off this afternoon without the usual barrage of tears and protestations; she and Hunter had finally made love last night, albeit hurriedly and with a minimum of foreplay, before he'd passed out from too much sun and liquor.

Caroline looked toward the balcony of her suite as she removed her white lace cover-up, then lay back in her chair. She'd been hoping this holiday would reawaken the easy passion she and Hunter had once shared. But Hunter was preoccupied with work; she was preoccupied with the children; their friends were always around. The reality was that she and Hunter had spent very little time alone together this week. Not exactly the romantic getaway she'd been hoping for.

"Ooh, interesting bathing suit you have on," Rain said, adjusting the top of the tiny hot-pink bikini she was spilling out of. "Very retro."

Caroline glanced down at her black-and-white one-piece swimsuit and smiled. She didn't know Rain all that well, so she was never quite sure how to take such compliments: *Love that just-got-out-of-bed look you've got going on with your hair. Look at you with those wide pants — so brave of you to buck the trends. Wish I could wear such a big print — you flat-chested girls have it so easy.* She looked around the crowded pool. "Where are the guys?"

"Golf," Rain said.

"One of the few activities your mother deemed safe enough for her precious son," Becky said, then looked away, so as not to invite comment.

You can't let her get to you, Caroline wanted to tell her sister-in-law, but stopped when she realized she'd been telling her that for years. Telling *herself* that ever since she could remember. But it was a losing battle. Her mother was a force of nature. There was no getting away.

"Excuse me," Rain called, beckoning a young, dark-haired waiter toward them. "Who wants a gin and tonic?" she asked the others.

"Sounds good," Peggy said.

"Count me in," Becky agreed.

"I'll have a Coke," Caroline said.

"You will absolutely *not* have a Coke," Rain said. "It's our last day. I forbid it. Four gin and tonics, *por favor.* This one's on me, ladies."

Minutes later, they were leaning back in

their chairs, sipping their drinks. "So, what's everyone up to when we return to civilization?" Rain asked.

"Back to work," Peggy said. Peggy worked at San Diego General Hospital.

"Don't know how you do it," Rain said. "Dealing with sick people all day. Doesn't it get to you?"

"Well, I don't actually deal with patients. I'm in administration."

"What about you?" Rain asked, swiveling toward Becky. "Ready to resume the job hunt?"

Caroline held her breath as Becky's shoulders stiffened. Steve had let slip that Becky had recently been fired from her job as an accounts manager for a local ad agency after a major client bolted to the competition, a fact that Becky had been hoping to keep under wraps until she found a new position. Of course, Caroline already knew about it; her mother had called with the news as soon as Steve confided it.

"This might be a good time to concentrate on getting pregnant," Mary had told her daughter-in-law, as if the reason she and Steve hadn't conceived was Becky's lack of concentration.

"At least you don't have to worry about money," Rain said. "Jerrod tells me that

Steve is doing *verrrry* well these days."

"We're managing," Becky said. She downed what was left in her glass and signaled the waiter for a refill. "Who's joining me?"

"I'm game," Rain said.

"What the hell. Why not?" Peggy agreed.

"Only if it's my turn to treat," Caroline said, still nursing the drink in her hand. She'd never been much of a drinker, especially in the afternoon. Still, it was their last day in Rosarito, for once she didn't have a child hanging on her arm or a baby balanced on her hip, and she didn't want to be perceived as a stick-in-the-mud. She was still one of the girls. She still knew how to have fun.

She was more than just a mother.

"I guess it's just more of the same for you," Rain said to Caroline, as if she'd sneaked a peek into her brain.

"Sorry? More of the same?"

"Staying home, looking after two little kids. I'd go crazy with the lack of adult stimulation. It must turn your brain to mush. I think you're amazing. I really do."

Caroline tried not to bristle at the subtle insult embedded in the compliment or at having to defend her decision to be a stay-at-home mom. "It's only for a few more years. Then I'll go back to teaching."

"Another job I could never do. Especially math. It's so boring."

"I don't find it boring at all . . ."

"Really?" asked Rain, eyes wide with wonder.

"I guess everything must seem pretty dull when you compare it to modeling," Peggy said, as the waiter returned with a fresh round of drinks. "Jerrod says you're still in a fair bit of demand . . ."

"More than a fair bit. And I'm offered way more jobs than I'm able to accept because of all my charity work. Plus Jerrod travels so much, and he likes me to go with him, so I'm limited in what projects I can take on." She leaned in, motioning with her hands for the others to do the same, as if she were about to impart a great secret. "We made a pact when we got married that we'd never spend more than two nights apart. That's what put the kibosh on Jerrod's first marriage, you know. Made him especially vulnerable to women like me." She gave a smile that could only be described as dazzling. "My husband has an insatiable libido, and I'm happy to say he's finally met his match." She tossed her head back, her honey-blond hair cascading halfway down her back, then held that position, as if waiting for a photographer to snap her picture.

"I didn't realize he had to travel that much," Caroline said, although what she really wanted to say was "Oh, God, no. Please let's not talk about that." She didn't want to discuss Rain's sex life or her role in the dissolution of Jerrod's previous marriage. She didn't know much about either Rain or Jerrod other than that Jerrod was the lead director of a major mining corporation, and he and Hunter had become friendly when Hunter's firm was hired to handle a recent acquisition. Rain was fun to be around, in large part because you never knew what outrageous thing she was going to say next, but she and Rain would never be bosom buddies. In Hunter's words, "a little of her went a long way."

"Every month we're off somewhere new and exciting," Rain was saying. "Alaska, Vancouver, South America. Visiting mines. Meeting with local dignitaries. These last five years have been quite the adventure."

"No time for kids, I guess," Peggy said.

"God, no. Besides, Jerrod already has three with his first wife. That's more than enough." She made a face. "I don't know. Children have never been my thing. They're just so . . ."

"Boring?" asked Caroline.

Rain laughed. “Kind of like math.”

“I don’t think children are boring,” Peggy said.

“That’s because you have them. You *have* to feel that way. But we know the truth, don’t we, Becky?”

Once again Caroline found herself holding her breath, understanding that Rain likely knew nothing of Becky’s situation. The two women had met only a week ago and Becky wasn’t in the habit of discussing her fertility problems with relative strangers. Or with anyone, for that matter.

Caroline looked toward her sister-in-law, who acknowledged her glance with a roll of her eyes before turning away. They’d been close once, more like sisters than sisters-in-law. But Becky, fueled by her mother-in-law’s constant comparisons, had grown increasingly distant over the years, more so after Samantha’s birth. She’d tried to hide it, but it was pretty obvious she regarded Caroline’s fecundity as something of a personal affront.

Caroline took another sip of her drink, leaned back in her chaise, and closed her eyes. She was exhausted. Who knew that relaxing could be such hard work?

“Time for more sunscreen,” a voice said. “Your nose is getting burned.”

Caroline opened her eyes to see Peggy's face looming above hers. "What?"

"You're getting a bit red."

Caroline bolted upright, knocking her canvas bag off her chair, its contents spilling onto the concrete. "I must have fallen asleep. What time is it?"

"Five after four."

"Shit. I was supposed to pick up Michelle at four." She scrambled to retrieve the items that had escaped her bag, then pushed herself to her feet. "Where is everyone?" she asked, looking around.

"Becky had a headache, so she went back to her room about half an hour ago. Rain had an appointment for a massage."

"Well, I hate to leave you here alone . . ."

"No problem. I've had enough lounging. Time to go upstairs and take a nap." Peggy slipped her hand through Caroline's and together they headed for the lobby.

"I can't believe I passed out like that. Did I miss anything?"

"You mean with Little Miss Met-His-Match? No, thankfully she spared us further details. For a minute I thought we were back in high school."

The two women laughed. Caroline was still chuckling when she picked up Michelle.

"You're late," the child cried, causing the

chuckle to die in Caroline's throat.

The raven-haired young woman holding Michelle's hand shot Caroline an accusing glance. "See? I told you your mommy didn't forget about you."

Caroline checked her watch. "It's only a few minutes . . ."

"Michelle was getting quite anxious."

"I would never forget about you," Caroline assured her daughter repeatedly on the elevator ride back to their room.

"I'm not going to kids' camp anymore," Michelle said as they walked down the long hall toward their suite.

"Well, we're leaving first thing in the morning, so you don't have to." Caroline fumbled in her canvas tote for her keycard, almost walking into a service cart loaded with towels and linen. "Shit. Where is it?"

"You said a bad word."

The damn thing must have fallen out at the pool, Caroline thought as they approached their suite, then waited for Hunter to answer her knock on the door. "What — again?" she could almost hear him say. She'd already lost one keycard, earlier in the week. Good thing they were so easy to replace. She knocked again. "Hunter?" She rested her ear against the door, heard the shower running. "Great. Perfect time for a shower."

Hunter was notorious for both the frequency and the length of his showers. "Looks like we'll have to go back to the lobby and get another card."

"I don't want to go back to the lobby."

Caroline remembered the service cart. Probably the housekeeper had a master keycard. "Come with me," she said to Michelle.

"No." The child pulled her hand out of Caroline's reach, then sank to the floor, her back against the door, her arms crossed in protest.

"Okay, then. Don't move. I'll be right back." She raced around the corner, almost colliding with the uniformed woman coming out of an adjacent room, her hands full of towels. "*Perdóname, dama.* I'm sorry to bother you but I can't find my keycard. I was wondering if you could let me into my room."

The woman nodded, dropped the towels onto the cart and followed Caroline around the corner.

Michelle was gone.

"Michelle?" Caroline looked around frantically. "Michelle?"

The door to her suite opened. Hunter stood before her, a large white towel wrapped around his hips, water clinging to his chiseled chest, a bemused look in his eyes. "Relax. She's inside."

Caroline breathed a sigh of relief. The housekeeper tucked her master keycard back into her pocket and retreated down the hall. "Thank you," Caroline called after her.

"Mommy said a bad word. And she was late," Michelle announced as soon as Caroline stepped inside the living room.

"By all of five minutes," Caroline explained.

"I'm sure Mommy's very sorry."

"And Mommy has apologized repeatedly," Caroline said. "Where's the baby?"

"She's not a baby," Michelle said.

"In her crib, playing with her toys," Hunter said. "Happy as a clam."

"We went hunting for clams," Michelle said as Caroline crossed into the children's bedroom.

"Did you? That sounds like fun."

"I hate clams," Michelle said.

Of course you do, Caroline thought, approaching Samantha's crib. Her younger daughter was already standing up, a huge grin on her sweet face, her arms extended in welcome. Caroline lifted her out of her crib, hugged her tight. "Hi, my sweet thing."

"She's not a sweet thing. *I'm* your sweet thing."

"You're *both* my sweet things."

Samantha leaned her head against Caroline's shoulder, her breath soft against her mother's neck. *At least I got one good one,* Caroline recalled her mother saying to one of her friends, the words still having the power to wound after all these years. Not that her mother had been abusive or neglectful. If anything, she'd been overprotective, hovering over her daughter like a circling wasp, watching her like the proverbial hawk. Unlike Steve, who was granted freedoms Caroline could only dream of. But while she had her mother's attention, it was Steve who had her affection, and both children knew it, ensuring that they would never be close. Caroline had made a silent vow that she would never be anything like her mother. She wouldn't be overprotective. She wouldn't be judgmental. She would never show favoritism.

As if to prove her point, she leaned over to ruffle Michelle's hair. "I love you," she told her.

"I don't love *you,*" said Michelle, squirming out of her mother's reach and running from the room.

"Well, that's too bad, because I love *you,*" Caroline called after her.

"What's too bad?" Hunter asked from the

doorway.

Caroline lowered Samantha to the floor, then walked into his waiting arms. "I'm a terrible mother."

He laughed and pulled her closer, the dampness of his bare chest permeating her white lace cover-up. "Next time we leave the kids at home."

At eight o'clock, their sitter still hadn't arrived.

"Where is she?" Caroline asked. "She's been so prompt all week."

"Relax. She's probably in the elevator as we speak."

Caroline stepped onto the balcony and stared down at the garden restaurant below. Almost all the tables were occupied. Colored lanterns flickered from overhead wires. Soft music played. A slight breeze stirred. Samantha and Michelle were both asleep. It was shaping up to be a perfect evening for this, their last night in paradise.

Except the sitter was late.

"Are the others there yet?" Hunter asked, coming up behind her, his arms snaking around her waist.

"I don't see them. Oh, wait. There's Rain."

"What on earth is she wearing?"

"You mean, what *isn't* she wearing?" Caroline corrected. "I think she forgot her top. Did you know her husband is quite the stud?"

"Really? She told you that?"

"I believe *insatiable* was the word she used."

Hunter made a face. "Hard to picture."

"Let's not," Caroline said, as Jerrod suddenly appeared beside his wife, the two of them looking up and waving. Caroline waved back, felt Hunter do the same. "Maybe we should call the front desk, find out what's up." She stayed on the balcony, watching Steve and Becky join Jerrod and Rain as Hunter went back to the living room to phone. "Well?" she asked upon his return.

"She's not coming."

"What do you mean, she's not coming?"

"Apparently we canceled."

"What? What are you talking about? We did no such thing."

"I told them that. But that's what their records indicate. They're trying to find us someone else."

"How long will that take?"

"They said it should only be a few minutes."

Caroline shook her head in dismay, noting that Peggy and Fletcher had just arrived. As if on cue, everyone at the table turned toward them.

"We'll be down soon," Hunter called out, although Caroline doubted anyone could hear him over the music and chatter. The phone rang. "There you go. Problem solved."

Except it wasn't solved. The sitters registered on the hotel's roster were all booked and the concierge was unable to find anyone else on such short notice, unless they were willing to wait until ten o'clock.

"So much for that." Caroline slumped to the sofa, kicking off the recently purchased high heels that Peggy had christened Caroline's "fuck me" shoes.

"No. We're not going to let this ruin our anniversary dinner."

"We can't wait till ten o'clock."

"We don't have to," Hunter said. "We'll go, have dinner, come right back."

"What are you talking about? We can't leave the kids alone."

"We're not leaving them alone. We'll be right downstairs. It's just like at home, when the kids are in bed and we're sitting in the backyard."

"It's not the same."

"How is it different?"

"For one thing, this *isn't* our backyard. If

the kids were to wake up, if they started crying, we wouldn't be able to hear them."

"How many times did they wake up all week when the sitter was here?"

"That's beside the point."

"The sitter said they never woke up once."

"This is the same sitter who claims we canceled?"

"Nothing's going to happen," Hunter insisted.

"You go," Caroline said.

"Without you?"

"Yes. You go. Bring me back something to eat."

"This is our anniversary dinner, Caroline. I'm not going without you."

"All right. How's this? We call the restaurant and explain what happened, and tell everyone they can either join us up here for room service or come up later for dessert. I'm sure they'll understand."

"*I* don't understand. We're not talking about leaving the grounds. We're talking about going downstairs. For a couple of hours. You don't think you're being a little overprotective?"

"Overprotective?" Caroline pictured her mother lurking close by, waiting to pounce.

Hunter shrugged. "Forget it. I shouldn't have said that. It's disappointment talking, that's all. It's just that . . . well . . . I had something kind of special planned."

"It can still be special," Caroline protested weakly.

Hunter sank to the sofa beside her, took her hand in his. They were silent for several seconds. "Okay, listen. I have an idea." He paused, gathering his thoughts. "We go downstairs . . ."

"Hunter . . ."

"We go downstairs," he repeated, a little louder the second time, "have dinner with our friends, and take turns checking on the girls every half hour. How's that?"

Caroline's head was spinning. She was horrified at his casual comparison to her mother, having spent her entire life determined to be anything *but* like her mother. And she didn't want to disappoint him, especially when he'd gone out of his way to plan something special. The restaurant was literally right under their noses. They wouldn't be gone long. "I don't know . . ."

"You *do* know. We'll be right downstairs, we'll check on the kids every thirty minutes, they won't even know we're not here."

"You promise everything will be all right?"

Hunter took her face between his hands and kissed her tenderly on the lips. "I promise," he said.

FIVE: THE PRESENT

"Mom? Mom, are you home?"

Caroline heard the front door open and the words race through the downstairs hall and up the ivory-carpeted stairs toward her bedroom, as if actively searching for her.

"Mom?"

Caroline opened her mouth to speak, but thought better of it and said nothing. If she didn't answer, maybe Michelle would assume she wasn't home and go away. Although she knew even before she heard the footsteps on the stairs that Michelle was unlikely to give up so easily. Her daughter was as relentless as she'd always been.

"Mom?"

Caroline could feel Michelle standing in the doorway, peering into the darkness of the bedroom, her eyes burning into her back.

"Mom?" Michelle said again, flipping on the overhead light. "What's going on?

Didn't you hear me?"

"I heard you," Caroline said.

"You heard me but decided not to answer?"

"I . . . ," Caroline began, then stopped when she could think of nothing significant to add.

"What's the matter? Are you sick?" There was something vaguely accusatory in Michelle's tone.

Caroline shook her head. It was a tone she was used to.

"Then what are you doing? Why didn't you answer me? Why were you just sitting here in the dark?"

Caroline shrugged. She hadn't noticed the darkness. When had that happened? "What time is it?"

"Almost seven o'clock."

"What are you doing here?" Caroline asked.

"What do you mean, what am I doing here? You invited me to dinner, remember?"

"You said you were busy." Caroline swiveled around on the bed to face her daughter, surprised as she always was by how thin Michelle was, and biting down on her lower lip to keep from voicing this thought out loud.

"I was," Michelle said. "Then I thought

you might . . . Never mind what I thought. What's going on? Bad day at school?"

"I didn't go to school."

"Why not?"

"Just didn't feel like it."

"You didn't feel like it?" Michelle repeated, taking a few tentative steps into the room. "That doesn't make sense. You always feel like it."

"I didn't feel like it today."

"Why not?" she asked again.

"I don't know."

"You don't know?"

Caroline shrugged. Was Michelle going to repeat everything she said? "I don't know what you want me to say."

"I want you to tell me what's going on. You're acting very weird. Did you have a fight with Dad or something?"

"No."

"Is this about Mackenzie?"

"Mackenzie?"

"Dad's new baby," Michelle said with more than a hint of annoyance, as if they'd been over this many times — and perhaps they had.

"No."

Michelle stood at the foot of the bed, shifting from one foot to the other and looking everywhere but at her mother. "So, what happened? You sounded normal this morning on the phone when you were lecturing me about my responsibilities. And you're dressed for work, so you were obviously intending to go." Her eyes drifted to the newspapers strewn across the unmade bed. "Was it the article? The pictures? I mean, you can't be too surprised. This happens every year. You've kind of learned to go with the flow . . ."

"It's not the article or the pictures."

"Then what?"

"I don't know."

"You've been sitting here all day and you have no idea why? I don't believe you."

"Michelle . . ."

"Mother . . ."

"Please, Michelle. I don't want to argue with you."

"I don't want to argue with you either."

"Then let's just drop it, shall we?" Caroline pushed herself off the bed and took Michelle in her arms, hoping to silence her. Instantly she felt her daughter stiffen. Caroline took a deep breath, forced a smile onto her face. "So, where do you want to go for dinner?"

"How about that new raw place over on Bayshore?"

"Raw? As in not cooked?"

"It's all organic. Very healthy."

"I'm sure it is. Just doesn't sound all that . . ."

"Forget it," Michelle said.

"No. I'll give it a try."

"Never mind," Michelle said. "I'm not very hungry anyway."

The words hung suspended in the air like smoke from a stale cigarette. Caroline wondered if it had always been this way between them. The truth was that Michelle had been needy and difficult from birth, characteristics that Samantha's disappearance had only exacerbated. And the needier she'd become, the more Caroline's resentment grew. The more she'd clung, the more Caroline pulled away. The more Caroline pulled away, the more Michelle's resentment grew. Their relationship had devolved into a vicious cycle of push-pull, one retreating just as the other was reaching out. For every step forward, it seemed they took two back.

My fault, Caroline thought. *Everything, my fault.*

"I had a phone call this morning," she ventured cautiously. Maybe if she stopped shutting Michelle out, her daughter would welcome her back in.

"From . . . ?" Michelle stuck her thumbs

into the side pockets of her tight jeans, dark green eyes narrowing.

"A girl in Calgary."

"Calgary?"

"It's in Canada."

"I know where Calgary is, Mother. I'm not an idiot."

"Of course you're not an idiot. I didn't mean to suggest . . ."

"Who do you know in Calgary?"

"I don't know anyone."

"Is she a reporter?"

"No."

"You're not making any sense."

"You're not giving me a chance. Maybe if you stopped interrupting me . . ."

Michelle let out a deep sigh. "Okay. Sorry. Let's start again. You got a call from some girl in Calgary. Does she have a name?"

"Lili."

"Lili . . . ?"

"I don't know her last name. She wouldn't say."

"She wouldn't say," Michelle repeated. "Is this girl the reason you're acting so peculiar?"

"She doesn't think Lili is her real name," Caroline said, ignoring Michelle's question and looking directly into her daughter's eyes. "She thinks her real name is Samantha."

Michelle's shoulders slumped. "Shit."

"She thinks she's your sister."

"Oh, please. Don't tell me this." Michelle's eyes widened in anger. She began pacing back and forth in front of the bed, her arms shooting out in all directions, like an explosion of fireworks. "Don't tell me you believe this crap."

"I believe *she* believes it."

"Mother, for God's sake. This sort of thing happens every time they update those stupid sketches. People calling to say they've seen Samantha in line at the grocery store, psychics claiming they know where to find her, crazies boasting that they're holding her prisoner in some underground bunker. You've been dealing with these nutcases for years. And now some girl calls you from Calgary and says she thinks she's Samantha and you flip out? You know better than this. You know she's full of shit. Even if *she's* crazy enough to believe it . . ."

"This is different."

"*How* is it different?"

"She offered to take a DNA test."

"What?"

"She thinks we should go for a DNA test, to find out one way or the other."

"Whoa, whoa, whoa," Michelle said, stopping dead in her tracks. "What are you saying? That she's coming to San Diego?"

"No." Caroline replayed the conversation with Lili in her mind and then relayed it in its entirety to Michelle.

"Tell me you're not seriously considering going to Calgary."

"I've been thinking about it."

"No, you haven't."

"You asked what I've been doing all day. That's what I've been doing — thinking about it."

"You're not going to Calgary, Mother."

"Why not?"

"Why not? *Why not?*"

"What would be so terrible?"

"I don't believe this. I just don't believe it."

"Think about it for a minute, Michelle. What harm could it do? I go to Calgary, I meet this girl, we do the test, we find out one way or the other."

"*You* think about it. You go to Calgary, you meet this girl, who's probably a raving lunatic with her own agenda, maybe even a butcher knife — you ever think about *that*? — and you take the test and it turns out negative, which it will, you know it will, and then you come home all upset . . . for what?

Why would you do that to yourself? To us? *Again,"* she added for emphasis.

"Because that way we'd know for sure."

"I *already* know for sure."

"That's because you didn't talk to her. You didn't hear her. There was something about her voice . . ."

"Samantha was barely two years old when she disappeared. She could say 'mama' and 'dada' and maybe a few dozen other words, most of which nobody could understand —"

"I understood," Caroline interrupted, the threat of tears causing her voice to wobble.

"My point is," Michelle continued, "that there's no way you could recognize Samantha's voice if you heard it today. You're fooling yourself if you think otherwise. The odds against her being Samantha are astronomical. This girl, whoever she is, be it con artist, psychopath, or just poor deluded soul, is definitely not my sister. And you're not going anywhere near her."

"Sweetheart, I understand your concern and I love you for it, but . . ."

"But nothing." Michelle pushed her long brown hair away from her forehead and stared at her mother. "You've already made up your mind, haven't you?"

"It just makes sense to me, the more I

think about it."

Michelle moved toward the phone. "That's it. I'm calling Dad."

"What? No! I don't want you to call him."

"Why not? You don't think he has the right to know?"

"We don't know anything yet."

"We know you're going to Calgary. Maybe he'll want to go with you."

"He won't."

"Of course he won't. And do you want to know why? Because he's not a crazy person, that's why." She lifted the phone into her shaking hand.

"Please don't call your father."

"Why not?"

"Because I'm asking you not to. Please, Michelle . . . Micki . . ."

Michelle lowered the phone. "What did you just say?"

"I . . ."

"You called me Micki. You never call me Micki."

"I know."

"You hate that name."

"It doesn't matter."

"What — you think that if you call me Micki, I'm suddenly going to come around, that I'm that easy to manipulate?"

"No, of course I don't think that."

"You don't think, period. Shit." Michelle tossed the phone onto the bed. She shook her head, opened her mouth to speak, then shook her head again. "All right. Fine. I won't call him."

"Thank you."

"When are you thinking of going?"

"Tomorrow."

"Tomorrow," Michelle repeated.

"Apparently there's a flight in the morning that gets into Calgary around noon."

"I see. Have you already booked your ticket?"

"No."

"But you're going to."

"Yes."

"Do you have a passport?"

"A passport?"

"It's Canada, Mother. You need a passport."

"I have one."

"And winter boots?"

"Boots?"

"It's Canada in November. You need boots."

"I'll be all right."

"How long are you planning to stay?"

"Probably a couple of days. I don't know for sure."

"You *do* know this Thursday is Thanksgiving."

"I'll try to be home by then."

"Grandma Mary is expecting us for dinner."

"Oh, God."

"I'm not going to be the one who has to explain to her why you aren't there."

"I'll be there. I'll go, meet this girl, take the test, come home."

"You really think it's going to be that easy?"

Caroline shrugged. "Please try to understand, sweetheart. I've spent the last fifteen years regretting one decision. I don't want to spend the next fifteen regretting another."

Michelle sank down on the bed. A noise halfway between a sigh and a scoff escaped her throat.

"What?"

"I was just wondering if you'd be going to all this trouble if it had been me, and not Samantha, who'd disappeared that night."

Caroline felt the words form a sword and pierce her heart. Instinctively, she reached for Michelle. "Oh, God. You can't really think . . ."

Michelle jumped to her feet, resumed her pacing. "It doesn't matter what I think, does it? You've proved that over and over. You proved it again tonight. My opinion doesn't matter. It never has. I don't know why I'm surprised. I should be used to it." She turned and bolted from the room.

"Michelle!" Caroline raced after her daughter, following her down the hall and into her bedroom. She watched her pull an overnight bag out of her closet and toss it onto the green-and-white comforter on her bed. "What are you doing?"

"What does it look like I'm doing?" Michelle walked to her dresser, opened the top drawer, and threw a handful of undergarments into the bag. "A couple of days, you said?"

"What are you talking about?"

"One sweater should be enough." She threw a navy wool turtleneck into the bag. "The jeans I'm wearing will be fine. And I have that ski jacket Dad bought me in Aspen last year. It should be in the closet downstairs. Hopefully Calgary won't be absolutely buried in snow."

"Stop," Caroline said, stilling her daughter's hands before she could add more items to the bag. "You can't come with me."

"I can't? Why not?"

"Because . . ."

"You don't want me to come?"

"It's not that."

"Then what is it?"

"You said it yourself. It's a crazy idea. *I'm* crazy."

"All the more reason for me to go with you."

"No."

"Don't give me a hard time, Mother. 'Whither thou goest,' and all that crap."

"Michelle . . . Micki . . ."

"Give it up, Mother. It's not going to work this time. So what's it going to be? Are we going to Calgary tomorrow or not?"

Caroline saw the determined set of her daughter's jaw and the angry hurt in her eyes. She knew it was pointless to argue. "I'll book the tickets," she said.

Six:
Fifteen Years Ago

"Did I tell you that Jerrod got us tickets for *Dance with the Devil*?" Rain said, casting her heavily blue-shadowed gaze around the table before bringing it to rest on Caroline.

"What's that?" Caroline asked, sneaking a glance in the direction of her suite and then at her watch. She put down her fork and pushed away what was left of her lobster dinner, which was most of it. She'd been too nervous to eat. It was almost time to check on the kids.

"They were fine when I checked on them thirty minutes ago," Hunter whispered under his breath, his lips barely moving. "They're fine now. Finish your meal."

"*Dance with the Devil?* It's only the hottest show on Broadway," Rain said, answering the question Caroline had already forgotten she'd asked. "It's impossible to get tickets, especially on Thanksgiving weekend. But Superman here managed to do it." She threw a proprietary arm across her husband's shoulders, causing her breasts to all but leap out of her dress.

"So you'll be spending Thanksgiving in New York," Becky said. "Lucky you."

Rain flashed her best veneer-enhanced smile. "What are you guys up to?"

"My mother always has Thanksgiving dinner at her place," Steve said.

"You can just imagine how much I'm looking forward to that," Becky said.

Steve glared at his wife. "Let's not start."

"Stop looking at your watch," Hunter told Caroline.

"You know what my darling mother-in-law said to me last Thanksgiving?" Becky said, continuing without waiting for a response. "She'd just been to a funeral and I made the mistake of asking how it had gone, and she said, and this is a direct quote: 'It was a lovely affair. Her daughter selected a beautiful coffin. Much nicer than the one you had for *your* mother.' "

There was a collective gasp from around the table.

Although not from Caroline, who was used to such remarks.

"I assure you she said no such thing," Steve protested.

"That's exactly what she said."

"You're exaggerating. As usual."

"And you're defending her. As usual."

"So, what are we all thankful for?" Peggy interrupted, a forced chirp in her voice. "Come on. Three things, not including health, family, or friends. We'll just assume you're thankful for those."

"Never assume," said Becky.

"Oh, this is fun," Rain said, clapping her hands. "Can I start?"

Peggy opened the palms of her hands, indicating that Rain had the floor.

"Well, first, obviously, I'm thankful we'll be spending Thanksgiving in New York and not at some horrid family function, no offense intended." Her smile drifted from Becky to Steve before ultimately landing on Caroline. "Second, I'm thankful for the new necklace Jerrod bought me." She patted the impressive diamond sparkler at her throat. "And third, I'm thankful gray hair doesn't run in my family. Your turn," she said to Caroline.

Caroline struggled to keep her hands away from her head. She'd never noticed any gray hairs, but then, she really hadn't been paying close attention. "I'm thankful for this past week," she said, nodding toward her husband. "I'm thankful to be celebrating ten years of relative wedded bliss," she continued, recalling her brother's words.

"What do you mean, *relative*?" Hunter asked, a mock frown on his lips.

"I'll drink to *relative,*" Jerrod said, raising his glass of champagne as the others followed suit, stretching their glasses toward one another in a congratulatory toast.

"Careful," Rain warned. "You can't cross hands or it's bad luck."

"Really? I've never heard that," Becky said.

"Go on," Peggy instructed Caroline. "One more thing you're thankful for."

Caroline tried to come up with a third reason to be grateful other than family, health, and friends. Surely she could think of something. "I'm thankful for the ocean," she said finally, glancing in its general direction.

"Seriously?" Rain asked.

"I'm thankful the San Diego real estate market is so strong," Steve said, not waiting to be asked. "I'm thankful I was able to persuade Hunter to let us join you here in beautiful Rosarito to help you celebrate." He glanced pointedly across the table at his wife. "I'm especially thankful that my mother is such a great cook."

"You're so full of shit," Becky said.

"Is our mother not a great cook?" Steve asked Caroline.

"Our mother is indeed a great cook," Caroline agreed. "And you are also full of shit."

Everybody laughed, although Steve's laugh was muted and his hazel eyes were as lifeless and hard as stones.

"Your turn, Becky," Rain said.

"I'm sorry, everyone. I've had this terrible headache all afternoon, and it seems to be getting worse." Tears clouded her eyes. She made no move to hide them or brush them aside. "If you'll excuse me," she said, pushing back her chair and getting to her feet.

"Oh, sit down," Steve said. "You're fine. Don't be such a prima donna."

"Fuck you." Becky turned and stomped away.

There was a moment of stunned silence.

"Shouldn't you go after her?" Fletcher asked Steve as he calmly finished off the last of his champagne.

"What — you think I'm as crazy as she is?"

"I should go check on the kids," Caroline said, as eager to get away as Becky had been.

"Hurry back." Hunter stood to kiss her cheek before she left.

"Oh. So sweet," Caroline heard Rain say as she was walking away.

An elevator was waiting, its doors open,

when Caroline reached the far side of the lobby. She stepped inside and pressed the button for the sixth floor. So far the evening had proved less than stellar: first the mix-up with the babysitter, then her guilt at leaving the kids alone, followed by her brother and sister-in-law's unpleasant bickering. That they no longer seemed to care who heard them was not a good sign. Caroline exited the elevator, doubting her brother's marriage would survive the year, let alone a decade.

She hurried down the long corridor, convinced with each step that she heard her children's anguished cries bouncing off the walls. But when she opened the door to her suite, she heard nothing except the reassuring hum of silence. She tiptoed into their bedroom, pausing in the doorway for her eyes to adjust to the dark, then moved toward Michelle's bed.

The child lay sleeping on her side, her mouth partly open, the covers bunched awkwardly around her waist, her Wonder Woman doll trapped inside their folds. Caroline carefully extricated the doll and drew the sheet up over her daughter's shoulders, depositing the doll on the pillow next to her head. *You're such an angel when you sleep,* she thought, fighting the urge to kiss her cheek. *If only you could save some of that sweetness for when you're awake.*

She swiveled toward Samantha's crib and leaned over its side, a deep sigh escaping her lungs.

Samantha lay on her back, her little arms raised above her head and bent at the elbows, as if she had literally surrendered to sleep. *Hunter was right,* she thought. *I've been silly to worry.*

The phone rang, its shrill sound a bayonet slicing through the stillness. Caroline bolted for the living room, grabbing the offending object before it could ring again and pressing it tight against her ear. "Hello?" She should have phoned the front desk, told them to hold all calls. What if the phone had rung when she wasn't around? What if it had woken up the children? What if they'd cried out for her? What if they'd panicked when she hadn't come running?

"Is this a bad time?" asked the voice on the other end. "You sound peculiar."

"Mother?" Caroline could barely hear her own voice over the beating of her heart. She thought of the conversation at dinner and suppressed a shudder. Was it possible her mother had sensed they'd been talking about her? She'd always claimed to have eyes in the back of her head, and ears everywhere, that nothing ever escaped her. When Caroline was little, this thought used to terrify her. If she was being honest, it still did. "Is everything all right?"

"Do you care?"

"What do you mean? Of course I care."

"Is that why I haven't heard from you all week?"

"Well, I . . ."

"I'm not complaining, you understand. Just stating facts. I know you're very busy partying. At least I have one child who is considerate of his mother's feelings."

That's because he's still laboring under the misconception that you have any, Caroline thought. "Steve's a good son," she said. A good son and a lousy husband.

"Too bad you didn't have boys."

Caroline almost laughed, remembering her mother's spontaneous outburst when she'd phoned from her hospital bed to tell her of Samantha's birth. "Another stinking girl!" her mother had exclaimed.

"I just called to wish you a happy anniversary," she said now.

A wave of guilt swept over Caroline. She was being too hard on her mother. The woman wasn't going to change. It was up to Caroline to change the way she reacted to her. She had to be more generous, less judgmental. "Thank you."

"I have to say I'm surprised. I thought Hunter would be bored to tears by now."

This time Caroline did laugh, although the sound was muted and caught in her throat. *You can't make this stuff up,* she thought. "I'm sorry — are you saying I'm boring?"

"Don't put words in my mouth. Hunter just strikes me as the type of man who gets bored easily. Stop being so sensitive."

"I should go, Mother. Everybody's wait —" The line went dead in Caroline's hands before she could finish the sentence. She shook her head and hung up, then immediately picked up the phone again and pressed the number for the front desk, telling them to hold all calls until further notice. She doubted there would be any more calls, but she couldn't take that chance. Her mother usually insisted on having the last word.

She did one final check on the girls before leaving the suite. Neither had been disturbed by her mother's call. "Just boring old me," she said as she closed the door behind her and stepped into the hall. A waiter in a white jacket was walking toward her, wheeling a dinner cart. He stopped a few doors away from her and knocked.

"Room service," he called out as Caroline passed by.

"Everything all right?" Hunter asked when she returned to the restaurant.

"Everything's fine." Caroline noticed that there were now two empty seats at the table. "Where's my brother?"

"He gave in to peer pressure soon after you left and went to see if he could persuade Becky to come back," Peggy said.

Good luck with that, Caroline thought, as a trio of handsome young musicians approached their table. "What's this?" she asked, as two of the men knelt at her feet and raised their guitars in the air.

"Happy anniversary," Hunter said.

"Isn't this just the most romantic thing ever!" Rain exclaimed.

"You're not bored with me, are you?" Caroline whispered to Hunter as the musicians began their soft serenade.

"Bored with you? Where on earth would you get that idea?"

Caroline shook all remaining thoughts of her mother out of her head. She caressed her husband's cheek. "I love you," she said.

"Ah," said Rain, "so sweet."

Half an hour later, the singers had finished their songs, and dessert — flaming crêpes suzette — had been ordered. "I should go check on the kids before it arrives," Hunter said.

Caroline smiled, grateful she hadn't had to remind him.

"And I need a sweater," Rain said, resting a manicured hand on her impressive cleavage. "The girls are getting chilly."

Caroline watched her husband and Rain go their separate ways at the restaurant's entrance, Rain to one wing, Hunter to the other.

"Well, that was a lovely little surprise," Peggy said.

"It was," Caroline agreed.

"Hunter certainly knows his way around a grand gesture."

"He certainly knows how to make the rest of us look bad," Fletcher groused good-naturedly. "Not that there are many of us left."

"Yes, it's starting to feel a bit like musical chairs around here," Jerrod concurred.

"Think your brother and Becky will ever come back?" Peggy asked.

Caroline shook her head. "I wouldn't be surprised if they've already checked out. Frankly, I don't know why they wanted to come at all."

"Maybe they hoped a romantic holiday

might be good for their marriage."

Caroline couldn't argue with that. Hadn't she been hoping the same thing for hers?

Two waiters approached.

"Would it be too much trouble to hold off on dessert until the others get back?" Caroline asked them. "They should only be a few minutes."

In reality, it was more like fifteen.

"Sorry I was gone so long," Hunter said as he reclaimed his seat. "I waited forever for an elevator, then finally gave up and took the stairs. The kids are sound asleep," he continued before Caroline could ask. He looked around the table. "Where is everyone?"

As if on cue, Rain suddenly appeared, Steve at her side. "Look who I found in the lobby," she said, gathering her newly acquired shawl around her.

"I was about to send out a search party," her husband said.

"I forgot I'd already packed the damn thing. Had to unpack my whole suitcase to find it."

"Serves you right for being so organized," Peggy said. "I haven't even started packing."

"I take it you couldn't convince Becky to come back," Caroline said to her brother.

Steve shrugged as he pulled out his chair. "Women," he said to the men present. "Can't live with 'em, can't shoot 'em."

"Nice talk," Caroline said.

"Kids okay?" Steve asked Hunter.

"Kids are fine."

The waiters returned and everyone watched in silence as one prepared the crêpes while the other set them ablaze, the flames stretching like angry claws toward the darkened sky.

"Home, sweet home," Hunter said, waving the keycard in front of the door to their suite. The small light at the lock flashed red, indicating that the door remained locked. He staggered slightly as he tried again and got the same result. "That's weird. It was working fine earlier."

"Try mine," Caroline said. She'd gotten a new one before dinner.

He did, and it worked. "Stupid thing," Hunter muttered, throwing the keycard down on the coffee table as they entered the living room, then flopping down on the sofa.

"Maybe you had it too close to your cell phone."

"Maybe. Come sit with me," he said.

"I'll just check on the kids."

"The kids can wait two minutes."

Caroline walked over to the sofa and sank down beside her husband. He quickly surrounded her with his arms and kissed her neck, his breath warm and carrying the trace of at least one drink too many. The drapes were open and the reflection of the light from the outside lanterns danced on the walls, mixing with the soft glow of the moon. "So, did you enjoy your anniversary after all?"

"I did."

"Liar," he chided.

"No. It was lovely. It was."

"You hardly touched your dinner."

"I wasn't that hungry."

"You were worried about the kids."

"I got over it."

He kissed her neck again. "Did you enjoy your serenade?"

"Very much."

"Were you surprised?"

"I was. I didn't realize you were such a romantic."

"I can't take all the credit. It was actually Steve's idea."

"Really? Too bad he can't come up with any good ideas where Becky is concerned." Caroline's hand moved to the front of her husband's pants. "And speaking of coming up . . ."

Hunter stilled her hand. "I'm really sorry, babe. I think I may have overdone it with the celebratory toasts."

"Oh, dear." Caroline tried to keep the disappointment out of her voice. She'd been looking forward all day to making love to her husband, had been fantasizing about prolonged foreplay, maybe even trying something new. "Maybe there's something I can do about that."

Hunter moved her hand away from his groin. "Sorry, sweetheart. Not that I wouldn't appreciate the effort but I'm afraid you'd just be wasting your time."

"We could try, see what happens."

"Please don't make me feel worse about this than I already do," he said, effectively ending the conversation.

Caroline withdrew her hand, sat up straight.

"Now you're angry."

"Just disappointed."

"We can do it in the morning."

Sure, Caroline thought. *When the kids are up and we're hurrying to pack and check out.*

"And tomorrow night."

When you're exhausted from driving and the kids are cranky and we're unpacking and you're preoccupied with getting back to work.

"And every night after that for the rest of our lives," Hunter said, giving her his best little-boy smile. "Please, Caroline. I'm really sorry."

"I know. Me, too." She pushed herself off the couch. "I'll go check on the kids." Once again she found herself in the doorway of the girls' bedroom, waiting for her eyes to adjust to the dark. *So much for romance,* she thought, moving toward Michelle's bed and stepping on something hard.

Wonder Woman, she realized, picking the doll up off the floor and returning her to the pillow beside Michelle's head. The child immediately swatted the doll away with her hand, although she didn't wake up. *Another rejection,* Caroline thought, crossing over to Samantha's crib.

When she didn't see her immediately, Caroline assumed that the toddler had merely shifted positions, that she'd somehow turned herself around in her sleep, as she often did, her head now at the opposite end of the crib, her feet where her head should be.

Except her feet weren't there either.

Caroline leaned in closer, her eyes trying to pierce the darkness, her fingers grasping at the covers, finding nothing but an empty quilt.

Samantha wasn't there.

No, this can't be, Caroline thought, panic filling her lungs. *It's impossible. It can't be.*

She moved quickly to the light switch and flipped on the overhead light, then raced back to the crib.

It was empty.

"Samantha?" she called out, wondering if her daughter had somehow managed to climb out of the crib. She fell to her knees, checking under it in case Samantha was lying unconscious on the floor.

She wasn't there.

"Samantha!"

"Mommy?" Michelle sat up in bed, rubbing her eyes as Caroline began spinning around in helpless circles.

"Samantha!" Caroline called again, hysteria clinging to the name, as she raced through the living room into the master bedroom.

"What's going on?" Hunter asked, emerging from the en suite bathroom.

"She's not there! She's not there!"

"Mommy?" Michelle cried, coming up behind her.

It was then that Caroline's rising panic

broke loose, exploding violently into the air and filling the suite with screams.

Seven:
The Present

The plane touched down in Calgary at precisely twelve minutes after noon. Caroline's forehead had been pressed against the window of the small aircraft ever since they'd left San Diego, her eyes following the gradual muting of the sky as it dulled from bright blue to steel gray over the course of the flight.

"It looks like we've landed on the moon," Michelle said from the seat beside her, probably the most words she'd uttered all trip.

It certainly looks cold, Caroline thought, noting the large piles of shoveled snow on the ground along the edge of the runway. She was glad Michelle had persuaded her to wear boots, even though they weren't lined and likely weren't waterproof. She was also glad her daughter had insisted she bring her heavy down coat, a coat she'd purchased on impulse immediately following her divorce and had rarely had occasion to wear. In fact, she was glad that Michelle had insisted on accompanying her, even though it gave her one more thing to worry about. Maybe worrying about Michelle would take her mind off the insanity of what she was doing.

"Coming?" Michelle asked from the aisle as the plane was emptying.

Caroline scrambled to her feet, grabbing her coat and overnight bag from the overhead bin. She hadn't slept more than a few hours all night and she was exhausted. Also hyper. *Not a great combination,* she thought, following Michelle to the front of the plane. She thanked the flight attendant, then struggled to catch up to her daughter, who was walking very purposefully, her bag thrown across one shoulder, her arms swinging at her sides. *Does she always walk this fast?* Caroline wondered. *And has she always been so thin?*

She's so thin because all she eats is raw fish and vegetables, she thought with her next breath. Or maybe it was the bulky down jacket that was making her hips seem so narrow, her thighs so inconsequential.

"Holy crap," said Michelle, the words disappearing into tufts of steam upon contact with the frigid air. "How does anyone live here? It must be forty below."

Caroline shifted her weight from one foot to the other, her legs growing numb inside her thin wool pants, as they waited in a small line of travelers for a cab. "The Fairfax Hotel on Stephen Avenue Walk," Caroline directed the driver as they climbed into the backseat.

"Is it always so cold here?" Michelle asked. "My ears are frozen."

"It takes some getting used to," the cabbie said pleasantly, his Pakistani accent melodic and thick. "Summer is very nice."

"Too bad Lili didn't call in July," Michelle said to her mother.

They didn't speak again until they reached the hotel half an hour later. The drive into the city had been as uneventful as it was uninteresting. A flat landscape covered in snow. Michelle was right, Caroline thought. It did feel as if they'd landed on the moon.

The hotel was an old gray stone building, maybe ten stories high. Caroline paid the cabdriver in American dollars and they hurried into the lobby to escape the bitter wind. The lobby was surprisingly warm, the walls painted eggshell beige, the carpet a rich weave of brown and gold. Brown leather sofas and chairs were strategically placed throughout the large room, and a round oak table stood in the middle of the rug, a huge arrangement of colorful silk flowers at its center. But Caroline noticed only the empty sofas and chairs.

"She's not here," Michelle said, giving voice to Caroline's thoughts.

They approached the reception desk. "I'm Caroline Shipley. I have a reservation," she told the young man behind the counter. He had curly blond hair and a gap between his front teeth that seemed to widen when he smiled.

He typed something into the computer in front of him. "Yes, here you are. You're booked for one night, possibly two. Is that correct?"

"Yes, that's right."

"Wait a minute," Michelle said. "We're not actually going to check in, are we? I mean, what's the point? She's not here."

"What else would you have me do? There isn't another plane till tomorrow."

"Is there a problem?" the clerk asked.

"No," Caroline told him. "We're good."

"We're good and crazy," Michelle said, not quite under her breath.

"Could you see if there are any messages for me?" Caroline asked.

The young man glanced back at his computer. "No. Nothing."

"You're sure? Could you look again?"

Michelle groaned audibly. "There are no messages, Mother."

"No messages," the clerk repeated. "Do you prefer smoking or nonsmoking?"

"Smoking," Michelle said.

"Nonsmoking," Caroline said, their voices overlapping.

"Come on, Mom. Give me a break."

"If you have to smoke, you'll do it outside."

"I'll freeze to death."

"Better than dying of cancer."

"Nice one, Mother."

"Nonsmoking," Caroline said to the waiting clerk.

"King-size bed or two doubles?"

"Two doubles," Caroline and Michelle said in unison.

The clerk pushed a piece of paper across the counter. "If you'll just fill this out and sign here. And I'll need an imprint of your credit card."

Where are you, Lili? Caroline was thinking as she handed over her Visa card. She glanced around the lobby, her eyes seeking out every nook and cranny in case the girl was hiding, waiting for the right moment to announce her presence. Or maybe she knew the young man behind the desk. Calgary wasn't that big a city. It was entirely possible Lili had come to the hotel, recognized the clerk, and made herself scarce before he spotted her. But she saw no one. "Have you noticed anyone hanging around the lobby? A young girl, about seventeen . . . ?"

"Sorry. I just started my shift."

"She isn't here," Michelle said. "She's not coming."

"You don't know that."

"You said she'd be here waiting."

"Maybe something came up. Maybe she got delayed."

"Or maybe she's not coming."

Caroline pushed the completed form back to the clerk, noting the unobtrusive security camera mounted on the wall behind his head. Maybe if they'd had security cameras at the Grand Laguna . . . But that was fifteen years ago, she reminded herself, before such precautions became the norm. And it was Mexico, where even today such measures were haphazardly taken. "I'm expecting either a visit or a phone call from a girl named Lili," she told the clerk, pushing such thoughts from her mind. There was no point in speculating about what might have been, and even less in torturing herself about what never was.

"Is there a last name?" the clerk asked.

"Just call us if anyone shows up," Michelle said.

"Certainly. Can you describe her?"

Caroline pictured the sketches in yesterday's paper. "She's a pretty girl, brown hair, blue eyes, a strong jaw . . ." *Hunter's jaw,* she thought.

"We don't know what she looks like," Michelle interrupted. "Just call us if you see some strange girl hanging around."

"And if anyone phones," Caroline added, bristling at Michelle's dismissive tone, "please connect them to our room immediately."

"Of course. Would you like one keycard or two?"

Caroline hated keycards, had hated them for fifteen years. Maybe if she hadn't lost her keycard that awful day, she wouldn't be here now.

"Make it two," Michelle said.

The young man placed the keycards in a small white envelope and handed them to Caroline. "You're in room 812. Enjoy your stay."

"You didn't have to be so rude," Caroline told her daughter as they waited for the elevator. "He probably thinks we're nuts."

"We *are* nuts."

The elevator doors opened and the two

women stepped inside and turned to face forward. Michelle leaned over to press the button for the eighth floor. "Wait," Caroline cried, her hand reaching out to prevent the door from closing.

"What is it?"

"Someone just came into the lobby."

Michelle stepped in front of Caroline. "For God's sake. That woman is a hundred and ten years old." She stepped back as Caroline let her hand fall to her side again. "Get a grip, Mother," Michelle said as she pressed the button and the elevator doors closed.

The room was large and traditionally furnished, with two double beds occupying most of the center space. The carpet was soft and brown, the bedspreads a silvery beige, the papered walls a subtle flowery print. A large-screen TV sat on the bureau across from the beds. A desk stood on the opposite wall, close to the window overlooking the pedestrian walkway that was Calgary's main street. Caroline stared down at the parade of people braving the elements. The cold weather didn't seem to bother them, she thought, shedding her heavy coat, and trying to make out the faces beneath the ubiquitous winter hats and scarves. Was one of those people her daughter?

"She's not there," Michelle said, as if reading her thoughts.

Caroline sighed. "Which bed do you want?"

In reply, Michelle threw her bag onto the bed closer to the bathroom. "So, what now?"

"I think I'll go back to the lobby, wait there."

"Is that really necessary? We already told the guy at the desk to call us if she . . ."

"You can stay here."

"As if," Michelle said, following her mother to the door. "You do realize that somebody somewhere is having a good laugh at your expense."

It won't be the first time, Caroline thought, heading for the door. She'd been betrayed before.

They returned to their room at four o'clock, having seen no one who even remotely resembled Samantha. By four-thirty, it was already growing dark. By five, the only light came from the streetlamps along Stephen Avenue Walk and the television across from the beds on which they were sitting. The TV was on CNN: a disgruntled man in North Dakota had gunned down his boss and six coworkers after being fired from his job earlier that afternoon. "Maybe we should order room service," Caroline said, turning on the lamp and reaching for the menu, almost knocking the phone off its hook. She stared at it, as if willing it to ring. But it remained stubbornly silent.

"I'm not really hungry," Michelle said.

"We haven't eaten all day. You have to have something."

"I said I'm not . . . Fine. I'll eat. What are my choices?"

Caroline scanned the menu. "They have steak, hamburgers, prime rib . . ."

"Really, Mother? Prime rib?"

"You used to love prime rib."

"I haven't eaten red meat since I was twelve years old."

"You need protein . . ."

"I don't eat meat."

"How about fish? They have a tuna melt."

"Tuna smothered in cheese. No, thank you."

"What about a BLT?"

"I don't eat bread."

"For God's sake, Michelle . . ."

"Look. Just order me a bowl of fruit."

"They have milk shakes."

"Are you kidding me? Am I a child?"

"I don't know. You're certainly acting like one."

"Why? Because I like what I like?"

"You don't like *anything.*"

"I like sushi. Do they have sushi?"

"No. And maybe you're eating too much raw fish. You'll get mercury poisoning."

"Oh, for fuck's sake, would you just stop?"

A phone rang.

"My God," Caroline said.

"Relax," Michelle told her. "It's my cell." She reached into her purse and pulled out her cell phone. "It's Dad," she said, glancing at the caller ID.

"Don't answer it," Caroline urged.

"Yeah, right. Hi, Dad."

"Don't tell him where we are."

"Yeah, I'm sorry I haven't called. I'm in Calgary with Mom."

"Shit," Caroline said, listening as her daughter explained to Hunter where exactly they were and what they were doing there.

"No, I'm not kidding." Michelle held the phone toward her mother. "He wants to talk to you."

Caroline shook her head, refused to take it.

"He's pretty upset," Michelle said, returning the phone to her purse minutes later. "He wants you to call him."

"He's not my husband anymore. I don't have to talk to him if I don't want to."

"Now who's acting like a child?"

"Are we ordering dinner or not?"

Michelle snatched the menu from her mother's hands. "Fine. I'll have the house salad, no dressing, just a wedge of lemon, and a spinach and parsley smoothie, no yogurt."

"Sounds yummy," Caroline said, rolling her eyes and relaying Michelle's order to room service, along with her own order of a steak with fries, a side salad, a slice of cheesecake, and a large Coke. Not that she wanted any of it. She just wanted to make a point. Although she was no longer sure what that point was.

"Just so you know, I'm sorry about the way things turned out," Michelle said at the end of the mostly silent meal. "I was hoping she'd at least have the decency to call."

"Me, too. Thanks for coming with me, for being here."

"Well, I couldn't very well let you come alone."

Caroline reached across the portable table the waiter had set up to pat her daughter's hand, but Michelle's hands were already moving toward her lap. She wanted to ask what was going on in Michelle's life, how she really felt about Hunter's new baby, if she was dating anyone special, if she'd decided whether or not to return to school, if she had any idea what she wanted to do with her life, but she was afraid to disturb this moment of guarded peace. "Peggy tells me you're doing a great job at the hospice," she said, choosing the safest option.

Michelle shrugged. "I don't do all that much."

"She said you have a real way with the patients."

"We don't call them patients. We call them residents."

"Oh."

"Patients are waiting for a cure," Michelle explained. "Residents are waiting to die."

Caroline took a moment to absorb the casual distinction. "That can't be easy for you."

"The court didn't give me a whole lot of choice, did it? Do you believe in God?" Michelle asked in the same breath.

"What makes you ask that?"

"I was just thinking of this woman at the hospice," Michelle said. "She isn't that old. Fifty-ish. A former drug addict, but then she got religion and turned her life around. Everything was starting to look up. She got a job, met this guy, then boom, she got cancer. I was sitting with her the other day and she asked me to read the Bible to her. So I opened it, just randomly. And it's this passage from Luke about the Prodigal Son. Do you know it?"

"It's been a long time since I read the Bible."

"Well, Jesus is telling a group of people this story about a wealthy landowner who has two sons. And one day he decides to give them each a lot of money. One son takes the money, then immediately takes off. 'See you around, Dad. Nice knowing you.' And off he goes. But the other son, he stays put, saves his money, works hard. Years go by. The father doesn't hear boo from the one who left. And then one day, he's back. And guess what? He's dead broke. Spent every last dime. Pissed it all away on cheap wine and loose women. 'Dad,' he says. 'I've sinned, but I've come back home.' And what does his father do? Does he cast him aside? Does he lecture him, tell him he's no longer welcome?" Michelle paused dramatically. "No. He welcomes the ingrate back with open arms. He even throws a huge feast to celebrate his return. And the other son says, 'Hey, wait a minute, that's not fair. I'm the one who stuck by you all these years. Don't I deserve a little party?' But the father says no. He doesn't see it that way at all. And according to Jesus, the father is right. According to Jesus, it's better to welcome one sinner back into the fold than to honor the ones who never strayed in the first place." She shook her head. "I don't get it. Do you?"

Caroline felt the full weight of the parable fall across her shoulders, like a heavy woolen blanket. "I know you feel I haven't always been there for you," she began. "And I'm sorry if I've let you down . . ."

"Wait a minute. You think I was talking about me and Samantha? About you?"

"Weren't you?"

"I was talking about Jesus."

"I'm sorry. I just thought . . ."

"Well, you thought wrong."

"I'm sorry."

"Not everything is about you."

Caroline bit her tongue to keep from apologizing again.

"What difference does it make anyway? It's all so lame," Michelle pronounced. "God, religion, heaven, hell. It's just a load of crap."

"Michelle . . ."

"Don't worry. I don't tell that to the residents." She pushed herself away from the table and stood up. "I'm going outside for a smoke."

"Do you have to?"

"I won't be long." She fished inside her purse for her cigarettes, held up the package triumphantly.

"It's dark . . . it's cold."

Michelle retrieved her jacket from the closet, throwing it over her shoulders as she opened the door. "You don't have to worry. I'll be back."

EIGHT: FIFTEEN YEARS AGO

The hours immediately after Caroline discovered that Samantha was missing were a blur of tears, screams, and veiled accusations. "Samantha!" she screamed repeatedly over Michelle's terrified cries. "Samantha, where are you?" She raced through the suite, Michelle nipping at her heels like a frightened puppy. "No, no, no, no, no, no, no."

"What the hell is going on?" Hunter demanded, coming out of the bathroom, his shirt off, toothbrush in hand.

"She's gone. Samantha's gone."

"What are you talking about? How can she be gone?" He ran into the children's bedroom, emerging wide-eyed and ashen-faced. "Where the hell is she?"

"Oh, God. Oh, God." Caroline was on her hands and knees, searching the closet, under the coffee table, behind the drapes. "She's not here. She's not here."

"That's impossible. She *has* to be here."

They searched the master bedroom, then searched the entire suite again.

"Mommy," Michelle kept crying. "Mommy, what's wrong?"

A terrifying thought crept into Caroline's brain. Michelle had always been jealous of her baby sister. Was it possible she'd done something to harm her? Caroline had heard stories of resentful siblings dangling babies out of second-story windows. Was it possible that Michelle . . . ? The thought was too horrifying to finish. She rushed to the window between Michelle's bed and the crib. But the window was too high for Michelle to reach on her own and besides, it was securely locked and impossible for a child to open, let alone close and re-lock. Even so, Caroline threw it open and leaned well over its side, her eyes desperately searching the ground below. The restaurant was right there. Surely someone would have seen or heard a child fall.

Maybe Samantha had woken up and somehow managed to climb out of her crib, then when she couldn't find her mother, opened the door and wandered down the hall.

Caroline ran out of the bedroom and flung open the door to their suite. She raced down the long corridor, screaming: "Samantha! Samantha, baby, where are you?"

Doors along the corridor opened, people warily poking their heads out, asking what was wrong.

"Have you seen my baby?" Caroline demanded of each curious face. Was it possible Samantha had made her way to the elevators and managed to press the call button? Could she have stepped inside and somehow reached one of the lower buttons? Had she proceeded unnoticed across the lobby and out into the night? Could she, right now, at this very second, be out there in the dark, stumbling blindly on her chubby little legs, toward the ocean? "Where are you, baby?" Caroline cried. "Where are you?"

And then Hunter was beside her, Michelle balanced precariously on the inside of his arm. He wrapped his other arm around his sobbing wife and led her back to their suite. Then he called the front desk, told them his child was missing, and instructed them to call the police.

"But where can she be?" Caroline asked over and over again. "You just checked on her half an hour ago."

"She was sound asleep," Hunter assured her, repeating the same thing to the hotel manager when he arrived twenty minutes later, having been roused from his bed at home.

"You left your children alone in the room?" the portly, middle-aged Mexican man asked, not even attempting to mask his disapproval. "We offer a babysitting service . . ."

"The sitter never showed up," Hunter said.

The hotel manager lifted his cell phone to his ear, muttered something into it in Spanish.

"We checked on them every half hour," Hunter told him.

"We never should have left them alone," Caroline said.

"Our records show that the request for a sitter was canceled," the manager stated, lowering his cell phone to his lap.

"Obviously a mix-up," Hunter said. "We never canceled."

"We never should have left them," Caroline said again.

"Where are the police?" Hunter asked. "We're wasting precious time."

"They are coming," the manager said. "They have to come from Tijuana . . ."

"Shit." Hunter jumped to his feet. They were gathered in the living room. Michelle had fallen asleep on the sofa, her head in her mother's lap.

"I assure you we are doing all we can in the meantime. We have every available staff member searching the premises."

"Someone's taken her," Caroline wailed softly. "Someone's taken my baby."

"Can we go over this once again?" the manager asked. "To make sure I understand and can help with the police investigation."

"It's our anniversary," Hunter began, his voice low and steady, despite having already told the manager everything they could about the evening. "We'd arranged for a sitter, the same thing we've done every night since we got here a week ago, but she didn't show, and our friends were downstairs in the restaurant waiting, so we thought . . ."

"*You* thought," Caroline interrupted.

Hunter continued as if she hadn't spoken. ". . . that since the restaurant was right downstairs . . . It's right under our window, for God's sake . . . We thought it would be safe . . ."

"*You* thought," Caroline said again.

"We checked on them every half hour."

"The last time you checked was when?"

Hunter glanced at his watch. "About an hour ago now."

"Oh, God," Caroline said.

"If she's anywhere in the hotel," the manager said, "we'll find her."

"And if she's not, if someone took her," Caroline said, trying to muzzle her growing hysteria so as not to wake Michelle, "she could be anywhere by now."

"Who would take her?" the manager asked. "How would they have gotten inside the room? You said the door was locked when you got home."

"I don't know how," Caroline said, looking to her husband for an answer.

"You lost your keycard," Hunter said.

Caroline tried not to hear the hint of accusation in his voice.

"When was this?" the manager asked.

"This afternoon. At the pool. I dropped my purse. Everything fell out. I didn't realize I'd lost the damn thing until I got back upstairs . . ."

"This wasn't the first time you lost one," Hunter said.

"That's right. I lost one earlier in the week," Caroline confirmed, her voice shaky. "Oh, God — you think someone might have picked it up and used it to steal my baby?"

"Can you think of anyone who might have done this?" the manager asked, the same question the police asked when they finally arrived almost half an hour later.

"Did you notice anyone suspicious, perhaps someone following you around?" the police asked.

"No one," Caroline said, her body growing numb with fear and fatigue. Every time she answered one of their relentless questions, she felt her energy dim, her voice grow weaker. Almost two hours had passed since they'd returned to their suite. It was after midnight. A search of the hotel and its grounds had thus far proved fruitless. Samantha was gone. By now she could be anywhere. "Can't you issue an Amber Alert?"

"We're not in California," Hunter said, his voice betraying his impatience. With the police. With their questions. With her. "They don't have Amber Alerts in Mexico."

"We've notified the border patrol to be on the lookout for anyone traveling with a small child," one of the officers said. Caroline had initially thought there were two policemen, but now she saw that there were three, two of them looking barely out of their teens, one closer to middle age. All had black hair and piercing, judgmental eyes. The younger two wore uniforms of navy pants and white shirts; the oldest was dressed in street clothes, gray pants, and a rumpled short-sleeved shirt he hadn't bothered to tuck in.

Caroline thought of the thousands of people who snuck across Mexico's border into California every year, and her body filled with despair. The border was so close, and they'd already lost so much time. If someone had wanted to sneak her daughter into the United States, she was long gone by now. The greater likelihood was that whoever took her was still in Rosarito, that he'd taken her somewhere close by for his own perverse purposes. The police were conducting room-to-room searches of both wings of the hotel. "There was a waiter," Caroline said with a shudder, her mind's eye filling with the image of a man in a white jacket pushing a portable dinner table down the hall. "Room service. I passed him in the corridor after I checked on the kids. He stopped a few doors down."

"What time was this?"

"Around nine o'clock."

"We'll check on it," the hotel manager said, already speaking into his cell phone.

"And I saw a housekeeper on the floor at four o'clock. No," she amended immediately, "it was closer to four-fifteen. I told her I'd lost my keycard and asked if she could use her master key to let me inside."

The manager nodded, relayed this information to the person he was speaking to.

"Just how many people have access to master keys?" Hunter asked.

The hotel manager lifted his shoulders in an exaggerated shrug. "Many people — the senior staff, housekeeping, the clerks at the reception desk, the valets who bring your luggage to your rooms. The same as in hotels in America."

Caroline noted the defensiveness in the manager's voice.

"So the last time you saw your daughter was . . . when exactly?" the oldest officer asked Hunter.

"Nine-thirty."

The officer turned his gaze to Caroline. "And you checked her again at ten?"

"No. We were leaving in a few minutes, so Hunter said it wasn't necessary." She glanced accusingly at her husband, who immediately looked away. In truth, it had been more like ten minutes, she realized. Would those ten minutes have made a difference?

"So it would appear your daughter disappeared sometime between nine-thirty and shortly after ten o'clock."

"Yes," Caroline and Hunter said together.

"And that you were the last person to see her," the officer said to Hunter.

"Yes," Hunter said, his eyes growing opaque with tears.

The phone rang. One of the younger officers directed Hunter to answer it.

Caroline felt a sudden surge of hope. Was it possible Samantha had been kidnapped and was being held for ransom? Was it the kidnapper on the phone, calling with his set of demands? *Whatever you want,* Caroline thought. *We'll give you all the money we have. Just bring my daughter back to us, unharmed.*

"Hello?" Hunter said, listening for several seconds before lowering the phone to his chest. "It's your brother," he told Caroline. "He's calling to make sure everything is okay. Apparently the police just searched their room, told them a child had gone missing . . ." His voice caught in his throat. He hung up the phone without saying anything further.

Minutes later, Steve and Becky were banging on their door. The police ushered them inside. Peggy and Fletcher arrived soon after, Rain and Jerrod only seconds behind them.

"My God, what happened?" Becky asked, rushing to Caroline's side, her voice as shrill as an alarm clock, jolting Michelle from her sleep.

"Mommy!" the child cried, sitting up and burrowing into her mother's chest.

"Where's Samantha?" Becky asked.

"Oh, God," Peggy said, eyes darting frantically in all directions.

"It's Samantha?" Rain asked. "Samantha's the child who's missing?"

"How can that be?" Jerrod asked. "You checked on her every half hour."

"The eight of you were having dinner together?" one of the officers asked.

Caroline could no longer differentiate between the various voices. She felt as if someone had lowered a giant glass bell jar over her entire body, like that author who had committed suicide by sticking her head in an oven. What was her name?

"Breathe," she heard Peggy say as she sat down beside her and put her arm across her shoulder, although the invisible jar prevented Caroline from actually feeling her touch.

"Yes," Jerrod answered the officer. "In the garden restaurant directly below. You can see it from the window." He walked to the window and pointed. "Yes. There. You can actually see our table."

"What was the name of that writer?" Caroline asked Peggy. "The one who committed suicide by sticking her head in an oven?"

"What did she say?" Becky asked.

"Sylvia something, I think."

"Sylvia Plath," Peggy told her.

"Right."

"Why is she talking about Sylvia Plath?" Rain asked.

"I think she's in shock," Peggy said. "Caroline? Caroline, are you okay?"

"Samantha's gone," Caroline said.

"I know."

"I should never have left her."

"Mommy, I have to go to the bathroom," Michelle said.

"I'll take you," Peggy offered.

"I want Mommy to take me." Michelle's hands wrapped around her mother's neck, breaking through the invisible glass shield.

Caroline felt the air being squeezed from her body, as if she were being strangled. "Please, somebody," she cried. "Get her off me."

Everyone's eyes focused immediately on Caroline.

"I'll take her," Becky said quickly, lifting the squirming youngster into her arms and carrying her into the bathroom, Michelle screaming in protest.

The police continued to ask variations of the same questions for the next hour, to which the group gave variations of the same answers. "Did any of you accompany your friends when they went to check on their daughters?" one of the officers asked.

"No," they answered.

"Why do you ask that?" Steve said.

"What are you implying?" Hunter asked.

Caroline knew why they were asking. Her husband had been the last person to see Samantha. Was it possible that something had happened on his watch? Could he be in any way responsible for their daughter's disappearance?

No, he wasn't responsible, she decided, answering her own question. Still, it was at Hunter's insistence that they'd left their girls alone. Which made him responsible after all.

Except I can't blame him, she thought in her next breath. *I gave in. I went along. I'm just as guilty. This is my fault, too.*

"What happens now?" Hunter asked as the police were closing their notepads and preparing to leave.

"You go to bed, try to get some sleep," the oldest of the officers answered. Caroline thought she'd heard one of the other officers refer to him as Detective Ramos, but she wasn't sure. "We'll meet again in the morning."

"You expect us to sleep?"

"Probably not," Ramos conceded. "But it

would be a good idea to try." He checked his watch. "It's almost two A.M. Nothing more will be accomplished tonight. We'll resume our search in the morning and contact the local papers if we haven't found your daughter by noon."

"That's it?"

"The border has been notified. Officer Mendoza will be posted outside your door all night in case anyone tries to contact you. We'll follow up, check on the waiter you saw in the hall and the housekeeper you talked to, conduct interviews with the entire staff. But this will all take time. Please, Mr. and Mrs. Shipley. Try to get some sleep. Your daughter needs you." His eyes fell on Michelle, who was once again fast asleep in her mother's arms, then circled the room, sizing up its occupants. "Obviously I need all of you to be available tomorrow."

"We're supposed to be leaving tomorrow," Rain said.

"Clearly that's not happening," Peggy said, her voice a sharp rebuke.

"Of course not. I didn't mean . . ."

"Mr. Shipley, do you have a picture of your daughter that I can borrow?" Officer Ramos interrupted.

Hunter reached into his wallet, removed a small photo of Samantha from behind his driver's license. "I'm sorry. It's a few months old."

"Beautiful child," Ramos said, tucking the picture into the pocket of his shirt. "I assure you, we'll do everything in our power to get her back to you."

"Do you want us to stay here tonight?" Becky asked Caroline after the police and the hotel manager had left.

"No," Hunter told their friends. "Ramos is right. It's going to be a long day tomorrow. Get some sleep. We'll see you in the morning."

Caroline watched her friends approach in single file to kiss her cheek or give her a hug. But she felt nothing. Her baby was gone. Someone had entered their suite and taken her while she and her husband were downstairs enjoying crêpes suzette. She should never have let him persuade her to leave their daughters alone. If she'd stood her ground, none of this would be happening.

Her brother and Becky were the last to leave. "You're sure you want us to go?" Becky asked again.

Caroline nodded. Steve leaned in to take her in his arms. "Please don't call Mom," she whispered.

"I won't."

But even as he was saying the words, Caroline knew he'd be on the phone first thing in the morning. *Please, God,* she thought, *let us find Samantha before then.*

NINE:
THE PRESENT

The phone rang at just past six-thirty the next morning. Caroline reached across the bed and answered it before it could ring a second time. "Hello?" she whispered, glancing toward the other bed and watching Michelle turn over in her sleep.

"It's me," Lili said.

"Thank God. Where are you?"

"Can you meet me?"

"Of course. When?"

"Now."

"Where?"

The girl gave Caroline an address. "Come alone." The line went dead.

Caroline threw herself out of bed and jumped into her clothes, taking less than a minute to brush her teeth and splash some cold water on her face. She scribbled a brief note for Michelle — *Back soon. Don't worry* — then snuck out of the hotel room and hurried down the hall, boots in hand. She gave no thought to what she was doing or that no one would have any idea where she was. She gave only fleeting thought to the fact that Lili knew she wasn't alone.

She raced down eight flights of stairs and pushed her way through the lobby doors onto the street, her boots now on her feet, although she had no memory of having put them on. A cab was idling on the other side of the road, but even after she waved frantically in his direction, the driver remained stubbornly where he was. She ran across the street, slipping on the icy road and almost falling before she reached him.

"Where to?" he asked as she climbed into the backseat. Caroline recognized him as the same man who'd driven her and Michelle to the hotel from the airport the day before, but she quickly dismissed the coincidence. "I am not familiar with any such place," he said when she gave him the address.

Caroline wondered if the girl was playing with her, leading her from one dead end to another in some sort of elaborate sick joke. "Can you check? Please, I'm in a hurry."

"My GPS, she's not working." Reluctantly, the cabbie pulled a map from his glove compartment and unfolded it, studying it carefully before dropping it to the seat beside him. “Ah, yes. Now I see it.”

Except he couldn’t find it, and they drove around for almost twenty minutes until it became obvious even to Caroline, who didn’t know the city but *did* recognize the same snowdrift after they’d passed it for the third time, that they’d been driving around in circles.

“Am lost,” the driver admitted finally, pulling to a stop and checking the map again.

“Please,” Caroline begged. “I’m already very late.” Would Lili decide Caroline had changed her mind about meeting her and leave? Would she call the hotel again, wake up Michelle?

“Ah, here it is,” the driver said, jabbing at the map with his index finger. “I know now. Is not so far away.”

“Hurry. Please.”

“Don’t worry. We be there in five minutes.”

Except they’d already been driving around for almost half an hour, the morning rush hour had begun, and they soon found themselves mired in a traffic jam several blocks long. “Looks like an accident,” the cabbie said with a shrug. “What can you do?”

“Is there another route we could take?”

Without a word, the driver did an illegal U-turn and sped down a side street, gunning the engine and throwing up a cloud of snow in his wake.

Caroline heard the sirens before she saw the police car. "No," she muttered. "Please, no."

"Where's the fire?" the policeman asked, approaching the car and leaning into the front seat, his helmet covering his head and face except for his dark eyes.

I know those eyes, Caroline thought, as the taxi driver handed over his license and registration.

"We've already had one terrible accident here this morning," the officer continued. "Not ten minutes ago, a teenage girl was hit by a speeding car as she was crossing the street."

"Is she all right?" the cabdriver asked.

Caroline felt a scream building in the back of her throat. Was it possible that girl was Lili?

"Afraid not." The officer removed his helmet, revealing a head of thick, black hair. He stared accusingly at Caroline, as if she were the one responsible.

"Detective Ramos?" Caroline whispered, the scream in her throat gaining traction and filling her mouth like bile.

"This is your fault," he told her. "You should never have left her alone."

The scream shot from Caroline's lips into the surrounding air.

"Mom?" a voice called from somewhere above her head. "Mom? Mother, wake up!"

Caroline bolted up in bed, her eyes darting around the hotel room, trying to bring it into focus. "What's happening?"

"You're having a nightmare."

"What?"

"You were having a nightmare," Michelle said, relegating it to the past tense. "God, look at you. You're soaking wet."

Caroline swiped at the pool of sweat between her breasts. She pushed a clump of damp hair away from her forehead.

"You scared the hell out of me," Michelle said. "What were you dreaming about?"

Caroline shook her head. "I can't tell you."

"What do you mean, you can't tell me? Why the hell not?"

"My mother always said it's bad luck to tell your dreams before breakfast because the bad ones will come true."

"Since when did you start listening to Grandma Mary?" Michelle asked.

She was right. Caroline had spent a lifetime trying to ignore her mother's unsolicited advice. "I'll tell you after breakfast," she said anyway.

Except that by the time they'd finished their coffee, Caroline had forgotten all but a few vague details of her nightmare. "It was one of those frustrating dreams where you keep trying to get somewhere but something keeps getting in your way. I probably should have realized it was a dream when I saw the cabdriver."

"What are you talking about?" Michelle asked.

"And Detective Ramos."

"Who's Detective Ramos?"

"You wouldn't remember."

They spent the morning sitting in the lobby of the hotel on the off chance that Lili would finally turn up, then called for a taxi to take them to the airport when she didn't. As the cab pulled away from the curb, Caroline took a last look down the snow-lined street.

"She's not there, Mother."

"I know."

"She never had any intention of showing up."

"You're right." Was she? "Maybe we should have waited longer."

"And miss our flight? Besides, you left her a note."

Caroline felt a pang of guilt and looked

into her lap. She'd thought she was being discreet when she'd left that note for Lili with the reception desk.

"Stop worrying. I'm sure she'll contact you again," Michelle was saying as they settled into their seats on the plane. "She'll have some sort of sob story, of course, a reason she couldn't meet you. Then she'll promise to make it up to you. She'll offer to come to San Diego. Of course she'll need money. Yada, yada, yada. It's like those Internet scams from Nigeria. They're transparent as hell, but you wouldn't believe how many people fall for those things."

I'd believe it, Caroline thought, but said nothing. She wished Michelle would stop talking. She'd made her point, her point being that her mother was an idiot. Caroline leaned her head back in her seat and closed her eyes. After a few minutes, Michelle took the hint and they spent the duration of the flight in silence.

Hunter was waiting for them when they pushed through the heavy, opaque glass doors into the arrival area of San Diego International Airport. He was wearing a lightweight navy suit and a blue-and-yellow-striped tie, having come straight from the office. "What the hell were you thinking?"

he demanded, grabbing their overnight bags as he led them toward the parking lot.

"Oh, just feel that glorious warm air," Michelle said, doffing her heavy jacket.

"You don't have to carry my bag," Caroline told her former husband. "I can manage."

"I've got it, Caroline. Just answer the question."

"We're not in court. I'm not on the witness stand. And you already know what I was doing."

"Some girl phones, tells you she's Samantha, and you go running? You honestly thought there was a chance this girl was our daughter?"

"I guess I did."

"She didn't show up, did she? She didn't even call."

"You know she didn't," Caroline said. Michelle had obviously phoned her father from the Calgary airport, relayed the depressing details of their trip, and told him what flight they'd be on.

"How much did that little escapade cost you anyway?"

"What difference does it make?"

"Last-minute tickets don't come cheap, as we know from past experience. They had to set you back a pretty penny."

"A pretty penny? Who says things like that anymore?" Caroline said, annoyed at Hunter's proprietary attitude. They were no longer husband and wife, a decision he'd made for the two of them a dozen years ago. What right did he have to question her expenses? They reached his cream-colored BMW. "Anyway, I'm sure the pennies aren't nearly as pretty as the ones you spend on a new car every year."

"I lease," he reminded her. "And I'm still paying alimony, if I'm not mistaken . . ."

"Have you ever been?" Caroline interrupted.

". . . which gives me some rights . . ."

"Please," Michelle said. "Do you have to argue about this now?"

"No," Caroline said. "I'd be more than happy to take a cab."

"Get in the car," her ex-husband directed, throwing the two overnight bags into the trunk and climbing behind the wheel as Michelle crawled into the backseat, leaving the front seat empty for her mother.

Reluctantly, Caroline took her place beside her former husband, trying not to notice how handsome he looked. As good as ever. Maybe even better. His hair had yet to turn gray or thin out, and his waistline was as trim as it had always been. If anything, the years had sharpened his features, emphasizing the prominence of his cheekbones, which in turn emphasized the fullness of his lips. "How's the baby?" Caroline asked in an effort to clear her head of such disconcerting thoughts.

"She's fine," Hunter said, paying the attendant and pulling out of the parking lot. "Don't change the subject."

"I wasn't aware we had a subject."

"Just tell me what happened. Everything. From the beginning."

Caroline wasn't sure what beginning he was referring to exactly, but the one thing she *was* sure of was that it was pointless to protest further. Hunter was a good lawyer, maybe even a great one. If there was one thing he knew, it was how to argue. And if he couldn't win outright, he'd wear you down over time. Might as well get it over with, she decided, starting with Lili's phone call. She watched his face as he listened, his expression changing from curiosity to disbelief to flat-out anger. When she reached the part about leaving a note for Lili with the reception desk when they checked out of the hotel, he was already halfway out of his seat, his entire body swiveled toward her.

"Watch where you're going," she cautioned.

Hunter returned his attention to the road. But even in profile his outrage was formidable. "And you didn't even think to call me about this?"

"Why would I do that?"

"I don't know. Maybe because Samantha was my daughter, too."

Caroline blanched at Hunter's use of the past tense. "What are you saying? That you would have come with me?"

"I might have. You didn't give me that chance."

"Because you wouldn't have come. You would have said it was a wild-goose chase and I was a fool to even consider it, just like you did when I went to Tacoma and Miami. Be honest, Hunter. There's no way you would have gone to Calgary. Or that Diana would have let you go," she added, drawing a measure of satisfaction when she saw him flinch. She'd heard from multiple sources that his much younger wife had him wrapped around her little finger and that he rarely made a move without her okay.

"That's not the point."

"What *is* the point?"

"The point is that we could have talked it through. We *should* have talked it through."

"We don't talk, Hunter. We never have."

"That's ridiculous. We were married for

twelve years. You're saying we never talked?"

"*You* talked. I listened."

"That's bullshit and you know it."

"Face it, Hunter. You're a bully. In court and out."

"And you're a victim. Like always. It's the same old shit."

"Guys, please," Michelle pleaded from the backseat. "Can we not do this?"

"You should have phoned me," Hunter repeated, either unmindful or uncaring of his daughter's request. "You should have told me what was happening. You should have given me the option. Admit it."

"Only if you admit that there's no way you would have gone with me," Caroline said, once again standing her ground, something she wished she'd done more often during their dozen years together. Maybe if she had, they wouldn't be having this stupid argument. Samantha would never have gone missing.

"Well, I guess we'll never know," Hunter said.

"*I* know."

"Right. Because you know everything."

"I know there's no way Hunter Shipley would have taken a few days off work for something as unimportant as his family."

"Okay. That's enough. You're way off base."

"Really? How many days did you take off work after Samantha disappeared?" Caroline knew she was being unreasonable, but the words escaped her mouth before she could stop them, pushed out by fifteen years of repressed rage.

"Mom," Michelle said. "Let's just drop it, okay?"

"How many days, Hunter? Thirty? Twenty? Ten?"

"I stayed . . ."

"Seven whole days," Caroline said. "You stayed one whole week."

"That's not fair."

"Really? How fair were you? Leaving me alone in Mexico to deal with everything."

"I asked you to come home. I begged you, for God's sake."

"And I begged you to stay." *Please, Hunter,* she'd begged. *Just give it a little more time.* The same way she'd begged when he told her he was ending their marriage.

"The investigation was going nowhere. The police had pretty much made up their minds that we were behind Samantha's disappearance. There was nothing more to be accomplished by staying . . ."

"You left me," Caroline said, no longer

sure if she was referring to the time he left Mexico or the time he left for good.

"I hired a private detective . . ."

"Whom you fired after three months."

"Because he was getting nowhere."

"Because he was costing you a *pretty penny.*"

"Goddamn you, Caroline," Hunter muttered.

"Goddamn *you,*" she said in return.

Michelle fell back against her leather seat, the movement creating an audible *whoosh.* "I need a drink," she said.

TEN: FIFTEEN YEARS AGO

"Tell me you're not seriously considering going home," Caroline demanded of her husband.

"It's something we *have* to consider," Hunter said. "It's been almost a week."

"It's been five days."

"And the police are no further ahead than they were the night Samantha disappeared."

"That's not true. They have leads . . ."

"They have nothing." Hunter plopped down on the sofa in the living room of their suite, running his hand through his thick brown hair in frustration.

Caroline walked to the window, stared down at the restaurant below, spotting her mother and Michelle having lunch under one of the multiple red umbrellas. Her mother had insisted on coming to Rosarito as soon as Steve had called her with the awful news. She'd burst into their suite and immediately wrapped Caroline in a tight, almost suffocating embrace. Caroline had instantly reciprocated, gratefully clinging to her mother, her entire body going limp. "Mommy," she heard herself sob into the silk shoulder of her dress.

"How could you let this happen?" her mother said.

"We have to look at this realistically," Hunter was saying now.

Caroline wanted to walk over to where he was sitting, slap him hard across the side of his head, and shout, "How's this for realism?" Instead, she stopped pacing and waited for him to continue.

"It's been five days," he reiterated. "The police have searched the hotel and grounds at least a dozen times and found nothing. The guests have all been investigated and cleared . . ."

"There's that man who had a collection of pornography on his computer . . ."

"The pictures were all of grown men. And his alibi checked out: he and his friends were at a nightclub down the beach when Samantha disappeared. They have a roomful of witnesses."

"Samantha didn't just *disappear,*" Caroline said, tired of the euphemism that implied her daughter had somehow magically vanished into thin air. "She was abducted. Someone took her." She burst into a flood of angry tears. How many tears could one body hold? How many could she spill before she drowned in them?

Hunter was immediately at her side, his arms moving helplessly around her, as if seeking a safe place to land.

"Don't," Caroline said before he could touch her.

He backed off and returned to the couch, although he remained standing.

"Go on," she said, trying, and failing, to keep the edge out of her voice. "We were being *realistic.*" She knew she was hurting him, pushing him further away every day. But he deserved to be pushed, to be hurt. This was his fault. Samantha was gone because of him.

And now he was talking about going as well. Leave the scene of the crime, return to San Diego, resume their normal life. Except they'd come here with two children, and they'd be leaving with one. Their lives would never be normal again.

"There's nothing more we can do here," he argued. "We've searched everywhere. We've told the police everything we know. We've gone over everything that happened that night a thousand times. We've answered all their questions. It's obvious they don't believe us. It's obvious they're starting to think we had something to do with it."

"What is it they think we did? Do they think we kidnapped our own child?"

The look in Hunter's eyes told Caroline it was worse than that.

"They can't seriously believe we murdered our daughter."

"I think that's exactly what they believe. Which is one of the reasons I want to get the hell out of Mexico."

"But if they believe that, what makes you think they'll let us leave?"

"Because they need proof to hold us and they don't have any."

"They don't have any because we didn't do anything," Caroline said, growing dizzy from going around in so many circles. Was Hunter right? Could the police really believe they'd murdered Samantha? Instead of searching for their little girl, were the police busy gathering evidence to implicate her and Hunter? If so, maybe he was right — nothing more would be accomplished here. They were jeopardizing not only their freedom but their lives. Maybe they should *get the hell out of Mexico* before it was too late. "What about that waiter from room service who nobody has seen since that night?"

"The police claim they're looking for him."

"You don't think they are?"

"Let's just say I don't think they're looking very hard."

"Why not, for God's sake?"

"Because they've already decided we're guilty," he said again. "This happens all the time, Caroline, and not just in Mexico. I see it every day. The police think they know who's responsible, so they get tunnel vision. They ignore other suspects and discount any evidence that doesn't support their position."

"What about the housekeeper?" Caroline persisted. "She had a master keycard. She could easily have gotten inside. Or the babysitter who was with the kids every night. You saw how she loved Samantha. Maybe she couldn't have children of her own. Maybe . . ."

"The housekeeper was at home with her family. The babysitter was on another assignment."

"They could have had accomplices . . ."

"Yes, they could have," Hunter agreed, sinking back down on the sofa. "But the police aren't looking for accomplices. They're looking at us. They're saying we're the ones who canceled the babysitter . . ."

"Which we didn't."

". . . that you were the one who phoned the front desk and told them not to put any more calls through to the room . . ."

"Because my mother had phoned and I didn't want anyone else to call and disturb the girls."

"It doesn't matter why. It just matters that it looks suspicious."

"How is that suspicious? Oh, God. It's hopeless. We'll never find her. We'll never get her back."

"It's not hopeless," Hunter said, his posture saying otherwise. "I've already talked to the senior partners at my firm. They think we should hire a private investigator, which I'll do as soon as we get home . . ."

"I can't do it. I can't go anywhere until I find my baby."

The phone rang. Hunter picked it up. "Yes," he said instead of "hello." Then, extending his hand toward her: "It's Peggy."

Caroline took the phone from his outstretched hand.

"How are you?" Peggy asked.

"Not good."

"Do you want me to come back?"

Yes, Caroline thought. "No," she said. Peggy hadn't wanted to leave Rosarito, but she had two children of her own to get back to. She had a job, responsibilities, a life.

Rain and Jerrod had been the first to go, leaving as soon as the police gave their okay, off to spend Thanksgiving in New York. Caroline didn't begrudge them their plans. They weren't close friends, and there was nothing they could do here. Besides, Rain's concern had verged on the spectacular, her sympathy so overwhelming that it left little room for Caroline to feel anything but numb. In truth, she'd been glad to see them go.

She was equally relieved when her brother and Becky followed suit the next day, the tension between the two having become unbearable after Mary's arrival. Peggy and Fletcher were the last to leave. "We're just a phone call away," Peggy had said then.

"What's happening?" she asked now.

"Apparently the police think we did it."

"That's ridiculous. What are you going to do?"

"Hunter wants us to go home."

"Maybe that's not such a bad idea."

"I don't know. He's called a press conference for this afternoon," Caroline said, feeling sick to her stomach. The world press had jumped on the story of Samantha's disappearance, and Hunter had decided they should sidestep the seeming incompetence of the Mexican police by appealing to the international community for help. At first Caroline had resisted taking her grief public, but Hunter was insistent that a mother's tears would go a long way toward getting Samantha back, so how could she refuse? The police were against them talking to the press, and had been successful so far in keeping the reporters at bay, claiming that such publicity would only hinder their investigation. But Hunter was convinced that they were only concerned about looking bad. Besides, he argued, the police thought that he and Caroline were guilty of murdering their own child. So, screw them.

"Let me know how it goes," Peggy said before hanging up.

"I guess we should start getting ready," Hunter said.

Caroline understood that he was referring to the press conference, but she wasn't sure what he meant by "getting ready."

"Maybe brush your hair, put on a bit of makeup," he explained, answering the question in her eyes.

Caroline ran a disinterested comb through her hair and applied a bit of waterproof mascara to her swollen eyes. She changed out of her shorts and oversized shirt into a modest beige sundress. Her skin was tanned, effectively hiding the blotches caused by days of constant crying, and she'd lost at least five pounds, unable to eat much or keep anything down. Still, when she looked at herself in the mirror, she was surprised to see a seemingly calm and controlled, albeit haunted-looking, woman staring back.

"Mommy!" Michelle shouted as the door to their suite opened. The child rushed into the room, throwing herself at her mother's knees and almost knocking her down.

"Hi, sweetheart," Caroline said, staring down at the deep purple fingerprints now spread across the bottom half of her dress.

"I had blueberry pie for dessert," Michelle announced.

"You'd better change," Hunter said.

Caroline returned to her bedroom and riffled through the closet. The beige sundress was pretty much the last clean article of clothing she had with her. The only other thing she could wear, besides shorts, bathing suits, or evening wear, was a blue-and-white-striped miniskirt and a sleeveless blue T-shirt.

"*That's* what you're wearing?" her mother asked when Caroline returned to the living room.

Caroline brushed aside her mother's words with a wave of her hand. What possible difference did it make what she wore?

Hunter scooped Michelle into his arms. Caroline noticed the child's hands had been washed clean. "Ready?" he asked, heading for the door.

As ready as I'll ever be, Caroline thought.

She spent the next two days in bed, poring over the papers and watching the news on TV.

"Haven't you had enough of that crap?" Hunter asked, throwing the last of his shirts into his suitcase and zipping it up, then depositing it by the bedroom door.

"Did you see this?" Caroline held out the latest edition of the *Los Angeles Times,* which her mother had brought back to the room earlier in the day. "We made the front page."

"Ignore it."

"Easy for you to say. You come off rather well, all things considered."

"Sweetheart, please . . ."

"You're the *handsome man barely holding himself together,*" she read. "You're the one *clinging tight to his daughter* while I'm the one who's *aloof* and *standing ramrod straight.*" She scoffed. "Who knew good posture was such a bad thing?"

"Don't do this to yourself . . ."

"They even comment on the shine in my hair, *as if she'd just come from the hairdresser,*" Caroline read, almost choking on the words. "I haven't washed my hair in a week, for God's sake. The stupid reporter doesn't know shine from grease."

"You can't let it get to you. You'll make yourself sick."

"Oh, and of course, we were out *cavorting with friends at a nearby restaurant* when it happened. God forbid they leave that part out." *Or mention that it was at your insistence,* she thought, her attention temporarily diverted by something on television. Their ill-fated press conference was once again being broadcast around the globe. "Oh, there I am again, still ramrod straight." *I* do *look aloof,* she thought. *My hair* does *look shiny. My skirt* is *very short,* as another paper had pointed out the day before.

We're asking for your help, Hunter said from the TV, his voice cracking.

If anybody out there knows anything, anything at all, Caroline continued, taking up the reins, her own voice surprisingly steady and clear, *if you think you might have seen Samantha, or have any clues as to her where-*

abouts, please contact the police immediately.

We just want our daughter back, Hunter said, his obvious emotion in direct contrast to his wife's eerily cool demeanor.

In fact, Caroline had been dangerously close to fainting. Her deliberately calm exterior masked an interior that was collapsing in on itself, like an imploding building. The steeliness of her voice had been the only thing keeping her upright.

Why did you leave your children alone? a reporter shouted out.

Is it true the police consider you a suspect?

Have you hired an attorney?

Is it true you're planning to leave Mexico?

"So," Caroline said, glancing at his suitcase, "you're all packed?"

He nodded. "It's not too late to change your mind and come with us."

"I'm not going anywhere."

"Caroline, please. Don't make me leave you here alone. If anything were to happen to you, I don't think I could live with myself."

"Nothing's going to happen to me. I'm a big girl. This is my decision. You don't have to feel guilty about leaving." Caroline knew he felt as guilty as she did about Samantha, maybe even more so. She'd heard him crying in the bathroom last night when he thought she was asleep. She'd even considered getting up and going to him, clinging to his side and crying with him, but she didn't. She couldn't. "You should go now. My mother will be getting anxious." Caroline pictured her mother waiting in the coffee shop with Michelle, repeatedly checking her watch.

"Please come with us."

"I can't."

"Michelle needs you."

"My mother will take good care of her."

"*I* need you."

Caroline said nothing.

The phone rang. Hunter walked to the side of the bed and picked it up. "Yes. Okay. I'm on my way." He replaced the receiver. "At least come downstairs, say goodbye."

"I've already said goodbye."

Hunter approached the side of the bed, shifting his weight from one foot to the other. "Don't I even get a kiss?"

"Hunter . . ."

"You have to stop blaming me," he said, his voice a plea. "This isn't my fault."

Caroline scrunched the paper in her hands into a tight little ball and hurled it angrily at the TV before jumping to her feet. "Not your fault? Really? Because I distinctly remember it was you who insisted that we leave the girls alone, that I was overreacting, that I was sounding just like my mother . . ."

"I never said that."

"You promised they'd be safe . . ."

"And I will be sorry to my dying day . . ."

"Sorry isn't enough."

"What do you want me to do?"

"I want you to find our daughter!"

"You don't think I want the same thing?"

We're asking for your help, Hunter was appealing from the TV in yet another repeat of the press conference. *We just want our daughter back.*

"How could you let this happen?" Caroline asked him, hearing her mother's voice echo through the room. She could tell by Hunter's face that he'd heard it, too.

"I'll call you when we get home," he said, picking up his suitcase and walking out of the room.

ELEVEN: THE PRESENT

"You're late," Mary said instead of hello.

"Happy Thanksgiving," Caroline said, ignoring the rebuke and giving her mother a kiss on the cheek. "I brought dessert." She held out the box containing the pumpkin pie she'd picked up from the gourmet grocery store on the way over.

Her mother made no move to take it from her. "Store-bought," she said with a lift of her well-plucked eyebrows, making the words sound vaguely obscene.

Caroline closed the front door behind her. "I thought you liked Nicola's pies."

Mary shrugged. "They're all right. Overpriced, like all their stuff. Steve and I prefer their apple to their pumpkin."

"They didn't have apple."

"Well, I guess when you leave things until the last minute . . . I'm surprised they were even open."

"Sorry. It's been a little hectic . . ." Caro-

line peered over her mother's shoulder into the empty living room. "Where is everyone?"

"No one's here yet."

"So I'm the first to arrive?"

"You're still late," her mother said.

Caroline sighed. "What do you want me to do with the pie?"

"Put it in the kitchen," Mary said, exiting the foyer for the living room.

Caroline proceeded down the hallway toward the kitchen at the back of the tidy bungalow. "Something smells good," she said, inhaling the aroma of roasting turkey and depositing the pumpkin pie on the counter. The small room had changed very little over the years. Despite new appliances and an update from laminate to granite countertops, it was essentially the same kitchen she remembered from her childhood: a slightly elongated square with a table and four chairs in front of a large window that overlooked a tiny backyard. Peering into the darkness, she pictured the old clothesline on which her mother used to air-dry the family's freshly laundered clothes. When Caroline was little, Mary would secure her to that clothesline with a long rope tied around her waist. "Stop squirming. It's for your own protection,"

she'd insist when Caroline tried to wiggle out of its grasp. Steve, of course, had endured no such curbs on his freedom. When Caroline had protested this unfairness to her mother and argued that she, too, should have the freedom to play unfettered on the streets with her friends, Mary pointed out that Caroline *had* no friends.

"It was nice of you to invite Peggy and Fletcher," Caroline said now, entering the living room.

She and Peggy had met in high school and bonded immediately, both being what is commonly referred to as "late bloomers." "Misfits" was probably the more accurate term. Both girls had been shy and flat-chested, more interested in books than boys, although maybe that was because the boys in their class were more interested in the less-bookish, better-developed girls. They were also both fatherless: Peggy had lost her dad to cancer when she was twelve, and Caroline lost her dad to her parents' acrimonious divorce a year later. Even though her father had tried for the better part of a year to maintain regular contact with his children, Mary had made that all but impossible, canceling agreed-upon visits at the last minute and scuttling proposed outings. Influenced by his mother, Steve had eventually refused to have anything to do with his father at all. The poor man had finally given up and moved to upstate New York, where he'd been killed in a car accident when Caroline was fifteen. "Couldn't have happened to a nicer guy," Caroline remembered her mother remarking to one of her bridge cronies. "Good riddance to bad rubbish." The usual assortment of bitter clichés that were Mary's stock-in-trade.

"You look nice," Caroline said to her mother in an effort to banish such unkind thoughts. It was Thanksgiving, after all. She was supposed to be awash in gratitude, not wallowing in past grievances. She sat down on the high-backed green velvet chair opposite the floral print sofa on which her mother was perched. "Is that a new dress?"

Mary patted the curls of her freshly streaked hair, styled the way she'd been wearing it for as long as Caroline could remember. *Short and sassy,* she liked to say. Although *short and stiff* was the better description, the tight curls kept in place by a daily deluge of hairspray. "A present from your brother," she said, caressing the folds of her silk print shirtwaist.

"That was very nice of him," Caroline said, trying to keep the shock out of her voice.

"Yes. He's very generous."

He should be, Caroline thought, *since he lives here rent-free and doesn't lift a finger to help out.* "Where is he anyway?"

"He had a business meeting."

"Really? On Thanksgiving?"

"You know your brother. Always working on something."

Always working the angles, Caroline thought. Although the angles hadn't been working for him for some time, his life having pretty much gone off the rails in the decade since he and Becky had divorced. First the real estate market had come crashing down. Then he'd lost his job. A string of disastrous investments had cost him pretty much everything he had left, including a newly purchased waterfront condo he'd bought at the height of the market and been forced to sell less than a year later at a substantial loss. His mother had attributed each successive failure to a combination of bad timing and worse luck, and had welcomed him back home with open arms. He'd been camping out in his old bedroom for the past three years, doing little but playing copious amounts of poker, drinking copious amounts of alcohol, and watching even more copious amounts of TV.

Ironically, he'd perked up, albeit briefly,

when Becky had come back into his life. She'd moved to Los Angeles immediately following their divorce, only to return four years later, having been diagnosed with terminal cancer. It turned out that the headaches that had plagued her for years were the by-product of a slow-growing but ultimately fatal brain tumor. She'd contacted Peggy, who had recently been appointed director of the newly opened Marigold Hospice, and shortly after that Becky had moved to the hospice, where she died two months after that. Surprisingly, Steve had been at her bedside every day, a sadly classic case of *too little, too late* and *you don't know what you've got till it's gone.*

"So, what's been doing?" Caroline asked her mother.

"What should be doing?" her mother asked in return.

Caroline shrugged. Her mother obviously wasn't going to make this easy. "I don't know. Have you seen any good movies?"

"I don't go to movies. You know that."

"Actually I didn't. I thought you loved movies."

"I used to. But they're all so violent now."

"What about bridge? I know you like that. Win any tournaments lately?"

"Not with Paula Harmon as a partner,

that's for sure. I don't know where her head is these days. I think she's losing it. We went down two tricks the other day when everyone else in the room made an overtrick. Then she got all defensive when I very gingerly tried to point out what she'd done wrong."

Caroline tried imagining her mother's "gingerly" attempt to correct her partner.

"What are you smiling about?"

"Nothing. Sorry," Caroline said, finding it odd to be apologizing for smiling. "I read somewhere that bridge players always think they're better players than their partners."

"What's that supposed to mean?"

"I . . . Nothing. It was just something I read."

"Well, it's stupid."

The doorbell rang.

Thank God, Caroline thought, jumping up and hurrying to the front door.

"Hi, there. Are we late?" Peggy asked as she and Fletcher stepped inside.

"Right on time," Mary said, coming up behind Caroline and accepting a bouquet of long-stemmed yellow roses from Peggy and a bottle of expensive white wine from Fletcher. "I'm so thrilled you could make it. Caroline, could you please put these gorgeous flowers in a vase? Don't forget to trim the stems." She handed them to Caroline with scarcely a glance in the roses' direction.

"Thank you so much for inviting us," Peggy said, following Mary into the living room as Caroline walked toward the kitchen.

"Fletcher, maybe you could open the wine," Caroline heard her mother say in an almost coquettish tone of voice.

"Okay. Where does she hide them?" she muttered as she searched through the cupboards for a vase.

"Talking to yourself again?" a male voice asked from behind her. "I hear that's the sign of a crazy person."

"Shit," Caroline exclaimed as she spun around to face her brother. He was sitting in one of the kitchen chairs, one long leg crossed over the other. "You scared me half to death. Where did you come from?"

He pointed in the direction of the bedrooms.

"I thought you were at a business meeting."

"I was. Snuck in twenty minutes ago. Thought I'd have a nap, but your scintillating conversation with Mother kept getting in the way. You might try the cupboard over there." Steve pointed toward a high cupboard above the stove.

Caroline had to stand on her tiptoes to reach the shelf, her fingers stretching toward the neat row of glass vases. "I don't suppose it would occur to you to help."

"It's much more fun to watch you struggle," he said as the heavy vase almost slipped through her fingers. "You sure you want that one?"

Caroline carried the vase to the sink where she filled it with water, then unwrapped the roses.

"Don't forget to trim the stems," Steve said with a wink.

She located a large pair of scissors in the top drawer next to the sink and proceeded to snip an inch from the bottom of each long stem, her brother chuckling all the while. She noted that he was having trouble focusing. "I see someone started celebrating a little early."

"And I see you brought pie."

"Pumpkin."

"I prefer apple."

"So I've heard." She finished trimming the roses, arranged them in the vase, and then picked it up and carried it into the hall. "Coming?" she asked her brother.

"Wouldn't miss it for the world."

"Steve, sweetheart, is that you?" Mary

asked as Caroline and her brother approached. "I thought I heard your voice."

"Happy Thanksgiving, Mother," Steve said, walking into her embrace. "Fletcher . . . Peggy. Good to see you again."

"How are you, Steve?" Fletcher asked.

"You're looking well," Peggy added.

"As are you." Steve dropped into the chair Caroline had occupied earlier.

Caroline deposited the vase on the coffee table in front of the sofa and stood back to admire it. "The flowers are so beautiful."

"They are. But why did you pick that vase?" Mary asked. "Surely there was a nicer one . . ."

"I tried to tell her," Steve said.

"This vase is perfect," Peggy said.

Mary sniffed at the flowers. "It's such a shame that roses don't smell anymore."

"Why is that, I wonder?" Steve asked. "And more to the point, what's everybody drinking?"

"Fletcher and Peggy brought a lovely bottle of Chardonnay. So thoughtful." Mary glanced pointedly at Caroline before pouring her son a glass and placing it in his outstretched hand.

"I wouldn't mind some," Caroline said.

"Are you sure, dear? You know how you get when you drink."

"Excuse me?"

"Allow me," Fletcher said, jumping up and filling a glass for Caroline as the doorbell rang.

"That'll be Micki," Mary said, heading for the front door.

"What is she talking about?" Caroline asked Peggy. "How do I get?"

"She's just baiting you," Peggy answered. "Try not to bite."

"I'd like to bite her head off, is what I'd like to do."

"And we're off," Steve said, smiling from ear to ear.

"Sorry I'm late," Caroline heard her daughter apologize from the foyer. "I waited forever for a bus."

"Don't give it a thought. You're right on time."

"I was at the hospice," Michelle said, entering the living room and nodding hello to everyone.

"I thought you worked mornings," Mary said.

"I switched shifts with this girl who needed her afternoons free. So now it's every Monday and Thursday from four till eight. They let me leave a little early tonight because of Thanksgiving."

"You're such a good girl. I don't know

how you do it." Mary stroked her granddaughter's long brown hair. "It must be so depressing."

"You'd think it would be," Michelle said, "but it's actually not."

"So, how did everything go?" Peggy asked. "They were serving a turkey dinner for the residents and their families," she told everyone.

"It went well," Michelle answered. "Everyone seemed to enjoy it."

"*Enjoy* being a relative term," Steve said, "considering everyone there is at death's door."

"Well, you won't catch me going to one of those places," Mary said. "I intend to die at home."

"Who are you kidding?" Steve downed the balance of his wine. "You have no intention of dying. Ever."

"Oh, darling." Mary laughed, and Caroline found herself wondering if her mother would have been so amused had she been the one to make that remark.

"Well, thanks for everything you're doing," Peggy said to Michelle.

"And thanks for joining us," Mary added. "I was afraid your father would insist you spend Thanksgiving dinner with him this year."

"They're going to Diana's parents' house for dinner. Besides, they understand that I always spend Thanksgiving dinner with my Grandma Mary." She hugged her grandmother and Mary responded by throwing her arm around Michelle's tiny waist with genuine affection.

Caroline understood that their closeness was the result of the bond that had been forged between them in the months after Samantha's disappearance, when Caroline had been unavailable, first physically and then emotionally, and she hated herself for being jealous of their obvious connection.

"I'd say such good deeds deserve to be rewarded," Steve said. "Perhaps a glass of wine . . ."

"Perhaps not," Caroline said quickly. "She's not allowed any alcohol."

"Oh, come on. It's Thanksgiving."

"Yes. And we're very thankful she's not in jail."

"Nice one, Mother," Michelle said.

"Was it really necessary to bring that up?" Mary asked.

Caroline lifted her own glass of wine. "Well, we all know how I get when I drink."

"Well, that was a nice evening," Michelle said, following her mother into their house and closing the door behind her.

"Yes. Dinner was lovely."

"Grandma Mary's such a good cook."

"How would you know? You hardly touched a thing."

Michelle gave her mother a look that Caroline was only too familiar with. "I ate plenty."

Caroline said nothing. She was too tired to argue.

"You were pretty quiet all night," Michelle said.

"Sometimes it's safer that way." Caroline headed for the stairs.

"You're not going to bed, are you? It's not even nine-thirty."

"I'm tired. Your grandmother takes a lot out of me."

"Ever think you're being too hard on her?"

"No," Caroline answered honestly. "Never."

"Well, *I* think you are."

"Ever think you're being too hard on *me*?" Caroline had no wish to continue the conversation. All she wanted to do was climb into a steaming-hot bath and crawl into bed. "Are you staying here tonight?" she asked when she felt Michelle's footsteps on the stairs behind her.

"Don't you want me to? I can go to Dad's

if you'd prefer."

"That's not what I said."

"It's what you implied."

Caroline stopped at the top of the stairs. "Michelle," she said, her patience evaporating. "Please. Do what you want." She turned and walked down the hall toward her bedroom. Stepping out of her shoes and unzipping her gray slacks, she left them lying on the floor as she crossed into the bathroom, her bare toes burrowing into the plush carpet. She reached into the claw-foot tub and turned on the hot water, watching the steam fill the room, mercifully coating the mirror over the sink and blocking out her reflection. She pulled her white sweater over her head and dropped it to the floor, then unhooked her bra and removed her panties, watching her underwear float toward the small mint-green bath mat. She was climbing into the tub when the phone rang.

Quickly wrapping a large green towel around her torso, she returned to her bedroom and answered it.

"Don't hang up," the voice said before she could speak.

Caroline sank down on the bed, her heart pounding. "Lili?"

"I'm so sorry."

"Where were you? I flew to Calgary, waited all day and night . . ."

"I know. I wanted to come."

"Why didn't you?"

"I was on my way. Then, I don't know . . . I just chickened out."

"I don't understand."

"I was afraid."

"Of what? That you'd be unmasked as a fraud?"

"I'm not a fraud."

"What, then? That we'd take the test and you'd find out you were wrong?"

A second's silence. Then: "That I'd find out I was right."

"I don't know what to say. You're the one who contacted me . . ."

"I know."

"I believed in you, that *you* believed . . . that you honestly wanted to find out the truth . . ."

"I do."

"I did exactly what you said . . ."

"I know."

"I spent the night in a hotel, waiting by the phone, praying you'd call . . ."

"I said I'm sorry."

"I took two days off work."

"I'll make it up to you."

"How? I'm not flying to Calgary again."

"I'll come to you."

"What?" Caroline was suddenly aware of a figure standing in the doorway.

"Who are you talking to?" Michelle asked, stepping into the room.

Caroline waved her away.

"I said, who are you talking to? It's her, isn't it?" Michelle marched to the bed and wrestled the phone from her mother's hand. "I told you she'd call again," she said, eluding Caroline's frantic efforts to get the phone back. "Listen to me, you lying little bitch . . ."

"Michelle, please . . . Don't . . ."

Michelle ignored her. "I don't know who the hell you are or what sick game you're playing, but I swear that if you ever call this house again, if you try to contact my mother in any way, I will call the police and have you arrested. Do you hear me? This shit stops now. Am I making myself perfectly clear?" She paused for breath, then threw the phone angrily to the bed.

Caroline immediately lunged in its direction, grabbing it and pressing it to her ear. "Lili? Lili?"

"She hung up. And of course she blocked her number. There's no way to check . . ."

"What have you done?" Caroline stared helplessly at the phone, then at Michelle.

"What have I done? What have *I* done?"

"You shouldn't have talked to her like that."

"Really? How was I supposed to talk to her? *Oh, hello, Lili. Or would you prefer I call you Samantha? So nice to meet you. I've really missed having a sister.* Is that what you wanted me to say?"

"You didn't have to call her a liar."

"Why not? That's what she is."

"We don't know that."

"*I* know. And so do you. Didn't I tell you this was going to happen? Didn't I? What did she say? That she was sorry, that she'd make it up to you, that she'd come to San Diego . . . Shit, is that the water I hear running?" Michelle ran into the bathroom.

Caroline heard the bathwater suddenly shut off.

Michelle came back into the room, wiping her hands on the front of her black denim jeans. "Well, that was lucky. The damn thing was about to overflow. Good thing I was here."

"Good thing you were here," Caroline repeated without conviction.

"Yeah, well. Hurray for me. Another crisis averted." She pried the phone from Caroline's hand and tucked it into a back pocket of her jeans. "For safekeeping," she said. Then she walked to the bedroom door. “I’ll be in my room. Shout if you need anything.”

“I won’t need anything.”

“That’s what I figured.”

The next time Caroline looked toward the doorway, Michelle was gone.

TWELVE: FOURTEEN YEARS AGO

"Mr. Wolford will see you now."

Caroline smiled at the young woman, the youngest and prettiest of the three secretaries sitting behind the reception counter in the main office of Washington High School. Bidding a silent goodbye to the gum-chewing teenage girl slouched in the seat beside her, she pushed herself out of her uncomfortable wooden chair, one of four resting against the wall of the small waiting area in which she'd been sitting for the better part of twenty minutes. She tucked her hair behind her ears and straightened the creases of her dark blue dress, then followed the apple-cheeked young woman into the office of Barry Wolford, ignoring the veiled stares of the other secretaries, and almost crashing into a lanky six-footer who was just leaving the principal's office.

"What do we say, Ricky?" a man's voice boomed from inside the room.

"Excuse me," the boy said to Caroline, eyes resolutely on the floor.

"It was my fault," she acknowledged in return. *Everything, my fault.*

"Teenagers," Barry Wolford said, motioning for Caroline to sit down in the chair in front of his desk. He was about fifty and balding, with noticeable stains under the arms of his pale yellow open-necked shirt. "Close the door, please, Tracy."

A look of disappointment crossed Tracy's unlined face, causing her bright coral lips to turn down. No doubt she and the other secretaries had been hoping to catch snatches of the principal's interview with the infamous Caroline Shipley. Caroline had heard their whispers as she sat waiting for her interview. *Really? She thinks she'll get a job here? Wolford's out of his mind if he hires her. What would the parents think?*

"Sorry to have kept you waiting." Barry Wolford lowered his ample frame into the curved-back wooden swivel chair behind his cluttered desk. He cleared his throat and smiled. The smile was half-hearted at best, stopping well short of his eyes. Caroline immediately understood that this interview would go the same way as the ones she'd already endured at other high schools in the area over the last four months, which was not well at all.

She wasn't sure how many more such interviews she could subject herself to. It had taken all her courage and what was left of her self-esteem to put herself out there by re-entering the workforce. She knew there'd be opposition to hiring her, that the San Diego Unified School District Board would frown on her application, that there would be parental opposition to any school brave enough to take her on. But what choice did she have? She was going crazy sitting at home, wallowing in self-pity, waiting for the phone to ring with news of Samantha, news that never came. "So, I see you used to teach math . . ."

"At Herbert Hoover High School, yes. For four years. I've always loved math. My father was a math teacher . . ."

"I assume you've already spoken to someone at Hoover?" he interrupted.

"I did, actually, yes. There were no positions."

"I'm not surprised, considering."

"Considering?"

"You've been out of the workforce for a while now."

"Yes. Yes, I have. But I've kept up my skills . . ."

"That's admirable. But unfortunately for

someone like you, we seem to be enjoying a glut of teachers at the moment."

"So I've been told."

"Eager new hopefuls graduating every day. Hard to get back into the job market when you're competing against all these fresh young faces."

"On the other hand, there's something to be said for experience."

"I couldn't agree more," he said, and Caroline felt a surge of hope. "Mind my asking why you stopped teaching?"

Caroline swallowed. "Uh . . . the usual reasons, I guess. Family, children . . ."

"Yes, they can certainly slow one down."

"Well . . . that's not really what I meant."

"You're saying you quit to be a stay-at-home mother," Wolford said, rephrasing. He lifted his pen as if to jot this down, then lowered it without writing anything. "Nothing more rewarding than being a parent."

Caroline nodded.

"I have four children of my own." He turned several framed photographs on his desk in her direction.

"They're lovely," Caroline said, glancing at the smiling faces of his family.

"Not always easy, of course. But whoever said that being a parent was supposed to be easy?"

Caroline tried to smile, but managed only a twitch. She tried to tell herself that Barry Wolford was only making conversation, that his comments were innocent. Was it possible he had no idea who she was? Her picture had been all over the newspapers and television for more than a year. Last week had marked the first anniversary of Samantha's disappearance, and it seemed as if every paper in the country had made note of that fact. She'd even made the cover of *People,* standing blank-eyed and erect under the lurid headline WHATEVER HAPPENED TO BABY SAMANTHA? Her name was practically a household word, a synonym for bad parenting. Could it be that he really didn't recognize her?

"How many children do you have, if you don't mind my asking?"

"My daughter is six years old," Caroline said, straining to keep her voice steady.

"Sorry. I thought you said 'children,' plural," he prodded.

"Yes. Uh . . . is this relevant?"

"Only if you consider children relevant, I guess. Some people do. Some don't."

Caroline felt her stomach constrict. "I'm not sure I understand."

"What's the expression — out of sight, out of mind?"

"What exactly are you getting at, Mr. Wolford?"

"Just trying to figure out what motivates someone like you."

"Someone like me?"

"A woman who leaves two young children alone in a Mexican hotel room so she can go out partying with her friends . . ."

So he *did* know who she was, had known all along. He'd been toying with her, having cruel fun at her expense.

"Assuming, of course, that's the least of what she did."

Caroline jumped to her feet, although outrage kept her rooted to the spot.

"There are no jobs available to you here at Washington High," Barry Wolford said, standing up and looming menacingly over his desk. "Nor will there ever be, as long as I'm principal here."

"Why are you doing this? Why even bother setting up an interview?"

"Just wanted to meet the infamous Caroline Shipley, see if she'd actually have the gall to show up. Although I don't know why I'm surprised. Clearly you have no shame."

You're wrong, Caroline thought. *I have nothing* but *shame.*

"Frankly, I'd be surprised if any school in the city would consider hiring someone so irresponsible —"

"You have no idea what you're talking about."

"Really? I know that a woman who can't take care of her own children has no business around other people's. I know that she should be embarrassed to show her face around decent, God-fearing members of society."

"Go to hell," Caroline whispered.

"You first," he said.

Too late, Caroline thought as she fled the premises. *I'm already there.*

Even though it was a weekday, Balboa Park was crowded. It always was. The landmark destination was the heart of San Diego, and had been since the early twentieth century. It was filled with lush gardens, museums, theaters, and beautiful Spanish-style pavilions, as well as being the site of the world-famous San Diego Zoo. The park attracted thousands of people, both tourists and locals, every day of every week of every month. Caroline had come here often over the past year, walking the grounds and trying to lose herself in the crowds.

She sank onto a nearby bench. It wasn't that easy to lose yourself, she'd discovered. Despite being the eighth-largest city in the

United States and the second-largest city in California, with a population of close to 1.3 million people, San Diego was really a small town at its core. It was hard to get lost in a small town.

When she'd first returned from Rosarito, she'd spent entire days in the vast parkland, wandering from garden to garden, attraction to attraction, peering into the faces of each and every small child, searching for Samantha under a floppy cotton sunbonnet or snoozing in her father's arms, her head resting on his shoulder. How many times had she stolen a peek into a passing stroller, convinced she might encounter her daughter's sweet face? It was possible, wasn't it? *Wasn't it?*

Even if whoever had taken her had cut and dyed her hair, somehow rendered the child virtually unrecognizable, Caroline was convinced she would recognize Samantha instantly. A mother surely knows her own child, no matter what, no matter how many years have passed. *Dear God,* she thought now. *My baby has been missing for more than a year.*

"I'm sorry. Is there a problem?" a woman asked from somewhere beside her, her tone stopping just short of accusatory.

Caroline's eyes snapped into focus. A

young woman was sitting on the far end of the bench, breast-feeding an infant. Caroline must have been staring at her for some time without realizing it.

"I'm within my rights," the woman said. She was younger than Caroline, with long blond hair and deep bags under her eyes, probably from lack of sleep.

"Sorry. I guess I tuned out for a few minutes. I didn't mean to stare."

The woman's eyes narrowed. "I know you," she said slowly. "You're that woman whose baby disappeared in Mexico."

Caroline was immediately on her feet.

"Did you do it?" she heard the woman call after her. "Did you murder your own child?"

"You're very late," Caroline said when Hunter walked through the door at half past nine that night.

"Sorry. There was an emergency partners' meeting. It went on forever. I went to the gym after to unwind."

Caroline nodded knowingly. Hunter had been made a partner in his prestigious downtown law firm two months ago, but she doubted that was where he'd been. There had been too many emergency meetings, too many late nights unwinding at the gym. She found it interesting that her husband had received little of the vitriol that had come her way in the aftermath of Samantha's disappearance, that his career had actually advanced. And why not? Hunter's clients weren't the kind to be overly bothered by scandal. As long as he did his job, as long as he continued to negotiate successful deals and mergers, as long as he could be counted on to make them money, he was an asset, regardless of what was happening in his personal life. Ironically, the tragedy of losing his daughter had made him seem noble. It was left to Caroline to bear the burden of their guilt.

"What are you doing, sitting here in the dark?" He turned on the lamp beside the sofa and took off his jacket. Caroline put her hand over her eyes to block out the unwanted light. "Michelle asleep?"

"Yes."

"She give you any problems?"

"The usual. She wanted her Grandma Mary. Apparently she's a much better story reader than I am. You smell good," she added, an observation more than a compliment.

"Took a shower," he said, his voice casual. "I was pretty sweaty." He lowered himself into one of two beige tub chairs across from where Caroline sat on the gold-and-beige-striped couch. "How'd the interview go?"

"Not good."

"Sorry."

Caroline shrugged.

"Something will turn up eventually."

"I doubt it. It seems there are a lot of people who don't exactly relish the idea of someone who might have murdered her own child taking care of theirs. Imagine that."

Hunter sighed. "Maybe you've rushed things. Maybe it's still too early. Maybe you should go slower, start by putting your name on a list of substitute teachers . . ."

"I did that months ago," Caroline said testily, tired of all the maybes. "Phone's not exactly ringing off the hook."

"Well, December's an especially hard time of year."

December, Caroline repeated silently, thinking ahead to Christmas. Was it possible it was Christmas already? She'd spent last Christmas in Mexico, miserable and alone, waiting for some word of their daughter. She'd begged Hunter to come back down; he'd begged her to come home. Michelle needed her, he said repeatedly. *He* needed her. But how could she leave? How could she go anywhere without her baby?

No, she'd told him. She couldn't — *wouldn't* — go anywhere until Samantha was safely back in her arms.

But after two months of rude police questions and no answers, of lost opportunities and leads that went nowhere, of increasingly pointed accusations and decreasing results, she'd finally given up and returned to San Diego, alone and defeated. Except she wasn't really alone. Reporters were always lurking. People were always staring. Judging her. Finding her guilty.

"I was thinking maybe we should put up some decorations this Christmas," Hunter said. "Michelle's been asking about a tree."

Caroline tried to process what he was suggesting. The holiday season was upon them. Her mother had insisted on holding her usual Thanksgiving dinner, although it had proved to be a muted affair, none of the participants particularly thankful. Steve and Becky barely looked at each other, let alone spoke. Caroline and Hunter had little appetite for turkey and even less for each other. Their eleventh anniversary had come and gone without so much as a congratulatory kiss. And now here he was, talking about decorating Christmas trees as if it was the most natural thing in the world to be discussing such things, as if it was time to put away their grief, accept what had happened, and get on with their lives.

She lowered her head. She was being unfair and she knew it. Someone had to be practical; someone had to take care of the business of day-to-day living. Someone had to worry about Michelle, make sure her needs weren't forgotten. The child had every right to enjoy the glittery trappings of Christmas. Hunter was right to want to provide her with that opportunity. Caroline knew she should be grateful. He'd been so attentive to Michelle these past months, so patient, never raising his voice or losing his temper, as if trying to atone for his earlier lapses as a father.

She watched a sudden flash of worry shoot through his eyes. "What?" she asked. "What is it?"

Hunter pushed some hair away from his forehead, a signal that he was about to impart some information he considered important. "Listen. I have to tell you something and I need you to stay calm," he began.

Caroline felt her heart rate quicken. Was he about to come clean about where he'd been tonight, about the affair she suspected he'd been having? She was almost certain there'd been more than one such affair in the last year. She wondered how many times he'd betrayed her since her return from Mexico. But she wasn't sure she had the strength to deal with his honesty now.

"I spoke to Detective Ramos this morning," he said, catching her by surprise.

"This morning? Why didn't you tell me?"

"I'm telling you now."

"You called him?"

"He called me."

"What? Why? Have they found . . . ?"

"No."

"For God's sake, Hunter. Spit it out. What did the man say?"

"Apparently a member of the hotel staff was arrested yesterday for molesting his niece."

The words hit Caroline with the force of a well-placed punch to the stomach. She doubled over, the air rushing out of her lungs as she gathered her arms around her, her body rocking back and forth. "What do you mean, 'molested'?" she asked when she was able to straighten up and find her voice.

"What do you think I mean?"

"He raped her?"

"He 'interfered with her' is how Detective Ramos put it."

"And they think he might have 'interfered with' Samantha?"

"They don't know. They're still questioning him. So far, he's denied any knowledge of what happened to Samantha."

"Well, of course he'd deny it. But he was working at the hotel at the time she disappeared?"

"Yes."

"And nobody knew they had a child molester on the payroll?"

"How could they? He had no record. He'd never been charged with anything."

"But there's no question he molested his niece."

"Apparently not."

"Oh, God, Hunter. Do you think it's possible? Do you think . . . ?"

"I don't think anything until all the facts are in."

Caroline jumped to her feet. Damn him for thinking like a lawyer. "We need to go down there."

"What are you talking about?"

"We have to see this man. We have to confront him."

"They're not going to let us see him, Caroline. They're not going to let us talk to him. They're not going to let us anywhere near him."

"I don't care. I'm going down there."

"You're not going anywhere. This is exactly why I didn't tell you earlier. You're panicking, being irrational."

"So what are you suggesting? That we just sit here and do nothing?"

"There's nothing we *can* do. Detective Ramos promised to keep us informed."

"How reassuring." Caroline buried her face in the palms of her hands.

"Come to bed," Hunter urged after several minutes had passed.

Caroline shook her head, refusing to look at him. She was trying not to resent his composure, his skill at rationalizing and compartmentalizing, his resolve to stay calm and focused, to not let his emotions get the better of his common sense. How she envied his ability to throw himself into his work, to take refuge in a string of meaningless affairs. How she hated him for it.

Hunter waited another minute before reaching over and switching off the lamp. Caroline felt his arm as it brushed against her shoulder, but didn't open her eyes until she was certain he'd left, taking the sweet, soapy scent of his most recent betrayal with him.

THIRTEEN: THE PRESENT

"Okay. This morning I'd like to talk about some of the ways we can use mathematics in our daily lives," Caroline said, trying to generate a modicum of enthusiasm in her class of twenty-three tenth-grade students. The students, an almost equal mix of boys and girls, stared back at her, one face blanker than the next. "Now, I know that some of you don't think you'll have any use for algebra, or trigonometry, or geometry, or any kind of math at all, for that matter," she continued, thinking of Michelle's frequent pronouncements, "but, in fact, we use some form of math to solve problems every day. And if we don't, we should." She looked up and down the five rows of desks, hoping to catch at least one nod of confirmation, one glimmer of interest in a pair of glazed eyes, but finding none. "Let's take astronomy. An astronomer needs to apply the concepts of algebra and trigonometry in order to determine the distance from one planet to another, or to measure the distance between stars. Or a surveyor," she continued, realizing there probably weren't a lot of potential astronomers in the room. "A surveyor needs to determine precise locations and measurement of points, elevations, and areas for such things as mapmaking and land division." Another unlikely prospect. "Or on a simpler level, say we want to determine the height of a tall building or tree. We can do that by knowing the distance from us to the base of the building or tree. Everyone with me so far? Anyone?"

No one raised a hand.

"Okay, let's tackle a specific problem."

"Let's not," a male voice said from the back of the room. Joey Prescott, class cutup. Medium height, shaggy-haired, more muscles than brains.

"Okay, Joey," Caroline said, "suppose your mother wants to buy broadloom for a room that's twenty feet long and ten feet wide."

"What's broadloom?" Joey asked.

Caroline smiled. "Wall-to-wall carpeting."

"My mother doesn't like wall-to-wall carpeting. She likes hardwood."

There were a few chuckles from the front of the class and one outright guffaw from the back. Caroline knew the laugh well:

Zack Appleby, court jester to Joey's clown. "Zack," she said, staring the freckle-faced boy down, "how does *your* mother feel about broadloom?"

Zack stared back at her as if he'd never seen her before in his life. "Huh?"

"Come on, people. Did you all eat too much turkey last week?"

A hand shot up from the third seat of the second row.

Thank God, Caroline thought. At least someone was making an effort. "Fiona?"

"What was the question?" Fiona asked.

Caroline bit down on her bottom lip. "Your mother wants to buy broadloom for a room that's twenty feet long and ten feet wide."

"Her mother, too?" Joey shouted out. "Hope they have enough in stock."

More laughter. Even Caroline found herself chuckling. "The broadloom costs fourteen dollars and ninety-five cents a square foot," she continued, shifting her gaze from Fiona to the girl beside her, who was chomping aggressively on a strand of long blond hair. "Daphne, can you tell us how to determine the total cost of the carpet?"

Daphne shrugged and continued chomping.

You can do this, Caroline encouraged her silently. *All you have to do is try. I can help you, if you'll let me.*

She'd resumed teaching twelve years ago, following her divorce. It had taken two years after Samantha's disappearance for her marriage to finally limp across the finish line and another year after that to find a school principal brave enough to hire her. Unfortunately, the principal hadn't proved brave enough to keep her on, asking her to resign two years later, following the suicide of one of her students. Not that he blamed her, he'd explained repeatedly. He knew the boy's death wasn't her fault. But if word were to get out that a student in one of her classes had killed himself . . . if parents were to find out . . . if reporters were to get wind of it . . . with her history . . .

Not to worry, she'd told him, leaving without protest.

The following year she'd been hired to teach math at a high school in Golden Hill. She was asked to leave five years later, when the story of the boy's suicide did indeed make the news. Two years later, she'd found a position at Jarvis Collegiate, a medium-sized, underachieving high school located in East San Diego, and she'd been teaching there ever since, although with all the recent publicity, with every sordid detail of her life having been dredged up yet again, she didn't know how long it would be before she was once again asked to quietly resign.

Could she survive another devastating blow? Teaching was the one thing keeping her sane, the one area of her life where she felt any real satisfaction. And she was *good* at it. No — better than good. She had a genuine gift, a way of reaching even the most recalcitrant of pupils.

Not all of them, she reminded herself.

"You have to know how much carpet you need, right?" Caroline continued, breaking free of such disquieting thoughts. "So the first thing you have to figure out is the total area of the room." She wrote on the chalkboard behind her:

Area = length × width
= 20 × 10
= 200 square feet

Underneath that she wrote,

Cost = $14.95/sq. foot

"So, the total cost would be the area in square feet multiplied by the cost per square foot. Are you with me?"

Again, no response, no raised hand.

She pointed to the equation on the board. "Twenty times ten equals two hundred. Two hundred multiplied by fourteen ninety-five is . . . ?"

"Two thousand, nine hundred and ninety dollars," Rob Kearny shouted.

"Correct. Very good, Rob."

The boy proudly held his smartphone above his head.

"You're not supposed to have those turned on in class," Caroline reminded him, her elation short-lived.

"How else are you supposed to figure out the answer?"

"You might try using your head."

"Give head for Christmas," Joey Prescott exclaimed, and the rest of the class laughed uproariously.

Caroline suppressed a smile. "All right, class. Settle down. Is any of this making any sense at all? Does anybody have any questions?"

Addison Snider raised her hand.

"Addison?"

"Did you have a nice Thanksgiving?"

The room suddenly stilled, waiting for Caroline's response.

"It was very nice. Thank you. But I was referring to the lesson."

Caroline sensed movement from the far side of the room, saw Vicki Garner dropping something onto the desk of the girl behind her. "What's that? What did Vicki just hand you, Stephanie?"

"Nothing," Stephanie said, although her thin face said otherwise.

"Can I see it, please?"

Stephanie looked to the floor as she rose from her seat, extending the newspaper clipping in her hand toward Caroline.

Caroline knew even before she saw her daughter's sweet face staring up at her what she was holding. She set the article on her desk. She'd been expecting something like this. "Okay. You've seen the news and you obviously have a lot of questions, so let's get to them. What do you want to know?"

Silence. Clearly the class was as surprised by her direct question as she was for having asked it.

"Do you think you'll ever find your daughter?" Vicki asked quietly.

"I don't know. I hope so."

I think my real name is Samantha.

Daphne's hand shot into the air. "What do you think happened to her?"

"I think someone took her."

"Why?"

"I don't know."

"Do you think she's still alive?"

I think I'm your daughter.

"I don't know. I hope so," she repeated.

"What about that boy?" Joey asked from the back of the room. "The one who killed himself."

"What about him?"

"Did he really kill himself because of you?"

A wave of low murmurs rippled through the class. "Shut up, Joey," someone said.

Caroline struggled to stay calm, to keep her voice level. "No, it's not true."

"So what happened?"

Caroline took a deep breath, and then another. "He was one of my students. He was failing. Not just my class. All his classes." *I can't do this,* she thought, looking toward the clock on the wall, silently appealing to the bell to ring and rescue her. But it was only five minutes after ten. There were fifteen minutes left before the period ended. "He had a history of depression. I tried to help him, but . . ."

"How'd he do it?"

"He hanged himself."

The muttering got louder, spilling from one mouth to the next like a series of collapsing dominoes.

"Gross," Stephanie whispered.

"It wasn't your fault," Vicki said.

"You're a great teacher," Daphne added. "If you couldn't help him, no one could."

Caroline's eyes filled with tears.

"It's not fair they blamed you," Joey Prescott said.

Caroline sank into the chair behind her desk, her body limp with gratitude, her heart full of love for these children who'd somehow managed to survive into their teens relatively unscathed. For all their bravado, they were still naïve enough to believe that life was supposed to be fair.

"Okay, so in one basket we have four heads of cauliflower and five heads of lettuce costing eight forty, and in the other we have six heads of cauliflower and two heads of lettuce costing eight twenty, and our problem is to determine the price of one head of cauliflower and one head of lettuce. What do we do first?"

"Buy hot dogs," someone shouted out.

"Let *x* represent the cost of one head of cauliflower," Caroline said, ignoring the interruption and scribbling the information on the chalkboard. *If it's a quarter to two in the afternoon and there are five more minutes till the end of class and two more classes till the end of the day . . .*

"And let *y* represent the cost of one head of lettuce," Jason Campbell volunteered.

"Very good. Thank you, Jason."

The wall phone behind her desk rang, signaling a call from the office. Caroline excused herself to answer it.

"Did you hear — Joey Prescott asked her about that kid who killed himself?" someone whispered as she was turning her back.

"You're shitting me. What did she say?"

Caroline ignored the voices and picked up the phone. "Yes?"

"Sorry to interrupt," said the voice on the other end. "You have an emergency call."

Caroline hung up the phone. "If you'll excuse me," she said, leaving the room without explanation.

"Where's she going?"

"Maybe someone else offed himself."

She hurried down the long, stale-smelling corridor toward the main office, running through a list of potential emergencies, some far-fetched, others all too possible: Michelle had been arrested again, this time for driving drunk on the freeway; Caroline's mother had suffered a stroke; her brother had been shot by one of his gambling buddies when he couldn't make good on a bet; another of her students had indeed "offed" himself.

The secretary was waiting, an anxious look on her hawklike face when Caroline burst into the office. Caroline took the phone from the woman's outstretched hand. "She wouldn't give me her name," she said as Caroline lifted the phone to her ear.

If Michelle is five feet nine inches tall, weighs one hundred and eight pounds, drinks five times the amount of what she eats, has four unpaid parking tickets and one arrest for driving under the influence, how many more chances does she get to screw up her life?

"Hello?"

"It's Lili."

The room lurched to one side. The soft buzz of the overhead recessed lighting grew loud and insistent, like a nest of angry bees. "How did you find me?"

"I looked up where you work on the Web."

"It's on the Web?" Caroline looked toward the secretary, who was pretending to be reading something on her computer. How much of her life was out there for others to casually peruse? Was there anything left that was hers and hers alone?

"Is it all right that I called there? I was afraid to phone your house again."

"I'm sorry about what happened."

"It's okay. That was Michelle, right? I

understand why she'd be upset."

"Do you remember her?" *Can you tell me something,* anything, *about her that nobody else in the world would know but you and me, something that isn't on the Internet, something that would prove conclusively . . . ?*

"No. I wish I could say I did, but . . ."

"She thinks you're a fraud," Caroline said quietly.

"I'd probably think so, too, if I were in her shoes."

"So, what happens now? Were you really serious about coming to San Diego?"

There was a brief pause, a sharp intake of breath. "What choice do I have?"

Was the girl for real or was Michelle right? Caroline felt a sinking sensation in her gut, remembering Michelle's predictions. "And I suppose you want me to send you money . . ."

"No. I already told you, I don't want your money."

"Then how . . . ?"

"I don't know yet. I have to figure a few things out."

"So, when . . . ?"

"I'll get back to you. Do you have a cell phone?"

"I have one. I just never have it on. Michelle is always after me about it. She says it's ridiculous that —" She realized she was rambling and stopped abruptly, fishing inside her purse to retrieve her phone. She switched the power on and located her number. "Here. I have it." Caroline quickly relayed the number to Lili.

"I'll call you." The line went dead.

"Hello? Hello, Lili?" Caroline stood motionless, replaying the conversation over and over in her mind. *She must think I'm a moron,* she thought. *Who doesn't know her cell phone number? Who never has the damn thing on?* And then more thoughts: Did this girl really not want her money or was she just biding her time in an effort to maximize her potential payoff? She'd successfully baited the hook and Caroline had greedily snapped it up. All that was left was to reel her in. Was that what Lili was doing?

"Is everything okay?" the secretary asked.

Caroline handed back the school phone. "I'm an idiot."

"Don't say that. Just because you couldn't remember your cell phone number . . ." The secretary's face reddened. "You have a lot on your mind these days. All that stuff in the news recently . . ."

Caroline nodded, wondering if the principal had informed them of her past long ago or whether they'd just found out.

"The police in Mexico still have no idea . . . ?"

"Nothing."

Every lead Detective Ramos had collected over the last decade and a half eventually led to the same dead end; every suspect he'd pursued managed to evade his grasp. *If the police waste fifteen years on dead ends and Caroline endures fifteen years of false hope, how many more years will it take till she loses her mind altogether?*

"Just so you know, Shannon and I don't believe for a second that you harmed your daughter . . ."

"Not for a second," Shannon confirmed.

For the first time since she'd entered the office, Caroline became aware of the other secretary sitting at her desk. "Thank you." She gave both women her best attempt at a smile and began edging toward the hall. She had to get out of here before either of them said another word.

". . . or that you had anything to do with that poor boy's suicide."

Too late. She hadn't moved fast enough. Caroline felt the color drain from her face as the buzzing of angry bees returned.

"We were just saying it was so mean of that reporter to bring all that up again. As if you don't have enough on your plate . . ."

The room began spinning. The next thing Caroline knew, she was sitting on the floor, her back against the wall, her feet splayed out in front of her, the room performing cartwheels around her.

"My God, what happened?" Shannon cried.

"She fainted. Call the nurse."

"You're going to be all right," Shannon told her, kneeling beside her and patting her hand while they waited for the school nurse to arrive. "You'll see. Everything is going to be just fine."

Fourteen: Ten Years Ago

"Okay, everybody, listen up," Caroline said. "You only have two weeks left before your final exams . . ."

A collective groan emanated from the throats of the twenty-two eleventh-grade students in her final class of the day at Lewis Logan High.

". . . and I'd like to use these last few minutes to give you some suggestions that I think could help you make the most of your study time."

"How about just telling us what's on the exam?" one of the boys asked, right on cue. There was always one boy in every class who asked the same thing.

"The first thing you need to do is to organize your work so that you begin with the most challenging material right off the bat. I know that might sound counterintuitive, but you can't be afraid of it. Okay? Then you start dividing that material into small chunks that you can manage easily. You'll find that things aren't nearly as overwhelming when you start breaking them down."

"I think *I'm* having a breakdown," another boy said, and the class laughed.

Except for Errol Cruz, who sat in the last seat of the last row, chewing on the end of his pencil and staring out the side window, looking even more lost than usual. A skinny, somewhat delicate-looking boy with deep blue eyes and acne-scarred skin, he never laughed at the smart-alecky remarks of the other students or offered up any of his own. He never volunteered anything in class, although whenever Caroline called on him, he always had the correct answer ready. Occasionally he lingered after class to discuss the day's lesson or a challenging math problem he'd come across online. Or maybe he just hung around to delay going home. His father was said to be gruff and unpleasant, and neither parent had bothered showing up for the last set of parent-teacher interviews. According to his other instructors, Errol rarely completed his assignments and had almost no chance of making his year, which was a shame, because despite his failing grades, he showed a real aptitude for math. Maybe with a little more encouragement . . .

"It helps to begin each study session with a quick review of what you studied the day before," she continued, stealing a glance at the clock on the wall. Michelle had a dentist appointment at four o'clock and Caroline had arranged to pick her up from school at three-thirty. This meant she had to leave as soon as the bell sounded in order to drive to Michelle's tony private school in Mission Hills and get her over to their dentist, whose office was located on Washington Street, just east of Old Town, a fifteen-minute trip at the best of times, and likely twice that during rush hour. She had little time to waste. The school had been given strict instructions never to leave Michelle alone or unsupervised, but you could never be sure. "When you're reviewing, make sure to carefully read over each step in the procedure and use a Magic Marker to highlight the main concepts and formulas. If it helps, draw a diagram to make the concept clearer."

The bell rang. The class immediately began packing up belongings and filing out. "Goodbye, Ms. Shipley," someone said. "Have a nice night," said another.

"Thank you. You, too. Errol . . . ," she

called as the boy was shuffling out of the room.

He stopped, standing motionless in the doorway, head down, eyes directed at the floor.

"Do you have a minute?" She stole another glance at the clock. She had little time to spare. Michelle would be waiting. She couldn't be late.

The boy turned slowly back toward her, staring at a point just past her right ear, refusing to make eye contact. "Is there a problem, Ms. Shipley?"

"I was just about to ask you the same thing." She maneuvered her head into his line of vision. "I was watching you in class and I couldn't help noticing . . . Is there something wrong, Errol? You seem a little . . . I don't know . . . distracted."

More distracted than usual, she added silently.

Blue eyes shifted to the floor. A long pause, a swaying from one foot to the other. "No. I'm fine."

"Are you sure? Because you don't seem fine," Caroline insisted. "What is it, Errol? Please tell me. If there's something you don't understand . . ."

He said nothing, his hand brushing away some stray hairs that fell across his forehead.

Caroline thought she saw the fading remnants of a bruise above his right eye, but when she tilted her head to get a better look, he quickly pushed his hair back into place.

"Is everything all right at home?"

He shrugged. "Sure."

"You can talk to me, Errol," she said, hearing the clock ticking off the seconds on the wall behind her head. "You know that, don't you?"

"Yeah."

"About anything. Not just math." She glanced toward the door. If she didn't leave in the next minute, she had no chance of getting Michelle to her dentist appointment by four o'clock.

"You have to be somewhere," he said.

"No. That's all right. I have plenty of time."

"Nah, it's okay."

"Really. I have time."

"It's nothing. I'm good."

"Are you sure?"

The boy was already shuffling out of the room. "Yeah. No problem."

"Okay. Well, then, see you tomorrow."

"Bye, Ms. Shipley."

"Goodbye, Errol."

She watched him disappear down the hallway, then locked the classroom door behind her, trying to shake off unwelcome stirrings of guilt. Clearly, something was bothering the boy. Just as clearly, he didn't want to talk about it. What was she supposed to do? Sit on him? Force the truth out of him? Still, maybe with a little more prodding, a little more patience . . . She'd try again tomorrow, she decided, proceeding briskly to the parking lot.

Within minutes she was on the San Diego Freeway headed toward Mission Bay. At ten minutes to four, fully twenty minutes after she was supposed to arrive, she pulled up in front of Michelle's school to find her daughter, in the company of an older student, sitting on the school's outside steps, one knee sock up, the other curled around her ankle like a sleeping snake. Only ten years old and already she'd perfected her grandmother's look of world-weary disappointment. Caroline reached across the front seat of her black Camry and pushed open the passenger door.

Michelle waved goodbye to the other girl and sauntered down the steps. She climbed inside the car and pulled her seat belt into place without so much as a glance at her mother. "You're late," she said.

"You're late," the receptionist echoed as

Caroline approached the counter. Caroline felt a roomful of disapproving eyes fall squarely on her back. The waiting room, a large, pleasant space shared by three dentists, was crowded, the red plastic seats lining its white walls almost all filled.

"Sorry. The traffic was really bad."

"Dr. Saunders took another patient ahead of you. I'm afraid you'll have to wait."

Caroline nodded and retreated to a corner of the room where there was one empty chair. She sat down and Michelle promptly jumped into her lap. "Whoa, easy there," Caroline said.

"What's the matter?" Michelle asked.

"Nothing. You're just getting pretty heavy."

"Am I fat?"

"No, of course you're not fat. Who said you were fat?" Although there was no denying Michelle's propensity for junk food and sweets. It was a taste she'd developed in the aftermath of Samantha's disappearance, one indulged by her grandmother, who was always plying her with high-calorie treats. Caroline had been reluctant to say anything to either of them, reasoning that Michelle was just a child and her mother was, well, her mother. She knew this was a convenient rationalization, but she lacked the stamina to take on either one of them. A loud chewing sound suddenly reached her ears. "Is that gum in your mouth?"

Michelle's shoulders slumped as her eyes rolled toward the ceiling.

"Spit that out. You're at the dentist, for heaven's sake."

Michelle released a huge wad of pink bubble gum into the palm of her hand. "What do I do with it?"

Caroline looked around the room for a wastepaper basket but found none. "There's a bathroom down the hall." She gently pushed Michelle from her lap and rose from her seat. "Come on."

"I can go by myself."

"I'm coming with you."

"No."

"Yes."

"It's so embarrassing. You never let me do anything," Michelle said, loud enough to attract the attention of everyone within earshot, which was pretty much everyone in the room. "I'm not a baby. I'm a big girl."

"Just give me the gum and sit down," Caroline said, her face flushing, as if a brush fire were racing through her veins. She wrapped the gum in a tissue and approached the receptionist. "I'm sorry. Do you have somewhere I can put this?"

The receptionist held up the wastepaper

basket at her feet without speaking and Caroline dropped the tissue inside, sure that all eyes were upon her. But when she glanced around the room, she was relieved to see that most of the people were either engrossed in books they'd brought with them or browsing through the office's collection of out-of-date magazines.

A blond woman in a pale pink uniform entered the waiting room from one of the inner offices. "Mrs. Pearlman?" she called toward a middle-aged woman sitting next to the door. "Dr. Wang will see you now." Mrs. Pearlman promptly dropped the magazine she'd been reading onto the small table beside her and followed the pink uniform toward the inner offices.

Caroline immediately sat down in the freshly vacated chair, its seat still warm. Just as quickly, Michelle got up from her chair on the opposite wall and plopped down on her mother's lap.

"I'm hungry," she said.

Caroline reached to the table beside her for a fashion magazine and handed it to Michelle. "Here. Read this."

"Mommy, look!" Michelle exclaimed, pointing at the table, her eyes as round as circles.

Caroline stared at the stack of old magazines with mounting horror. There she was on the very top of the pile, standing ramrod straight at Hunter's side, the familiar picture having been taken during the course of their press conference in Rosarito. FIVE YEARS LATER, blared the headline of the magazine dated last November. WHERE IS SAMANTHA SHIPLEY?

"Why is your picture on the magazine?" Michelle asked, her finger stabbing at a tiny photo of her sister in the cover's upper right corner. "Is that Samantha?"

Caroline struggled to keep from screaming. She'd always been so diligent about keeping such headlines away from Michelle, making sure the child never caught so much as a glimpse of the newspaper and magazine coverage of either the event or its aftermath.

Not that Michelle had ever asked many questions; she'd accepted Samantha's disappearance the way a child accepts most things over which she has no control. In the beginning, she'd occasionally wondered aloud where Samantha was and when she was coming home, but after a few months even those questions had stopped. In the past year, she hadn't mentioned her sister at all.

And mercifully, the once-constant barrage of stories had also started to abate. But the five-year anniversary of the toddler's disappearance had marked a major milestone, resulting in renewed coverage. *Five years since I've seen my baby,* Caroline thought now, fighting back tears. How could that be?

"Mommy, why is your picture in the magazine?"

What could she say? What could she do? The damage was done. She'd been fighting a battle she couldn't possibly win. No matter how hard she tried, she couldn't protect Michelle forever from unexpected sightings such as this. It was June, the end of another school year. She'd naïvely thought they were safe until next November. When was she going to realize they were never safe?

"Where's my picture?" the child asked plaintively, her eyes scanning the magazine cover.

"Michelle Shipley?" a voice called out.

Caroline glanced up at the waiting dental hygienist. She'd never been so happy to see anyone in her life. "Off you go, sweetheart."

"Why isn't my picture in the magazine?"

"Because you're lucky," Caroline said. "It's a stupid magazine, and you don't want your picture in it."

"Michelle Shipley," the hygienist said again.

"Here she is." Caroline edged Michelle off her lap. "Go on."

"Aren't you coming?"

"I have to wait out here."

"I want you to come."

"You're a big girl, remember?"

"Your mother will come talk to the dentist after I'm done," the hygienist said.

As soon as Michelle was gone, Caroline jumped up from her seat and fled the room, the magazine crushed in her fist. She ran into the bathroom at the end of the hall and locked herself in the nearest stall, her hands shaking as her fingers fumbled for the story inside. And then there it was: FIVE YEARS LATER. WHERE IS SAMANTHA SHIPLEY?

The article began with a two-page photo spread of the Grand Laguna Resort, complete with pictures of the restaurant and pool area, a big **X** indicating the room from which Samantha had been taken. Three pages of photographs, rumors, and innuendos followed, most of the so-called sources unnamed. There were several pictures of Hunter and Caroline, together and separately, as well as a group photo of them with Peggy and Fletcher, Steve and Becky, Rain and Jerrod. There was even a picture of Michelle holding tight to her grandmother's hand as they were leaving the resort to return to San Diego. Caroline wondered how the magazine had gotten hold of these pictures, and who was behind the quote: *She seemed like the perfect mother, but then, you really never know other people, do you?* She suspected it was Rain — it sounded like the sort of backhanded compliment Rain would volunteer. She thought of phoning her and demanding an explanation, but she hadn't spoken to the woman in years. Once she and Hunter had divorced, friends like Jerrod and Rain had quickly disappeared from her life.

Caroline gobbled up the article voraciously and then read it twice more. She'd spent five years avoiding such stories, but now that one was actually in her hands, she couldn't tear her eyes away. It contained the usual recap of events: it was their tenth anniversary, the babysitter had mysteriously canceled, they'd left their two children alone while they went to celebrate with friends in the garden restaurant downstairs, Samantha had been snatched from her crib sometime between nine-thirty and ten o'clock that night, a number of suspects had been questioned and released, including one hotel worker who was currently in jail for molesting his niece. *The mother seemed distant,* a hotel employee was quoted as saying. *She was always late picking up her other daughter from our afternoon kids program.* "One time," Caroline said out loud. "I was late *one time.*" An unnamed police officer was also quoted: *We've always felt the family knows more than they're letting on.* "Like what, asshole?" Caroline yelled. "What more could we possibly know?"

The door to the bathroom opened. A pair of women's ivory pumps appeared in front of Caroline's stall. "Is everything all right in here?" a voice asked. "I thought I heard shouting."

Caroline's heart was pounding so rapidly she could barely speak. "Everything's fine," she managed to spit out. "I just caught my fingers in the door."

"Ouch."

Caroline held her breath as the woman busied herself at the sink. *What the hell is she doing for so long?* Caroline wondered, peering through the crack between the door and the stall support and watching as the woman applied a fresh coat of lipstick before fluffing her hair.

"You're sure you're okay?" the woman asked as she was about to leave.

"I'm fine, thank you."

Caroline waited until the door closed before bursting into tears. "Pull yourself together, damn it," she said, careful to keep her voice a whisper as her eyes returned to the magazine.

Of course the article also mentioned Caroline and Hunter's divorce, postulating that it was guilt that had driven them apart. It made no mention of his affair with a paralegal, which was what had hammered the final nail into the coffin of their marriage. Not that this affair had been any more significant than the ones that preceded it. Not that it had lasted any longer or was any more intense than the others. It was just the latest of a continuing series of affairs that had taken place in the aftermath of Samantha's disappearance. But while Hunter's infidelities might have contributed to their growing estrangement, it was undoubtedly her coldness, her unrelenting resentment that had been responsible for those affairs in the first place. Guilt had indeed driven them apart. And she was as guilty as he was.

More so.

Near the end of the article was a picture of Caroline outside Lewis Logan High, taken just after she'd resumed her teaching career. Beside it was a more recent photo of Hunter walking beside an unidentified young woman. Maybe a client or business associate. Maybe not. MOVING ON, read the caption beneath the pictures.

"Moving on," Caroline repeated angrily, tossing the magazine into the trash can beside the door on her way out of the washroom. If she was so busy moving on, why did she feel more stuck than ever?

FIFTEEN:
THE PRESENT

"You fainted?" Peggy's face reflected both confusion and concern.

"Well, I didn't exactly faint."

The two women were sitting at a corner table in Costa Brava, a Spanish restaurant on Garnet Avenue that was famous for its tapas. A big-screen TV on one of the restaurant's minimalist whitewashed walls was broadcasting a satellite feed of a Spanish soccer game that was being watched by a handful of enthusiastic fans at the bar. Shouts of "Olé" periodically pierced the air.

"One minute you were standing up, the next minute you were on the floor. That's fainting, as far as I'm concerned. Why didn't you call me?"

"I can't call you about every little thing."

"You don't call me about *anything* anymore. I hardly ever see you. It's a good thing your mother invited us over for Thanksgiving dinner."

"And wasn't that a treat?" Caroline looked out the window at the cloudless Saturday afternoon sky. She could almost hear the ocean roaring a few blocks away. "I'm terrified they're going to ask me to resign."

"That's not going to happen."

"Why not? It's happened before."

"All because of that stupid news story," Peggy said, shaking her head and swallowing the last of her wine.

"It was my fault."

"It was *not* your fault. Stop being so quick to accept the blame for everything."

"I don't think I could stand it if I lose this job."

"You won't. Your principal knew what had happened when she hired you."

"The story had died down by then. Now, thanks to all those stupid articles, it's back again. The damn thing just never goes away, does it? It's like herpes."

Peggy laughed. "Thanks for the image. Eat your lunch."

Caroline speared a forkful of black beans and rice, watching most of it slip back onto her plate. "My students have been talking about nothing else all week."

"So give them something else to talk about. Give them a surprise test. They love that." Peggy signaled the waiter for a refill of her wine. "Okay, I've been patient long enough. Are you ever going to tell me?"

"Tell you what?"

"Come on, Caroline. How long have we been friends? You don't think I know when you're keeping something from me?"

Caroline put down her fork and stared across the table at her friend. "Michelle told you about Lili, didn't she? She told you about Calgary."

Peggy leaned forward in her chair, her elbows resting on the table. "She didn't mean to let it slip. She assumed you'd already told me. The question is, why didn't you?"

"I'm sorry. It all happened so fast."

"It happened more than a week ago," Peggy corrected, obviously hurt. "What's up, Caroline? Don't you trust me?"

"Of course I trust you."

"Then why didn't you tell me?"

Caroline looked toward the ceiling, as if the answer might be hiding behind one of the low-hanging chandeliers. "I don't know. I guess I was afraid."

"Of what?"

"That you'd think I was crazy. That you'd try to talk me out of going."

"Well, you have to admit it's not exactly rational behavior. This girl calls you out of the blue, says she's Samantha, and off you fly to Calgary without a word to anyone —"

"She called again," Caroline interrupted. Now that Peggy knew part of the story, she might as well know all of it.

"Michelle told me that, too. She said she grabbed the phone right out of your hand, warned her not to call you again . . ."

"She called me at work."

"What? When was this?"

"Last Monday."

"What did she say?"

"That she'd come to San Diego for the DNA test."

"When?"

"As soon as she can work things out."

"What does that mean?"

"I have no idea."

"Does Michelle know?"

"No. I can't tell her. She'll go ballistic. She's so sure Lili is a fraud."

"And you're so sure she isn't?"

"I'm not sure of anything."

"Has she asked you for money?"

"No."

"Has she asked you for *anything*?"

"No."

"Which doesn't mean she won't."

"I know that."

"But assuming she doesn't," Peggy continued slowly, measuring out each word, "that leaves three possibilities."

"Which are?"

"One, that she honestly believes she could be Samantha; two, that she's a sadist who gets her jollies fucking with people's heads; three, that she's out of her mind."

"There's a fourth possibility."

"Which is?"

"That she really *is* Samantha."

Peggy stared at Caroline with eyes that were ineffably sad. "Oh, honey. You're the math wizard. The odds against that are just so astronomical."

"But there *is* a chance . . ."

"A tiny *fraction* of a chance . . ."

"A chance nonetheless," Caroline said forcefully. "How can I not take it?"

The waiter approached with Peggy's second glass of wine. Before he had a chance to set it on the table, she took it from his hand and swallowed one quick gulp, then another. "Go for it."

"Where have you been all day?" Michelle asked from the hallway even before Caroline had closed the front door. Ever since Michelle had intercepted Lili's phone call, she'd been watching her mother like a hawk.

"I met Peggy for lunch at Costa Brava."

"It's almost four o'clock."

"I went for a walk along the beach after. Why? Were we supposed to do something?"

Michelle laughed. "You mean like go shopping or to the movies? Like that's ever happened."

And we're off, Caroline heard her brother say. Not home two minutes and already her daughter had her on the defensive. She walked into the kitchen and poured herself a glass of water, drinking it down while silently counting to ten. She would not let Michelle get to her. She would be pleasant and calm. She would not rise to the bait. She would not bite. "That's a pretty blouse," she offered with a smile. Michelle was wearing a pair of denim shorts and a loose-fitting beige shirt. Her hair hung in a careless braid over one shoulder, and she wore no makeup except bright red lipstick that emphasized the cut of her cheekbones. "You look nice," Caroline said.

"Oh, God," Michelle moaned.

"What's the matter?"

"That means I'm fat."

"What?"

"Whenever you tell me I look nice, it means I've put on weight."

"No, it most certainly does not."

"Yes, it does."

"No. Do you know what it means?" Caroline said, fighting the urge to hurl her now empty glass at Michelle's head. "What it means is that I can never say anything nice to you, that you can never enjoy a compliment. Anything positive I say, you hear as negative. You only feel good when I say you look bad. How screwed up is that? How sad."

"What's sad is that you have no respect for my feelings. For me."

"What are you talking about? Where is this coming from? You're mad at me because I went out for lunch?"

"I'm mad because it didn't even occur to you to tell me where you were going. It would have been nice if you'd left me a note or something. So I wouldn't worry."

"There's no reason for you to worry."

"No, because it's not like you'd do anything crazy, like fly off to Calgary or something."

"Sweetheart, I promise you I'm not flying off anywhere."

"Then why are you being so secretive?"

"I'm not being secretive."

"Yes, you are."

"Well, then, I'm sorry. I don't mean to be. I guess I'm just not used to you being so concerned."

"Why? Because I don't have feelings?"

"Nobody said you don't have feelings."

"What *are* you saying?"

"I don't know," Caroline said, waving her hands in the air in total frustration. "I don't know what I'm saying. I have no idea what this conversation is about or why we're arguing. I know I had a nice lunch and a lovely stroll on the beach. I was actually feeling pretty damn good, and then I come home and all hell breaks loose."

"So this is my fault?"

"No, it's mine. Whatever it is. *Everything* is my fault. I get that. I accept it."

"My mother, the martyr."

"Okay, fine."

"I was worried, that's all. Can't I be worried?"

"If you were so damn worried, why didn't you just call me? I have a cell phone."

"Which you never have on. What's the point of having a damn cell phone if you never have it on?"

"I have it on." Caroline fished inside her purse for her phone and waved it in front of Michelle. "See? It's on."

Michelle's eyes narrowed. "You never have it on. Why is it on now? Who are you expecting to call? Does Lili have this number? Has she called you again?"

"For God's sake, Michelle."

"Let me have the phone."

"No." Caroline quickly dropped the phone back inside her purse before Michelle could grab it. "Enough. I've had enough." She marched into the living room, her purse tucked protectively under her arm, Michelle at her heels. They stood glaring at each other in the middle of the room for several seconds. "You know what I'd really like?" Caroline asked finally.

"No. What would you really like?"

"For once, just for once, I'd like us to have a nice, normal conversation. One without yelling and accusations. I've heard rumors that some mothers and daughters actually have them." Not that she'd ever had such a conversation with her own mother, Caroline recalled.

"Okay. Fine." Michelle lowered herself into the nearest chair. "Let the conversing begin."

Caroline sank into the other chair, set her purse on the floor, and waited for her daughter to continue.

"So how was lunch?" Michelle asked.

"Good."

"How's Peggy?"

"Good."

"How are her boys? I haven't seen them

in ages."

"They're fine. Kevin graduates high school this spring. Philip is doing very well at Duke."

"That's good."

More good. More silence.

"What about you?" Caroline asked.

"What do you mean?"

"Any thoughts about going back to school?"

Michelle shifted uncomfortably in her seat. "I'm thinking about it."

"Really? What are you thinking?"

"That I might go back next fall."

"Any school in particular?" Caroline tried not to sound too enthusiastic. Michelle had dropped out of Berkeley in the middle of her second year, having changed majors twice. She'd dropped out of UCSD the following year, after only one semester.

"Dad thinks I should finish college, then apply to law school."

"Does that interest you?"

"I don't know. Maybe."

"There wouldn't be any problems because of . . . ?"

". . . my DUI?"

Caroline nodded.

"The deal is that once I finish my community service, they'll expunge my record.

Anyway, I haven't made any decisions yet."

"I think you'd make a great lawyer."

"Why? Because I'm good at arguing?"

"Because I think you'd be good at whatever you set your mind to."

"Really?"

"Really."

Another silence.

"Are you seeing anyone?" Caroline broached.

Michelle's response was a familiar roll of her eyes.

"Never mind. Forget I asked."

"I'm not seeing anyone," Michelle said. "I *was* seeing this one guy for a little while, but it didn't work out."

"That's too bad."

"No. He was a jerk. All he wanted to do was get high and have sex."

Sounds perfect, Caroline thought, having done neither in years. "I hope you use protection . . ."

"Oh, God. Do I look like a complete imbecile?"

"You were arrested for driving under the influence," Caroline reminded her, the words out of her mouth before she could stop them.

"And we were doing so well."

"Sorry. I shouldn't have said that."

"No. I deserved it. It wasn't the smartest decision I ever made."

"I just don't understand."

"I know that," Michelle said sadly.

"Then enlighten me. What made you get behind the wheel of the car that night? What were you thinking?"

"We've been through this a million times. I think the whole point is that I *wasn't* thinking."

"You could have killed someone. You could have *been* killed."

"I'd only had a couple of drinks. I didn't think they'd go to my head like that."

"You're such a smart, beautiful girl," Caroline persisted, unable to stop herself, "and you keep doing all these self-destructive things. You quit school; you drive drunk; you smoke; you don't eat . . ."

Michelle jumped to her feet. "That's right. I'm a total fuckup. Unlike your other precious daughter, who I'm sure would have turned out perfect."

"Whoa. Wait a minute . . ."

"No. *You* wait a minute. It's my turn to ask *you* something."

Caroline held her breath.

"What if it had been me that night?"

"What are you talking about?" Caroline asked, although she already knew the answer. "What night?"

"The night Samantha disappeared. What if it had been me?"

"Oh, God. Michelle . . ."

"Would you have spent fifteen years mourning my loss every damn second of every damn day? Would you have let your marriage fall apart? Would you have flown off to Miami . . . to Tacoma . . . to Calgary? Would you have been so desperate to believe the word of an obvious con artist? Tell me, Mother. Would you have given a shit if it had been me?"

"You can't be serious."

"And you haven't answered my question."

"Because it's so ridiculous. I love you more than anything in the world. You know that."

"Still not an answer."

"What do you want me to say? I would have been distraught, for God's sake . . ."

"As distraught as you were when you discovered Samantha was missing?"

"I don't understand. This was never a competition."

"No, it certainly wasn't." Tears filled Michelle's eyes, and she raised her chin to keep them from falling. "A competition is when everyone has a shot at winning. And I was always going to come in second, wasn't I?"

"That's not true."

"It *is* true. Samantha was the golden girl. It was true fifteen years ago, and it's even truer now. Just the remote possibility you might see her again makes you happier than I ever could."

"That's so unfair." Caroline lowered her head. The next thing she heard was the sound of the front door slamming.

SIXTEEN: SIX YEARS AGO

"When did she check in?" Caroline asked.

"Yesterday morning," Peggy said.

"Why didn't you call me right away?"

"I couldn't until she gave me permission."

"I had no idea she was even back in town."

"I don't think anyone did except your brother."

"Steve knows?"

"He was here all morning."

"Really?"

Peggy shrugged, as if to say, *Go figure.*

"How is she?"

"She's here, isn't she?"

"Here" was the Marigold Hospice on Harney Street in Old Town, a block from the Old Abode Chapel. The hospice was a two-story red brick building that had once served as a drop-in center for the homeless. It had been converted into a facility for the terminally ill two years ago, and Peggy had left her job at San Diego Hospital to become its first director.

"How long does she have?" Caroline asked.

"No way of knowing for sure. The average length of stay is anywhere from three days to two weeks. But you never know. Some last months; others don't last a day. We've had one resident here for almost a year. You just never know."

"Did you tell her I was coming?"

"I did. She seemed pleased."

The phone at the reception desk rang. The young Asian volunteer picked it up at the end of its first ring. "Good afternoon. Marigold Hospice," she announced. "Amy speaking. How can I help you? Yes. I'll transfer your call." She pressed a series of buttons on the keypad, then replaced the receiver.

Seconds later, a buzzer sounded, signaling that someone was at the front door. Amy stretched toward the big red button on the wall that released the lock and admitted a family of four to the glassed-in foyer. She promptly rose from her seat and opened another door into the beautifully appointed reception area, where Caroline and Peggy were standing in front of four large, overstuffed chairs. The chairs were grouped around a coffee table, in front of a gas fireplace and a large-screen TV. "Would you mind signing in, please?" Amy directed the man and woman to the guest register.

"Why do we have to sign in?" asked their son, a towheaded boy of about five.

"Safety precaution," Amy told him. "In case of a fire, we need to know how many people are in the building."

"Come on, kids," their mother said. "Let's go see Grandpa."

"Do you know what room he's in?" Amy asked.

"Oh, yes. Thank you." The family disappeared down the interior hallway.

"You allow children?" Caroline asked Peggy.

"Children, dogs, cats. You name it. Whatever makes people feel more at home. You're doing a great job, Amy," Peggy told the young volunteer.

"Thank you, Mrs. Banack."

"So are you," Caroline told her friend.

Peggy brushed off the compliment. "Speaking of jobs, I should get back to mine. Becky's in room 104." She sighed. "Just be prepared. She doesn't look quite the way you remember."

Caroline took a long, deep breath and entered the interior hallway. Standing in front of the closed door to room 104, she took another deep breath, straightened her shoulders, and knocked.

"Come in," called the weak but familiar voice.

Caroline pushed open the door, careful to keep her emotions from registering on her face. Not that this was difficult. Her natural physical reaction when confronted with a tragedy of any sort was to shut down. Her face would go blank; she would get almost preternaturally calm. A defense mechanism, Peggy had once explained, although the press never failed to excoriate her for it, tarring her with the labels "cold" and "unemotional," when the exact opposite was true.

The room was in relative darkness, the only light coming from whatever late-afternoon sun had managed to penetrate the draped window on the far wall. A TV across from the bed was tuned to an all-news channel, a constant scroll of the day's headlines streaming across the bottom of the screen. In the middle of the room was a hospital bed, and in the middle of the bed sat Becky, a gaunt figure wearing a quilted blue housecoat and a short dark wig that sat a little too low on her forehead.

"Caroline," Becky said in greeting, muting the TV and waving her former sister-in-law toward the easy chair next to the bed. A second chair, this one high-backed and uncomfortable-looking, stood in front of the bathroom.

"Whose stupid idea was this?" Caroline said, the door swinging shut as she approached the bed and leaned in to give Becky a kiss on the cheek. She fought the urge to straighten the wig, fearing that such an intimate gesture might be perceived as presumptuous.

"Definitely not mine," Becky said. "Sit down. You look terrific. As always."

"Thanks." Caroline touched her own hair self-consciously.

"It's really nice to see you again. How have you been?"

Caroline lowered herself into the light brown leather lounger, deciding to focus on Becky's eyes, which were the same intense brown they'd always been. "I'm fine. I'm so sorry you have to go through this."

"Don't be. It's not your fault."

"I wish I'd known."

"You couldn't have done anything."

"I could have been there for you."

"Really? Would you have moved to L.A.?"

Caroline was silent.

"Sorry," Becky said. "I don't mean to sound ungrateful."

"I deserved it. It's such a cliché, telling

someone you'll be there for them when you both know you won't be."

"I certainly wasn't there for you," Becky said. There was no need for clarification. Both women understood exactly what she was referring to.

"You had a lot of things on your plate," Caroline said.

"And we weren't exactly close at that point."

"Not like we used to be," Caroline acknowledged. "I never quite understood what happened."

"What happened," Becky repeated. "Your mother. Your brother. Your mother."

Caroline smiled.

"How *is* the dragon lady?"

"Still breathing fire."

"Yeah. That woman will outlive even Keith Richards. Sorry, I shouldn't talk like that. She *is* your mother."

"That's all right. It's hard to argue with the truth."

Although the truth was that, in more ways than not, Becky was exactly like Caroline's mother. She was stubborn, opinionated, and unforgiving. Once you entered her bad books, you stayed there. Neither woman would budge an inch. Mary had never forgiven Becky for persuading Steve to elope to Las Vegas without a word to anyone until the deed was done. Becky had never forgiven Mary for not welcoming her into the family with open arms. It hadn't helped that she'd made absolutely no attempt to win Mary over. Mary liked to be wooed almost as much as she liked to nurse a grudge, and Becky hadn't given her that satisfaction. Steve, an outwardly strong man whose confident swagger belied a surprising weakness at his core, had been caught in the middle, his allegiance constantly vacillating between the two. The marriage was doomed from the start. The fact that it had managed to survive a full three years after the breakup of Caroline's own marriage was a constant source of amazement to her.

"So fill me in on everything," Becky instructed. "How's Michelle?"

"She's okay."

"Just okay?"

"She's a teenager. What can I say?"

"Things still strained with Hunter?"

"We manage. Apparently he's seeing someone."

"No kidding. Is it serious?"

"According to Michelle, it is. She says they're talking marriage."

"How do you feel about that?"

"No feelings one way or the other," Caroline lied.

"Do you think they'll start a family?"

"Probably. From what I understand, she's a lot younger than Hunter."

"And how do you feel about that?" Becky pressed.

"I can't do anything about the fact that she's younger."

"I meant about Hunter starting another family."

"I know."

Becky nodded understanding. "What about you?"

"What *about* me?" Caroline asked.

"Are you seeing anybody?"

"God, no."

"Why not? You're a beautiful woman. You're smart. Interesting. I'm sure you could have guys lining up."

"A lineup of men is the last thing on my mind."

"What *is* on your mind?" Becky asked.

"Actually, I try *not* to think most of the time."

"Probably a good idea. So what do you do when you're not thinking?"

"I eat, sleep, go to work. The usual."

"You went back to teaching?"

"Finally found someone brave enough to hire me."

"You've had some bad luck."

"Guess we all have." Caroline looked toward the TV. Her eyes had adjusted to the dim light. They had yet to adjust to Becky's sunken cheeks and pasty complexion. "I understand my brother's been here."

"Yeah. I called him yesterday, after I checked in. Checked in to check out," she said with a wry chuckle.

"I'm surprised you called him."

"Why?"

"Well, neither of you was exactly the other's biggest fan."

Becky shrugged, her head falling back onto her pillow. "We needed to talk. I owed him that."

Caroline waited for her to continue and was almost relieved when she didn't. Whatever unresolved issues Becky and Steve had between them were none of her business. If Becky felt she owed Steve an explanation or an apology for slights either real or imagined, then who was she to argue? If wiping her marital slate clean allowed Becky to die in peace, then she was entitled to the opportunity. Caroline only hoped her brother was mature enough to listen to whatever his ex-wife had to say. "Is there anything I can do for you, anyone you want me to call?"

"No. I never had a lot of friends. You were

pretty much it."

"I'm sorry we lost touch."

"It wasn't you."

Caroline nodded. Becky was right. It hadn't been Caroline who'd pulled away. For whatever reasons, their friendship had hit a speed bump after Samantha's birth, and it had pretty much crashed and burned after she'd disappeared, both women too preoccupied with their own problems to make the effort necessary to get it up and running again.

"I owe you an apology," Becky said now.

"For what?"

"I was so jealous of you. Your perfect marriage, your perfect children, the way you just popped those babies out. You had the perfect life."

"Not so perfect, as it turned out."

"No. I'm sorry."

"It's not your fault," Caroline said, repeating Becky's words.

Becky closed her eyes.

"Do you want me to leave and let you get some sleep?"

"No. Please stay. There are things that need to be said."

Caroline remained in her seat, saying nothing, watching Becky's chest rise and fall with each labored breath.

"You didn't deserve what happened," Becky said after a long silence.

Caroline shrugged, even though she knew Becky wasn't watching. She pushed back the tears that threatened.

"Not just Samantha disappearing, but everything that happened afterward. The suspicions, the accusations, the way the press treated you . . ."

"I don't care about any of that."

"You lost everything — your marriage . . . your friends . . ." She opened her eyes. "What am I talking about? I treated you just as badly. Worse — I was supposed to be family."

Caroline shook her head, dislodging the tears that had been hovering. "Please don't feel guilty."

"I think about her, you know. Samantha. Not a day goes by that I don't picture that sweet little face and wonder what happened to her, how her life turned out."

"You think she's alive?"

"Don't you?" Becky asked, pushing herself back to a sitting position.

"I don't know."

"Oh, Caroline. You mustn't give up hope." Becky reached for her hand, her fingers fumbling for Caroline's. "You want to know what I think? I think Samantha's alive. I think she's alive and beautiful and happy."

Caroline gasped, her breath catching in her throat, blocking further sounds.

"I don't think she was taken by some pervert," Becky continued, clutching tight to Caroline's trembling hand. "I don't think she was murdered or sold to a pedophile ring, like the papers speculated. I think whoever took her was just desperate for a baby, like I was, and that she's being well cared for and loved."

Caroline realized how badly she wanted to believe what Becky was saying. "You really believe that?"

"I really do."

Caroline felt a flurry of faint hope flutter in her breast. "Thank you."

"No. Don't thank me."

"Thank you for what?" Steve asked from the doorway.

Caroline turned toward the sound of his voice. She'd been caught so off guard by both Becky's pronouncement and the fervency with which it had been uttered that she hadn't heard the door open. She saw Steve leaning against the doorframe, resplendent in a pale blue shirt and black pants. "Becky thinks Samantha is alive. She thinks she's being raised by a good family who loves her."

"Well, she's always been a bit clairvoyant, so let's hope she's right." He walked to Becky's bedside and gave her a kiss on the cheek, then leaned in to kiss his sister, whispering in her ear. "She's been saying some pretty strange things. Try not to let her upset you." He straightened back up, dragged the other chair to the side of the bed, then reached over to adjust Becky's wig. "That's better," he said with a gentleness that surprised Caroline.

Too bad he hadn't shown such tenderness toward her when they were married, she thought. Maybe if he had, they never would have divorced. There wouldn't be all these unresolved issues between them.

"I'm glad you're here," he said to Caroline. "I told Becky she should call you. She has all this guilt she's been carrying around, thinks she deserted you in your hour of need," he continued under his breath. "Anyway, I wasn't sure she'd listen to me. She never used to," he said, speaking to Becky now. He smiled, although the wattage of his killer smile was noticeably dim. "Are you hungry?" he asked his former wife.

Becky shook her head, then winced in obvious pain.

"What hurts?" Steve asked.

"Everything. You'd think I'd be used to it

by now."

"I'll call the nurse," Caroline said.

"Don't," Steve said. "I have something that'll work better than any pain medication she'll give you." He pulled a small plastic bag out of the side pocket of his pants and waved it in front of them.

"Is that what I think it is?" Caroline asked.

"Mexico's finest." Steve put the bag in his lap and pulled some small squares of paper from his back pocket.

It was Caroline's turn to wince, as she did every time someone mentioned Mexico. "You can't be serious about smoking dope in here."

"Of course I'm serious. There's no good reason for Becky to be in pain. Not when there's a simple solution." He sprinkled some weed onto one of the square pieces of paper and licked its sides together.

"Simple and illegal," Caroline protested.

"Then let them arrest me," Becky said, her voice surprisingly strong, as Steve lit the fat cigarette and took a long drag before holding it to his ex-wife's lips.

Caroline watched Becky open her mouth and inhale deeply.

Steve extended the joint toward his sister. Caroline shook her head. "Come on," he told her. "It'll do you good."

Caroline hesitated before taking the joint from his outstretched hand. She couldn't remember the last time she'd smoked a joint, deciding it had probably been in college. Hunter had never approved of getting high, although he had no such reservations about drinking, something he did often in the months after Caroline had returned home from Rosarito.

"So, what do you think?" Steve asked, taking another drag before returning it to Becky's lips. "Good stuff, no?"

"Great stuff," Becky answered, falling back against her pillow and closing her eyes.

"*Smelly* stuff." Caroline pushed herself out of her chair and walked to the window, cranking it open and waving the sweet-smelling smoke toward the outside. "If anyone were to walk in . . ."

"Nobody's going to walk in without knocking first."

"You did."

Steve's response was to take another drag, then pass the joint back to her.

"Where do you get this stuff anyway?" Caroline asked, inhaling deeply and holding the smoke in her lungs until she thought she would burst.

"I have a guy," Steve answered.

Caroline nodded, beginning to experience

a pleasant sensation at the nape of her neck, as if her head was about to separate from her body. Steve always "had a guy." Ever since they were teenagers, Steve had managed to find someone to help him shortcut the system, whether it was to buy him alcohol when he was too young to do it himself, or supply him with illegal drugs, or front him the money for a seat at a high-stakes poker game. And, of course, if things didn't go quite according to plan, or if they went south altogether, there was always their mother to come running to his rescue.

Their mother — the biggest "guy" of all.

"Feeling better now?" Steve asked Becky when there was nothing left of the expertly rolled joint but a burning ember between his fingertips.

"Hmm," Becky muttered, drifting toward unconsciousness.

"It's pretty powerful stuff," Steve said to Caroline. "She'll probably sleep for a while. You don't have to stay."

"Neither do you."

"On the contrary. It's the least I can do."

Yes, you've always been very good at doing the least, Caroline thought, wondering what had provoked her brother's change of heart but reluctant to question it.

"I hope she didn't upset you too much,"

Steve said. "I know that wasn't her intention."

"She didn't. Actually, if anything, she did the opposite. I've been concentrating so much on the negative lately, obsessing on all the bad things that could have happened to Samantha. And she gave me hope."

"Well, then, it's good she called you."

Becky stirred, opened her eyes. "Is Caroline here?" she asked, as if unaware of their earlier exchange.

"Right here," Caroline told her.

"Caroline?"

"Yes."

"I'm so sorry."

"I know."

"Forgive me," she said.

"There's nothing to forgive."

"Did you hear that?" Steve asked his former wife as she drifted back toward oblivion. "Caroline says there's nothing to forgive." He kissed her softly on the lips, then slouched back in his chair. "I'm the one who should be begging for forgiveness. I was such a prick."

"You just weren't a good match," Caroline offered, trying to be kind.

"Poor Becky," he said, gently stroking her arm. "You deserved better."

Didn't we all? Caroline thought, pushing

herself out of her chair and floating toward the door, her head lost in a drug-filled cloud. When she looked back, her brother was hunched over Becky, whispering soft words in her ear, still stroking her arm.

Seventeen: The Present

Caroline woke up the next morning with a headache, the result of a night spent arguing with Michelle, their earlier altercation having spilled over into her dreams. She swung out of bed, her head pounding with each step as she padded toward the bathroom and gobbled down two extra-strength somethings, then returned to bed. Remnants of her disturbing dreams hovered just out of reach, as stubbornly elusive as the daughter who provoked them. Half an hour later, her head was still pounding, keeping time with the beating of her heart. She thought of Becky, how she'd ignored her headaches until it was too late. She wondered if she, too, could be nursing a tumor, and if anyone would be there to mourn her loss, as Steve had mourned his former wife. Would Hunter be filled with similar remorse for the shabby way he'd treated her? Would Michelle regret her harsh words, her blistering accusations?

"Okay. Enough of that." She showered and dressed, then went downstairs, made a pot of coffee, and retrieved the Sunday paper from outside her front door. She was sitting at the kitchen table, working on the crossword and enjoying her third cup of coffee, the caffeine having mercifully reduced her headache to a dull throb at her temples, when Michelle entered the room. Her daughter was wearing a black leotard and a hot-pink cropped top with the logo TRACK FITNESS stenciled in bold black letters across her chest, her hair pulled into a high ponytail and tied with a ribbon the same color of pink as the laces of her sneakers. She poured herself a cup of coffee and drank it standing up in front of the sink.

"Good morning," Caroline said.

"Morning."

"I didn't realize you were here."

"What else is new?"

Caroline's headache returned full force. "It's just that I didn't hear you come home last night."

"No, you were pretty much dead to the world when I looked in on you."

"You looked in on me?"

Michelle rolled her eyes as she finished her coffee and deposited her empty cup in the sink. "I'm off to thc gym."

"Don't you think you might be overdoing the exercise? I read somewhere that too much aerobic exercise can actually shorten your life."

"Funny. I heard the same thing about reading." Michelle headed for the front door.

"Michelle, wait." Caroline followed after her. "Can we talk about what happened yesterday?"

"I think we've probably talked enough, don't you?"

"You made some pretty strong accusations."

"Forget I said anything. It doesn't matter."

"It *does* matter. You have to know I love you, sweetheart. More than anything in the world . . ."

"I do," Michelle said. "Really. I do. Now I have to go or I'll be late for my class."

"Wait," Caroline said again, reluctant to let her daughter leave, but not knowing what else to say. She ducked into the living room and grabbed her purse from the floor where she'd left it the previous afternoon. "Can you pick up some coffee? We're almost out." She fished inside her purse for her wallet, withdrawing a twenty-dollar bill and handing it to Michelle. "Wait," she said again, as her daughter was turning to leave. "Something else we need?"

"My phone," Caroline said, her hand searching the bottom of the bag. "Where's my phone?"

"How should I know?"

"Did you take it? When you came home last night . . ."

"Why would I take your phone, Mother?" Michelle asked, shifting her weight from one foot to the other. "You probably just put it somewhere . . ."

"I haven't touched it."

"Well, neither have I."

"It was in my purse. I forgot to take it out when I went upstairs."

"Which means I took it?"

"Give me back my phone, Michelle."

"Give it a rest, Mother," Michelle said before opening the front door and jogging down the front walk to the street.

Caroline slammed the door after her, as Michelle had slammed it the day before. She dumped the contents of her purse onto the gray slate floor, watching her wallet, comb, lipstick, sunglasses, and an assortment of crumpled tissues fan out across the foyer. No phone. "Damn it, Michelle."

How would Lili get in touch with her now? What if she'd already called? What if

Michelle had answered and repeated her threat to call the police? Would Lili have known such threats were groundless? Would she risk calling again? Would she try the house or get in touch with her at work, as she had before?

Or would she just give up, decide it wasn't worth the effort, and never call again?

"How could you be so stupid as to leave your purse lying around?" she castigated herself, retrieving the items from the floor and returning them to her leather bag.

The phone rang.

"Lili?" Caroline wondered aloud, scrambling to her feet and racing into the kitchen, slamming her hip against the brass knob of a cabinet as she grabbed for the phone and pressed it to her ear. "Lili?"

"Caroline?" a man's voice said.

The voice was vaguely familiar, although Caroline couldn't place it. "Who is this?"

"It's Jerrod Bolton."

"Who?"

"Jerrod Bolton," the man repeated with a chuckle. "I realize it's been a long time . . ."

"Jerrod Bolton," Caroline repeated, a picture slowly forming in her mind's eye. "Jerrod Bolton," she said again, seeing his face clearly now, although he remained as nondescript as the last time she'd seen him standing beside his glamorous wife in Mexico. Why was he calling? "Jerrod, my goodness. This is a surprise. How are you?"

"I'm fine. I was wondering if we could meet for lunch."

"Why?" Caroline asked.

He laughed. "I see we're not going to waste any time beating around the bush."

"Why do you want to meet for lunch?" Caroline persisted. "Is something wrong?"

A brief pause, then, "There are some things I'd like to discuss with you."

"Such as?"

"I'd rather not talk about them over the phone."

"Sounds ominous."

"Sorry. I don't mean it to. I've just learned some things I thought might interest you."

"What sort of things?"

"The sort of things one doesn't discuss over the phone. Can we meet?"

"Does Hunter know you're calling me?"

"No. And I'd prefer you didn't say anything to him, at least for the time being."

"I don't understand."

"And I'd be happy to explain. At lunch. Today, if you're available."

"Where?"

"Darby's, over on Sunset Cliffs. Say twelve o'clock?"

Caroline repeated his words silently in her head, trying to make sense of them. Why did he want to see her again after all these years? Why didn't he want Hunter to know? What possible things could he have learned that would interest her?

"Caroline, are you still there?"

"Darby's, over on Sunset Cliffs," she said. "Twelve o'clock."

Darby's was a typical Southern California beachfront restaurant: large, casual, airy, and inviting. Light walls, dark hardwood floors, a giant swordfish mounted on one wall, half a dozen strategically placed televisions broadcasting an endless stream of surfing videos, a giant bar in the center of the room staffed by beautiful young women in tiny black dresses that barely covered their high, firm backsides.

Caroline approached the reception counter and looked around the main room, already crowded with midday diners. She didn't see anyone resembling Jerrod Bolton, although she reminded herself that fifteen years had passed since their last encounter and he hadn't been all that memorable to begin with.

She tried not to think about the possible things he'd learned in the interim that might hold any interest for her, as such speculations invariably proved wrong. It was always the one thing you *hadn't* thought of, the one possibility you *hadn't* considered. How many times had Hunter told her to stop worrying about what *might* be and concentrate on what *was,* to forget suppositions and deal strictly with the facts? And the fact was that she hadn't seen either Jerrod Bolton or his wife in fifteen years. So why did he want to see her now? What could he possibly have to tell her that would benefit her?

"Can I help you?"

Caroline looked at the short but shapely young woman with waist-length black hair and deep burgundy lips who was smiling at her expectantly. "I'm looking for Jerrod Bolton," Caroline said. "I think he has a reservation . . ."

"Oh, yes. Mr. Bolton. He's on the patio. Right this way."

Caroline followed the young woman as she maneuvered her way in staggeringly high heels through the close-together tables of the main dining room to the patio outside at the back.

"Caroline," she heard a man call over the sound of the ocean waves, the easy authority of his voice rising above the screech of the seagulls swooping across the sand.

"Over here."

Jerrod Bolton was standing beneath a navy canvas umbrella, half in, half out of his white plastic chair, waving her over. In the years since she'd last seen him, he'd put on a few pounds and lost most of his hair, the shine of his now bald head accentuated by the loud orange-and-white-flowered print of the Tommy Bahama shirt he wore. Other than that, he was as nondescript as ever, Caroline decided as she walked toward him. If she hadn't been expecting to see him, she doubted she would have recognized him. It was strange: he'd been part of the worst, most difficult time of her life, and yet she might have passed him in the street a thousand times over the past fifteen years without even knowing.

"You're looking as beautiful as ever," he said as she approached. He took her hands and pulled her forward to kiss her on both cheeks. "The way the French do," he said with a grin.

"How've you been?" Caroline asked, sitting down.

"Wonderful. Health is good. Business is great. I can't get over how lovely you look. Really, you haven't changed a bit."

She was wearing only a minimal amount of makeup and a shapeless yellow sundress.

The humidity was playing havoc with her hair. “I doubt that’s true.”

“It’s true. Trust me.”

Why should I trust you? Caroline thought.

The waiter approached.

“What would you like to drink?” Jerrod asked.

Caroline shrugged. She normally didn’t drink in the afternoon, and she didn’t know much about wine.

“How about some champagne?” he asked, not waiting for her answer before ordering a bottle of Dom Pérignon.

Caroline knew even less about champagne than she knew about wine, but she knew that Dom Pérignon was one of the most expensive champagnes you could buy. “Are we celebrating?”

“You might say that.”

“What would *you* say?”

He smiled. “That having lunch with a beautiful woman is reason enough for celebration.”

Was he coming on to her? Was that the reason he’d phoned? “How’s Rain?” she asked pointedly.

“Sharp as a tack,” he said with a smile. “And about as pleasant.”

“Excuse me?”

“We’re separated.”

"Oh." Caroline sank back in her chair.

"You seem surprised."

"I guess I am. You seemed so crazy about each other."

"*I* was crazy about *her.* She was just crazy." He winked.

"I'm sorry," Caroline said, ignoring the wink. While she and Rain had never been close, she had no interest in sitting here listening to him bad-mouth the woman. She'd heard enough bad-mouthing when Steve and Becky were going through their divorce. "You sound as if you're having a difficult time."

"I admit it hasn't been easy."

Was that why he'd called? Because he needed a shoulder to cry on? Did he have no one else to confide in?

The waiter returned with their champagne, popped the cork expertly and efficiently, and poured two glasses.

"To fresh starts," Jerrod said, clicking his glass against hers.

Caroline reluctantly brought the glass to her lips and took a sip, feeling the bubbles tickle the tip of her nose. "I'm sorry, Jerrod. I don't mean to be rude, but why am I here?"

"You've never heard of two old friends getting together?"

"I haven't seen you in fifteen years," Caroline reminded him. "Even then, you were more Hunter's friend than mine."

"Yes, well, so much for that."

"So much for what?"

"You really have no idea what I'm talking about," Jerrod stated more than asked. He took another sip of his champagne.

"I really don't."

The waiter approached with their menus.

"Do you mind if I order for us?" Jerrod asked. "They make the most fabulous shrimp salad. I really think you'll love it."

Caroline nodded, feeling her appetite already disappearing. If this was the way Jerrod had behaved during his marriage, then all her sympathies rested with Rain. It was a wonder their union had survived as long as it had.

"Two shrimp salads. And could we have some bread, please? Thank you."

"You said on the phone that you'd recently learned some things that might interest me," Caroline said as soon as the waiter retreated.

"Absolutely true."

"Are you going to tell me what they are or are you going to make me guess?"

"It's about your former husband and my soon-to-be-ex-wife."

"What about them?"

"You still haven't guessed?"

"I'm lousy at guessing games."

"They were having an affair," he said matter-of-factly.

"They were having an affair," Caroline repeated, trying not to laugh. The man was out of his mind. Hunter had always seemed oblivious to Rain's obvious charms. And even in the unlikely event that he and Rain *had* been involved, what difference did it make to her now? She was no longer Hunter's wife. Other women were no longer her problem. Diana was the one Jerrod should be talking to. Hunter was her headache now.

The waiter set a breadbasket on their table. "Try the olive bread," Jerrod instructed her. "It's the best in the city." He took a slice and slathered it with butter. "I really thought you knew about it, or at the very least suspected."

"When exactly did this affair supposedly take place?"

"Fifteen years ago."

Caroline felt a numbness begin to worm its way into the pit of her stomach. "Fifteen years ago?"

"And there's no 'supposing' about it. Rain admitted to the whole sordid thing. Frankly, I think she was relieved to finally get it off her chest. A chest that, I have to admit, I shall dearly miss."

Caroline felt the numbness starting to spread throughout her body. She'd known that Hunter had been cheating on her repeatedly in the aftermath of Samantha's disappearance, but she'd never in her wildest dreams thought one of those affairs might be with Rain. "You mean after he got back from Mexico?"

"After. Before. *During.*" Jerrod popped the piece of olive bread in his mouth and chewed vigorously.

The numbness took root in Caroline's lungs. She couldn't breathe. "Wait. You're saying they were sleeping together *while* we were in Rosarito?"

"Happy anniversary." He raised his glass in a toast, then immediately set it back on the table. "Sorry. I don't mean to be glib. You don't deserve that. You were clearly as duped as I was."

"And Rain just blurted all this out?"

"Blurted out a lot more than that. As I said, I think she was relieved to finally come clean."

"What exactly did she tell you?"

"That while we were in Mexico, she and Hunter were together whenever they had the chance, that they'd even snuck away during your anniversary dinner, that they were going at it hot and heavy while your husband was supposedly checking on Samantha . . ."

A strangled cry escaped Caroline's lips.

"I wasn't going to tell you. Water under the bridge and all that. What possible good would your knowing this do after all this time? But with all the recent stuff in the news, I couldn't get you out of my head. I know it doesn't change anything, but I guess I thought you had the right to know."

Caroline jumped to her feet. "I have to go."

"What? No, wait. You haven't eaten. I thought we might go for a walk on the beach later, maybe take in a movie . . ."

Caroline stared at him in disbelief. "Son of a bitch," she whispered, running from the patio.

Jerrod might be right about Hunter and Rain, but if what he said was true, he was wrong about it not changing anything.

It changed everything.

EIGHTEEN: FIVE YEARS AGO

The phone was ringing, interrupting a nightmare in which Caroline was being pursued down a dark corridor by a man wearing a hockey mask and brandishing a large butcher knife. "Shit," she cried, sitting up in bed and trying to orient herself to her surroundings. She was in her room, in her bed, the odor of stale popcorn hanging in the air like cheap cologne. It was dark, except for the light coming from the TV on the opposite wall. On the screen, a terrified young woman was being chased through a cornfield by a knife-wielding lunatic. The digital clock beside her bed read 1:35.

"*Fright Night* will continue in a moment," announced the disembodied voice from the TV as Caroline muted the sound and reached for the phone, her heart pounding, her adrenaline pumping. Being chased by a knife-wielding psychopath was never a good thing; phone calls in the middle of the night were almost as bad.

"Hello?"

"You better get over here," Hunter said.

"What's wrong?"

"It's Michelle. She's . . ."

"Oh, God."

"Take it easy," her ex-husband said, his voice instantly softening. "She's fine."

Caroline's mind struggled to focus, to arrange the events of the evening in some sort of order. It was Saturday night; Michelle was at a party; Caroline had spent the night alone, watching horror movies in bed, a bowl of homemade popcorn in her lap. At some point during the nonstop carnage, she'd obviously fallen asleep. Michelle had just as obviously missed her one o'clock curfew. What was she doing at Hunter's apartment?

"I don't understand," Caroline said, her brain unable to make sense of the situation, her head threatening to explode.

"She's drunk."

"What?"

"You'd better get over here."

Caroline glanced down at her butter-stained nightgown, then back at the clock. It was late. She was in bed. Michelle was unharmed. The fact that her fifteen-year-old daughter had been drinking was worrisome, but it wasn't exactly a medical emergency. "Can't she just stay there tonight? I'll come get her first thing in the morning."

"Now," Hunter said, then hung up the phone.

Caroline stared at the receiver in her hand. "Aye, aye, Captain." Reluctantly she tossed off her covers and climbed out of bed. "What's the damn urgency?" she muttered as she pulled on a pair of jeans and exchanged her nightgown for a lightweight gray sweatshirt. She was almost at the front door, car keys in hand, when she realized she didn't know where she was going. "I don't know your address," she told Hunter on the phone moments later.

Mercifully, there was little traffic at that hour and Caroline soon found herself in the formerly sleazy but now trendy downtown neighborhood known as the Gaslamp Quarter, her eyes searching the rows of beautifully restored Victorian buildings for her ex-husband's address. When they were married, Hunter wouldn't have considered living in this part of town, filled as it was with tattoo parlors, porn shops, and tenements on the verge of collapse. But the last decade had seen such old eyesores supplanted by shiny new art galleries, boutiques, and upscale restaurants. It had become the "in" place to be and be seen, so it was only natural that Hunter had recently purchased a condo here. Caroline opened her car window and breathed in the cool night air. Even at almost two A.M., music from several of the nearby clubs could still be heard, the throb of a lone bass guitar spilling out onto the street like an errant heartbeat.

Caroline located Hunter's address and pulled into the first available parking spot, which was almost a full block away. It was October, and a slight breeze was blowing in from the ocean. She probably should have thrown on a jacket before she left the house, she was thinking as she walked briskly down the street. But Hunter seemed in such a damn hurry. What was the rush, for God's sake? Why was he so anxious to get Michelle out of his apartment?

They were waiting for her in the rose-colored lobby, Hunter looking attractively disheveled in a pair of tight jeans and a white T-shirt, Michelle looking vaguely green around the gills, her long, uncombed hair hiding all of her face except for her eyes, eyes that were glaring at her mother with unabashed hostility.

"Are you all right?" Caroline asked her, ignoring Hunter, whose feet she noticed were bare.

"Get her home and into bed," Hunter said, as if Michelle's condition was somehow Caroline's fault.

"I don't understand. What happened?"

"It's late," he said, already turning toward the elevators. "We'll talk tomorrow."

"Hunter . . ."

"Can we just go home?" Michelle wailed.

Caroline watched Hunter step inside the waiting elevator, then led her daughter out of the lobby and down the street, Michelle shrugging her mother's arms off her shoulders as soon as they reached the sidewalk. Glancing back at Hunter's building as they walked toward her car, Caroline saw a shadowy figure peeking out at them from behind some curtains about five stories up. Had Michelle created such a disturbance that she'd awakened Hunter's neighbors? Was that why he'd been so anxious to get rid of her?

"I'm not an invalid," her daughter said when Caroline tried to help her into the car.

"No, you're fifteen and you're drunk," Caroline said, unable to keep her anger at bay any longer. "What the hell happened tonight?"

Michelle hunkered down in her seat, said nothing.

"What happened?" Caroline persisted,

starting the engine and pulling away from the curb. "What were you doing at your father's? And put your seat belt on," she added when the seat belt signal started beeping.

Michelle dragged her seat belt across the low scooped neck of her tight powder blue T-shirt.

"That's not what you were wearing when you left the house," Caroline said, recalling the more modest black blouse her daughter had been wearing earlier. "Start talking, Michelle. What's going on?"

Michelle groaned.

"That's not an answer."

Michelle bolted upright in her seat. "You want answers? Fine, I'll give you answers. Did you know Daddy and Diana have set a date?"

"That's a question, not an answer," Caroline shot back, fighting to stay in control.

"And that she's all of twenty-one."

"Your father's girlfriends are none of my concern." *Dear God — twenty-one?* "Nor are they the issue here."

"Did you hear what I said? They're engaged. They're getting married in June."

"Again, none of my concern."

"So it doesn't bother you that he's getting married again?"

"It's not exactly unexpected."

"Or that they're planning this big wedding with more than two hundred guests and at least ten bridesmaids?"

"They told you that?"

"Not exactly."

"How exactly?"

"I heard them."

"What? When?"

"Before they knew I was there."

"I don't understand. How didn't they know you were there? You're saying you snuck into your father's apartment?"

"I have a key. It's not exactly sneaking in when you have a key."

"What were you doing there in the first place?"

Michelle shrugged and leaned her head back against the headrest, closing her eyes.

"Oh, no," Caroline said. "Nobody gets to sleep around here until we get to the bottom of this. Now start at the beginning," she instructed. "You went to a party at Chloe's. You got drunk."

"It's not like I was plastered. I just had a few drinks."

"You're fifteen years old! You shouldn't be drinking at all. Where were Chloe's parents?"

"How do I know?"

"You told me they'd be home."

"Yeah, well, I lied. Guess you should have checked."

"I guess I should have. You can add it to the list of my failings."

"Yeah, poor you."

"Except this is not about me. It's about you."

"I know. I know. I'm a horrible daughter and a horrible person . . ."

"Nobody said you're a horrible person *or* a horrible daughter."

"You don't have to say it. I can feel it. I feel it every damn day."

Caroline stopped the car in the middle of the road and swung around in her seat to face Michelle. "What are you talking about?"

"You think I don't know what a disappointment I am to you? God, no wonder I drink."

"You're saying it's my fault you got drunk?"

"Of course it's not your fault. Nothing's ever your fault."

From behind them, a car started honking. Caroline checked her rearview mirror. "Damn it. Where did he come from?"

"It's downtown Saturday night, Mother. You're not the only person on the road."

Caroline threw the car back into drive and pulled to a stop at the curb, then shut off the engine.

"Really?" Michelle whined. "We're doing this now?"

"We're doing this now," Caroline said, turning her daughter's question into an answer.

"I don't feel well. I just want to go home."

"Then tell me what you were doing at your father's."

"Chloe's party was boring, so a bunch of us decided to head over to Maxie's."

"Who's Maxie?"

"Not who. What." Michelle rolled her eyes, as if to say, *Don't you know anything?* "It's a club." She waved her hand in its general direction. "A few blocks down."

"How'd you get in? You're fifteen."

"I know how old I am. You don't have to keep telling me." This time she rolled not only her eyes but her whole head. "I have a fake I.D."

"You have a fake I.D.?"

"Everybody does."

"*Not* everybody does. *I* don't."

"Because you don't need one," Michelle said, as if this should be self-explanatory. "You're old, for fuck's sake."

"Okay, that's quite enough."

"Do you want to hear the rest of the story or not?"

Caroline said nothing. She turned her right hand palm up, as if giving Michelle the floor.

"We went to Maxie's. We were dancing. It was hot. I started feeling kind of sick, so I left. Dad's place was right around the corner, and I figured I could stay there tonight. I was planning to call you. *So you wouldn't worry,*" she emphasized. "I have a key, like I told you. So I let myself in. I was tiptoeing down the hall, 'cause I didn't want to wake him up in case he was sleeping, and that's when I heard them."

"You heard your father and this . . . this Diana person talking about their wedding."

"Yeah. Well, not at first. At first I just heard them, you know . . . groaning and stuff."

Shit, thought Caroline, trying not to remember the variety of noises Hunter used to make when they were having sex.

"Then Diana said something like, 'Is it going to be this good once we're married?' and Daddy said, 'Even better.' And I think that may have been when I threw up."

"You threw up?"

"That's when they realized I was there."

"You threw up?" Caroline repeated, fighting the urge to throw her arms around Michelle and smother her face with kisses.

"Dad freaked."

"I'm sure he did."

"He jumped out of bed and started running around the room like a crazy person. And Diana was screaming for him to put some clothes on, 'cause he obviously forgot he was naked. Anyway, that's when he called you, told you to come and get me. Okay? Are you satisfied now?"

"Yes," Caroline said, stifling a laugh before it could escape her throat. *Very.*

"Can we go home?"

"Is she really only twenty-one?"

"I think she's closer to thirty. Can we please go home now?"

Caroline restarted the car's engine. "I love you," she said.

Michelle was still sleeping at noon the next day when Hunter phoned to talk about what had happened and to apologize for his behavior.

"I understand you're getting married," Caroline said.

A second's silence, then, "I was going to tell you . . ."

"Have you set a date?"

"June nineteenth. We thought it best to

wait a while. Until things calm down."

Caroline knew he was referring to the barrage of articles that were likely to start appearing over the next few weeks, stories marking the upcoming tenth anniversary of Samantha's disappearance. *What would have been their twentieth anniversary had they stayed married,* Caroline thought. Reporters would be eager to pounce on any new tidbit, however unrelated it might be to the original event. When Hunter and Caroline had divorced, it made the Milestones column of every national magazine in the country. His remarriage to a younger woman would certainly add more fuel to what was already an unquenchable fire.

"I'm sorry," he said again before Caroline hung up.

She didn't realize she was crying until she felt the tears funneling between her lips. She brushed them away with the back of one hand and reached for the small pad of notepaper she kept by the kitchen phone with the other. *Gone to Nicola's,* she scribbled, referring to the small grocery store several blocks away where she sometimes shopped despite its exorbitant prices. "If you want to know what grocery stores will be charging in the future," Peggy had once quipped, "shop at Nicola's today." *Back soon,* she added.

Not that they needed anything, Caroline thought as she was walking down the street. More that she just needed to get out of the house. And she could use the exercise. She couldn't help having noticed how good Hunter still looked, how he'd kept himself in such great shape, while she'd let herself go a little, first giving up her membership in the gym they used to frequent together, then abandoning the treadmill she once kept in her walk-in closet and used daily, and not bothering to replace it when it stopped working.

She entered Nicola's, grabbed a small green plastic basket from beside the front door, and began walking up and down the aisles, stopping at the produce section and lifting an avocado, mentally measuring its ripeness.

"Is everything all right?" she heard someone ask.

Caroline spun around, finding herself face-to-face with a handsome man of about forty. Well, not exactly handsome, she decided, assessing the thinning dark blond hair that fell into his light brown eyes, and the deep creases surrounding his too wide mouth, everything just a little off. Still, there was something very appealing about him.

"Excuse me?"

"You have a choke hold on that avocado," he said. "Is there a problem?"

Caroline quickly dropped the avocado into her basket. "I guess I just drifted off for a few minutes. I'm sorry." Why was she apologizing? She didn't know this man. She didn't owe him an explanation, let alone an apology.

"No need to apologize," he said, as if reading her thoughts. "You seem to know your produce," he continued with a smile. "Maybe you could help me out." He extended a cantaloupe in her direction. "I never know when one's ripe or not."

Was he coming on to her? "Are you asking me to feel your melon?" she asked, amazed at the flirtatiousness in her voice. It had been so long since she'd engaged in this sort of banter with a man. Not since Hunter. And now he was getting married. To a woman at least a decade her junior. A woman with whom he'd been having great sex when their inebriated fifteen-year-old daughter showed up unexpectedly and threw up in his doorway. And Caroline hadn't had sex in eight years. She hadn't so much as looked at another man since Hunter left. How fair was that?

"Why don't we start with a cup of coffee?" the man asked. "My name is Arthur Wainwright, by the way."

"Caroline," Caroline answered, deliberately omitting mention of her surname. She dropped her basket onto a stack of hothouse tomatoes and followed the man out of the grocery store to the Starbucks around the corner without another word.

Nineteen: The Present

"Son of a bitch!" Caroline was shouting as she sped north on Mission Boulevard toward the upscale neighborhood of La Jolla. "Son of a bitch!" She slapped the palm of her hand against the steering wheel, causing it to bark in protest, then used the back of her hand to wipe away the tears that had been falling down her cheeks ever since she'd left Jerrod Bolton standing open-mouthed beside his table on the patio of Darby's. "How could you do this, you miserable son of a bitch?"

She glanced to her right, saw the driver in the car beside her regarding her with a mixture of concern and fear. "Mind your own damn business," she hollered at him through the closed window of her passenger door, and he quickly turned away.

Did he recognize her? Would she read about her strange behavior in tomorrow's papers? Was he even now snapping pictures of her surreptitiously with his cell phone, pictures that would wallpaper the Internet come morning? *Mother of missing child Samantha Shipley has public breakdown in the middle of busy thoroughfare.*

"I don't believe it," she muttered, speeding up and switching into the right lane when Mission Boulevard morphed into La Jolla Boulevard, keeping an eye out for her exit. "I don't believe it."

What don't I believe? she asked herself in the next breath. That Hunter had cheated on her? That was a laugh. Of course Hunter had cheated on her. Many times and with many different women. But with Rain? Had Hunter really cheated on her with a woman he'd dismissed as a lightweight, saying on more than one occasion that "a little of her went a long way"? How little? Caroline wondered now. Exactly how far had she gone?

"Clearly all the way," she announced to her startled reflection in the rearview mirror. So she *did* believe Hunter could have slept with Rain. How could she not have suspected as much before? She thought back to that night in the garden restaurant of their hotel in Rosarito, remembering that Hunter and Rain had excused themselves from the dinner table at the same time, Rain ostensibly to get a sweater, Hunter to check on the kids. Her mind's eye watched them go their separate ways at the entrance to the restaurant, although that deception could have been easily staged and just as easily remedied. She watched them return approximately fifteen minutes later and only moments apart, Hunter supposedly delayed because of a slow elevator, Rain because she'd had to unpack her entire suitcase to find her sweater.

Except Rain hadn't been unpacking and Hunter hadn't been checking on the kids. Instead they were together, going at it like a couple of horny teenagers while someone was entering Caroline's suite and absconding with her baby. And Hunter hadn't said a word. Not to the police. Not to her. Not then. Not for fifteen years. What else hadn't he told her? "Damn you, Hunter! Damn you to hell!"

Caroline left La Jolla Boulevard at Torrey Pines Road, barely noticing La Jolla Natural Park as she sped past the leafy enclave. She didn't see the police car sitting at the side of the road, didn't register the officer's presence until he was in full pursuit, didn't realize the sirens blasting were meant for her until she saw the red lights flashing in her rearview mirror and watched the uniformed cop cut in front of her and wave her to a stop at the side of the road.

"Any idea how fast you were going?" he asked as Caroline lowered her window.

"I'm sorry," she said. "I didn't realize . . ."

"License and registration," he directed.

Caroline grabbed her purse from the passenger seat and fished inside it for her wallet, extending it toward the policeman, who looked shockingly young beneath his helmet.

"Take it out of your wallet, please."

"Oh. Sorry." She had trouble opening the wallet, and even more difficulty extricating her license, her trembling fingers refusing to cooperate. She took a deep breath, lowered the wallet to her lap, then tried again.

"You nervous about something?" the officer asked, his voice an accusation.

Caroline shook her head, apologized again. Ever since her experience with the Mexican authorities, when they'd all but accused her of being complicit in the disappearance of her daughter, she'd experienced terrible anxiety whenever she was around police officers. Her heart would pound, her hands would break into a sweat, her breath would escape in short, painful bursts. "Here," she said, finally managing to free her license and registration from their plastic confines.

The officer checked her face against her photo, paused for a second over her name. "You're Caroline Shipley?" he asked. *Did you murder your child?*

Caroline turned away, unable to respond.

"Ma'am?"

"Yes, I'm Caroline Shipley."

"You were going twenty miles over the limit," he told her.

"Twenty miles," she repeated numbly.

"Have you been drinking?"

"Drinking? No." Would the officer insist she take a Breathalyzer test and would the tiny sip of champagne she'd taken earlier register on it? What would he say if she refused to comply? Would he haul her off to jail, as had happened with Michelle only months ago? She could see the headlines now: *Mother of missing child Samantha Shipley arrested for driving drunk.* Or worse: *All in the Family: Mother and sister of missing child Samantha Shipley both face charges of driving under the influence.*

"Please stay in the car," the policeman said, returning to his vehicle and feeding her information to headquarters. "I'm afraid this is going to cost you," he announced upon his return, handing back her license and registration along with a speeding ticket for three hundred dollars. "Mind telling me why you were in such a hurry?"

I was rushing to confront my ex-husband about his affair with the wife of his former business associate, a woman who was supposedly helping us celebrate our tenth anniversary when, all the while, she was actually fucking my husband. In fact, she was fucking him when he was supposed to be checking on our children, possibly even mounting him at the very moment that our youngest child was being lifted from her crib and spirited away. And I was in such a damn hurry because too much time has already been wasted as a result of his lies, lies he told me, lies he told the police, lies he's been telling the world for fifteen fucking years. "Just taking a drive," she said instead.

The officer sighed. "Well, slow down. You don't want to kill someone." *Did you murder your child?*

Caroline tossed the ticket, along with her license and registration, into her purse. She would return the license and registration to their proper compartments in her wallet when her hands stopped shaking. "Thank you," she told the policeman when she couldn't think of anything else to say.

He stepped back and she threw the car into drive and pulled back onto the road, watching the officer in her rearview mirror as he returned to his vehicle. Had he known who she was or was his scowl indiscriminate, the one he used on all reckless drivers?

"Damn you, Hunter Shipley," she said as she pressed down on the accelerator, careful to keep within the posted speed limit as she continued toward Hunter's new home. "This is all your fault. I should give you the fucking ticket."

Torrey Pines Road twisted into Torrey Pines Drive, its magnificent mini-mansions overlooking the ocean. It had always been Hunter's dream to own property here, in what the residents of La Jolla referred to as the "Jewel" of San Diego. And now, due to a combination of hard work and a rich young wife, here he was. *Some dreams do come true,* she thought ruefully, pulling her car into the driveway of the wood-and-glass, ultra-modern two-story home and shutting off the engine. "Damn you, Hunter," she whispered as she got out of the car, repeating the words silently as she hurried up the stone walkway to the massive oak front door.

She rang the bell, then banged on it with the tail of its bronze dolphin knocker. "Hurry up, you miserable son of a bitch."

The thought suddenly occurred to her that he might not be home. It was the weekend, after all. Maybe he and Diana had taken their two young children for a stroll along the beach, or a drive up the coast. Maybe she'd sped all this way, incurring a three-hundred-dollar ticket, for absolutely nothing.

The door opened. A young woman with flawless skin, long blond hair, and a baby on one slender hip stood before her, blue eyes wide with alarm. "Caroline?"

"Diana?" Caroline had actually never met the woman who was Hunter's second wife. She'd seen pictures of her, heard Michelle casually extol her beauty, but nothing had prepared her for how lovely the young woman actually was. *Like a little porcelain doll,* she thought, feeling fleshy and oafish in her presence. In comparison, the baby in her arms was more Cabbage Patch doll than china, red-faced and wrinkly, although Caroline could see traces of Hunter, *traces of Samantha,* in her huge, almond-shaped eyes. She turned away, fighting the urge to grab the child from her mother's arms and run.

"Is something wrong?"

"Where's Hunter?"

"Has something happened to Michelle?" Diana's soft voice resonated with concern.

"Michelle's fine. I need to speak to

Hunter."

"What's going on?" her ex-husband called from somewhere inside the house.

"Caroline's here to see you," Diana called back. "Come in," she told Caroline, ushering her inside and closing the front door behind her.

"I need to talk to you, you son of a bitch," Caroline yelled in his general direction. Her eyes swept across the huge circular front hall and up the winding staircase to where Hunter stood, looking down on them from the second-floor landing.

Within seconds he was at her side. "What the hell is going on? What are you doing here? Is Michelle . . . ?"

"You were fucking Rain, you miserable son of a bitch?" she exploded as he took a step back. The baby in Diana's arms began to whimper.

"Whoa. Hold on a minute. Lower your voice."

"Don't tell me to lower my voice . . ."

"Take the baby upstairs," he directed his wife, who complied immediately and without question. "Calm down," he said to Caroline.

"I will not calm down."

"Then you'll have to leave."

"Oh, really? You gonna throw me out? You

gonna call the cops? You really want the world to know you were fucking another man's wife while someone was making off with your child?"

The color drained from Hunter's face, like milk from a straw. He raised his hands in surrender. "I just want you to calm down and lower your voice. I'm prepared to discuss this . . ."

"You're prepared to discuss this?" Caroline repeated incredulously. "After fifteen years, you're *prepared to discuss this*?"

"Come into the living room. We'll sit down, talk about this like two rational adults." He motioned toward the large sun-filled room on his right.

Caroline almost laughed as she followed him into the tastefully furnished living room whose wall of front windows overlooked the ocean. Did he know how ridiculous he sounded? Didn't he realize she'd ceased being a rational adult fifteen years ago? She sank into the overstuffed pillows of the aubergine velvet sofa. He remained on his feet, hovering over the gold brocade armchair to her left.

"What is it, exactly, that you think you know?"

"I know you were fucking Rain . . ."

"Do you think you could stop using that

word . . . ?"

"No, I don't fucking think I can stop using that fucking word," Caroline told him, watching him wince. "It's a good word. A great word. And I don't fucking *think* I know anything. I know, for a fucking fact, that you were fucking Rain Bolton. You're not really going to try to deny it, are you?"

Hunter looked on the verge of doing just that, then thought better of it. "All right. Fine. Yes. I had an affair with Rain. But that was after we got back from Mexico, when you didn't want anything to do with me."

"Liar!" Caroline snapped.

"Caroline . . ."

"I spoke to Jerrod Bolton today. He called me, told me that Rain had confessed the whole thing. They're getting a divorce, by the way. You can be very proud of yourself."

Hunter sank into the armchair, said nothing.

"You made me think it was my fault, that you were leaving me because you couldn't live with the blame you saw in my eyes every day. That it was my coldness that drove you into the arms of other women. When the truth was that you'd been sleeping with other women all along. *Before* we went to Rosarito. *After* we came home. *While* we were there."

"Okay. Okay. You win. I'm a total shit. Is that what you want to hear me say?"

"I already know you're a shit. I don't need you to tell me," Caroline shot back. She pushed her hair away from her face, shaking her head with the memory of their last night together. "When I think of how I begged you, pleaded with you to stay, promised you that things would be different if you'd just give me another chance . . ."

"You didn't want that. Not really. We both knew that. We both knew it was over, that it had been over for two years." He rubbed his forehead. "I don't understand what possible good can come of talking about this now."

"You really don't get it?"

"If it's an apology you're after . . ."

"I don't want your damned apology."

"Then what *do* you want?"

Caroline ignored the question. "You were sleeping with Rain," she reiterated.

Once again Hunter raised his hands in surrender. "Yes. I believe that fact has already been stipulated to."

"And you were sleeping with her *while* we were in Rosarito."

"Yes."

"On the night of our tenth anniversary."

"Yes, dammit."

"No swearing, please," Caroline said, because she couldn't help herself. "And you were with her when you were supposedly checking on our children."

"You and I had been taking turns checking them every half hour, for God's sake. You'd just been up there. You said they were fine."

"They *were* fine," Caroline said angrily. Was he implying otherwise?

"I don't know what you want me to say." Hunter stared up at the bleached wooden beams that stretched across the high ceiling, as if he half expected an answer might be buried in their grain.

"I want you to tell me why you kept this a secret for fifteen years, why you didn't say anything when the police asked you . . ."

"What was I going to tell them, Caroline? That I hadn't actually checked on my kids because I was busy screwing my friend's wife?"

"Yes," Caroline said. "That's exactly what you should have told them."

"How would that have helped? Think about it. Our baby was gone. You were hysterical. The last thing you needed to hear was that I was being unfaithful. I couldn't tell you. I couldn't hurt you that way . . ."

"Don't you dare try to pull that kind of

crap with me. Not now. I'm not buying it anymore. You weren't thinking about my feelings or what I needed. What I needed was the truth. This wasn't about me. It was about you. *All* about you."

"Okay. Have it your way. It was all about me. I just don't understand what difference rehashing this makes now. It doesn't change what happened *then.*"

"It might not have happened at all," Caroline said, "if you'd been where you were supposed to be. Samantha might still be with us."

"You don't think I know that? You don't think I've been living with that guilt for fifteen years?" Hunter buried his face in his hands. "You don't think I hold myself responsible for what happened? That I don't regret my choices, my actions, everything I *did,* everything I *didn't* do, every minute of every day? I shouldn't have insisted we go out that night. I shouldn't have been carrying on with Rain. I shouldn't have lied to you or the police. And I'm so sorry, Caroline. Sorrier than you'll ever know."

Caroline fought the impulse to feel sympathy for him. His feelings of guilt, his apologies, however heartfelt, were immaterial and irrelevant. All that mattered were the facts.

"I checked the kids at nine o'clock," she

stated without inflection. "You told the police you checked them again at nine-thirty. We got back to the room a little after ten, so the police, all of us, we naturally assumed that whoever took Samantha had taken her during that thirty-to-forty-minute time frame, but in fact it could have happened earlier. Whoever took her had since nine o'clock, not nine-thirty, to grab her and get away."

"Even so . . ."

"It changes the entire time frame. Thirty minutes, Hunter. Thirty minutes the police didn't bother looking into, thirty minutes of not checking into the whereabouts of hotel employees and guests, thirty minutes that were ignored by officials at the Mexican border, thirty extra minutes for whoever took her to get away without a trace."

"We don't know that for a fact."

"No," Caroline conceded, pushing herself to her feet. "And thanks to you, we never will. Too much time has passed. It's too damn late." She walked out of the living room into the large circular foyer.

Diana was standing at the foot of the stairs, her baby in her arms, her two-year-old son clinging to her side.

"Daddy," the boy squealed, running toward his father and crashing against the side of his legs.

Hunter reached down and scooped his son into his arms. The boy stared shyly at Caroline, and she watched Samantha materialize behind the smile that slowly spread across his face.

"Oh, God," she cried.

"I'm so sorry," Hunter said.

"You have a beautiful family," Caroline whispered, throwing open the door and fleeing the house.

Twenty: Five Years Ago

"You never told me your last name," Arthur Wainwright remarked over coffee at Starbucks.

"It's Tillman," Caroline said, her maiden name slipping off the tip of her tongue before she even realized it was there. She thought of correcting herself, then decided against it. He obviously didn't know who she was, and she'd likely never see him again. So why spoil a pleasant encounter by revealing her true identity? "Caroline Tillman."

"Caroline's a nice name," he said. "Unlike Arthur. God only knows what my mother was thinking."

"You don't like Arthur?"

"It's okay. Just so old-fashioned."

"You definitely don't run into many Arthurs these days," Caroline agreed, wondering what she was doing here with this man, this Arthur Wainwright. "But it's a strong name. It must have meant something to her."

"The only thing that meant anything to my mother was where her next drink was coming from."

"She was an alcoholic?"

"A mean-spirited one at that."

Caroline almost laughed. "Mine is a mean-spirited narcissist."

"To mothers," Arthur said, clicking his paper cup against hers.

Caroline realized she was having a good time. It had been a long time since she'd enjoyed the company of a man, a long time since she'd allowed herself that kind of indulgence. "What do you do?" she asked.

"Banking consultant."

Caroline nodded. It was the kind of job that Caroline had never fully understood.

"What about you?" he asked before she could think of a follow-up. "What occupies your time when you're not squeezing melons?"

"High school teacher. Mathematics."

"Mathematics? Really? I find that fascinating."

"You do? Why?"

"Because there aren't that many women who teach math. At least not in my experience. Women teach languages and history, not algebra and geometry."

Caroline thought back to her own math teachers in high school. He was right. None of them had been women. "My father was a math teacher. Maybe that's part of it."

"Maybe. But I suspect there's more."

"Like what?"

"I don't know. You strike me as someone with very deep thoughts, so maybe it has something to do with a desire to make sense of the world."

"You think I have deep thoughts?" Caroline couldn't help feeling flattered.

"Don't you?"

"I try not to," she said, grateful when he laughed.

"There's just something so wonderfully definitive about mathematics," he continued. "It's so clear. So true. What was it Keats said? *Truth is beauty. Beauty truth. That is all ye know on earth and all ye need to know.*" He shrugged self-consciously. "Something like that anyway."

"A banking consultant who quotes the Romantic poets," Caroline said. "Interesting."

"My wife was an English major."

Caroline lowered her cup of coffee to the small round table between them. "You're married?"

He hesitated. "Widower." He cleared his throat. "Five years and I still have difficulty saying that word."

"I'm sorry. Had she been sick?"

"Not a day in her life. Healthy as a horse until the moment some drunken asshole plowed into her when she was walking our six-year-old daughter to school."

"Your daughter . . ."

"Killed instantly."

"My God. How awful."

"Eight o'clock in the morning and the guy's already drunk out of his mind. Didn't even realize he'd hit anyone until the police showed up to arrest him. God, I hate alcoholics. Anyway," he said, snapping back to the present, "this isn't exactly the kind of first date repartee I had in mind."

"Is this a first date?"

"I was kind of hoping."

"It's been a long time since I've been on a date," Caroline conceded, returning her coffee cup to her lips. "I'm divorced," she offered. "About eight years now."

"Kids?"

"A daughter. Michelle. She's a teenager. Not a particularly easy one." Caroline felt a twang of guilt. Arthur's daughter was dead, mowed down by a drunk driver on her way to grade school, along with his wife. Who was she to complain about a difficult teenager? She fought the urge to tell him about Samantha.

"You and your ex get along?" he asked, stopping her just in time.

"Not really. Well, sort of, I guess," she amended. "We're not enemies or anything like that."

"That's good."

"Not really friends either."

"Guess you wouldn't be divorced if you got along great."

"He's getting married again in June," Caroline confided. "Big wedding. All the trimmings."

Arthur lowered his chin and raised his eyes, clearly relieved he was no longer the center of the conversation. "And how do you feel about that?"

"I don't really have feelings about it, one way or the other. No, that's not true," she said in the same breath. "To be honest, I'm a little pissed."

"Because you still love him?"

"Because his fiancée is considerably younger than I am."

He laughed.

"Still think I have deep thoughts?"

"I think your ex is a jackass for letting you go."

Caroline shook her head. "Yeah, well, you don't know me very well."

"I'd like to."

She leaned forward, rested her elbows on the table. "Why?"

"Why?" he repeated. "Well, for starters, you're beautiful, smart, and more than a little mysterious. Always an intriguing combination."

"You think I'm mysterious?"

"Lady, I think there's all sorts of stuff going on inside that lovely head."

Her turn to laugh. "What if it turns out to be empty?"

"Not a chance," he said.

"You're not from California, are you?" she asked, feeling slightly flushed and taking refuge in the traces of an East Coast accent she heard lurking inside his vowels.

"Utica, New York," he said. "I moved here after . . . Been here four years now."

"I take it you like it here."

"What's not to like? Sunshine almost every day, a temperature that rarely strays more than ten degrees from moderate, the Pacific Ocean, Mexico on my doorstep."

Caroline felt the coffee cup slip between her fingers at the mention of Mexico. Arthur's hand shot out to catch it before it fell to the floor.

"Well, that was close," he said, wiping the sudden spray of dark liquid from his muscular forearm.

"Sorry about that."

"Something I said?"

"No. Although you *do* have quite a way with words."

"I do?"

"A temperature that rarely strays more than ten degrees from moderate; Mexico on my doorstep," she quoted, forcing the word "Mexico" from her mouth, feeling it wobble as it left her tongue.

"I said that?"

"You did."

"Well, it's the truth. In my humble opinion, Southern California is as close to paradise as anywhere on earth."

"I guess."

"So, tell me more about Caroline Tillman," he said. "Does she like sports, movies, traveling?"

"She likes baseball. I know a lot of people think it's kind of boring, and I guess it can be. But I love it — all the statistics and stuff. Keeping track of the hits and runs and errors, how many strikeouts, all that. It's kind of . . . I don't know . . ."

"Poetic in a mathematical kind of way?" he offered.

Caroline laughed again, finding Arthur Wainwright more appealing by the minute.

"What about traveling?"

"I haven't really done much since my divorce."

"Guess it's hard when you're a single parent."

Caroline shrugged. "Maybe I'm just not very adventurous. What about you?" she asked before he could contradict her.

"I'm partial to all of the above. Sports, movies, traveling."

"What's your favorite place you've ever been to?"

"Barcelona," he said immediately. "It's a gorgeous city. And I'm a sucker for all things Spanish. Which is probably why I like Mexico so much. You like Mexican food?"

"Not really. Sorry."

"No need to be sorry. What kind of food *do* you like?"

"I like pasta."

"*I* like pasta," he echoed. "And I just happen to know this great little Italian restaurant over on Harbor Drive. We could go there for lunch. Are you hungry?"

"I'm starving," Caroline said.

He jumped to his feet. "Shall we go?"

Once again, Caroline followed Arthur Wainwright wordlessly onto the street.

■ ■ ■ ■

"What do you mean, you're not coming home for lunch?" Michelle demanded over the phone half an hour later. "What am I supposed to do?"

Caroline stared at her reflection in the mirror of the restaurant's tiny ladies' room, pushing her hair behind one ear while holding her cell phone to the other. "I don't know. Make yourself an omelet."

"I don't eat eggs."

"So have a sandwich."

"I don't eat bread."

"Since when don't you eat eggs or bread?"

"Since at least a year ago. When are you coming home?"

"I don't know. Later." Caroline fished inside her purse for her lipstick.

"When later?"

"I don't know."

"Where are you?"

"At this little Italian restaurant on Harbor Drive."

"What little Italian restaurant?"

"What difference does it make?"

"Who are you with?"

"A friend I ran into."

"You don't have any friends."

"Yes, I do." *No, I don't,* Caroline thought. *Except for Peggy.* All her other friends had vanished with Samantha's disappearance. And what would Peggy make of what she was doing, not only having coffee with some man she'd met over a stack of fruit and vegetables, but now lunch as well? Would she say that Caroline was merely reacting to the news about Hunter's marriage plans, or to her growing concerns about Michelle, or to the fact that she hadn't gotten laid since the last time she and Hunter had made love, which was, coincidentally, the night he told her he was leaving? Maybe a combination of all three? And while Arthur Wainwright wasn't the first man she'd found attractive since Hunter's departure, he was the first one who seemed to "get" her. Of course, it probably helped that he didn't have a clue who she really was. *He thinks I'm mysterious,* she thought. "I have to go, sweetheart."

"Wait . . ."

"I'll be home later."

"What do you mean, you're not coming home for dinner?" Michelle whined. "And where have you been all afternoon? I've been calling and calling. What's the point of having a cell phone if you're not going to have it on?"

"I'm sorry, sweetheart. It's just that I ran into some friends I haven't seen in a long time . . ."

"More friends?" Michelle asked. "Who are all these friends, all of a sudden?"

"You wouldn't know them." Caroline leaned into the small mirror over the white porcelain sink in the bathroom of Arthur Wainwright's studio apartment and checked to see if having sex for the first time in eight years had made any noticeable difference to her appearance. "Look, I won't be late. Just order a pizza or something."

"I don't eat pizza."

Caroline ran her hands through her hair and down her cheeks, letting them slide toward her bare breasts, mimicking the path Arthur's hands had traced earlier. "How about Chinese?"

"Why don't you just tell me to swallow a gallon of lard?"

"For God's sake, Michelle. Order whatever you want. Sorry," she apologized immediately, trying not to lose the wonderful calm she'd felt before leaving Arthur's bed to call her daughter. "Why don't you phone Grandma Mary? I'm sure she'd be thrilled to have dinner with you."

"You want me to phone Grandma Mary? Now I know something's going on."

"There's nothing going on. I'm just going out with some old friends."

"Fine. Leave your phone on."

"Why?"

"In case I need to contact you."

"You won't need to contact me."

"How do you know? Something could happen . . ."

"I'll leave my phone on," Caroline said, experiencing an all-too-familiar spasm of guilt in her gut. She took another look in the mirror and tried to recapture her earlier elation, the feel of Arthur's fingers gently caressing her flesh, the wetness of his tongue as it glided across her bare skin before disappearing between her legs, the expert way he'd brought her to climax even before he entered her.

"Everything all right at home?" he asked when she returned to the bedroom. He was lying naked in the king-size bed, the once crisp white sheets bunched around his torso.

Caroline turned off her phone, tossed it on top of the puddle of clothes on the floor, and slid in beside him. "Everything's fine," she said.

Twenty-One: The Present

"What's the matter?" Peggy asked, opening the door to her sprawling bungalow in the quiet, somewhere-between-artsy-and-rundown district of Hillcrest.

"Can I come in?" Caroline asked from the doorstep.

Peggy stood back to allow her entry.

"Who is it?" Fletcher called from somewhere inside the house.

"It's Caroline," Peggy called back. "What happened? You look terrible. Are you sick?"

"It's been quite a day." Caroline followed Peggy into the living room, sitting down on the comfortable brown sofa across from a couple of mismatched chairs, one a grayish tweed, the other a pink and blue floral print. The walls were yellow, the carpet navy, the coffee table some sort of distressed wood. Nothing belonged together, yet curiously, everything worked. Much like the marriage of Peggy and Fletcher, the only couple from that ill-fated trip to Rosarito whose relationship was still intact.

"What's going on?"

"I saw Jerrod Bolton this morning."

"Jerrod Bolton? As in Jerrod and Rain?"

"He called me, asked me to meet him. Did you know Rain and Hunter were having an affair?"

"What? When?"

Fletcher walked into the living room, looking surprisingly put together for a relaxing Sunday afternoon in tailored black dress pants and a blue-and-white-striped shirt. "Hi, Caroline. I didn't know you were dropping by."

"Hunter and Rain have been having an affair," his wife told him.

"What?"

"Fifteen years ago," Caroline qualified. "They were sleeping together while we were in Mexico."

"I thought Hunter didn't even like Rain," Fletcher said.

"And Jerrod just called you out of the blue to tell you this?" Peggy asked.

"Apparently Rain confessed that she and Hunter not only had an affair, but had been sleeping together when we were all in Rosarito, right under our noses. He said he's been debating with himself for months about whether or not to tell me. Then with all the recent publicity about it being the fifteenth anniversary . . . You honestly had no idea?"

Peggy and Fletcher shook their heads in unison, the shocked expressions on their faces convincing Caroline that they were telling the truth.

"I'm not sure I understand the point of telling you this now," Fletcher said. "It happened so long ago, you and Hunter have been divorced for years . . ."

"They were together the night Samantha disappeared."

"What?" said Peggy.

"What?" echoed Fletcher.

"Our anniversary dinner?" Caroline asked, as if she still couldn't quite believe it. "When she went to get a sweater and he was supposedly checking on the kids?"

"They were together?" Peggy said, repeating the question in Caroline's voice.

"He didn't check the kids," Caroline said. "Which means nobody looked in on them for more than an hour."

There was a long pause.

"So Samantha could have been taken up to half an hour earlier than anyone considered," Peggy said.

"Are you sure about this?" Fletcher asked.

"Maybe you should talk to Hunter."

"I just came from Hunter's. He confirmed it."

"Shit," said Fletcher, lowering himself into the pink and blue floral chair.

"Shit," said Peggy, mimicking her husband as she sank into the grayish tweed.

They remained that way, three points on an invisible triangle, for several minutes. Caroline stared at her friend's kind face and, for the first time, realized that Peggy was wearing eye makeup, that her hair was freshly washed and curled, and that she was wearing the turquoise silk dress she reserved for special occasions. "Oh, my God. You were getting ready to go out."

"We have a wedding," Fletcher said, almost apologetically.

"I'm so sorry." Caroline jumped to her feet, ran to the front door.

"Caroline, wait," Peggy said, running after her. "We still have time . . ."

"No," Caroline told her. "It's a wedding. You can't be late. It's bad luck."

"You just made that up."

"Go to your wedding," Caroline told her. "I'll be fine."

She ran to her car and backed out of the driveway, waiting until she was around the corner to pull over to the curb and burst into tears. She wasn't sure why she was crying, whether the tears stemmed from learning about Hunter's affair with Rain or the knowledge that this discovery had come too late to make a difference. Would knowing at the time that he and Rain were together when he was supposedly checking on the kids have changed anything? Would the Mexican police have been able to uncover the truth about Samantha's disappearance if they had been aware of the possibility that she'd been taken from her crib a full half hour before the time they'd originally considered? Or would they have been just as clueless?

Her sobs increased in strength and volume until her entire body was shaking. And she realized she wasn't crying because of Hunter's betrayal or even because the truth had come along too late to make a difference.

Fifteen years after her daughter had been stolen from her crib, Caroline was crying because there was still only one truth that mattered: Samantha was gone.

"Where the hell have you been?" Michelle demanded as soon as Caroline stepped through her front door.

Caroline dropped her purse to the floor

and walked into the living room, each step an ordeal, as if she were wading through quicksand. "Please, Michelle. We can't keep doing this. I don't have the strength."

Her daughter was right behind her. "You disappear for hours . . . you don't call . . ."

"How can I call? You took my fucking phone."

"Nice one, Mother. Where have you been?"

Might as well get this over with, Caroline decided, understanding that her daughter wasn't about to let it go. "I went to see your father."

"That was hours ago."

"What do you mean? How do you know that?"

"Dad phoned. He was concerned, said when you left you seemed very upset . . ."

"How insightful of him. Did he tell you *why* I went to see him?"

"He said he'd leave that up to you."

"Insightful *and* thoughtful."

"Can we skip the sarcasm? Are you going to tell me or not?"

"About why I went to see him? No. I think I'll toss that ball back into his court."

"About where you've been for the last three hours," Michelle corrected.

"I went to see Peggy."

"That was two hours ago. I called there," Michelle explained before her mother could ask.

"You shouldn't have done that. They had a wedding . . ."

"She said you'd already been there and were probably on your way home. But you weren't, were you? So I'll ask again, where have you been?"

"It's no big mystery, Michelle."

"Then why are you making it one?"

"I just drove around for a while. I ended up in Balboa Park."

"Balboa Park? On a Sunday afternoon? With all the tourists?"

"Yes. I like it there. I used to go there a lot."

"When?"

"Years ago. After . . . It doesn't matter. I'm home now."

"About time," her mother said, entering the living room and brushing past Caroline, sitting down on the sofa, a cup of tea in her hand. "I made tea, if anybody wants some."

"Mother!" Caroline exclaimed. "What are you doing here?"

"I called her," Michelle said.

"Why?"

"Because I was worried about you."

"You were worried about me, so you

called my *mother*?"

"She tells me you've been acting quite irrationally lately," Mary said.

"I haven't been acting irrationally . . ."

"You've been conversing with some crackpot who claims to be Samantha, you've flown off to Calgary . . ."

Caroline spun angrily toward Michelle.

"Don't you dare be angry with Micki," her mother said. "She confided in me because she's concerned about you, the way most daughters are concerned about their mothers."

Caroline shook off her mother's barb with a shake of her head.

"And now you disappear for half the day without telling anyone where you are. After what happened the last time you vanished like that, I don't think you can blame any of us for being worried," Mary said. "I certainly hope we won't be reading about today's exploits in tomorrow's papers."

Caroline pictured herself flying across the room and knocking her mother to the ground with one well-aimed punch to the jaw. "Low blow, Mother. Even for you. Now if you'll excuse me, I think I *will* have some of that tea." She walked out of the room and into the hall, head high, shoulders back, praying she wouldn't give Mary the satisfaction of tripping over her own feet.

"You shouldn't have said that," she heard Michelle tell her grandmother.

"She needs to be reminded. You did the right thing, calling me," Mary said in return. "You're a good girl, darling. Don't let anyone try to tell you otherwise."

Divide and conquer, Caroline thought. Her mother's favorite technique, her way of asserting dominance, maintaining control. And why not? It had always worked for her.

Caroline walked into the kitchen to find her brother sitting on the counter beside the sink, looking slightly disheveled in a pair of torn jeans and a lime green short-sleeved shirt. His hair, too long and jutting out over the top of his collar, made him look as if he'd just been roused from bed, which perhaps he had. "Already poured you some," Steve said, holding a china cup toward her. "A bit of milk, no sugar. Correct?"

"She brought you along for reinforcement?"

"I left the straitjacket in the car. What can I say? Have some biscotti. They're delicious." He pointed to the plate of biscotti on the kitchen table.

"I see she made herself at home."

"That's our girl. So, is it true?"

"Is what true?"

"That you're in the middle of some sort of breakdown?"

Caroline took a long sip of her tea. "I'm not having a breakdown."

"But you *have* been talking to some crackpot who claims she's Samantha?"

"What if she's not a crackpot?"

"Still doesn't make her Samantha."

"How can you be so sure?"

"Think about it, Caroline. What are the odds?"

"What difference does it make what the odds are?"

"I'm the gambler in the family," he reminded her. "You don't bet against the house, the house in this case being common sense."

"Since when have you had any of that?"

Steve slid down off the counter. "Let's not make this personal. I'm not the enemy here."

"No," Caroline conceded. "The enemy's in there." She looked toward the living room.

"You don't think you're being just a little hard on her? She was there for you, you know. After Samantha disappeared. You were down in Mexico. She moved in, looked after Michelle. And after you got back and were such a basket case. She was pretty much all the mother that kid had."

"And look how well that turned out."

"It hasn't been easy these past fifteen years. For any of us."

"Did you know?" Caroline asked.

"Know what?"

"That Hunter and Rain were having an affair."

Her brother looked toward his scuffed brown shoes.

"You *did* know."

He hesitated. "I suspected."

"How? Why?"

"I don't know why. Just a gut feeling, I guess. I saw the way she looked at him, the way he looked at her, when they thought no one was watching. Plus the way he was always putting her down when she wasn't around. Like he was trying to hide how he really felt. It just made me wonder. And then the night Samantha disappeared . . ."

Caroline felt her breath catch in her lungs. "The night Samantha disappeared . . . . What?"

Another moment of hesitation. "I saw them."

"What do you mean, you saw them? You saw them together? When?"

"Hold on. Hold on," Steve cautioned. "I

didn't say I saw them *together.*"

"What *are* you saying?"

"It was after I'd gone back to my room to try to talk some sense into Becky, you know, try to talk her into coming back to the table, but of course she wouldn't listen, and I was about to leave the room, I'd opened the door, and that's when I thought I saw Hunter walking down the hall. And I remember wondering what he was doing over in our wing. And then, when I ran into Rain in the lobby, I just put two and two together . . ."

"And kept the answer to yourself."

"What was I going to say, Caroline? *Happy Anniversary. I think your husband's having an affair!* I didn't know that for a fact. It might *not* have been Hunter I saw. He and Rain might *not* have been together. Even if they had, it might have been perfectly innocent."

"Well, they *were* together and it damn sure wasn't innocent. Instead of checking on the kids, my darling husband was, in fact, screwing a woman who was supposed to be my friend, and if you'd told the police what you saw . . ."

"I told them what I *knew,* which unfortunately was nothing. Even if the man I saw *was* Hunter, even if he and Rain *had* been together, I had no reason to believe he hadn't checked on the kids when he said he did."

He was right. Still Caroline wasn't ready to let her brother off the hook so easily. "You should have told me."

His answer was as direct, as forceful, as an arrow to the heart. "You shouldn't have left your kids alone."

The simple statement took her breath away. She doubled over, gasping, the teacup slipping from her hands and dropping to the tile floor, shattering into a hundred tiny pieces.

She heard the shuffle of feet moving toward her. "What's going on in here?" Michelle asked over the ringing in her ears.

"My God, what have you done?" her mother said, scrambling to pick up the broken slivers of china.

"I'm sorry, Caroline," her brother was saying. "I shouldn't have said that. You know I didn't mean it."

Don't be sorry, Caroline thought, feeling her knees about to give way. It was the truth, after all. He'd just said the same thing she'd been telling herself for the past fifteen years.

Which was when the doorbell rang.

"I'll get it." Steve excused himself, running for the front door as if he'd literally been saved by the bell. He returned as Michelle was helping Caroline into one of the chairs grouped around the kitchen table. "There's someone named Lili here to see you," he told his sister. "She says you've been expecting her."

Twenty-Two: Five Years Ago

The phone was ringing.

Caroline reached toward the nightstand beside her bed and lifted it to her ear, noting it was barely 6:30 A.M. Was it Arthur? Calling so early because he wanted to check in on her before she left for work, to tell her how much he missed her, even though it had been less than twenty-four hours since they'd been together?

But instead of Arthur's soothing baritone, it was Peggy's husky alto she heard. "Have you seen the morning paper?" she asked before Caroline could say hello.

"No. Why?"

"I'm coming over," Peggy told her. "Don't look at the paper. Don't answer your phone. Don't check your computer until I get there."

"What are you talking about? What's going on?"

"I'll be there in ten minutes."

"Wait . . . what . . . ?" The phone went dead in her hand. Caroline sat there staring at it for the next several minutes. "What just happened?" she whispered, heading for the bathroom as the phone rang again.

Don't answer your phone, she heard Peggy say. *Don't check your computer. Don't look at the paper.*

"Why not?" she asked out loud, ignoring the phone's persistent ring as she washed her face and brushed her teeth, then pulled on a bathrobe and headed down the hall.

Michelle sat up in bed as Caroline passed her room. She rubbed her eyes and stared accusingly at her mother. "Who keeps calling?"

"Just some idiot making crank calls. Go back to sleep. You don't have to be up for another half hour."

"As if I'll be able to sleep," Michelle whined, pulling a pillow over her head as Caroline closed the door to her room.

Don't look at the paper, Peggy admonished in Caroline's head as she ran down the stairs to the front door, throwing it open and lifting the morning paper into her hands.

EVERYTHING, MY FAULT, read the headlines in bold black letters, and beneath it, a picture of her smiling face. Caroline had never seen the picture before, although she knew exactly when it had been taken because she recognized the Starbucks logo in the window behind her head.

"No. Please, no."

She carried the paper into the kitchen and spread the front section across the table, the phone resuming its awful ring as her eyes flitted from one terrible paragraph to the next, from one damning statement to another. It was all there. Every indiscreet word she'd uttered; every heartfelt confession she'd made. Her deepest secrets laid bare in black and white for all the world to read: her guilt at having left her children alone, her continuing despair at the loss of her younger child, her complaints about her narcissistic mother and difficult older daughter, Hunter's upcoming nuptials to a "considerably" younger woman that left her feeling "pissed," even the details of her last night with her former husband, when he'd told her he was leaving and she'd abandoned all reason and pride and begged him to stay. *I pleaded with him not to leave me.*

She flipped to page ten, where the story continued, covering her return to teaching and the subsequent suicide of one of her students. *I feel so guilty,* she was quoted as saying beneath another candid photo of her laughing. *Everything that's happened. It's all my fault. Everything, my fault.*

"This can't be happening," she said, watching the printed words blur and disintegrate, only to regroup and return in larger, bolder type than before. "Please just let this be an awful dream."

Ten minutes later Peggy was on her doorstep. She took one look at Caroline's ashen complexion and gathered her into her arms. "Tell me everything."

"Everything all right at home?" he'd asked as she returned to the bedroom, cell phone in hand.

"Everything's fine." She'd turned her phone off and tossed it onto the pile of clothes lying on the floor. Then she'd climbed into bed beside him, burrowing into his side, allowing his strong arms to surround her. It had been a long time since she'd been in bed with a man, even longer since she'd felt safe. "Well, as fine as it can be where my daughter is concerned," she continued. "Like I said, she can be difficult."

"I guess it's hard being an only child."

Caroline's eyes filled with tears and she tried to look away. Arthur's hand, gentle on her chin, stopped her, forcing her eyes to his.

"What's the matter?"

Caroline hesitated. "She wasn't always an only child."

"I'm not following."

"I haven't been completely honest with you."

He waited, said nothing.

"I'm not sure I know where to start."

Again he waited, his silence urging her to continue.

"My last name isn't Tillman," she admitted. "It's Shipley."

"Caroline Shipley," he said, a slow smile spreading across his face. "Should I know that name? Are you famous?"

"More like infamous."

"Caroline Shipley," he repeated, eyes narrowing, then opening wide with recognition. "Oh, my God. The woman whose daughter disappeared . . ."

"Yes — 'oh, my God' — that's my middle name." She waited for him to pull away in horror, but instead he gathered her even closer into his comforting embrace.

"Thank you," she whispered, clinging to him.

"For what?"

"For not being repulsed by me."

"Why on earth would I be repulsed? I lost a child of my own, remember? I can only imagine what you went through. What you're going through . . ."

She was crying in earnest now. "It'll be ten years next week. I can't believe it. Ten years."

"Do you want to talk about it?"

She shook her head, not because she didn't want to talk about it but because she was afraid that if she started talking, she wouldn't be able to stop.

"I remember how guilty I felt after Jenny and Lara died," he was saying, speaking more to himself than to her. "Survivor's guilt, I think they call it. I kept thinking that if only I'd been there, if I'd driven Lara to school that day, if I'd been walking beside them, I could have saved them. Or maybe it wouldn't have happened at all. They'd still be alive."

"Or you might have been killed, too."

"I didn't care. I wanted to die. I'm sure you felt the same. You blame yourself, you think it was your fault . . ."

"It *was* my fault," Caroline said, encouraged by his openness, his understanding of her pain. "Everything, my fault."

"It wasn't."

"I left my children alone in a hotel room.

So I could have dinner with friends." The words began spilling from her mouth, as she'd known they would, a decade's worth of suppressed guilt and rage. She told him everything, embellishing facts already known, sharing the feelings of shame and despair she'd kept bottled up inside for ten years. She talked about her treatment by the Mexican police, their suspicions that she and Hunter were responsible for whatever had happened to Samantha. She took the blame for the deterioration of her marriage, for her strained relationship with Michelle. "They tell you it gets easier with time," she said. "But it doesn't. If anything, the opposite is true. It gets worse. Life just keeps piling on more and more for you to feel guilty about."

"Like what?"

That was when she told him about Errol, the boy in her class who'd committed suicide, and how her school principal had subsequently asked her to resign.

"He had no right to do that."

"I knew something was wrong, you know. With Errol. I could see it in his eyes. I tried to talk to him, get him to open up. I think he was on the verge, but then I looked up at the clock. Michelle had a dentist appointment and I knew how upset she'd be if I was late. And he noticed. He was such a sensitive boy. He clammed right up, insisted he was fine, told me he'd see me the next day. So I let him go. I went to pick up Michelle. And he went home and hanged himself."

"You had no way of knowing what he'd do."

"I knew he was vulnerable. Errol's dead because of me, because I wasn't there for him. Just like Samantha is gone because I wasn't there for her. I'm the common denominator in this equation. It's all my fault. Everything, my fault."

He shook his head. "I'm so sorry."

"For what? You have nothing to be sorry about. Not where I'm concerned anyway."

He kissed the top of her head, burying his face in her hair. Neither of them said another word until Caroline reluctantly announced it was time for her to go home. Michelle would be waiting and there was school the next morning.

"Will I hear from you again?" she asked as she was leaving his apartment.

"Count on it," he said.

"I'm such an idiot," she said to Peggy, her fingernails scratching at Arthur's byline. Except his name wasn't Arthur. It was

Aidan. A much trendier name. She almost laughed.

They were sitting at the kitchen table. Peggy had made a pot of coffee and taken the phone off the hook.

"You couldn't know."

"I should have been suspicious. It's so obvious, thinking back."

"How is it obvious?"

"The way we met, for starters. One of those 'meet cute' situations you only see in the movies. He probably engineered the whole thing, counted on his charm to win me over."

"He couldn't have known it would work."

"Why not? It's probably worked before. I'm sure I wasn't his first target." Caroline shook her head, remembering. "If it hadn't, I'm sure he would have tried something else later. Lucky for him, I was so easy. I should have known," she said again. "The way he quoted Keats. What banking consultant does that? What banking consultant says things like 'Mexico on my doorstep' and 'a temperature that rarely strays ten degrees from moderate'? He probably got that out of some travel brochure. And what the hell's a banking consultant anyway? Does such a job even exist?" She jumped to her feet. "He said he had a wife and daughter who'd been killed by a drunk driver. Did he make that up? Did he actually invent a dead child in order to worm his way into my confidence? Was it all a ploy to get me to confide in him by pretending to confide in me?"

Peggy shook her head. "I guess we'll never know."

"He played me. Oh, how he played me. Played on my emotions, my sympathy. Not to mention he flattered me, told me I was mysterious, that I had deep thoughts."

"You *are* mysterious. You *do* have deep thoughts."

"Are you planning to write a story about me, too?" Caroline asked.

"And a sense of humor," Peggy added, reaching for her friend's hand.

"How could he betray me like this?"

"He's a reporter. It's what they do."

"Do they all sleep with their subjects for a story?"

"Interesting that he fails to mention that. And at the risk of sounding prurient, was he any good?"

"He was great," Caroline confirmed. "More's the pity." She poured herself another cup of coffee and returned to her chair. "What's it saying online?"

"More of the same. *Lots* more of the same. Don't read it."

"Why not? Everyone else will."

They heard Michelle's footsteps descending the stairs. In the next second, she was standing in the doorway, still dressed in her flannel pajamas. "I thought I heard voices," she said, staring at Peggy. "You're here awfully early. Is something wrong? Why is the phone off the hook?" She replaced the receiver. Immediately, the phone started ringing. "Are you kidding me? What's going on?" Her eyes landed on the morning paper spread out across the kitchen table. "Is that a picture of you?" she asked her mother, dragging the paper toward her. "Shit. What is this?"

Caroline walked to the phone and picked it up. It was her mother. "What have you done?" Mary demanded.

"Are you out of your mind?" her brother shouted over the extension. "You spilled your guts to a reporter?"

Their call was followed by an even angrier one from Hunter. "What the hell is the matter with you?"

There came in quick succession at least a dozen calls from various magazines and newspapers across the country; a request from the producers of *60 Minutes* for a televised interview; an appeal from Howard Stern for her to be on his popular radio show. Both Barbara Walters and Diane Sawyer were seeking a one-on-one; Oprah was eager to talk, as was Katie Couric and someone with the unlikely name of Maury Povich. She hung up on all of them. "Who the hell is Maury Povich?" she asked Peggy. Then, to Michelle: "You should get dressed. You don't want to be late for school."

"Yeah, sure. Like I'm going anywhere near school today."

"Michelle . . ."

"Sorry, Mommy dearest. Am I being 'difficult'?"

"I'm the one who's sorry," Caroline said. "I should never have said those things."

"Why shouldn't you? That's what you believe, isn't it? That I'm a pain, a blight on your existence . . ."

"I never said that."

"You might as well have. Anyway, it doesn't matter."

"It *does* matter. I love you, sweetheart. You know that."

"Yeah, right," Michelle said. "Anyway, I'm not going to school today. Think I'll go over to Grandma Mary's. *She's* always happy to see me."

"Michelle, please . . . ," Caroline began as her daughter marched out of the room.

The phone rang again. This time it was

the school where Caroline worked, informing her that they thought it best she take a few days off, that her classes would be handed over to a substitute teacher, and that the principal would like to meet with her sometime later in the week.

"I'm going to lose my job," she said, hanging up the phone.

"They can't just fire you," Peggy said.

"They can. But they won't have to. I'll go quietly."

"No. You can't give up without a fight."

"I have no fight left," Caroline said.

Peggy scrunched the front page of the paper into a tight ball and flung it to the floor. "That bastard. Are you going to sue?"

"On what grounds? Those are pretty direct quotes. I'm sure he has it all on tape." She winced at the thought of her every word, every sigh, every groan being secretly recorded.

"Son of a bitch. Don't you want to call and confront him?"

"I think I've said quite enough."

"At the very least, you could tell him to fuck off."

"And read about it in tomorrow morning's paper?"

"It might be worth it."

The phone rang. Without a word, Caroline reached over and ripped the phone wire from the wall.

TWENTY-THREE: THE PRESENT

Whatever Caroline had been expecting, it wasn't this.

For fifteen years, she'd been fantasizing about what it would be like to see Samantha again, and how their reunion would play out. In the beginning, she'd imagined the two-year-old, all jowly cheeks and jiggling thighs, running toward her with abandon, her arms stretched out in front of her, joyous cries of "Mommy" rushing from her bow-shaped lips as she flung herself into her mother's desperate embrace. As the years slipped by, the fat cheeks and plump little torso had thinned and elongated, so that by the time she turned ten, the Samantha of Caroline's imagination had morphed into a living, breathing Disney princess, all blond hair and sparkling blue eyes, but still with the face she'd possessed as a toddler, a face Caroline knew she would recognize instantly. And after shyly assessing each other from a distance, Samantha would smile and throw herself into Caroline's arms, permitting her mother's fervent kisses and returning them with her own.

The teenage years had proved more difficult to imagine. It grew harder to imagine or predict the changes puberty would bring. Would Samantha be short or tall, fat or thin, small-breasted or voluptuous? Would her hair be brown or gold, long or short? There were the sketches in the newspapers, of course, updated approximations from the experts, based on such tangibles as bone structure and shape of the eyes. But what about the intangibles, the things that couldn't be measured? Caroline had always hated intangibles.

Look at Michelle. She'd changed so much over the years. The once plump little girl who adored all things sweet had grown into a slender young woman for whom sugar was the dietary equivalent of a four-letter word. There was little to connect the person she was today to yesterday's child. Only her eyes had remained constant: demanding, angry, needy. *Look at me,* those eyes shouted across the years. *Look at me.*

But one thing Caroline was certain of: no matter what changes time had wrought over the last fifteen years, she would recognize

Samantha on sight. And Samantha would know her. Mother and child would collapse, sobbing, into each other's arms. One look and all the years would instantly melt away.

None of which happened.

"There's someone named Lili here to see you," her brother said. "She says you've been expecting her."

"You've got to be kidding me," Michelle exclaimed as Caroline ran from the room.

And now here they stood, staring at each other from opposite sides of the front door, and there were no lightning bolts of recognition, no cries of "Mommy!", no joyous embrace. Just two strangers sizing each other up, trying to find hints of themselves in each other, to uncover lost or forgotten memories. But instead of answers and certainty, there were only questions and more uncertainty.

"Caroline?" the girl asked.

Caroline nodded, feeling the others crowd in behind her, four pairs of eyes bearing down on one young girl, trying to determine if she was one of their own.

The girl was tall and slim, although it was hard to tell how slim because of the oversized winter coat she was wearing. Her hair was dark blond, its ends dyed the same shade of navy blue as her eyes, its loose curls stopping just short of her shoulders. She wore no makeup and her skin was as pale and opaque as the sky of a Calgary winter. A pretty girl on the verge of being beautiful, as Caroline had been at that age. And she had Hunter's jaw, as the sketches in the papers and on the Internet had suggested. In fact, she looked more like the artists' renderings than she did either Hunter or Caroline. And she didn't resemble Michelle at all. There was nothing about either girl's face that suggested they were even vaguely related, let alone sisters.

"You're Lili," Caroline stated, her voice stronger than she'd anticipated.

"I probably should have called first."

"No, that's okay."

"I was afraid to, in case I chickened out again."

"You're here. That's what's important. Come in." Caroline backed up to allow Lili entry, stepping on Michelle's toes as she did so, hearing Michelle curse underneath her breath. "Maybe you could give us a few minutes alone," she suggested to her daughter, mother, and brother.

"Not a chance," Michelle said, speaking for the three of them.

Caroline ushered the girl into her living room, resigned to their presence. Maybe having them around was a good thing. Maybe it would force her to be more objective, less emotional, not allow her desire for a happy ending to overtake her common sense.

"Let me have your coat," Steve offered. "Don't think you'll be needing that in here." Lili unbuttoned her coat and slipped it off her shoulders, handing it to Steve. "I'm Caroline's brother, by the way," he said, draping the heavy coat over the banister and taking the small overnight bag from her hand before following the rest of the group into the living room. "And this is Caroline's mother, Mary, and her daughter, Michelle."

Lili nodded hello to each of them as they arranged themselves in a loose pentagon around the coffee table, Mary and Steve occupying the two chairs, Lili and Caroline sitting side by side on the sofa, Michelle standing off to one side, leaning against a wall, hands across her chest, studying Lili as if she were an alien being.

Caroline was also staring at Lili, trying to uncover the one genetic detail that might prove whether or not this was her child. But there was nothing she could point to conclusively. She looked for a gesture, a nervous tic, a common family mannerism, but there was nothing. Just a pretty girl with Hunter's jaw. Was that enough?

"Did you have a good flight?" Caroline asked her.

"It was okay. A little turbulent." Her voice was deeper than it had been over the phone, closer in tone to her own. Did that mean anything?

"Are you hungry? Can I get you something to eat?"

"I'm not hungry. Thank you."

For several seconds, nobody spoke.

"So," Steve said, breaking the silence, "you really think you're Caroline's long-lost child?"

Caroline held her breath, waiting for Lili's answer.

"I wouldn't have come if I didn't think there was a chance."

"And now that you *are* here?" he pressed. "Do you like what you see?" He motioned around the well-appointed room.

"Steve, please . . ."

"I don't want your things," Lili said.

"She hasn't asked for anything," Caroline told her brother.

"Not yet," Steve said.

"How did you pay for your plane ticket?" Michelle asked. "I thought you didn't have any money."

Lili glanced down at her lap. "I charged it

to my mother's credit card."

"Lucky girl, having so many mothers to choose from," Michelle said.

"Does she know you're here?" Caroline asked.

"I left her a note saying I'd be gone for a few days, telling her not to worry."

"She'll be going out of her mind," Caroline told her, reliving her own panic when she realized her daughter was missing. "You should call her."

"I will. Later. After we know for sure."

"And when will that be?" Steve asked.

"When they get the results back from the DNA test they're planning to take," Michelle said, pushing herself away from the wall and heading for the hallway. "If you'll excuse me a minute."

"Where are you going?" Caroline asked, but Michelle didn't answer.

"How do you go about taking a DNA test?"

"I'm not sure," Caroline said. "I'll ask Peggy. She'll know."

"Peggy?" Lili asked.

"Friend of Caroline's," Steve answered. "She was there the night my niece disappeared. Tell me. Do you remember anything about that night at all?"

Lili shook her head.

"She was two years old," Caroline reminded him.

"I *wish* I could remember something," Lili said. "I've tried. But I can't. The first thing I remember is playing with one of my dolls and one of its legs breaking off. I was probably three or four."

"Do you remember where you were living then?" Caroline asked, recalling that Lili had said they'd moved around a lot.

"Rome, I think. My father owned an import-export business that had offices all over the world. We were always traveling."

"And when did you first suspect you might not be who you thought you were?" Steve asked.

Caroline was actually grateful that Steve had taken over the questioning. She didn't trust her own voice, and his questions allowed her to focus on the girl's reactions.

"Like I told Caroline on the phone," Lili said, glancing briefly in Caroline's direction, "I'd always felt as if I didn't quite belong. I don't look anything like anyone else in my family and our interests are so different."

"In what way?" Michelle asked, returning to the room, although she remained in the doorway.

"Well, my brothers are real jocks, and I'm not."

"Not particularly shocking," Steve said.

"They're not really interested in school. And I love it. Especially math."

A slight groan escaped Caroline's lips.

"How convenient," Steve said.

"Convenient?"

"You've undoubtedly read that my sister is a math teacher."

"Yes. That's one of the things that made me suspect . . ."

"And the other things?"

"I've already discussed this with Caroline."

"Discuss it with me."

Lili swallowed, twisting her hands in her lap. "Well, the most obvious thing, of course, is the sketches on the Internet."

"She *does* look like the sketches," Caroline said.

"Half the teenage girls in America look like that sketch."

"She has Hunter's jaw."

They heard a car screech to a halt in front of the house.

"Speak of the devil," Michelle said.

Caroline pushed herself off the sofa and ran to the front window. "What's he doing here?"

"I called him."

"What? When?"

"A few minutes ago. I caught him as he was leaving the gym, told him to get over here as fast as he could. Looks like he broke the sound barrier."

"You shouldn't have called him."

"Why not? Don't you think he has the right to meet his own flesh and blood? You're anxious to meet your father, aren't you, Lili? Or would you prefer we call you Samantha?"

"I'd prefer to wait until we find out the truth," Lili said.

"Which will probably take at least a few days," Michelle calculated. "Tell me, where are you planning on staying in the interim? Excuse me," she said, walking to the front door without waiting for an answer.

"Welcome home," Steve said with a smile.

"How'd you get here so fast?" Caroline heard Michelle ask her father as he stepped inside the foyer.

"You said it was urgent. What's going on?" Hunter asked in return.

"See for yourself."

Hunter entered the living room, looking warily around. "Steve," he acknowledged in greeting. "Mary."

Caroline looked toward her mother. She'd

been so quiet since Lili's dramatic entrance that Caroline had almost forgotten she was there.

"What's going on?" Hunter asked again, this time of Caroline, his gaze shifting to the young girl sitting on the sofa. "Who is this?" he asked warily, although his eyes said he already knew.

"This is Lili," Caroline said. Then, to Lili. "This is Hunter, my ex-husband."

"And quite possibly, your father," Michelle elaborated. Her tone indicated she didn't believe for a second that that was possible.

"This is the girl who phoned you? The one you flew to Calgary to see?" Hunter proceeded cautiously into the room. "Stand up," he directed Lili.

Lili got to her feet. Hunter drew within inches of her, circling her slowly, studying her face from every angle as Caroline watched him, holding her breath.

"Well?" Steve asked as Hunter took a few steps back. "What's the verdict, counselor?"

Hunter shook his head. "I don't know. I just don't know." He looked toward Michelle, then back at Lili. "The two of you don't look anything alike."

"They never did," Caroline reminded him. "She has your jaw."

"Well, I guess that settles that," Michelle said. "She has Dad's jaw. Pretty definitive evidence, if you ask me. Don't think we even have to bother with some pesky little DNA test. The prodigal daughter has returned. Let the celebrations begin."

"You sound so angry," Caroline said.

"I *am* angry. Some girl calls out of the blue and claims to be Samantha and the two of you are so blinded by your fantasies and your guilt that you throw reason out the window and welcome her with open arms . . ."

"Nobody is doing that," Hunter protested.

"She's come all this way," Caroline began. "What harm could it do to take the test . . . ?"

"What harm?" Michelle demanded. "How many times do we have to go through this? Do you think I enjoy having my mother made a fool of — *again*? Haven't you suffered enough humiliation? Have you forgotten what happened five years ago when that reporter — ?" She broke off. "What's the use? You never listen to me."

"Who are you, really?" Steve asked Lili, picking up where Michelle left off. "What is it you want? Money? Publicity?"

"No."

"You think that by showing up here, by

playing on my sister's vulnerability, her desperate desire for some sort of closure, you'll make a name for yourself, maybe be interviewed on TV? Have your fifteen minutes of fame?"

"That's not why she's here," Caroline said. *Was it?*

"I don't want fame. I don't want publicity," Lili said. "I just want to know the truth. We'll take the DNA test. If it's negative, I'll be on the first plane out of here." Her voice broke, the first sign that she was as nervous and confused as the rest of them.

"We need to ease up a bit here," Caroline said to the others. "This is a big risk she's taken. Leaving her family, flying here on her own. It's pretty amazing when you think about it."

"What's amazing is how naïve you still are," Michelle said. "And she still hasn't answered my question: where are you planning to stay till the test results are in?"

Lili shrugged, her lower lip trembling. "I don't know. I guess I thought . . ."

"You'd stay here?" Michelle asked.

"Of course she'll stay here," Caroline said.

"Mother, for God's sake . . ."

"You'll stay here," she told Lili.

"I can't. Not if it's going to cause trouble."

"A little late for that, don't you think?"

Steve said.

Hunter turned toward Caroline, his eyes filled with both hope and pain. "You really think there's a chance in hell she could be Samantha?"

"Oh, please," said Michelle, making fists in the air. "You're as bad as she is."

"What say *you,* Mother?" Steve asked. "You've been curiously quiet throughout all this. It's not like you to be so restrained."

"Mother?" Caroline said, growing alarmed. "Are you all right?"

"It's her," Mary said softly.

"What are you talking about?" Steve protested.

"She looks just like you did at that age," Mary told Caroline.

"You're crazy," Steve said. "She doesn't look anything like Caroline did as a teenager."

Mary got up from her chair and approached Lili, reaching for the young girl's chin, turning her head from side to side. "I'm not sure what it is exactly," she said. "You're right. The features aren't the same. But it's Caroline. I can see it."

"Are you sure?" Caroline asked.

"It's her," Mary said firmly. "It's Samantha."

Twenty-Four: The Present

"So, what happens now?" Steve asked after several seconds of stunned silence, voicing the question on everyone's lips.

"I'll call Peggy first thing in the morning," Caroline said, remembering that Peggy and Fletcher were at a wedding and probably wouldn't be back until late. "See if she knows where to go for a DNA test."

"Oh, please," Michelle said. "Hasn't anybody here ever heard of the Internet?" She left the room. Seconds later, her footsteps could be heard running up the stairs.

"I'm really sorry," Lili apologized to Caroline. "She seems so upset."

"Can you blame her?" asked Steve. "It's not every day your sister returns from the dead."

"Let's not get off track here, people," Hunter interjected, in full lawyer mode. He glanced toward Lili, who sat perched on the edge of the sofa, her hand resting in Mary's lap. "We won't know anything until we take a DNA test and the results either confirm or deny. So I suggest we call it a day, get a good night's sleep, Caroline will speak to Peggy first thing in the morning, and we'll proceed from there. There's little to be gained from further speculation or discussion. And *nothing* to be gained from telling anyone else about this. The last thing we want is for the press to hear about it. Are we agreed? Are we clear?"

"Clear," Steve said, although the question had been directed at Caroline.

"I'm not going to tell anyone," Lili said.

"You have to call Calgary," Caroline told her. "Your mother . . ." She stopped, the word sticking in her windpipe, like an errant piece of hard candy.

"I forgot about her," Hunter said. "She doesn't know you're here?"

Lili shook her head.

"Caroline's right," Hunter said. "You'll have to call her."

"What do I tell her?"

"The truth."

"You really think that's a good idea?" Steve asked. "What if she calls the police?"

"I guess that's a chance we'll have to take."

"She wouldn't do that," Lili said.

"Certainly not if she has anything to

hide," Mary said, not quite under her breath.

"Is there anything you can tell us that might make me a believer?" Steve asked Lili. "Anything at all that you remember from that night . . . ?"

Lili shook her head.

"She was only two years old," Caroline reminded her brother.

A phone rang, a muffled collaboration of Beyoncé and Jay-Z emerging from Hunter's pocket. He shrugged sheepishly and answered it, turning away from Caroline as he spoke. "Hi, babe."

Caroline felt an unexpected and unwanted twinge in the pit of her stomach at such easy intimacy. He'd never called her "babe."

"Yes, I'm fine. Sorry I haven't called. I'm at Caroline's. Something unexpected came up. I'll tell you about it when I get home."

"I thought we weren't supposed to tell anyone," Steve reminded him.

"You can't expect me not to tell Diana," Hunter protested, returning the phone to his pocket. "This affects her, too."

"He's right," Caroline said, her eyes boring into Hunter's. "It's not good to keep secrets from your wife."

Hunter had the good grace to look embarrassed. "I should go."

"Don't you want to know what I found out?" Michelle asked, re-entering the room and holding up a piece of paper. "It seems there are a whole slew of places in San Diego that test for DNA, including a clinic right here in Mission Hills. Unfortunately, results take three to five business days, which means we're kind of stuck with each other for the next little while."

"Talk to Peggy," Hunter said to Caroline. "See if she can speed things up." He turned to leave, then stopped. "You want to stay at my place in the meantime?" he asked Michelle.

"Nah. Think I'll stay here." She glanced at Caroline. "You don't mind if I stick around, do you, Mom?"

"Of course I don't mind," Caroline said, although in truth, there was a part of her that *did* mind, that had been hoping Michelle would spend the night, maybe even the next few days, at her father's, thereby allowing Caroline to concentrate on Lili, get to know her better without Michelle's negative energy hovering.

"Not quite ready to give up my room just yet," Michelle said.

"Nobody's asked you to give up your room."

"Oh, right. She can sleep in her old room."

"Michelle . . ."

"It used to be your nursery. Mom insisted on keeping the crib and everything for years, but now it's a guest room," she explained to Lili. "It has a foldout sofa. Not that comfortable, but since I doubt you'll be staying long . . ."

"I think that's quite enough, Michelle," Mary said firmly, holding tight to Lili's hand.

"Grandma Mary?" The shock in Michelle's voice bounced off the living room walls.

Mary let go of Lili's hand and rose to her feet. "Your father is right. There's no point in further discussion. We need to get some rest and carry on in the morning. Steve, darling, I think it's time we went home."

Steve was instantly on his feet. "Your wish, as always, is my command."

Mary bent down to kiss Lili's cheek. "Good night, sweetheart."

"Sweetheart?" Michelle repeated incredulously. "Just like that?"

"Goodnight, Micki," her grandmother said. "Try to behave."

"What the hell was that?" Michelle asked after they were gone.

"That was your grandmother," Caroline told her, recognizing Mary's ingrained habit of playing one family member off against another. The woman simply could not help herself. "Welcome to my world."

"What did she say?" Caroline asked Lili as she hung up the phone.

"She was pretty upset." Lili sat down across from Caroline at the kitchen table. The remains of the cheese omelet Caroline had made for dinner sat congealing on their plates. Michelle, of course, had declined to eat. She'd been holed up in her room with the door closed ever since the others left. "She wants me to come home."

"You told her no," Caroline stated, replaying Lili's end of the conversation in her mind.

I'm in California. I'm fine. Please don't worry.

"Tell me what she said."

I'm with Caroline Shipley. You know, the woman whose little girl was stolen out of her crib in Mexico fifteen years ago? I know you think I'm crazy, but I think I might be that girl.

"She said I'm being ridiculous, that *she's* my mother."

I have to know one way or the other. I have to know for sure.

"She said she wants me home immediately or she'll call the authorities."

We'll take a DNA test in the morning. I'll

have the results by the end of the week.

"Do you think she will? Call the authorities, I mean?" Caroline asked.

"I don't know."

I'll call you tomorrow. Please try to understand. I have to do this.

"At least she knows you're all right."

I love you.

"She was crying."

Goodbye, Mommy.

"This can't be easy for either of you," Caroline said, the word *Mommy* echoing in her ears, a word directed at another woman, a word she'd been denied hearing from Samantha's lips for fifteen years.

Mommy, Mommy, Mommy.

"What can't be easy?" Michelle asked, materializing in the doorway.

Caroline jumped. "You scared me."

"Forgot I was here, did you?"

"Would you like something to eat?" Caroline said, refusing to take the bait.

"Let me think," Michelle said, surveying the leftover omelets on their plates. "Greasy fried eggs smothered in processed cheese. How can I resist?" She opened the fridge, withdrew a green apple and took a large bite. "What can't be easy?" she repeated.

"I phoned Calgary," Lili told her.

"Your mother give you a hard time?"

"She doesn't understand why I'm doing this."

"She's not the only one." Michelle pulled out a chair between Caroline and Lili and straddled it, crunching on her apple. "So, what's she like? Your mother?" she asked pointedly.

"She's really nice," Lili answered, tears filling her eyes. "Quiet. A little shy. She likes crossword puzzles and watching cooking shows on TV. She's a really good cook."

"Does she have a job?"

"No. We're pretty much it. She home-schooled my brothers and me, nursed my father when he got sick."

"She sounds awful," Michelle dead-panned. "No wonder you're so anxious to leave."

"Michelle . . ."

"So, you want to know what I found out about this whole DNA business?"

Caroline sighed, grateful for the reprieve. "Please."

Michelle struggled to read her writing. "Well, it appears you have two choices, a private test option and a legal test option."

"What's the difference?"

"In a legal test option, the sample collection is witnessed, which, I assume, is the one you'd want. It's the one that would stand up in court."

Caroline looked to Lili. They nodded in unison.

"Okay, so, you go to the clinic and they take a buccal swab specimen — don't know if I'm pronouncing that right — which is a fancy way of saying a mouth swab, from each of you. Painless, relatively non-invasive, takes just a few seconds, you've seen it a million times on TV. 'This sample contains cells, and most cells in our body contain a full set of genetic information in the form of DNA.' That's short for de . . . oxy . . . ribo . . . nucleic acid," she said, struggling with the long word. "For sure I didn't pronounce that one right. Anyway" — she continued reading from her notes — " 'DNA is essentially a genetic blueprint, much like a fingerprint, and is unique to each individual.' You know that already, right?"

Again Caroline and Lili nodded together. "Is there more?" Caroline asked.

"Oh, yeah. Lots more. 'At the lab, the DNA is extracted from the cell and specific regions of the DNA are amplified by a process known as PCR, also known as polymerase chain reaction' — how's that for a mouthful? — 'which are then examined carefully. The DNA pattern of the child is then compared to the *alleged* mother,' " she continued, putting her own emphasis on the word *"alleged."* " 'Because a child's genes are inherited from her biological parents, examination of the child's DNA will conclusively determine whether the *alleged* mother is the true *biological* mother of said child.' " She took an emphatic bite out of the apple in her hand. "So — how do you like them apples?"

"Very interesting."

"Just thought you might appreciate knowing what you're in for."

"Thank you."

"Yeah, sure. Anytime." She leaned forward, resting her chin on the high back of the kitchen chair she was straddling. "So, potential sister-of-mine, has being in the old house tweaked any new memories?"

"Michelle . . ."

"What? That's a perfectly natural question. I'm just curious about whether or not being here, in this house, has jogged her memory."

"I wish it had," Lili said. "I was actually hoping it might."

"Yeah? No such luck. I mean, you were only a baby, right? I don't have any memories of being two either. You want to know what my first memory is?" The question was obviously rhetorical and she continued without waiting for a reply. "It's being in Disneyland. I was three and we were in the Magic Kingdom and I wanted to go on one of the rides — think it might have been Pirates of the Caribbean — but Mother here said the line was way too long and she couldn't stand for hours waiting."

"For God's sake, Michelle, I was pregnant."

"Oh, right. Forgot about that. Anyway, I threw this major tantrum. I screamed so much that we had to leave. And that's my first memory."

As well as her first grudge, Caroline thought. A grudge she'd been nursing ever since. God, did her list of grievances never end?

"You want to know what else I remember?"

Another rhetorical question. Another long-standing grudge about to be revealed. Another example of Caroline's failure as a mother.

"I remember the day she brought you — well, maybe you, maybe not — home from the hospital, and you were so small and beautiful and I wanted to hold you, but she wouldn't let me."

"I wouldn't let you hold her because you

said you were going to throw her in the garbage," Caroline interrupted, angry now.

"Really? I said that?" Surprisingly, Michelle's face broke into a wide grin.

"In no uncertain terms. *Let me have her. I'm going to throw her in the garbage.*"

And then suddenly Caroline was laughing at the memory of Michelle's angry, scrunched-up little face, and Michelle was laughing with her, and soon even Lili was laughing. And the three women sat at the kitchen table, laughing until they cried.

Twenty-Five: The Present

"How come you never moved?" Lili was asking.

She and Caroline were sitting on opposite sides of the sofa bed, the bed having been pulled out and outfitted with clean white sheets and a lightweight rose-colored blanket. Lili was clutching one of two down-filled pillows to her chest, her eyes continually moving up one off-white wall and down another, skittering across the surfaces of several abstract lithographs, like a spider.

Caroline shrugged. It was a question she'd asked herself many times over the years. "I don't know. I thought about it a lot, even came close to selling a few years ago. But something always stopped me. Guess I just got used to being here."

What if Samantha came back? What if she were to come looking for me and I was no longer here?

"I think Michelle hates me," Lili said.

"No. It's *me* she hates."

"She doesn't hate you. She loves you."

"Well, she has a funny way of showing it sometimes."

"I think she's just trying to protect you."

"And I think you should probably get some sleep. It's been a long day. It'll be even longer tomorrow." Caroline climbed reluctantly to her feet. While part of her desperately wanted to stay, another part of her recognized the danger of getting too attached. Could she really afford to lose another daughter, even one that was never really hers?

"Do you have any old pictures?" Lili asked before she reached the door.

In answer, Caroline changed direction and went to the walk-in closet opposite the sofa bed. She pulled open the bottom drawer of the built-in dresser and removed three old photo albums, two of which she'd rescued from the garbage bin at her mother's house right after her father had moved out. Lili immediately cast aside the pillow she'd been holding to gather the albums in her lap. She opened the top one, her arm brushing against Caroline's and sending a spasm of chills throughout Caroline's body, like an electric shock.

A young man and woman stared up at

them from the first page of the album, their arms uncomfortably resting around each other's waists, their faces blank. "Are these your parents?" Lili asked.

"That's the happy couple, all right."

"Your dad's really good-looking."

"Yeah. He was." The sight of her father brought tears to Caroline's eyes. Or maybe it was the feel of Lili's shoulder pressing against hers. She ran a gentle finger over her father's handsome face.

"He's dead?"

"Long time ago."

"Your mother never remarried?"

Caroline shook her head, burrowing even closer into Lili's side as she turned the page. "I haven't looked through these albums in years."

A large photograph of Caroline's mother holding a baby filled the center of the next page. Mary was wearing a pink-and-white-striped sundress, and her hair was styled in the familiar tight helmet of curls she still sported today. The baby in her arms was maybe three months old and almost totally bald. "Is that you?"

"It is. Apparently I was hairless for almost a year. My mother actually took me to the doctor to make sure I wasn't . . . follically challenged."

Lili turned toward Caroline and smiled. "Hard to believe you didn't have hair. It's so beautiful now."

"Thank you. So is yours." She fought the almost overwhelming impulse to run her hand through Lili's blue-tipped, shoulder-length hair.

"It's really different than my mother's . . . than Beth's," Lili said, using the woman's given name for the first time. "Her hair is much coarser than mine, much curlier. Even curlier than your mom's. And it's darker."

"And your father?"

"He was like you were . . . follically challenged. Even before the chemo." She fell silent, casually examining the next several pages: pictures of Caroline as a baby in her father's arms, as a toddler walking with him along the ocean's edge, then sitting proudly beside him as he held his newborn son. "And this is obviously your brother."

"Yeah. He was a beautiful baby. Lots of hair."

"Are these all of him?" Lili flipped through the rest of the album till the end. "Where are you?"

Caroline pointed to the picture on the very last page. "I think that's my arm."

Lili chuckled and opened the second album. It was filled with photographs of

Steve: Steve with his mother, with his father, with both parents. There were some pictures of the whole family, although Steve was always the focus. Even when Caroline was included, she was somehow separate — *standing aloof and apart,* she couldn't help notice.

Lili opened the last album, the one Caroline had put together herself. "There you are," Lili said, indicating a picture of Caroline in a long mint green dress standing beside an awkward-looking boy in a dark blue suit.

"Oh, God. My senior prom. Me and Michael Horowitz. I was about your age." She stared at the picture, then over at Lili, then back at the picture, hoping to see the resemblance her mother had been so sure of.

"What do you think?" Lili asked, clearly thinking the same thing.

"Hard to tell."

"I don't really see it."

"Well, it's not the greatest picture. Green isn't exactly my color."

The next pictures were of Caroline's wedding.

"Wow — you and Hunter are sure a gorgeous couple."

"I guess we were," Caroline agreed.

"Did you get divorced because of me? Because of what happened with Samantha, I mean?"

Another question Caroline had asked herself repeatedly. Would she and Hunter have divorced had Samantha never been taken from them? Or had what happened only speeded up the process? "I think it was bound to happen sooner or later."

"Because Hunter was cheating on you?"

"You know about that?"

"It was on the Internet."

"Well, I guess his cheating was part of it," Caroline said, answering Lili's question. "Combined with what happened in Mexico, well . . . People handle grief in different ways and those ways aren't always compatible. And guilt and blame are two very powerful weapons. Weapons of intimate destruction," she said with a wry smile.

"But you're friends now?"

"Well, I wouldn't exactly call us friends, no. But we don't hate each other. That's something. And of course, we have a child — children — together."

"Is that Michelle?" Lili pointed to a picture of a sleeping infant with both hands raised above her head, her pose identical to Samantha's the last time Caroline saw her. She was wrapped in a blanket and wore a pink woolen cap sporting a large GAP logo. Her mouth was turned down in a natural frown.

"That was the day we brought her home from the hospital."

There followed pages of pictures of Michelle as she grew from frowning infant to somber-looking child. Soon the serious-faced little girl was joined by her golden-haired, sweet-faced sister. "Samantha," Lili said, her eyes proceeding cautiously from one photo to the next.

Picture after picture of Samantha, Caroline realized, interspersed only intermittently with photos of Michelle. She tried to tell herself it was because Michelle would never sit still long enough to have her picture taken or had run out of the room whenever a camera materialized in her mother's hands, or that she would always make silly faces or do something to make Samantha cry. But was that really the reason pictures of Samantha were by far in the majority?

"I don't have any pictures of me as a baby," Lili said, interrupting Caroline's reveries.

"None at all?"

"My mother . . . *Beth* said they got lost during one of our moves."

"I guess that's possible. You said you moved around a lot."

"My brothers' baby pictures didn't get lost. Just mine." Lili reached across the bed for her overnight bag. "There's nothing until I was about six years old. My mother — Beth — always claimed she was hopeless with a camera." She unzipped the top of the bag and extricated half a dozen pictures from a side compartment. "Meet the Hollister family," she said, dropping the first photograph into Caroline's trembling hands: Lili as a fair-haired little girl sitting beside two smaller dark-haired boys. "That's me and my brothers. See? We don't look anything alike. And this is my father. *Tim.* Before he got sick, of course. I don't look anything like him at all. And this is my . . . This is Beth." She passed Caroline a picture of an attractive woman with frizzy dark hair, wide-set eyes, and an engaging, if somewhat wary, smile. "My brothers look just like her. Don't you think so?"

Caroline scraped her memory to determine if she'd ever seen Beth or Tim Hollister before. She tried to picture them poolside at the Grand Laguna Hotel in Rosarito or sitting at the next table in the garden restaurant. Maybe she'd smiled at them as she passed them in the hotel lobby one afternoon. But no such memories existed.

The last two pictures Lili showed her were of the entire family. Lili was right — she stood out like the proverbial sore thumb. Mother, father, and two sons formed a tight little group, while Lili stood shyly off to one side.

Standing ramrod straight. Aloof and apart.

"It's a nice-looking family," Caroline said, returning the photographs to Lili.

"Do you know what she said to me? Beth, I mean? On the phone earlier, before I hung up."

"What did she say?"

"That she was glad my father isn't alive to see what I'm doing. That it would break his heart." Her voice trembled to a stop. She took several long, deep breaths and bit down on her lower lip to still its quivering.

Caroline said nothing. What could she say? She knew all about broken hearts. Words couldn't heal them. She was about to step forward and take Lili in her arms when Michelle poked her head into the room.

"So, how's the family reunion going?" she asked. "Enjoying your little jaunt down Memory Lane?"

"Lili was just showing me pictures of her family in Calgary," Caroline said.

"Would you like to see them?" Lili shyly

extended them toward Michelle.

Michelle took the pictures from Lili, studying each one in turn. "Your brothers are really cute."

"Yeah, they are. I don't really look like them . . ."

"No, you don't," Michelle agreed. "Well, it's late. I'm going to bed."

"Sleep well, sweetheart," Caroline said.

"Aren't you coming?"

"I guess." Reluctantly, Caroline walked toward the door. "Are you all right? Is there anything you need?" she asked Lili.

"No. I'm fine."

"If you get hungry . . ."

"She knows where the kitchen is," Michelle said.

"If you can't sleep or you think of anything . . ."

"She knows where to find you."

"I'm just down the hall," Caroline said anyway.

"I'll be fine," Lili said. "Thanks for everything. I really appreciate it."

"Sleep well," Caroline said.

"We'll see you in the morning," Michelle told her before shutting the bedroom door. She proceeded briskly past her mother down the hall to Caroline's room.

"Where are you going?" Caroline asked,

trailing after her daughter into her room.

"I'm sleeping with you tonight."

"What? No."

"What? Yes." Michelle unfurled the nightgown she had tucked away under her arm. "Don't argue with me."

"But why?"

"Why?" Michelle repeated. "For the same reason I'm sleeping with this." She pulled a large knife out from underneath the mattress.

Caroline gasped. "What are you doing with that? Where did you get it?"

"From the kitchen. Where do you think? I put it here earlier."

"Well, put it back."

"No chance. It's staying right there." She returned it to its previous position.

"That's just absurd. Don't you think you're being a little overdramatic?"

"Better dramatic than dead."

"You can't actually think Lili intends to harm us?"

"I don't know what to think and neither do you. She seems sweet enough, I'll grant you that, but you never know. We have no idea who she really is. What if she robs us blind and takes off in the middle of the night?"

"Then I guess you'd be right about her."

Michelle shook her head. "Has it ever occurred to you that I'd rather be wrong? That a big part of me hopes she really *is* Samantha? That I'd give anything to have my sister back?"

Caroline took a deep breath. The truth was that it *hadn't* occurred to her. She'd been so caught up in her own feelings that she hadn't even considered what Michelle might be going through. "I'm sorry," she said softly.

"Apology accepted," Michelle said, pulling back the covers. "Now can we please get some sleep?"

TWENTY-SIX: THE PRESENT

When they woke up the next morning at just past seven A.M., Lili was gone.

"Well, at least we're alive," Michelle said, standing behind her mother in the doorway to the spare room. "Guess we should check the silverware."

"Lili?" Caroline called, trying to stem the too familiar panic that was rising in her gut. "Lili? Where are you?" She raced down the stairs and into each of the first-floor rooms. "Lili?"

"Relax," Michelle told her as she clomped down the steps after her, Lili's overnight bag in her hand. "I doubt she'd go anywhere without this."

"Lili?" Caroline called again, running back into the kitchen, her eyes searching the backyard. "Where the hell is she? Where could she have gone?"

"Maybe I should check this thing for explosives." Michelle began riffling through the bag. "Here's her passport." She opened it to its picture page. "Yep, that's her, all right. Lili Hollister. Born August 12, 1998. Correct me if I'm wrong, but I'm pretty sure Samantha was born in October."

The doorbell rang.

Caroline froze. She pictured a policeman standing outside her front door. *I'm sorry to have to inform you, but there's been an accident . . .*

"The prodigal daughter returns yet again," Michelle said, pushing past her mother into the hall and opening the door.

"Sorry," Lili said sheepishly. She was wearing the same jeans she'd had on the day before and a T-shirt emblazoned with a picture of Kate Moss. "I just wanted to feel the warm air. I didn't realize the door would lock automatically."

"How long have you been standing out there?" Caroline asked, ushering Lili into the foyer and glancing up and down the street before closing the door.

"Not long. I woke up really early, about five. Couldn't get back to sleep. So I got dressed and came downstairs, waited for the sun to come out, then stepped outside and got locked out. I didn't want to wake you up so early, so I went for a walk."

"A walk? Where?"

"Just around. This is a really beautiful neighborhood."

"Did you see anyone?"

"A couple of joggers."

"Lovely," Michelle said. "Any of them happen to have cameras?"

"I don't understand. Did I do something wrong?"

"Of course not," Caroline said. "It's just that sometimes we've caught reporters hanging around . . ."

"They hang out in the street . . . behind bushes . . . inside grocery stores," Michelle said pointedly.

"Not to mention the neighbors," Caroline said, cutting her off. "They don't mean to be nosy, but . . ."

"It's probably better if you don't take any more early-morning walks," Michelle advised.

"It would be quite the media circus if this were to get out," Caroline said.

"I'm so sorry. I wasn't thinking."

"You're sure about that?" Michelle asked.

"Michelle, please."

"I already told you I'm not interested in publicity. Is that my overnight bag?"

"And your passport." Michelle handed them both over to Lili.

"We didn't know where you'd gone,"

Caroline started to explain.

"I'm really sorry if I worried you."

The phone rang.

"And so the start of another fun-filled day," Michelle said, returning to the kitchen and answering the phone in the middle of its second ring. "Shipley Home for Wayward Girls. Michelle speaking. How can I help you?" She extended the phone toward her mother. "It's Dad."

"Hey," said Caroline in greeting.

"Have you spoken to Peggy?"

"Not yet."

"Call me after you speak to her." He hung up.

Caroline stared blankly at the phone in her hand. "Yes, sir. I'll take care of that immediately."

"You don't think it's a little early to be calling anyone?" Michelle asked, as Caroline pressed the digits of Peggy's phone number.

"Why don't you make us some coffee?" Caroline suggested.

"I can do it," Lili offered.

"I'll do it," Michelle said.

Peggy answered the phone immediately. "What's wrong?" she said instead of hello.

Caroline immediately filled her in on the events of the last twenty-four hours.

"Holy shit," Peggy said. "How can I help?"

"Do you know anyone at the San Diego DNA Medical Clinic in Mission Hills?"

"I don't think so. But let me ask around and get back to you. What time were you thinking of heading over there?"

"As soon as it opens. Probably around nine."

"Make it ten. It'll give me more time to make some calls. I'll meet you there."

"You don't have to do that."

"You couldn't stop me if you tried. Besides, you'll need a witness, right?"

"Yes."

"I'll see you at ten."

The clinic occupied the bottom floor of the modern white stucco, two-story building located at 40 Upas Street. Hunter was already waiting in the building's lobby when Caroline, Michelle, and Lili arrived.

"You really didn't have to come," Caroline told him — the same thing she'd told him on the phone after talking to Peggy. While all DNA clinics tested for paternity, the clinic in Mission Hills was one of the few in the state that also offered maternity testing. Mothers, it seemed, were generally expected to know their own children.

"I want them to test me, too," Hunter said.

"They don't need . . ."

"I want them to test me, too," he repeated, as if she hadn't spoken.

"Okay. If you think it's necessary."

"I think it's necessary."

"Why don't they test all of us?" Michelle said. "Maybe I'm not really your daughter either."

"Michelle," Caroline and Hunter said in unison.

"Sorry — a failed attempt at levity. But hey, you guys — a gold star for presenting a united front. I think that's a first."

Hunter turned his attention to Lili. "How are you this morning, Lili? Did you sleep well?"

"Yes, thank you."

"She was up kind of early, did some exploring of the neighborhood," Michelle said.

"You let her go for a walk?" Hunter asked Caroline.

"I —"

"That's probably not such a good idea," he told Lili. "If the press were to get wind of this . . . I think it's best that you stick around the house until we get the results of the test."

The front door opened and Peggy marched into the lobby. She was wearing a pair of gray slacks and a pearl pink blouse, and was obviously dressed for work. She walked directly over to Caroline and hugged her. "How are you holding up?"

"I'm okay."

"The rest of you?"

"Just peachy, thank you," Michelle said.

Peggy's gaze moved past Hunter and Michelle to the girl at their side. "This must be Lili."

"Lili," Caroline said, "this is my friend, Peggy."

"Very nice to meet you," Lili said.

"What do you think?" Hunter asked. "You knew Caroline when she was seventeen. Do you think they look anything alike?"

"I don't know," Peggy said, all but swallowing Lili's face with her eyes. "They're different, but at the same time, there's something so familiar . . . I just don't know."

"Excuse me, but isn't that what we're here to find out?" Michelle asked.

"Micki's right," Hunter said, snapping back into lawyer mode. "There's no point in speculating. Let's just get on with it. Were you able to talk to anyone?"

"I made a few calls," Peggy said, "and I finally managed to connect with the person in charge. He said he'll do everything he can to get the results back to you in a timely fashion."

"He understands the need to be discreet?"

"He does. He gave me the name of his most trusted technician, said she's been with the clinic ever since it opened."

"Then shall we proceed?" Hunter asked, opening the door to the inner reception area.

"Ready?" Caroline asked Lili.

"Ready or not," said Michelle.

The test went exactly as Michelle's notes had outlined. After Hunter paid all charges in advance, they proceeded to an inner office where an unsmiling middle-aged woman collected buccal swabs from Caroline, Hunter, and Lili. If she recognized any of them, she gave no sign, although the receptionist kept sneaking peeks in their direction. Peggy then signed the witness forms, and they were told they'd have the results back from the lab in three to five business days.

"Well, that was pretty anticlimactic," Michelle said as they were leaving the clinic.

"I assume we'll have the results by the end of the week," Hunter said, ushering them through the outer door.

"Never assume," Michelle intoned solemnly. "Didn't you once tell me that's one of the first rules of law?"

"Nice to know you occasionally listen to your old man," Hunter said, kissing her on the forehead. "Anyway, I've got to get going. Call me if you hear anything. Immediately," he added unnecessarily.

"Of course." Caroline watched her former husband walk toward his car. *Out of one life and into another,* she thought, finding his ability to compartmentalize nothing short of amazing.

"I better get a move on as well," Peggy said. "Monday's always a bitch. Are you coming in today?" she asked Michelle.

"From four to eight."

"Good. See you later." Peggy gave Caroline another hug. "You heading off to school?"

"No, I called in sick. Told them I might be coming down with something."

"You *are* looking a little green around the gills."

"I'm fine," Caroline said, although the truth was that she *was* feeling kind of queasy. While the DNA test had been as quick and painless as advertised, the simple swab had taken more out of her than she'd thought it would.

"And you," Peggy said, turning toward Lili. "You seem like a nice girl. Very composed and mature for your age. Whatever the test results, I really hope your intentions were good. Because my friend here has been through a hell of a lot, and if it turns out this is some sort of scam, well" — she flashed Lili her most beatific smile — "I just might have to kill you."

"She's kidding, of course," Caroline said quickly.

"Don't be too sure," Peggy said.

It was Michelle's turn to smile. "Guess we'll find out in three to five business days."

TWENTY-SEVEN: THE PRESENT

"Need some help?" Lili asked, entering the living room to find Caroline struggling to put together the six-foot-tall artificial Christmas tree that had been stuffed in a cardboard box in the basement, like Count Dracula in his coffin, for the past five years.

"I think I've almost got it," Caroline said. "Just this top part here." She stretched on the tips of her toes to attach the final clump of plastic branches, then stood back to survey her handiwork. "There. How does it look?"

"A bit squished."

"Yeah, well, it's been cooped up in a box for a long time, so . . ." She started pulling on the ends of the branches, turning some up, some down, twisting them this way and that until they began to fall more naturally. "There. That's better. What do you think?"

"Starting to look good."

"Luckily the lights come already attached," Caroline said, plugging the extension cord into the wall socket and watching hundreds of miniature white bulbs sparkle to life, like tiny stars. "And voilà! The magic of Christmas."

"It's beautiful."

"It'll look better once we get all the ornaments on." Caroline glanced toward the bags of Christmas decorations on the floor.

"You lugged all this stuff up by yourself?"

"Well, Michelle's at the hospice, you were in your room, I had all this energy . . ."

Lili knelt down and reached into one of the bags, pulling out a small box containing a dozen silver balls. She lifted one into her hand, staring at her distorted reflection in its shiny surface.

"Go ahead," Caroline urged. "Put it on the tree."

"Can I?"

"Please."

Lili hesitated. "Maybe we should wait till Michelle comes home."

Caroline shook her head. "She was never very interested in this sort of stuff. That's one of the reasons I stopped bothering. Every year I was dragging the damn thing up from the basement, and every year she'd find another excuse not to help decorate it — she didn't like artificial trees, she'd ruin her manicure, she was going out with friends . . . Eventually I thought, *Why am I doing this?* It wasn't like Michelle was tree-deprived. Her father had one — a *real* one. So did my mother. Hers was artificial, but it came completely decorated already, so . . ."

"You're not very close with your mother, are you?" Lili interrupted, hanging the silver ornament on one of the tree's middle branches and watching the bough bend slightly with its weight.

"Sorry if it was so obvious."

"She seems nice."

Don't be fooled, Caroline thought, but she refrained from saying it out loud. "She has her moments." She opened another box of ornaments, this one filled with red-and-white-striped balls.

"She and your brother look pretty tight."

"I guess some women make better mothers of sons than they do daughters."

"My mother always says that boys are much easier than girls," Lili said.

Caroline blanched at Lili's use of the word "mother."

"Sorry," Lili apologized immediately. "I mean *Beth.*"

"No need to apologize." Caroline swallowed once, and then again. "She's been a good mother to you, hasn't she?"

"Oh, yeah," Lili said easily. "A little strict, maybe, definitely old-fashioned, but I always felt loved. That's something I've never questioned. It's what makes what I'm doing now so hard."

"If it helps, I think you're being very brave," Caroline told her honestly. "And I want you to know that no matter how the test turns out, whether you're my daughter or not, I believe you acted honorably. I don't think you're a con artist. I don't think this is some sort of scam. I think you're a sweet and lovely young girl that any mother would be proud to call her own."

Tears filled Lili's eyes. "Thank you. That means a lot."

They spent the next several minutes decorating the tree in silence. "I called her again," Lili said, opening a bag containing half a dozen plastic Santas with flowing cotton beards.

"You called Beth? When?"

"After we got back from the clinic. I should have told you."

"How is she?"

"She's kind of freaking out about everything. Especially after I told her we'd taken the test."

"What did she say?"

"She insisted I come home immediately."

"What did you tell her?"

"That we should have the results back in a few days, that you have a friend who's trying to expedite things. That's the right word, isn't it? Expedite?"

"It's the right word."

"I left out the part where she threatened to kill me." Lili smiled to indicate she didn't take Peggy's threat too seriously.

"Sorry about that."

"It's all right. She's just being protective. Like Michelle. I understand."

"Did Beth say anything else?"

It was Lili's turn to take a deep breath. "She said that if I don't come home, she's coming to get me."

"What?"

"She said that if I'm not on a plane to Calgary first thing in the morning," Lili elaborated, "she'll be on the first one to San Diego in the afternoon."

"I don't understand. She doesn't even know where you are."

"She knows."

"How?"

"I told her."

"You told her?"

"I had to. She was threatening to contact the FBI and the Mounties and the local police, and whoever else she could think of, and if she does that, then for sure the papers will get wind of it and all hell will break loose."

"Do you think she'd do that? Come here, I mean?" Would Beth really take that chance? Caroline wondered. And if Beth was willing to come to San Diego, what did it mean? That she was confident the test results would prove that Lili was exactly who her passport said she was: Lili Hollister, born August 12, 1998, and not Samantha Shipley, born in mid-October of that same year? Surely Beth Hollister wouldn't risk crossing the border and exposing herself to criminal charges if there was any chance that Lili was not her child.

Unless she was no longer thinking rationally. Unless the fear of being exposed, of losing the child she'd raised as her own, had literally driven her out of her mind.

I've been her, Caroline thought. *I did lose my mind.*

Was Beth just as desperate?

"I don't know," Lili was saying. "I'm causing so much trouble. Maybe it *would* be better if I went home. We've taken the test. It's been witnessed. You could just call me with the results."

"No, you can't leave. Please. Please, you can't go until we know for sure." She couldn't allow Lili to return to Calgary before she knew the truth. If Lili *was* Samantha, she couldn't risk losing her again. If Beth was truly that desperate, who knew what she was capable of?

"So what do we do?"

"Maybe I could call her," Caroline offered, "try to make her understand . . ."

"I really don't think that's a good idea."

"No, you're probably right."

"Are you angry with me?"

"Why would I be angry?"

"What if I've put both of you through all this for nothing?"

They sat on the floor in silence for several seconds, the question flickering between them like a faulty lightbulb. "Are you hungry?" Caroline asked, hearing faint rumblings from her stomach.

"Starving."

"Feel like a pizza?"

"Double cheese, pepperoni, and tomato slices?"

"I'll make the call." Caroline scrambled to her feet and headed for the kitchen, forcing all troubling thoughts from her head. "You keep decorating the tree."

"Wow," Caroline said, taking a few steps back to admire the tree that was now dripping with ornaments, and almost stepping into the large pizza box containing two leftover slices. "It's gorgeous. You did an amazing job."

"The pinecones came in really handy for filling in the empty spaces."

"And I love these little glass slippers and ballerinas. I'd forgotten we had those."

"We just need an angel for the top."

Caroline began riffling through the remaining bags with one hand while balancing a half-eaten piece of pizza in the other. "One angel coming up." She located a glittery gold-and-silver cardboard angel that Michelle had made in grade school and held it up to the tree. "I think we're going to need a stepladder."

"Do you have one?"

"In the kitchen."

"I'll get it." Lili was halfway down the hall when Caroline heard a key turn in the lock and the front door open. She checked her watch. It was eight-thirty, which meant that Michelle was home from the hospice.

"What's going on?" Michelle asked from the entrance to the living room, her eyes sweeping across the room, registering the Christmas tree and the various bags and boxes littering the floor.

"I thought it would be nice if we had a

tree this year," Caroline said. "You want some pizza? There are a few slices left."

Michelle said nothing, the roll of her eyes answer enough. She approached the tree, her fingers reaching for one of the silver balls. "A little premature to be celebrating, don't you think?"

"I just thought it would be nice," Caroline said again.

Michelle nodded. "And it never crossed your mind that I might like to participate?"

Caroline fell silent. *One step forward. Two steps back.*

"You can put up the angel," Lili said brightly, returning to the living room with the small stepladder.

"Oh, thank you," Michelle said. "That's so considerate of you."

"Michelle . . ."

"There's some pizza left," Lili said. "I can heat it up for you."

"Well, aren't you just the sweetest, most thoughtful little sister in the whole universe?"

"Please don't take your anger at me out on Lili," Caroline implored. "It was *my* idea to put up the tree. *My* idea to decorate it. Lili said we should wait till you got home. *I'm* the one who said you wouldn't be interested."

"Because you think I enjoy being left out?"

"Because you've never shown any interest before."

"Because you always made it seem like it was such a chore," Michelle shot back, her anger escalating with each pronouncement. "Because it was so obvious your heart wasn't in it, that there was no reason to decorate a stupid tree and pretend to be happy, when how could we be happy if Samantha wasn't here to celebrate with us? God knows *I* wasn't reason enough. God knows *I* never made you happy." She tore the angel from Lili's hand and ripped it apart, tossing what was left to the floor. "And by the way, Lili, or Samantha, or whatever the hell your real name is, just so you know, there are no such things as angels. Because there is no such thing as heaven." She spun toward the hallway. "It's all one big crock. A scam — just like you."

"Micki, wait."

"What exactly am I waiting for?" Michelle said, turning back. "For you to acknowledge that I matter as much as my sainted sister, that my actual presence is as important to you as her memory?"

"That is so unfair."

"Is it? What's it going to take, Mother? Do I have to disappear for you to love me?"

Caroline sank to the floor, crushing what was left of the cardboard angel beneath her weight, as Michelle ran from the room.

Twenty-Eight: The Present

"It's me . . . Lili. Can I come in?"

"Can I stop you?"

Caroline overheard the exchange from the doorway of her bedroom. She'd been on her way to apologize to Michelle yet again — how many of their conversations over the years had consisted of futile attempts to explain and atone? — when she heard the sound of footsteps in the hall and peeked out of her room to see Lili tapping gently on Michelle's bedroom door.

She watched Lili disappear inside Michelle's room before tiptoeing down the hallway, then stood with her back pressed tightly against the wall, knowing she shouldn't be eavesdropping but unable to tear herself away.

"Are you okay?" she heard Lili ask.

"Sure," Michelle responded. "Why wouldn't I be?"

"You seemed really upset."

"I overreacted. Not that unusual. Sorry if it worried you."

"No, please. I'm the one who should be apologizing to you."

"What do you have to be sorry about?"

"We should have waited till you got home to decorate the tree."

"That wasn't your decision."

"Please don't be angry at your mother. She didn't mean . . ."

"I know. You don't have to explain."

"She loves you."

"I know that, too. It's just this dance we do. Guess we've been doing it for so long, it's become ingrained."

Silence.

"What is it you want, Lili? Did my mother ask you to come in here?"

"No. I was just hoping that . . . maybe . . ."

"Maybe . . . ?"

"We could talk?"

"You want to talk?"

Caroline pictured Lili nodding her head.

"What do you want to talk about?"

"I don't know. Whatever. I guess I was hoping maybe we could get to know each other better."

"We don't know each other at all."

"I'd like to. Get to know you," Lili said.

"Why? I doubt you'll be sticking around

long once we get the DNA results back."

"You're so sure I'm not your sister?"

"You have to admit it's a long shot. But what the hell? We'll know in a few days. No point speculating."

"Do you remember her at all?" Lili asked. "Samantha, I mean."

Another silence, longer than the first.

"You were five when she was taken," Lili pressed.

"So?"

"So, you should have some memories of her."

"Should I?"

"Don't you?"

"I guess."

"What was she like?"

"She was two years old."

"Two-year-olds have personalities. Was she funny? Quiet? Did she make you laugh? Did she cry a lot? Was she a happy baby?"

Caroline imagined a look of irritation spreading across Michelle's face. She held her breath, waiting for an explosion of sarcasm. Surprisingly, the voice that emerged was quiet and free of vitriol. "I remember this one time she found my mother's Velcro rollers and she stuck them all in her hair, and she was running around the house wearing nothing but a diaper and my mother's big, fuzzy pink slippers, with these crazy-looking rollers sticking out of her head at all these weird angles, and she looked so proud of herself, and my mother was laughing so hard, and I remember wishing I could make her laugh like that, and then getting angry and marching over and pushing Samantha to the floor and yanking the rollers out of her hair. And she started crying, and, of course, my mother got mad and yelled at me."

I'd forgotten all about that, Caroline thought, tears filling her eyes as she recalled the halo of Velcro rollers clinging to Samantha's beautiful little head and the sweet smile on her beautiful little mouth as she scurried happily from room to room. She could also see the look of rage on Michelle's face as she pushed her sister to the floor and began tearing the rollers from her hair.

"You were jealous," Lili said. "That's pretty normal. I have two younger brothers, and until they were born, I was *it,* as far as my parents were concerned. And then along came Alex, and then Max, and I stopped being the center of the universe. It took some getting used to."

"Is that why you're doing this? To be the center of the universe again?"

"What else do you remember about Samantha?" Lili prodded, ignoring Michelle's question.

"That's about it."

"Do you remember anything about that night in Mexico?"

Another silence, this one lasting so long that Caroline decided Michelle had no intention of answering it.

"I try not to," Michelle said finally.

"So you *do* remember something."

"I remember my mother screaming."

Caroline felt her breath seize in her lungs and she threw her hands over her mouth in order to stifle the gasp about to escape.

"That must have been terrifying."

"Must have been," Michelle repeated without inflection.

"What else do you remember?"

"I remember trying to hold on to her, and her pushing me away."

Caroline recalled Michelle's efforts to cling to her and her own feelings of being suffocated, the panic of not being able to breathe, her irrational fear that Michelle was leeching the air right out of her body. Had she really pushed the child away?

"I'm sure she didn't mean to . . ."

"Maybe not. Or maybe it didn't happen that way at all. Maybe I dreamt the whole thing. I was a child. Children get confused.

They imagine all sorts of crazy things. Look," she continued, unprompted, "even if it *did* happen, I don't blame her for pushing me away. I don't even blame her for not loving me the way she did Samantha. I give her a hard time about it, but I understand. I honestly do. Samantha was this beautiful, really easy baby, always smiling, always happy. She was just . . . lovable. And I was, as my mother has been known to say, 'difficult.' I was whiny. I was demanding. I was clingy. In a word, I was a brat." She paused, blowing a long, audible breath into the air. "I was a brat before Mexico. I was a brat after. I'm a brat now."

"I don't think you're a brat."

"Sure you do."

"Brats don't volunteer at hospices."

"They do when they've been ordered to by the courts."

"I don't understand."

"She hasn't told you?"

"Told me what?"

"About my arrest for driving under the influence, my court-ordered community service?"

"You were arrested for drunk driving?"

"You can add it to my list of failings. She really hasn't told you?"

"Not a word."

"Guess she's too ashamed."

"Maybe she didn't think it was her place to tell me."

"Maybe."

"Will you?"

"Will I what?"

"Tell me what happened?"

Once again, Caroline found herself holding her breath. Michelle had never confided in her about any of the details of that night. While she knew the facts of her daughter's arrest, and the fine print of the deal Hunter had worked out with the assistant district attorney, Michelle had always refused to discuss exactly what had happened, and Caroline doubted she would agree to talk to Lili about it now. She braced herself for a barrage of expletives, hoping she'd have time to make it back to her own room undetected before Michelle pushed Lili — physically or metaphorically — out into the hall.

"It's no big deal," Michelle surprised her by saying. "I mean, it *is* a big deal, I guess. It's just not much of a story."

Both Caroline and Lili waited for her to continue.

"I went to a party at this older guy's apartment. It wasn't a great party because everyone was getting high on weed, which is kind

of boring. You know how it is."
"I don't, actually."
"You're kidding me. You've never smoked weed?"
"Never smoked. Never drank. Never . . ."
"Had sex?"
"What's that?" Lili asked with a laugh.
"You're a virgin?"
"You sound surprised."
"You're seventeen."
"I wasn't even allowed to date until a year ago."
"Wow."
"Not that it mattered. We moved all the time. I was homeschooled. I didn't know anyone. So who was I going to date? It wasn't until my father died that my mother started relaxing her guard a little. She even let me dye the ends of my hair blue. And one day I was at the library and this guy kept looking at me, and I'm thinking that he's kind of cute and I start looking back, trying to flirt, and he walks over to me, and I'm wondering if he's gonna maybe ask me out, and instead he says I look just like these sketches on the Internet and . . ."
". . . the rest is history."
"Finish your story," Lili directed.
"Well, like I said, there's not much to tell. Everyone's getting high on weed, and I

don't know, weed's never been my thing, even though I smoke — I'm sure my mother told you that."

"She didn't have to."

"What do you mean?"

"I can smell it on your clothes."

"You can? Seriously? Shit."

"So, what happened? At the party."

"Well, this guy I know was there. Spencer. We'd gone out a few times. Well, no. We hadn't actually gone out. We just had sex a couple of times."

Caroline's head dropped toward her chest. *Dear God,* she thought.

"Anyway, he said he knew where the host kept his wine. And next thing I know, the two of us are in the kitchen and we've polished off almost this whole bottle, and our host finds us and he's beyond furious and he orders us out of the house. Apparently it was a really expensive wine his father had been saving for years. So we had to leave, and Spencer gets into his car, and I get into mine. Ten minutes later, the police pull me over and . . ."

". . . the rest is history."

"It's not like I even drink that much," Michelle continued. "It's just that whenever I do, I mess up big-time."

So maybe you shouldn't drink, Caroline

thought, half expecting to hear the words emerge from Lili's mouth. But Lili said nothing. *Obviously much smarter than I am,* Caroline thought.

"Anyway, my drinking days are over. I've learned my lesson."

Caroline allowed herself a small sigh of relief.

"Guess I'll have to switch to weed after all."

Fuck.

"And my father cut some deal with the assistant D.A., and that's how I ended up working at the hospice. I told you it wasn't very exciting. Or noble."

"I still think it's pretty amazing. I don't think I could do it."

"It's really not that big a deal. People die, right? You kind of get used to it. Except sometimes. Like today."

"What happened today?"

"We got this new resident. Kathy."

"What makes her different?"

"She's only twenty-nine. And she's all alone. Her mother died when she was a kid and her father remarried and she never got along all that great with her stepmother. The whole Cinderella story except she ended up with ovarian cancer instead of a handsome prince. Probably won't even make it till Christmas. It just got to me, the unfairness of it. I think that's one of the reasons I went so ballistic when I came home and saw you guys decorating the tree."

"I'm really sorry about that."

"Stop apologizing. It wasn't your fault."

"It wasn't *anybody's* fault."

"Which pretty much brings us back to where we started. Seems we've come full circle. Time to call it a night."

Caroline felt Lili moving toward the door and she pushed herself away from the wall, preparing to make a hasty retreat. "Thanks," she heard Lili say.

"For what?"

"For not telling me to get lost. For confiding in me. For making me feel, I don't know . . . almost like . . ."

". . . sisters?"

"I guess."

"You really sure you want to be part of this family?" Michelle asked.

Caroline ran down the hall to her bedroom before she could hear Lili's reply.

Twenty-Nine: The Present

She was lying in her bed, wide awake at just after six A.M., having tossed and turned most of the night, her mind vacillating between hope and despair, anticipation and dread. What would she do if the tests proved Lili was indeed Samantha? What if they proved she *wasn't*?

You really sure you want to be part of this family?

Michelle's words bounced against the side of her brain, increasing in volume with each repetition, filling her head like a stubborn cold, leaving her barely able to breathe.

Her daughter was right. The family that Lili would be returning to — if the DNA test revealed she was, in fact, Samantha — was severely splintered, if not irreparably broken. Caroline and Hunter were divorced; Caroline barely tolerated her mother; she had a strained relationship with her brother, a strained relationship with Michelle . . .

I'm the common denominator here, Caroline acknowledged, finally climbing out of bed an hour later, her body a collection of aches and stiff joints. *Everything, my fault.*

She threw a housecoat over her cotton pajamas and headed down the stairs, past Michelle's and Lili's closed bedroom doors. She walked into the kitchen, moving as if she were on automatic pilot, and made a pot of coffee, then poured a large mug even before the coffeemaker indicated it had finished brewing.

"Is there enough for me?" Michelle asked, shuffling into the room on bare feet and plopping down into a chair at the kitchen table.

Wordlessly, Caroline reached into the cupboard for another mug and poured her daughter a steaming cup, depositing it in front of her. "You're up early."

"Didn't get a whole lot of sleep. I take it you're not going into work today."

"I told them I'd be out for the rest of the week."

Michelle nodded. "Probably a good idea." She sipped her coffee, offered nothing further.

"I owe you an apology," Caroline said.

"For what?"

"Last night. The way I acted. You were

absolutely right to be angry." She opened the breadbasket at the far end of the counter, removed two slices of raisin bread, and dropped them into the toaster. "I should have waited for you to come home to decorate the tree, at least given you the chance to . . ."

"Say no? I would have, you know. Said no."

"I still should have waited, given you the choice."

"Yeah, well. What's done is done, right? Tree looks great, by the way."

"It does look nice, doesn't it?"

"Except for the missing angel on top. My turn to apologize. I'll go out later, pick something up."

"That would be nice."

"Except I don't believe in angels or any of that stuff, so I'll probably just get a star or a snowflake. Something like that. Is that okay?"

"Sounds good." The toast popped up. Caroline put the slices on a plate, opened the fridge, took out some butter, and applied it to the two browned surfaces. "You want a piece?" she asked her daughter, without thinking. "Sorry," she said immediately. "Forgot you don't eat bread."

"I'll eat the raisins," Michelle said.

"You mean, right out of the bread?"

"As long as they don't have butter on them."

Caroline studied the two slices of toast. "You can't have the raisins. They're the best part." She caught Michelle's grin as she sat down at the table and began dunking the toast in her coffee.

"Oh, gross," said Michelle.

"You didn't used to think it was gross."

"What are you talking about?"

"When you were little. You used to watch me dunking my toast in my coffee and insist on doing the same thing."

"I don't believe you."

"It's the God's truth. I swear."

"I don't believe in God."

"Yeah, well. It's true anyway." Caroline smiled at the memory. "You were this little thing, I don't think you were even two years old, but even then you were very clear about what you wanted, and what you wanted was to dunk your toast in coffee, the same way I did. So every morning I'd pour a little bit of coffee into your cup and we'd sit there and dunk our toast together. And one day, I was busy doing other things, and you came marching into the kitchen, quite indignant, and demanded, 'Where's my coffee?' "

Michelle chuckled. "You're making that up."

"I'm not. You were quite the character."

Michelle wiggled forward in her seat, intrigued. "How so?"

"Well, you were very verbal very early, and you used to keep up this steady stream of chatter about everything you were doing," Caroline said, warming to her subject, her mind suddenly flooded with memories. "I remember one time, you were maybe eighteen months old, and you tripped over something, and you said, 'Oh, I fell down.' And then you said, 'It's all right. I get up.' It was like you were narrating your life." She paused, watching the scene play out in her mind. "And there was this one afternoon I took you to the movies. You were maybe two and a half. I think it was *Clash of the Titans,* some movie like that, and there were maybe half a dozen other people in the audience and you talked the whole way through the picture, this little voice like chipped glass, describing everything that was happening on the screen. *Oh, look, Mommy. Andromeda's taking a bath. She's getting out of the bath. She's walking to the door. She's opening the door.* On and on. And when the movie was over, we were in the washroom and this woman was at the mirror and I apologized if your voice-over had disturbed her, and she smiled and said, 'It's okay. She was very informative.' "

This time Michelle threw her head back and laughed.

"And one time your father got a new car and I was terrified to drive it because you know how he is about his cars."

Michelle nodded.

"But one day I was driving and you were in your car seat and I had to back into this parking space and I was a nervous wreck. It must have taken me ten minutes to park the damn thing. I was going back and forth and back and forth, trying to squeeze into the damn space, and I was covered in perspiration, absolutely soaking wet by the time I finally managed it, and from the backseat came this little voice — 'Good job, Mommy!' And it made my day. It really did." She shook her head. "God, I haven't thought about these things in . . ."

"Fifteen years?"

Caroline got up from her seat and poured herself another cup of coffee. Michelle was right. Her memories of Samantha had been so all-consuming, they'd all but erased her memories of Michelle's early childhood. "You want some more?"

"Sure."

Caroline filled her daughter's mug and returned to the table, her conscience getting the best of her. "Listen. There's something I have to tell you."

"Oh, dear. It's never good when sentences begin that way."

"I overheard you last night, talking to Lili."

"You *overheard*?"

"I didn't mean to." Caroline stopped. "No, that's not true. I saw Lili go into your room and I deliberately listened in."

"You're telling me you eavesdropped?"

"Yes."

"That's such a funny expression — 'eavesdropped.' Wonder where it came from."

"You don't sound too upset."

Michelle shrugged.

"Or surprised."

Another shrug. "I knew you were there."

"You did?"

"You breathe through your mouth."

"I do?"

"Whenever you're anxious or upset."

"You knew I was listening the whole time?"

"Not the whole time, no. But at some point I just knew you were there."

"And you kept talking anyway."

"I was curious to hear what Lili had to say."

"You did most of the talking."

"Guess I did."

"Did you mean the things you said?"

"I don't know. I said a lot of things."

"You asked Lili if she really wanted to be part of this family."

Michelle opened her mouth as if to speak, then stopped, taking another sip of her coffee as Lili entered the room. "Speak of the devil. Although technically, of course, I don't believe in the devil. We didn't hear you come down the stairs."

Lili glanced toward the wooly pink bunny-festooned socks peeking out from underneath her blue-and-white-striped pajamas, as if they explained the silence of her approach. "Is there enough coffee for me?"

"I think there's still some left." Caroline got up and poured Lili a cup. "Milk? Sugar?"

"Black's good."

"I can make eggs, or there's cereal," Caroline offered.

"Maybe just some toast." Lili crossed to the counter and extricated two pieces of raisin bread from the bag before Caroline could do it for her. A minute later, she was sitting between them at the table, buttering her toast.

"Have you spoken to Beth this morning?" Caroline asked, realizing she was breathing through her mouth and coughing into her hands.

"I called, but nobody answered. Not her landline or her cell." Lili glanced at the clock on the wall. "I wouldn't be surprised if she's already on her way to the airport. She always likes to get places way early."

"Why would she be on her way to the airport?" Michelle asked. "Don't tell me she's coming here."

Caroline felt a stab of panic in her side. "What time would her plane get in?"

Lili shook her head. "I'm not sure."

"I'll check the Internet," Michelle offered, getting up from the table, "find out what flights are arriving from Calgary and when."

"I better call your father," Caroline said.

"I'm sorry this is getting so complicated." Lili began absently dunking her toast in her coffee.

"What are you doing?" Michelle asked, stopping dead in her tracks.

"Sorry." Lili immediately lifted the now-coffee-soaked piece of toast from her mug. "I guess it's kind of gross."

Tears filled Caroline's eyes, as if this simple gesture was the genetic "tell" she'd been looking for, all the proof she needed that Lili was indeed her child.

The phone rang.

"Maybe that's her," Michelle said.

Caroline moved quickly to answer it. "Hello?"

"Caroline. It's Arthur . . . *Aidan* Wainwright. Please hear me out."

She immediately slammed the receiver down.

"What happened?" Michelle asked. "You're white as a ghost. Who was that?"

Caroline leaned back against the counter, instinctively understanding that the reporter knew of Lili's existence and wondering how long it would be before the rest of the world found out.

"Mom? Who was that?" Michelle repeated.

Caroline put two and two together and came up with the only possible answer under the circumstances. "Trouble."

Thirty: The Present

"Here comes a taxi." Caroline backed away from the living room window, her heart pounding.

Michelle immediately moved to take her place behind the sheer curtains. "No. It's not stopping. Oh, crap."

"What's happening?"

"I just saw something move behind the big tree across the street."

"Another reporter?" Caroline was immediately back at the window.

"Probably."

"Shit. Looks like the vultures are circling."

"Are you serious?" Lili asked from her seat on the sofa.

"I'm afraid so," Michelle said.

"I don't understand. How would they even know . . . ?"

"Somebody must have tipped them off."

"You think it was Beth?" Lili asked Caroline.

"I don't know. You said she threatened to."

"I know, but . . ."

"But what?" Michelle asked.

"It doesn't make sense," Lili said. "She'll be here any minute. The last thing she'd want is a bunch of reporters waiting for her."

"Unless that's *exactly* what she wants," Michelle said.

"What do you mean?" Caroline and Lili asked together, their voices overlapping.

Michelle spun toward Lili. "You almost had me convinced, you know. Not that you were actually Samantha. But that you really believed you might be."

"But that's the truth."

"Is it? Or is it something else? You said before that this was getting so complicated, but maybe it's not complicated at all. Maybe it's what my uncle Steve suggested: a chance to get in on the action, to jump-start a career in show business, make the cover of *People*?"

"No," Lili protested.

"You know that's not true," Caroline said.

"I know it's no coincidence that your reporter boyfriend happened to phone this morning after five years. I know that the press isn't camped out on our doorstep because it's a slow news day. Somebody told them Lili was here, and why."

Caroline winced at the word "boyfriend," its sting as painful as if Michelle had physically struck her.

"Did you tell anyone?" Michelle asked Lili.

"No. Did you?"

"*Me?* Are you kidding? Shit. Here comes a truck from Fox News."

"Damn it," Caroline said. "Call your father."

"I've already called him three times."

"Call him again."

Michelle groaned as she pulled her cell phone out of her jeans pocket and punched in the number for Hunter's office. "Hi, Lucy. Sorry to bother you again, but . . . Yeah, I know he's with clients. He's been with clients all day . . ."

"Give me that." Caroline grabbed the phone from her hand. "Lucy, this is Caroline. I need to speak to Hunter immediately."

"I'm so sorry, but he's in a very important meeting," the secretary responded.

"Then. Get. Him. Out."

"Just a minute."

"Wow," Michelle muttered. "That was impressive."

"What's up?" Hunter said moments later,

his voice rushed and impatient. "I'm in the middle of a major deal . . ."

"And I've got a street filling up with reporters."

"What are you talking about?"

"Aidan Wainwright phoned me this morning."

"Who the hell is Aidan Wain . . . ? Oh, shit," he said, before Caroline could answer. "What did that jerk want?"

"I didn't give him a chance to tell me. But I suspect he was calling because he found out about Lili."

"You think she called him?"

"No. But it's possible that Beth . . ."

"Who's Beth?"

Caroline couldn't bring herself to say "Lili's mother." "Apparently she's on her way here from Calgary," she said instead, hoping to jog Hunter's memory.

"What the hell? When did that happen? Why didn't you call me?"

"We tried. Three times. You're in the middle of a major deal, remember?"

"What time is her plane arriving?"

"We're not sure. The direct flight from Calgary was delayed. Apparently there's a snowstorm. Anyway, she may not even be on the direct flight. And she's not answering her phone."

"You think she's the one who alerted the media?"

"It's possible."

"Okay. Look, I'll be there as soon as I can. In the meantime, don't answer the door. Don't answer the phone. Don't say a word to anyone."

"Of course I'm not going to say anything," Caroline began, but he'd already hung up. "What — am I an idiot?" she asked as she handed the phone back to Michelle. She'd taken her landline off the hook immediately after Aidan's phone call.

"Is he coming over?"

"As soon as he can. Try Beth again," she directed Lili.

Lili used her cell phone to place another call to Beth, shaking her head as a recorded voice announced the line was temporarily not in service. "She's probably still in the air."

"She's just waiting until more troops arrive," Michelle said, glancing back at the street. "The woman clearly knows how to make an entrance."

"You're wrong," Lili insisted. "The last thing she wants is for anyone to know about this. She just wants me to come home."

A car pulled up in front of the house and a woman with long, shapely legs and wavy blond hair emerged from the backseat, a microphone in her hand. A bearded man trailed after her, half a dozen cameras draped around his neck. "Damn it," Caroline said, her eyes following them up her front walk.

The doorbell rang.

"What do we do?" Lili asked.

"What *can* we do?"

It rang again.

"We just let them keep ringing?"

"They'll get the message eventually."

"It's like being held hostage," Lili said as the ringing continued on and off for the next five minutes.

"They know we're home," Caroline said. "They probably saw us at the window."

"Maybe we should close the drapes." Michelle indicated the heavy beige panels framing the sheer curtains.

"Maybe we should call the police," Lili said.

"Great idea," Michelle told her. "Let's make the story even bigger. Maybe we can make the national news." The doorbell rang ten more times in rapid succession. "God, aren't they ever going to give up?"

"Thought you didn't believe in God," Lili said with a smile.

"Shut up," Michelle said.

Caroline found herself stifling a laugh.
"What? What's so funny?"
"You're starting to sound like sisters."
"Okay, that did it," Michelle said, moving away from the window. "I'm out of here." She headed for the front door.
"Wait, Michelle. You can't go out there."
"Then I'll go out the back." She turned on her heel, heading for the rear of the house.
"Michelle," Caroline pleaded, following after her. "Please . . ."
"Relax, Mother. You won't even know I'm gone."
"You're being foolish . . ."
"*I'm* being foolish?" She pushed open the rear door.
A man was standing on the other side.
"Who the hell are you?" Michelle asked, startled.
"Dear God," Caroline said from behind her. "Shut the door, Michelle. Now."
"Caroline, wait," the man said, grabbing the door to keep it from closing. "I know you don't want to talk to me and I can't say I blame you . . ."
"Is this that fucking reporter?" Michelle demanded.
"I'm Aidan Wainwright."
"The creep who wrote that awful story?

Get the fuck out of here."

"You must be Michelle."

"You must be fucking kidding. Let go of the door, asshole."

"Look. I know you all hate me, but I think that if you go back and read that story again, you'll find it's not so bad. You actually come off very well," he said, speaking directly to Caroline. "I portrayed you in a very sympathetic light."

Caroline stared at the not-quite-handsome man she hadn't laid eyes on in five years, the man whose story, whose betrayal, had cost her not only her job but what was left of her self-esteem. His hair was shorter than it had been the last time she'd seen him, and graying slightly at the temples, but other than that, he looked essentially the same. She was somewhat mortified to realize she still found him attractive.

"Is it true?" he asked. "Is Samantha back?"

"I don't know what you're talking about."

"What's going on?" Lili asked, coming up behind Caroline.

"Is that her?" Aidan asked, pushing harder on the door, trying to worm his way inside. "Talk to me, sweetheart. Who are you? What's your story?"

"Get back in the living room," Michelle told Lili. "Now."

Lili spun around and ran out of the room.

"You might as well tell me, Caroline," Aidan said. "You know I'm going to write something anyway."

"First tell me who tipped you off," Caroline said.

"You know I can't betray a source."

"Really? You had no trouble betraying me."

"Not quite true. And if you think about it, I also did you a favor."

"A favor?"

"I gave you a forum, a place to vent . . ."

"Without my knowledge. Without my permission."

"You never would have given me permission."

"Doesn't that tell you something?"

"It was never my intention to hurt you, Caroline. I liked you. I really did. I debated with myself for hours about handing in that story. I knew there was a chance you wouldn't understand."

"A *chance* I wouldn't understand? Understand what, exactly? That you abused my trust? That you humiliated me? That you used me to further your ambitions, to increase the size of your byline?"

"You'd been carrying around this huge burden of guilt for so many years that it was crippling you," he argued. "I like to think I might have actually lightened that load."

Was he really so delusional? she wondered. But then, why should he be any different than everybody else? Sometimes delusions were all that carried you through life. "Don't you dare try to fool yourself into thinking there was anything noble about what you did," she told him, pushing such thoughts from her head. "I bet you have a tape recorder on in your pocket right this minute, don't you?"

He looked away, trying not to smile. "A girl shows up on your doorstep, claiming to be the daughter stolen from you fifteen years ago. That's one hell of a story, Caroline, even if it turns out she's not Samantha. Let me write it. Give me a chance to make things right."

"First tell me if you really had a wife and daughter who were killed by a drunk driver."

His sheepish expression was all the answer she needed.

"You piece of shit."

"Talk to me, Caroline. Give me an exclusive and I swear you'll come off more saintly than goddamn Mother Teresa."

Caroline stared into his not-quite-handsome face, relieved to discover that all she felt was contempt. Then she wrested the door away from him and slammed it in his face.

"You should have told him to fuck off," Michelle said later.

"Yes, it's always a good idea, telling a reporter to fuck off," Hunter said.

"Sometimes it's just better to take the high road," Caroline said.

They were gathered in her living room, waiting for Beth to arrive. Her plane had landed half an hour earlier, and she'd called Lili as soon as she cleared customs to tell her she was on her way. Lili had, in turn, told her about the growing number of media surrounding the house and asked whether she was responsible for their presence, something Beth vehemently denied.

"Is it true Samantha's come home?" a reporter had shouted at Hunter as he was climbing out of his BMW.

"When will you get the DNA results back?" another demanded as Caroline opened the door and pulled him inside.

"Did Wainwright say who tipped him off?" Hunter asked now.

Caroline scoffed. "And betray a source?"

"There's a cab coming down the street," Lili announced from the window.

Caroline, Hunter, and Michelle immediately jumped to their feet in anticipation. They took a collective deep breath as the taxi pulled to a stop in front of the house and a woman emerged from its backseat.

Lili turned toward Caroline. “It’s her.”

Thirty-One: The Present

Beth Hollister looked exactly like the photograph Lili had shown her — which meant she looked nothing at all like Lili, Caroline was thinking as she ushered the clearly distraught woman into the foyer. She was wearing a heavy black wool coat and carrying the same style overnight bag that Lili had brought with her a few days earlier. Her hair was thick and dark, more frizz than curl, and she was deathly pale. Whether this was the result of the Calgary winter or the clamoring horde of reporters that had descended upon her like a cluster of angry bees as she exited her cab, snapping pictures and flinging questions at her head like pebbles as she ran up the front walk, was impossible to tell. She lowered her bag to the floor, fear-filled brown eyes blinking rapidly as she looked around for Lili, then brimming over with tears when she saw her, and finally closing with relief as Lili rushed into her arms.

Caroline felt a pang of jealousy as she watched the two embrace. She fought the proprietary urge to jump between them and force them apart.

"Are you all right?" Beth asked Lili, smoothing some stray wisps of hair away from her forehead and holding her face in her hands.

"I'm okay. How about you?"

"About what you'd expect, under the circumstances."

"How are Alex and Max?"

"They're okay. Confused, of course. They don't understand how you could just take off like that."

Caroline inched forward. "Mrs. Hollister," she said, about to extend her hand when she realized that Beth wasn't about to release her grip on Lili. "I'm Caroline Shipley. This is my ex-husband, Hunter, and our daughter, Michelle. I'm so sorry about the scene out front."

"I don't understand. What are all those people doing here? Why would you think I called them?" Beth looked from Caroline to Hunter to Michelle, then back to Caroline.

"We didn't know what to think," Caroline said.

"If you didn't call them, who did?" Michelle asked.

The question lingered in the air, like a stale cooking odor.

"It doesn't really matter," Hunter said. "It's a moot point. Someone obviously tipped the vultures off and they're not going away anytime soon."

"This is such a nightmare," Beth said.

"Can I take your coat?" Caroline offered.

"No, thanks. We won't be staying long."

Caroline glanced uneasily in Hunter's direction, anxious at Beth's use of the word "we." "Why don't we go into the living room where we can talk?"

Beth remained rooted to the spot.

"Come on, Mom," Lili urged gently, and Caroline felt another stab of anxiety. "You came all this way."

"I came to take you home."

"Please," Caroline said. "Surely you can stay a little while."

"I told the cabdriver to come back in half an hour."

"Which doesn't give us a whole lot of time," Michelle said as they proceeded into the living room.

"Have you had anything to eat?" Caroline asked. "Can I get you some tea or coffee?"

"Some tea would be nice," Beth said, unfastening the top button of her coat. "If it's no trouble."

"I'll make it," Lili offered.

"*I'll* do it," Michelle said. "How do you take it?"

"Milk and a little sugar, thank you."

"Anybody else?"

"I'll have some," Caroline said. "Just a tiny bit of milk."

"I know how you take your tea, Mom."

"Why don't we sit down?" Hunter said, as if he still lived here.

Caroline and Hunter lowered themselves into the chairs as Lili and Beth, their hands still intertwined, positioned themselves on the sofa.

"You have a lovely home," Beth said.

"Thank you."

"And such a beautiful tree." She nodded in its direction.

"Lili helped decorate it," Caroline said, watching the tiny white lights sparkle. She'd pulled the drapes shut earlier in the afternoon in an effort to keep prying eyes at bay. The result was that the room, normally airy and bright, felt small and claustrophobic. The tree helped liven things up a bit. "Are you sure I can't take your coat?" she asked.

"I'm fine, thank you."

"How was your flight?" Hunter asked.

"Not bad once we finally got off the

ground."

"Yes, I understand there was quite a storm."

Really? Caroline thought. *We're talking about the weather?*

"We had to wait on the tarmac for more than two hours. They had to keep de-icing the plane. It was touch and go there for a while whether we'd actually take off."

Her voice was deep, almost husky, nothing at all like Lili's.

Caroline scanned Beth's face for anything that might connect her to the girl at her side, but found nothing that matched up. Their eyes were different colors, their noses different shapes. Beth's jaw was round and delicate whereas Lili's jaw was square and more sharply defined. Hunter's jaw. Caroline stole a glance at her former husband, wondering if he was thinking the same thing.

"The weather here is always so perfect," Lili was saying. "Sunshine every day."

"I would imagine that could get quite monotonous," Beth said.

"There are worse things," Hunter said with a smile.

"Yes," Beth agreed. "And, unfortunately, this is one of them."

So much for the weather, Caroline thought.

"Believe me, I understand how difficult this must be for you," she said.

"No more difficult than I'm sure it is for you. Having to relive such a painful time in your lives, having your hopes raised." She took a deep breath, releasing it slowly. "But they're false hopes. And it's just so unfortunate. You don't deserve this. You've been more than kind, more than understanding, listening to this nonsense, indulging Lili's fantasies . . ."

Caroline looked toward Lili. "I think she just wants to find out the truth. I think that's all any of us wants."

"The truth is that Lili is not your daughter," Beth said firmly. "I know that's not what you want to hear. I know that's not what you want to believe. I know you'd give anything if she were yours. And I know I'd feel exactly the same way if our situations were reversed. But I'm telling you — Lili is not Samantha." She forced Lili's face to hers, her fingers resting on Lili's chin, the chin that was situated in the middle of Hunter's jaw. "You are *my* child, *my* flesh and blood. And I'm sorry if you think I've failed you in some way . . ."

"You haven't failed me." Tears began streaming down Lili's cheeks.

"Then why are you doing this? Why are

you punishing me?"

"I'm not trying to punish you."

"Do you have any idea how insulting this is? That my own daughter questions my word? That she's all but called me a liar?"

"I'm not calling you a liar."

"Then stop this insanity right now and come home with me."

"Mrs. Hollister —," Hunter began.

"Come back to Calgary," Beth repeated, ignoring him. "Forget all this foolishness. These people are not your family. This man is not your father. This woman is not your mother. *I'm* your mother and I love you. You have to believe me. You are *my* child and I've loved you from the first moment I laid eyes on you."

"I love you, too."

Caroline felt an invisible hand reach into her chest and tear at her heart. The pain was so strong she almost cried out.

"Then get your things and let's get out of here. Please. Your brothers are very anxious. First their father dies, and then you take off without a word. They think they did something wrong. They miss you."

"I miss them, too."

"I know this past year has been hard for you. It's been hard on all of us since your father died. And maybe I haven't handled things very well. I know I've been impatient and angry a lot of the time, that I haven't given you the attention you need, the attention you deserve. I also understand that you're a big girl now, that you want more freedom, and I'll give you that freedom. I promise . . ."

"Mrs. Hollister . . ."

Beth swiveled toward Caroline and Hunter. "We've inconvenienced you quite enough already. I really can't thank you enough for your patience and hospitality. But things have gotten way out of hand. They've gone too far and lasted too long. And I have to insist that Lili and I leave here immediately." She rose to her feet, pulling Lili up with her.

Caroline was on her feet as well. "Beth, please. I know this whole episode is as unsettling, as surreal, for you as it's been for us. I understand your indignation, your outrage, your desire to return home as quickly as possible. But we're only talking about a few more days. Once we get the DNA results back from the lab, we'll know for sure . . ."

"I *already* know for sure."

"I don't," Lili said, wiggling out of Beth's grasp.

"Lili, for God's sake."

"I'm sorry," she cried. "I just can't go home with you. Not yet."

Caroline heard footsteps approaching and turned to see Michelle standing in the doorway, holding a tray with two mugs of steaming tea and a plate of shortbread cookies. She deposited them on the coffee table as everyone slowly sank into their former positions.

"Thank you, sweetheart."

Michelle squeezed into the chair beside her mother, then turned toward Beth. "Why are you really here?"

"Excuse me?"

"What do you want?" she asked. "What are you after?"

"Michelle, what are you doing?" Caroline asked.

"I don't understand," Beth said. "I think I've been very clear about what I want and why I'm here. I want this nonsense to end. I'm here to take my daughter home."

"You don't want money?"

"Money? No."

"You're not hoping to get some sort of book or movie deal out of this?"

"That's ridiculous."

"You're not interested in publicity, in having your fifteen minutes of fame?"

"Of course not."

"How about five minutes? You don't even want your name in the papers?"

"That's the last thing I want."

"Why? Do you have something to hide?"

"What?"

Caroline glanced toward Hunter, shocked to see a sly grin creeping into the corners of his mouth.

Michelle stood up and began pacing back and forth in front of the sofa. "Look, I was very skeptical when Lili first contacted my mother. I've been waiting for the other shoe to drop, the con to be revealed . . ."

"There is no con."

"I believe you," Michelle told Beth. "I really do. I saw your face when those reporters swarmed you outside. And I can see the love in your eyes when you look at Lili. You aren't faking. Nobody's that good an actress. So, I accept that this isn't some sort of sophisticated scam, that Lili is as genuine as she appears, that she truly believes there's a chance she could be Samantha. And as unlikely as I still think that is, and as firmly as you insist it isn't, I have to wonder why you're so anxious to spirit her away before the test results come back."

Beth was immediately on her feet. "That's it. I'm done." She fumbled inside her coat pocket, retrieving a small card along with her cell phone and calling the number listed on its front. "This is Beth Hollister," she said, her voice shaking. "I'm finished here a little earlier than I thought. Can you pick me up now? I'll meet you at the corner. Thank you."

"Please don't leave," Caroline said. "There isn't a flight to Calgary until morning. You can stay here . . ."

"That's not happening," Beth told her, her voice as flat as if it had been run over by a steamroller. She spun toward Lili. "I'll be at the Best Western Hacienda Hotel until tomorrow. Then I'm on the first plane home. I'm praying with all my heart that you'll come to your senses in time to be on that plane with me." She marched into the foyer, grabbing her overnight bag on her way to the front door.

"Mom?" Lili called, running after her. "Wait."

"Thank God," Beth whispered, wrapping Lili in a tight embrace.

Caroline watched them, holding her breath. Then she watched as Lili slowly extricated herself from Beth's firm grip.

"I'll call you as soon as the results come back," she said quietly.

Beth's face crumpled in a combination of resignation and disbelief. "I love you," she whispered. "Never forget that."

Then she opened the door, pushed through the phalanx of waiting reporters, and disappeared down the street.

Thirty-Two: The Present

Peggy called at one o'clock the next day. "I just had a call from the director of the clinic," she said without preamble. "He has the test results."

"The results are back?" Caroline asked, as if she might have misheard. "So soon?" Her heart started to flutter rapidly, as if a small bird were trapped inside her chest.

"He wants to know how you'd like to handle things."

"I don't understand."

"Apparently the media has been camped outside the clinic since seven A.M. He feels terrible because he suspects it might have been his receptionist who leaked the story, and he wants to make sure your privacy is protected."

"A little late for that, don't you think?"

"What's done is done," Peggy said, as pragmatic as ever. "The question is, what do you want to do now? He can courier the results over to you, or you can pick them up in person . . ."

Caroline's head was spinning. "I don't know what to do. There are reporters everywhere."

"What if *I* go?"

"What do you mean?"

"I can go to the clinic and pick up the report. Nobody's going to recognize me."

"You just can't leave work . . ."

"I'm the boss, remember? I have a meeting, but I can get away in about an hour. In the meantime you'd have to call the clinic and give Sid Dormer your permission. Tell his receptionist your name is Angela Peroni."

"Who?"

"It's his ex-wife's cleaning lady. He'll know it's you. You'll give him the okay; I'll pick up the results and bring them right over. Caroline? Caroline, are you there?"

"I'm here. Oh, God." She started laughing, although the sound that emerged was more of a crazed cackle. "It feels like we're in the middle of a spy movie."

"Are you all right?"

"I don't know. I wasn't expecting the results back so soon. I thought I'd have more time. Another day, at least."

"To do what?"

"I don't know. Prepare myself, I guess."

"You've been preparing for this for fifteen years," Peggy reminded her.

Caroline braced herself against the kitchen counter, her legs threatening to buckle under her. "What if it's not her?"

"Then we'll deal with it," Peggy said. "Look, the sooner I get to this meeting, the sooner I can leave, and the sooner we'll know one way or the other. Do I have your okay to pick up the results?"

"Of course you have my okay."

"Okay for what?" Michelle asked coming into the kitchen as Caroline was jotting down Dormer's number. She was dressed as if she was going to the gym, in black leotards and a white tank top.

"The test results are back," Caroline told her, punching in Dormer's number.

"Already? It's only been two days."

"Can I speak to Sid Dormer, please?" Caroline said into the receiver. "It's Angela Peroni."

"Who?" Michelle asked.

"Ssh. Hello, Mr. Dormer. Yes, it's most unfortunate about the media. I'm sorry, too. Peggy just phoned me. She says you need my permission in order for her to pick up the test results, so I'm giving it to you. Yes, thank you. She should be there in about an hour." She hung up the phone.

"God, this feels like something out of James Bond."

"What feels like something out of James Bond?" Lili asked from the doorway.

"The results are back," Caroline said as Lili turned a deathly white, her pallor a stark contrast to the dark blue of her denim shirt.

"The moment we've all been waiting for," Michelle said. "I'll call Dad." She reached for the phone, leaving messages for him at his office, at his home, and on his cell, telling him to get over there as quickly as he could. "Should I call Grandma Mary?"

"Let's wait," Caroline said. "There's no point in getting everybody all riled up until we know one way or the other."

"So what happens now?" Lili asked.

Caroline wondered how many times she'd heard that question these last few weeks, how many times she'd asked it herself. "Peggy is going to pick up the results in about an hour and bring them over. In the meantime, there's not much we *can* do. Except wait."

Michelle shrugged, broad shoulders reaching for her ears. "Looks like the gym is on hold. Scrabble, anyone?"

■ ■ ■ ■

"What kind of word is *ramet*?" Lili asked, studying the small wooden tiles Michelle had just laid across the Scrabble board.

"It's a word," Michelle answered.

"What's it mean?"

"I have no idea. But I don't have to know what it means. I just have to know it's a word."

"I've never heard of it."

"Are you challenging me?"

Lili looked across the kitchen table at Caroline, as if appealing to her to intervene on her behalf.

Caroline braced herself. It was never a good idea to challenge Michelle. About anything.

"What happens if I challenge you?" Lili asked.

"We look it up in the dictionary. If you're right, I lose a turn. If I'm right, you lose a turn."

"Okay, I challenge you."

Caroline reached for *The Official Scrabble Players Dictionary* on the table beside her, noting it was almost two decades out of date. How many new words had come into being since the last time she'd played

Scrabble? How many had been declared obsolete? "Here it is," she said, locating the word "ramet" between "ramentum" and "rami." "It means 'an individual plant of a clone.' "

"What does *that* mean?" Lili asked.

"Beats me."

"I'm right. It's a word," Michelle said. "You lose a turn." She beamed triumphantly.

Lili shrugged and Caroline smiled. Playing Scrabble had been a good idea, even though Michelle probably hadn't been serious when she'd suggested it.

"Your turn, Mom."

Caroline glanced down at her letters — two A's, each worth one point, a P, worth three, a Y, worth four, an E and an I, each worth one — then back at the board, stealing a look at her watch as she lifted the P from her rack. It was almost three o'clock. She wondered what was keeping Peggy. She should have been here by now.

"Mom?"

"Hmm?"

"You've been staring at that letter for five minutes. Are you going to do something with it or not?"

Caroline put the P down on a space that awarded her a triple-letter score, then followed it with an I, then an E and a Y on either side of the T Michelle had used to form "ramet," the Y landing on another triple-letter score. *"Piety,"* she announced. "That's nine points for the P, twelve points for the Y, and one each for the I, the E, and the T."

"Twenty-four," said Lili absently as Caroline's smile widened and Michelle's vanished altogether. "What?" Lili asked warily.

"You're good in math," Michelle said. "Of course you are."

"Not really."

"You don't have to try so hard." Michelle's frown shifted from Lili to Caroline. "She's already on your side."

"I'm not trying . . ."

"And you're not fooling anyone," Michelle said to her mother.

"What are you talking about?"

"I know what you're thinking."

"What am I thinking?" Caroline asked, genuinely perplexed.

"That this is the first of hundreds of board games the three of us will play together if your prayers are answered and it turns out that Lili is indeed Samantha. That this is what it's like to be a normal family." She leaned her head back and looked toward the ceiling. "Well, I hate to keep throwing a wet blanket over everything, I really do," Michelle continued, "but we're *not* a normal family. We haven't been a normal family for fifteen years. And we can't suddenly start pretending we are. *None* of what's happened is normal. And no matter what the test results show or how fervently you pray to a God who's obviously not there or Samantha would never have disappeared in the first place, it's never going to *be* normal." She stared at the words spread out across the Scrabble board. "And this is a stupid game." She swept the tiles off the board with the back of her hand, sending them scattering across the kitchen floor.

Lili was on her hands and knees immediately, scooping them up.

"Leave them," Michelle said. "It's my mess. I'll fix it."

"It's all right."

"I said *I'd* do it." Michelle quickly gathered up the remaining letters, slamming them on the table. "Told you I was a brat," she said, plopping back into her seat.

"No," Caroline said after a silence of several seconds. "You're right. This *isn't* normal. It's anything *but* normal. And this is clearly a very tense time. We're all a little on edge . . ."

"Really? Because you seem so calm."

"It's just my face."

"I'm really not very good at math," Lili said quietly.

Michelle's lips stretched into a reluctant grin. "Have you spoken to Beth since she got back to Calgary?" she asked, returning the Scrabble tiles to their small pouch.

Lili nodded.

"How is she?"

"The same. Upset. Angry. Sad."

Caroline pictured Beth as she'd seen her last night on the evening news, an obviously distraught woman shielding her face with her hands as she struggled to outrun the herd of reporters pursuing her.

Who are you? they'd demanded as she hurried toward the taxi idling at the corner. *What's your connection to Caroline Shipley? Can you tell us anything about what's going on in that house? Is it true there's a girl claiming to be Samantha?*

"Is she still being hounded by reporters?" Caroline asked.

"There was this one guy who followed her cab to the hotel. He even trailed her to the airport this morning, but she wouldn't talk to him."

Caroline didn't have to ask the reporter's name. She already knew.

The doorbell rang.

"Oh, God," Caroline whispered.

"Oh, God," echoed Lili.

"As if," Michelle said. "Someone going to answer that?"

Caroline took a deep breath and headed for the door, Michelle and Lili only steps behind.

"Open up, for God's sake," Hunter yelled from the other side as they approached.

Caroline quickly opened the door and Hunter shot inside, cameras clicking furiously behind him.

"Hunter," one reporter called. "Look this way."

"Can you tell us what's happening?" another demanded.

"Do you have the results back from the lab?"

Hunter slammed the door on their questions. "What's going on?"

"Where have you been?" Michelle asked, their questions overlapping. "I called hours ago."

"Meetings. What's going on?" he repeated.

"The results are back," Caroline said.

"You have the results?"

"Peggy's bringing them over."

"Do you know what they are?"

Caroline shook her head.

A line of perspiration broke out across

Hunter's forehead. "Okay. It's important to stay calm, no matter what the results show."

Caroline could see he was saying this as much for his own benefit as theirs. "Maybe we should sit down," she said, beckoning everyone toward the living room.

They were settling into their seats when they heard a car pull into the driveway, a door slam, and footsteps hurry up the front walk.

Caroline ran to the door and opened it, grabbing Peggy by the arm and pulling her inside the house, the reporters pelting the closing door with questions.

Can you tell us . . . ?

Is it true . . . ?

What's . . . ?

Caroline ushered her friend into the living room. Peggy wasted no time on unnecessary pleasantries. She withdrew a sealed white envelope from her brown leather bag and handed it to Caroline.

Caroline shook her head. "I can't. You open it."

"You're sure? Hunter?" Peggy asked.

"You do it."

Peggy tore open the envelope and removed the single sheet of paper. She scanned the page, then looked up at Caroline, her eyes filling with tears.

Caroline felt her entire body go numb. She knew that if the reporters waiting outside could see her right now, they would undoubtedly describe a seemingly calm, self-possessed woman with impeccable posture and an expressionless demeanor instead of a woman on the verge of total collapse, her stiffness the result of every fiber in her being struggling to keep her upright and in one piece. They wouldn't understand that if she were to release the breath she was holding tight inside her lungs it would rush out of her like air from a balloon, and she would twist violently off into space, gutted and empty.

She glanced from Peggy to Hunter to Michelle to the young girl who might or might not be Samantha. Ever since Lili's first phone call, Caroline had been cautioning herself not to get emotionally invested. She'd warned herself against letting her desire get the better of her common sense. But all that resolve had gone out the window the moment Lili appeared on her doorstep, and it had vanished altogether over the course of the last few days. Facts might be facts, but one of those facts was that she'd fallen in love. Emotions had firmly trumped common sense. One and one no longer made two. Even if the DNA tests proved conclusively that Lili was not her daughter, Caroline wasn't sure she could survive her loss.

So she stood silent, her body rigid and ramrod straight, her face a placid mask, waiting for Peggy to speak.

Thirty-Three: The Present

They were sitting on her bed, wrapped in each other's arms, watching the eleven o'clock news and trying to come to terms with everything that had happened since Peggy had torn open that sealed white envelope and changed their lives forever.

"Oh, God," Peggy had said, her eyes shooting from Caroline to Lili and then back to Caroline.

"What? Tell me."

"She's yours. She's Samantha."

What followed was a chorus of gasps, as tears of relief mixed with cries of disbelief. Shocked voices overlapped; bodies swayed, rocked, clung together, before ultimately collapsing under the sheer weight of those four words.

"I don't believe it."

"Are you sure?"

"Is it really true?"

"Let me see that."

"It can't be. There must be some mistake."

"It's here in black and white. Look for yourselves. There's no doubt."

"Oh, my God."

"It's you. It's really you."

"I don't believe it."

"Thank you. Thank you. Thank you."

"Are you absolutely positive?"

"My baby. My beautiful baby."

And then the voice of reality. As usual, Michelle's: "What do we do now?"

They'd called the police. The police promptly notified the FBI. They'd all come running, their arrival triggering a frenzy among the reporters still gathered outside.

"My name is Greg Fisher. I'm with the Federal Bureau of Investigation," the agent had informed the assembled media, standing outside Caroline's front door several hours later. "There has been a new development in the case of missing child Samantha Shipley. Please bear with us. We'll be holding a press conference at noon tomorrow. In the meantime, we ask that the family's privacy be respected."

Caroline had relayed to the authorities the events of the last several weeks — that she'd received a phone call from a girl calling herself Lili who lived in Calgary with her widowed mother and two younger brothers, that Lili harbored suspicions that she was really Samantha, that a dubious Caroline had flown to Calgary to meet her but Lili had failed to show, that last week she'd turned up on Caroline's doorstep, that they'd gone for DNA testing, that Beth Hollister had flown in from Calgary yesterday to take Lili home but Lili had refused to go and Beth had returned to Canada alone, that the tests had provided proof positive that Lili was indeed Samantha, the daughter who'd been stolen from her crib in Mexico some fifteen years earlier.

"She's yours," Peggy had said. "She's Samantha."

She's mine, Caroline had been repeating silently all day. *She's really mine.*

The FBI verified the results with the lab, then notified the Royal Canadian Mounted Police. The RCMP had, in turn, informed the Calgary police, who'd quickly arrested Beth Hollister and brought her in for questioning.

She'd been protesting her innocence ever since, even when confronted by the young girl she'd insisted so vehemently was hers. Caroline was still replaying their conversation in her head hours after the fact.

"How could you?" Lili had demanded of Beth when Greg Fisher finally allowed them to speak, their conversation relayed over speakerphone in her kitchen for Caroline, Hunter, and Michelle to hear.

"I didn't know. I swear," Beth replied tearfully.

"You swore you were my mother," Lili reminded her.

"I *am* your mother."

"You swore you gave birth to me. I asked you — how many times did I ask you? — if I was adopted. You said no."

"Because that's what your father insisted I tell you. Because he said it was better for all of us that way."

"Because he knew the truth."

"I don't know. I don't know."

"You *do* know. Stop lying to me."

Piece by piece, the truth slowly emerged: Beth and her husband had been trying unsuccessfully for years to have children of their own; one day Tim had come home with the news that he'd arranged for the private adoption of a toddler, an adoption that could come through at any time; they were living in Portugal when the adoption was supposedly finalized; her husband had immediately flown to the States to pick up their little girl, a child whose mother had purportedly abandoned her.

Lili was incredulous. "You weren't even a

little suspicious? A mother just happens to abandon her two-year-old daughter at the exact same time another two-year-old mysteriously vanishes from her crib in Mexico? The timing doesn't seem more than a little convenient? You actually believed it was a coincidence?"

"I didn't know anything about what happened in Mexico."

"It was all over the media. All over the world. How could you not know?"

"We were living in Portugal. I didn't speak Portuguese. I didn't read the international papers. We didn't even own a TV. I was pretty isolated. Your father brought home this beautiful little girl and assured me everything was legal. I had no reason to doubt him. He had all the necessary documents . . ."

"But at some point, you had to become suspicious," Greg Fisher had said from his seat at the kitchen table, his voice stopping just short of a sneer.

"I guess I knew something wasn't right," Beth admitted reluctantly. "But it's amazing how you can fool yourself when you want to. I wanted to believe that my husband wasn't lying, so I did. I wanted to believe that he hadn't . . ."

". . . stolen me from my crib in Mexico?"

"He didn't do that," Beth said with unexpected vehemence. "He was never in Mexico."

"Then he was working with someone who was," Greg Fisher said matter-of-factly. "Can you tell us who that might have been?"

Caroline's body tensed as Hunter leaned forward in his chair.

"I have no idea. Tim knew a lot of people . . . through his business. I'm ashamed to say they weren't all reputable."

"So at some point you *did* suspect I might be Samantha?" Lili interjected.

"Not until much later. We were living in Italy. I saw a newscast. I think it was the five-year anniversary of the kidnapping. They showed pictures of Samantha. It was pretty obvious. I panicked. I confronted your father, begged him to tell me the truth. He told me I was being ridiculous and to stop talking crazy, that talk like that would only arouse unfounded suspicions and we could end up losing you, even though he swore up and down you weren't Samantha. What choice did I have but to believe him?"

"Of course, since your husband passed away last year, we have only your word for all of this," the agent said. "Very convenient for you, under the circumstances, being able to put all the blame on a man who's no longer here to defend himself."

A muffled sob could be heard on the other end of the line.

"What made you return to the States?" Fisher asked.

"A combination of things. Tim's business . . . the boys . . ."

"You had two sons by then."

"Yes. Once we had Lili, I had no problem at all getting pregnant. Ironic, isn't it?"

"I'm sure the fact that ten years had passed was also a factor in your decision to come back. You assumed you were safe."

"I assumed my husband was telling me the truth."

"Is that why we moved to Canada?" Lili broke in, her voice an accusation. "Is that why we were homeschooled? Is that why we didn't have a computer, why our access to television was limited, why we moved every time we started making friends? Because you assumed Dad was telling the truth?"

"We arranged our whole lives around you. We did everything we could to protect you."

"To protect *yourselves,* you mean."

It was at this point that Caroline intervened in the questioning. "Why come to San Diego? You knew we'd gone for DNA testing. You knew what the results would show. Why would you keep insisting . . . ?"

"Because believe it or not, I was still clinging to the hope that Lili *wasn't* Samantha. And I thought if I could just get her to come home with me, she would put this silliness aside, and that even if the tests showed she *was* your biological child that it wouldn't matter, it wouldn't be enough to undo the fifteen years I spent raising her, loving her . . . I love you so much, Lili."

There was a second of silence.

"My name is Samantha."

A cry shot from Beth's lips like a bullet, traveling through the phone wires to pierce Caroline's heart. In spite of everything, for a moment she felt genuinely sorry for Beth. She knew what it was like to lose a child.

"Of course the minute I saw you with your parents and sister, I knew who you were," Beth continued. "Which just made me all the more desperate."

"What made you stay in Calgary?" Greg Fisher asked. "You could have taken your sons and disappeared. You had a lot of practice, and you had to know the police would be coming after you."

"Where would I go? How could I leave if there was even the slightest chance I might get my little girl back?"

The question lingered in the air even after the phone call ended.

"What's going to happen to her?" Lili asked. "Will she go to jail?"

"I don't know," Greg Fisher said. "Obviously, this is only the start of our investigation, and while I'm confident the Canadian authorities will cooperate thoroughly, it's been fifteen years, and we have no proof she's lying. We'll keep looking into things, of course. Maybe we'll eventually find out the whole truth of what took place that night. I'd certainly like to be there if and when that happens."

Hunter shook his head. "So we lose a child, our daughter loses a sister, our marriage falls apart, our lives are virtually destroyed, all because this woman wanted a baby and purposely ignored all evidence as to who that baby really was. And she gets away with it because it's been fifteen years, her husband is dead, and there's no proof she's lying."

"What matters is that we have Samantha back," Caroline said simply.

And suddenly she and Hunter were in each other's arms and he was sobbing on her shoulder. "I'm so sorry, Caroline. I'm so terribly, terribly sorry."

"I know."

"For everything."

"I know. Me, too." They cried together,

Hunter's tears wet against her cheek. For an instant, the years fell away. A miracle had brought their daughter back to them. Maybe another miracle could make them a real family again, albeit an extended one. She hugged him tight, inhaled his clean, soapy scent.

It was a scent she recognized all too well.

Caroline pulled out of his arms, understanding that he hadn't been in meetings when they'd tried to reach him earlier. *Some things never change,* she thought sadly. *No matter how many years pass.*

"What do we tell the reporters?" Michelle asked.

"Let me take care of that," Fisher volunteered. "I'll see you guys tomorrow." He handed Caroline his card. "Don't hesitate to get in touch with me anytime."

"Thank you."

Caroline's mother and brother arrived a short time after the police and federal agents had cleared out. "Samantha, darling," Mary cried, brushing past Michelle and enfolding the young girl in her tight embrace. "I knew it. Didn't I say right away it was you? Welcome home, darling. We have so much catching up to do."

"Hey," Steve said, inching forward. "What am I — chopped liver? Come on, sweetheart," he said, beckoning Samantha into his open arms. "Come to your Uncle Stevie."

A strangled cry escaped Michelle's lips as Steve hugged his long-lost niece.

"Don't be jealous, Micki," her grandmother said. "It doesn't become you."

"Mother, for God's sake," Caroline said. "This is hardly the time."

"She's no longer an only child," Mary argued. "She'll have to get used to it sooner or later."

"I should go," Hunter said. "Diana will be getting worried."

She has reason to be worried, Caroline thought.

"I'll come with you," Michelle said.

"You don't want to stay here?" Samantha asked.

"Nah. This is your night. You and my mother deserve some time alone together. I'll sleep at Dad's."

"I'll have her back first thing in the morning," Hunter said. "And if it's all right, I'd like to bring Diana and the kids along, introduce Samantha to her half brother and half sister before the press conference."

"There's a press conference?" Mary asked.

"At noon," Caroline told her.

"Let's hope it goes better than the last

one you gave."

A wry chuckle escaped Caroline's lips. "I think it's time you went home as well, Mother."

"What? We just got here."

"Yes. And now you're leaving."

Mary straightened her shoulders and opened her mouth, as if preparing to object.

"Caroline's right," Steve intervened. "We should go. It's been a very long day and I'm sure that Samantha is exhausted."

"I *am* tired," Samantha agreed.

"Then we'll clear out of here and let you get some rest. And who knows, maybe now that the pressure's off, you might actually start remembering things."

Once again, Mary embraced Samantha. "Good night, darling. Sleep well." She walked to the front door, opened it, and stepped outside.

"Can you tell us what's going on in there?" a reporter shouted.

"Don't ask me. I'm only the grandmother," Mary replied as Caroline shut the door after her.

"You can't let her upset you," she said to Michelle.

Michelle smiled. "Sure. Easy for you to say."

"I'll see you tomorrow."

"Goodbye, Mom."

"Good night, sweetheart."

"Good night, Samantha," Michelle told her sister. "Believe it or not, I really *am* glad you're back."

"See you tomorrow," Samantha said.

Caroline watched from the window as they climbed into Hunter's cream-colored BMW and drove away. "You hungry?" she asked Samantha when the two of them were alone.

"Starving."

"Too soon for another pizza?"

"It's never too soon for pizza."

They spent most of the night just staring at each other, as if they understood it was both too early and too late for words, that fifteen years of words had been lost and could never be recovered. After dinner they went upstairs and watched TV on Caroline's bed, listening to Greg Fisher on the eleven o'clock news as he announced there'd been a new development in the case of missing child Samantha Shipley and promising a press conference at noon the next day. "We should probably try to get some sleep," Caroline said, kissing Samantha's forehead. "It's going to be a big day tomorrow."

"Can I sleep with you tonight?" Samantha asked.

Silently, Caroline pulled back the covers and Samantha crawled beneath them. Then Caroline lay down beside her, watching her daughter sleep until morning.

THIRTY-FOUR: THE PRESENT

The press conference began at exactly twelve o'clock noon and was televised live around the globe.

It took place outside the main precinct of the San Diego Police Department. Caroline and Hunter sat in folding chairs on an improvised dais, Samantha between them. They faced at least a hundred reporters and photographers representing news outlets from across the country and beyond. Cameras zoomed in on their every gesture; tape recorders strained to capture each whispered aside. Conservatively dressed agents from the FBI stood behind them; uniformed officers surrounded them and kept overly enthusiastic camera operators from venturing too close. The chief of police approached the microphone that had been set up in the middle of the stage, waiting for the noise from the standing-room-only crowd to die down so that he could speak.

Caroline reached for Samantha's hand. "Are you okay?"

"I think I might be sick."

"I know how you feel."

"Really? You look so calm."

"I know," Caroline said. "I can't help it."

Samantha smiled, and several photographers immediately stepped forward to capture the moment, their cameras clicking furiously, like keys on an old-fashioned typewriter.

"Please take a step back," an officer warned.

"Take deep breaths," Caroline advised, inhaling and then exhaling, as if trying to lead by example.

"You're doing great," Hunter told them.

Caroline glanced toward her lap, her eyes surreptitiously scanning the crowd. She saw her mother and brother sitting in the first of more than a dozen rows of chairs, each row containing eight to ten seats, each seat occupied. Beside Mary sat Hunter's wife, Diana, with their two children, and behind them, Peggy and Fletcher.

One person was conspicuous in her absence.

"Where's Michelle?" Caroline had asked when Hunter and his new family arrived at the house earlier that morning.

"She was already gone when we woke up," Hunter said, seemingly unconcerned. "Left a note saying she was going to the gym. Said she'd head back here when she was done."

"Well, she didn't."

She still hadn't shown up by the time they were ready to leave for the police station. Caroline had left increasingly urgent messages on her voice mail. Michelle hadn't responded to any of them.

A dozen thoughts collided in Caroline's brain: Michelle had been far more upset than she'd let on; she'd slipped out of Hunter's house in the middle of the night, gotten drunk, borrowed a friend's car, been in an accident, gotten pulled over by the police, was sitting in a jail cell at this very minute, or worse, was lying in a ditch, unconscious and broken. Or maybe some lunatic had followed her, determined to add his own sick addendum to the news of Samantha's safe return . . .

"I don't see her," she whispered to Hunter now.

"Relax," he said, although a slight twitch above his right eye betrayed his own concern. "She probably just decided not to come."

I'll see you tomorrow.

Goodbye, Mom.

"Goodbye," not "good night."

Where could she have gone? Caroline was torn between anger and worry. Not that she blamed Michelle for wanting no part of this media circus. She didn't want to be here either.

She looked toward the police chief, an imposing middle-aged man in full dress uniform. She watched him tap the microphone, then clear his throat as the assembled gathering fell silent. She wondered again where Michelle could be.

"Ladies and gentlemen," the police chief began, "it is my privilege to be here today delivering this extraordinary news. As you're all aware, fifteen years ago a two-year-old girl named Samantha Shipley was stolen from her crib while the family was vacationing in Rosarito, Mexico."

While her parents were downstairs, *cavorting with friends,* Caroline added silently, recalling past headlines and imagining fresh ones.

"It's not every day such a case has the happy ending we've all been praying for, but today is one of those days. I'm thrilled to be able to report that Samantha Shipley has been found alive and well, and that she's here with us today."

A wave of excitement swept through the

crowd. Cameras clicked wildly as reporters jumped to their feet, their eager voices rushing the stage, like teenagers at a rock concert.

The chief of police raised his hands, pleaded for cooperation. "If you'll bear with me, please. Your questions will be answered shortly." After a minute, a strained silence resumed. "DNA tests have confirmed that the young lady behind me is Samantha Shipley, the missing daughter of Caroline Shipley and Hunter Shipley." He then introduced Greg Fisher, stiffly handsome in his navy blue suit and red-and-blue-striped tie, who supplied them with a quick overview of Samantha's fifteen years as Lili Hollister. He relayed much of what Caroline had told him the day before, detailing Lili's growing suspicions that she might, in fact, be Samantha Shipley, suspicions that brought her from Calgary, Alberta, to Southern California, culminating in her reunion with her birth parents. He admitted that the FBI knew very little at this time regarding the logistics of the kidnapping itself.

"Very little" being a euphemism for "nothing at all," Caroline decided. Again she scanned the crowd for Michelle. Again she saw nothing but the rapt faces of strangers.

"Samantha and her parents, Caroline Shipley and Hunter Shipley," Fisher continued, subtly acknowledging they were no longer part of the same unit even though they continued to share a last name, "have graciously agreed to come here today to answer your questions. I remind you that they are under no legal obligation to do so, and I would encourage you to be as polite and respectful in your questioning as possible." He turned toward them. "Please," he said, beckoning them forward.

Caroline, Hunter, and Samantha were greeted by thunderous applause as they rose from their seats and approached the microphone, tightly clutching one another's hands.

"How does it feel to have your daughter back?" one reporter called out immediately.

"How does it feel to be home, Samantha?" another shouted at the same time.

The questions proceeded fast and furiously:

"When did you first become suspicious that you were Samantha?"

"How did you go about getting in touch with Caroline?"

"Caroline, what were your first thoughts when Samantha contacted you?"

"Was your reunion everything you hoped

it would be?"

"Did you know instantly she was your daughter?"

"Do you prefer to be called Lili or Samantha?"

"What about your family back in Calgary?"

"Are you planning to stay in San Diego?"

"Caroline, have you spoken to Beth Hollister?"

"Do you have any plans to see her again?"

"What are your feelings toward her?"

"Would you like to see her go to jail?"

"Samantha, look this way."

"Hunter, over here. Big smile."

"Can we have a picture of the three of you embracing?"

"Samantha, do you remember anything about the night you were kidnapped?"

"Do you blame Caroline and Hunter for leaving you alone that night?"

"Do you think you'll ever find out what happened?"

"Caroline, do you feel you've been treated unfairly by the press?"

"Samantha, can we have a picture of you kissing your mother?"

"How do you feel about your parents' divorce?"

"Will you be living with your mother or

your father?"

And then suddenly, a familiar baritone floating above the crowd. "I don't see your other daughter anywhere. Is Michelle here?"

Caroline recognized the speaker immediately: Aidan Wainwright.

The word "bastard" was forming on her lips when Hunter squeezed her hand. "Michelle is a very private person," Hunter answered calmly. "She chose not to be here."

"Caroline, in the past you've described your older daughter as 'difficult,' " the reporter pressed. "Is she unhappy about her sister's return? Is that why she isn't here?"

Another squeeze of her hand, harder than the first. "She's not unhappy," Hunter said. "Just a little overwhelmed. As are we all."

"On that note," Greg Fisher said, "I think we'll call it a day." He waved off further questions. "I would remind you again that the Shipley family has been more than cooperative and ask that you give them the privacy they need and deserve. Any further queries you have can be directed to the police or the FBI. Thank you."

"I have something I'd like to add," Caroline said into the microphone, staring out at the assembled crowd.

"Of course," said Fisher, stepping back.

"Please. Go ahead."

Caroline looked directly at Aidan Wainwright, giving him her widest, most genuine smile. "Go fuck yourself, asshole."

And then the place went wild.

They arrived back at Caroline's to find at least a dozen reporters camped on the doorstep. "Way to go, Caroline," a female photographer called out as the police tried to shoo them away, first by appealing to their sense of decency, and when that didn't work, by posting an officer outside the front door and threatening to arrest anyone who set foot on the property.

"Michelle," Caroline called out as they stepped inside. "Michelle?"

"She's not here," Mary said as she and Steve followed Peggy and Fletcher into the foyer.

"Fuck," Caroline muttered.

"I think we've heard enough of that word for one day, don't you?" Hunter said, ushering everyone into the living room.

"I can't wait to see the headlines," Mary said.

"For what it's worth," Peggy said, "I thought Caroline was fabulous."

They tried Michelle's cell again. It went directly to voice mail. Hunter checked his landline at home, but there was no answer there either.

"Maybe we should call Greg Fisher," Caroline suggested.

"She probably just needs some time alone," Hunter said. "I think we should give her a few more hours before we bring back the FBI."

"I'll make coffee," Peggy volunteered. "And then I'm afraid I have to get back to work."

Caroline followed her into the kitchen. "Do you think I'm overreacting?"

"I think if anyone has a right to overreact, it's you."

"It's ironic, isn't it?"

"What is?"

"I've spent the last fifteen years obsessing about Samantha, wondering where she was, if she was still alive, if I'd ever see her again. And now I get her back, and Michelle disappears."

Do I have to disappear for you to love me?

"Caroline?" A small voice spoke from the doorway.

Caroline turned toward the sound. "Is this my fault?" Samantha asked. "Did Michelle go away because of me?"

"No, sweetheart. Of course not." Was Hunter right? Did Michelle simply need more time alone, time to digest all that had happened? Or were there other, more sinister forces at work?

Caroline sank into a kitchen chair, suppressing a shudder and trying not to imagine the worst.

At five o'clock, Michelle had yet to appear. "If we haven't heard from her by six, I'm calling Greg Fisher," Caroline told Hunter as he was heading out the front door behind his wife and kids.

"Hopefully that won't be necessary," he said.

She watched Diana making her way down the front walk, a baby in her arms, a small boy holding tight to her hand. "She's lovely," Caroline said, breathing in the remnants of Hunter's clean, soapy scent.

He nodded. "I've always had exceptional taste in wives."

"Yes. You're a very smart man." She watched a self-satisfied smile settle on his lips. "So try not to be so stupid this time."

Hunter's smile froze, then quickly thawed. "Guess I should be happy you didn't call me an asshole." He leaned in to give her a kiss on the cheek. "Call me when you hear from Michelle."

"Ditto," Caroline said, grateful he'd used

the word "when" and not "if."

She returned to the living room, where Samantha sat wedged between Steve and Mary on the sofa. "Am I the only one who's hungry?" Mary asked.

"Chinese?" Caroline suggested, realizing they hadn't eaten anything since breakfast. She was reaching for the portable phone on the coffee table when it rang. Caller ID identified the caller as the Marigold Hospice. "Hello?"

"She's here," Peggy said.

Thirty-Five: The Present

"I don't know why I didn't think of it sooner," Peggy was saying as Caroline burst through the front doors of the hospice twenty minutes later. "I keep forgetting she switched shifts. Mondays and Thursdays from four to eight. Of course she wouldn't miss it."

"Have you talked to her?"

"No. It's been a little frantic since I got here. One of the residents — Kathy — took a major turn for the worse. Apparently she's been very agitated all day and only calmed down when she saw Michelle, who's been with her ever since. I called you as soon as I found out."

"Where is she?"

"Upstairs. Room 205."

"Can I go up there?"

"Of course."

Caroline hugged her friend, then took the stairs two at a time. She slowed down when she reached the second floor, proceeding cautiously along the long corridor, the sound of piano music accompanying her. Room 205 was at the far end of the hall, past the open kitchen and dining area, and the so-called "great room" where the residents and their families could relax or watch TV. Right now, a middle-aged man and woman were sitting on the dark green leather sofa in front of the fireplace, engaged in quiet conversation, while a gray-haired woman played a selection of Christmas carols on the baby grand piano next to the window. In the corner, a beautifully decorated tree stretched toward the high wood-beamed ceiling.

Caroline realized she hadn't been here since Becky's death.

You want to know what I think? Caroline heard Becky say as she approached the closed door to room 205. *I think Samantha's alive. I think she's alive and beautiful and happy . . . I think whoever took her was just desperate for a baby . . . that she's being well cared for and loved.*

At least she had that to be grateful for, Caroline thought, regretting that Becky hadn't lived to see Samantha's safe return.

"Are you here to see Kathy?" a young woman asked. She had dark skin and close-cropped curly orange hair. The name tag clipped to her white nurse's uniform identified her as Aisha.

Caroline kept her voice low. "I understand that Michelle is in with her."

"Yes. Kathy's pretty low. It could be just a matter of minutes now."

"Excuse me, nurse," the woman who'd been sitting on the sofa said, approaching. "My brother and I were wondering if we could talk to you for a minute about our father."

"If you'll excuse me," Aisha said to Caroline.

"Of course." Caroline stood for a moment in silence, then took a deep breath and quietly pushed open the door to room 205.

Michelle was sitting to the right of the hospital bed, her back to the door, her hand clutching the skeletal fingers of the young woman lying in the middle of the bed. Classical music emanated from the radio on the nightstand. On the walls, at irregular intervals, were taped pieces of white paper bearing the words I AM BLESSED in large handwritten black letters.

I am blessed, Caroline repeated silently, deciding she should leave before Michelle saw her. Her daughter was safe. That's all she needed to know.

"Michelle," a soft voice cried out.

"I'm right here," Michelle answered. She reached over with her free hand to caress the young woman's forehead.

"You won't leave me?"

"I won't leave you."

"I'm afraid."

"I know. I'm here."

The young woman sighed, her breath rattling in the still air.

"Are you in pain?"

"No."

"Is there anything I can get you?"

"No. Just don't leave me."

"I won't. I'll stay right here."

"You promise?"

"I promise."

Tears filled Caroline's eyes and blurred her vision. Again, she tried to back away. Again, Kathy's voice stopped her.

"Michelle . . ."

"Yes?"

"What do you think happens after you die?"

"I don't know."

"Do you believe in Heaven?"

Caroline held her breath, waiting for Michelle's answer.

"Yes," Michelle said finally, "I do."

Caroline brought her hands to her lips to

prevent the cry she felt building in her throat from escaping.

"Do you think I'll go there?"

"There's absolutely no question in my mind."

"I haven't always been a good person. I've done things that God wouldn't like."

"We've all done things," Michelle said. "It's what makes us human and God . . . God."

"What do you think it's like? Heaven, I mean."

Michelle took a long, audible breath, her shoulders rising and falling with the effort. It was several seconds before she spoke. "I think Heaven is where the slate is wiped clean and all your past mistakes are forgiven," she began, her voice gaining strength and purpose as she spoke. "I think Heaven is the place where you become your best self, where you're everything you always wanted to be." She took another breath. "I think Heaven is the place where dreams come true."

"I like your Heaven."

"I do, too."

"Michelle . . ."

"Yes?"

"Thank you."

Michelle nodded.

"I'm going to close my eyes now."
"Okay."
"You won't leave me?"
"I'm right here. I promise."
The room fell silent. After a few minutes, Caroline watched her daughter release Kathy's hand and move to the red call button at the side of the bed. She pressed it, then resumed her seat, returning Kathy's hand to hers.
"What's happening?" the nurse whispered, coming up behind Caroline and pushing the door fully open. Michelle rose to her feet, her eyes connecting with Caroline's as Aisha walked briskly to Kathy's bedside and confirmed she was gone. "Thank you," she told Michelle as a second nurse entered the room. "You were wonderful. We'll take care of things from here."
"You *were* wonderful," Caroline echoed as her daughter stepped into the hall and closed the door behind her. She was still wearing her gym clothes.
"You've been eavesdropping again."
"Sorry."
"Don't be. You're getting pretty good at it."
"What you said to her was beautiful."
Michelle shrugged. "I don't believe any of it, you know. That stuff I said about

Heaven."

Caroline smiled. "It doesn't matter."

"I just told her what she wanted to hear."

"Whatever. I'm so proud of you."

Michelle shook her head. "Don't be." She turned and hurried down the corridor, through the great room, kitchen, and dining area to the stairs.

"Michelle, wait," Caroline called over the sound of piano music that trailed them down the stairs and into the main floor reception room. They stopped suddenly, both women temporarily startled by the sight of Caroline's face on the television screen above the fireplace. Even though the sound was off, the message she was delivering to Aidan Wainwright came through loud and clear.

"Guess that high road got a little lonely," Michelle said with a grin.

Caroline smiled. "I have to admit it felt great to get off it."

The volunteer receptionist, a tiny young woman whose pixie haircut took the edge off her very serious face, glanced from Caroline to the TV, then back to Caroline before blushing bright pink and burying her head in the book she'd been reading.

"Why weren't you there?"

"I'm sorry," Michelle said. "I was planning to come. Honestly."

"Where were you? We called and called."

"I went to the gym, worked out for a while. I had every intention of coming home and changing, going with you to the press conference. But, I don't know, I started walking and just kept going. I ended up in Balboa Park. I remembered you told me that you used to go there all the time . . . Anyway, I was just sitting there on one of the benches, trying to clear my head. I figured I still had plenty of time. When I finally checked my watch, it was almost noon. I knew I'd never make it home to change and get over to the precinct for twelve o'clock, so I didn't even try. Maybe that was my subconscious plan all along. I don't know. Instead I went to a sports bar and watched it on TV."

Caroline couldn't help being alarmed. "You went to a bar?"

"Don't worry. I just had a Coke."

"You had a Coke?" Caroline repeated, even more surprised. When was the last time Michelle had had a soft drink?

"And a whole bowl of peanuts. God — I'm so awful."

"You aren't awful because you ate a bowl of peanuts."

"That's not what I mean."

"You still aren't awful."

"I didn't go to the press conference . . ."

"Which ultimately worked out pretty well . . ."

"I didn't answer my phone. I knew it was you calling, but I let it go to voice mail."

"It doesn't matter."

"It *does* matter. The least I could have done was call."

"Okay, you should have called. Which makes you a little inconsiderate, but hardly awful."

"You don't understand."

"I understand that the girl I just watched comforting that poor woman upstairs may be many things — difficult included — but she is anything but awful."

"I'm so stupid . . ."

"You aren't awful and you aren't stupid." Caroline spun toward the receptionist. "Do you think you could give us a minute here, please?"

The volunteer immediately jumped out of her seat, breathed a big sigh of relief, and left the area.

"You're not stupid," Caroline said again.

"This is all my fault."

"*What* is your fault?"

"Everything."

"How can *anything* be your fault?"

"I was jealous and spiteful . . ."

"You were just being protective. Some girl calls out of the blue, says she's Samantha. You were right to be suspicious."

"I wanted her gone."

"That's only natural. It's going to take time to adjust . . ."

"I'm not talking about now," Michelle said.

Caroline felt her entire body go numb. She glanced from Michelle to the TV, saw herself standing ramrod straight in front of a microphone just prior to her outburst. MOTHER HURLS EXPLETIVES AT REPORTER scrolled across the bottom of the screen. "I don't understand. What are you saying?"

Michelle fell back against the nearest of the four overstuffed chairs. "I'm not talking about wanting Samantha gone *now,*" she repeated. "I'm talking about wanting her gone fifteen years ago."

A buzzer sounded, signaling that someone was at the front door, wanting to come inside.

Caroline felt seeds of panic sprouting in her chest. "What do you mean?"

The buzzer sounded again.

"Someone's at the door," Michelle said. "We have to let them in." She crossed over to the big red button on the wall by the front desk and pressed it, holding it down until the lock on the outside door released and a man and a woman stepped inside the glass foyer. Michelle held open the inner door into the reception area. "If you wouldn't mind signing in," she told the couple, who obliged without comment before heading down the main floor corridor.

"What are you talking about?" Caroline asked as soon as they were gone. "You couldn't have had anything to do with Samantha's disappearance."

"I resented her," Michelle said, her eyes brimming with tears. "She was so pretty and perfect. She never cried. She never did anything wrong. You'd get this dreamy look on your face whenever you saw her. Like you couldn't get enough of her. I remember wanting you to look at me like that, and thinking it would be so nice if she just went away . . ."

"You were a child. Just because you wished she'd disappear didn't give you the power to make it happen. You can't blame yourself . . ."

"You don't understand." Michelle shook her head in frustration.

"Then tell me. What am I missing here?"

"I was awake."

Caroline fell back against the desk as if she'd been struck. "What?"

"The night they took Samantha. I was awake."

"You were awake?" Caroline repeated, her brain struggling to catch up to her voice. "You know what happened? You saw who took her?"

Michelle's voice got very small, as if she were five years old again. "I don't remember what woke me up, whether I'd been dreaming, or whether I heard the door open and that's what woke me. I just remember lying in bed, and hearing someone moving around in the next room, and I was scared because, somehow, I knew it wasn't you. And they came into the room and I closed my eyes and pretended to be asleep. I felt someone brush past my bed and I opened my eyes just a tiny, tiny bit and I saw them take Samantha out of her crib and put her in some sort of carrying case. And then I closed my eyes again and kept them closed, even after I heard the door shut. I could hear the music coming from the restaurant outside, people laughing. I kept waiting for them to bring Samantha back. I didn't understand what was happening. Eventually I fell asleep. And next thing I knew, you were screaming."

Caroline fought to make sense of what she was hearing. "You saw someone take Samantha? Why didn't you tell us? Why didn't you say anything?"

"I did."

"What do you mean, you did?"

"Not to you. You were beyond hysterical. So was Daddy. He was yelling. Everybody was running around, shouting that Samantha was missing, and then the police came and the room was full of people. Your friends were there, and Uncle Steve and Becky, and people from the hotel. Everybody was talking at once. I was scared. I was confused. And . . . and . . ."

The volunteer receptionist suddenly reappeared, opening the glass door and poking her head slowly through the doorway, like a turtle cautiously emerging from its shell.

"Go away," Caroline said without so much as a glance in her direction.

The woman promptly withdrew.

"And then Grandma Mary came and took me home," Michelle continued without prompting.

"You told her," Caroline said, her voice flat. "You told your grandmother what you'd seen."

"She insisted it was all a dream, that I'd

been traumatized by what happened, that I was confusing fantasy and reality, and that I shouldn't say anything because it would only upset everyone even more. And time passed, and what can I say? I was a kid. Part of me was actually *glad* Samantha was gone. No more sweet little baby for everyone to fuss over. Just me. Somewhere in my twisted little five-year-old brain, I actually thought that with Samantha gone, I'd have you all to myself. So I pushed her out of my mind, convinced myself that Grandma Mary was right, that what I thought I'd seen was just a dream, a story I created after the fact, that what I saw happen hadn't really happened at all. At some point, I guess I just repressed the whole thing altogether. Until yesterday."

"What happened yesterday?"

"It all came rushing back. What I'd seen that night, what I heard. It wasn't a dream." Michelle stared at her mother. "I know what happened that night, Mommy," she said, a name she hadn't called her mother since she was a little girl. "I know who took Samantha."

Thirty-Six: The Present

It was after seven o'clock when they arrived home. They'd spent much of the last hour crying, their heads spinning from trying to make sense of the evening's revelations, but now their heads were clear and their eyes were dry. It was important to stay calm, to keep fury at bay. "You ready?" Caroline asked, turning off the car's engine and swiveling toward the girl in the seat beside her.

Michelle nodded.

Caroline gave her daughter's hand a reassuring squeeze. Then mother and daughter pushed open their car doors and exited the garage, cutting across the manicured lawn to the front door. A police car was sitting at the foot of the driveway, keeping the few still lingering reporters a respectful distance away. Hunter's BMW was parked a few houses down, just behind Steve's older-model Buick.

"Dad got here pretty fast."

Caroline nodded. She'd called from the car and told him to get his ass back to her house as quickly as possible.

"Get my ass back . . . ?" he was stammering as she disconnected the phone.

"Caroline," a reporter called out now, "do you have time for a few questions?"

"Anything you'd like to add to what you said earlier?" another shouted as she opened her front door and stepped inside.

She turned toward them. "Stick around."

"Stick around?" Hunter parroted from the foyer. "Did I just hear you tell a reporter to stick around?"

"Trust me," Caroline said. "This is worth sticking around for."

"You're back," Samantha said, joining them in the foyer, her relief at their safe return evident on her face.

"Can't get rid of me that easily," Michelle said, sniffing at the air. "What smells so good?"

"Grandma Mary ordered Chinese. There's lots left, if you want any."

"Shit."

"Is somebody going to tell me what's going on?" Hunter pleaded.

"In a few minutes." Caroline walked into the living room, noting the open cartons of

Chinese food and multiple empty beer bottles covering the coffee table. "As soon as everyone else gets here."

"Who else is coming?" Hunter asked.

"I invited a few more people," Caroline said. "Thought we should celebrate."

"Well, I wish you'd called and told me," Mary said from the sofa, where she was balancing a plate of food on her lap and struggling with a pair of wooden chopsticks. "I would have ordered more."

"That's all right. I don't think anybody's going to be too interested in eating."

"So," Steve said to Michelle as he reached over from his chair to pile some more noodles on his plate, "I understand you were at the hospice. I hear people are just dying to get in."

Michelle stiffened.

"Sorry. I guess you get that quite a bit," he said with a laugh.

"I'd like to see it sometime," Samantha said. "Maybe I could go with you one day."

"Sure."

"Are we really making small talk?" Hunter demanded. "Is that why I rushed over here like a lunatic? What the hell is going on?"

"I'm sorry," Caroline said. "It shouldn't be much longer."

"Who are we waiting for?"

A car door closed. Hunter crossed to the window. "I rushed over here for Peggy and Fletcher?"

"I thought they deserved to be here." Caroline walked to the door and beckoned them inside.

"Welcome," Mary greeted them. "Help yourselves to some Chinese."

"Thank you," Peggy said, looking anxiously around the room, "but no thanks."

"None for me," Fletcher said.

"A beer?" Steve held up a freshly opened bottle. "For some reason I'm getting the feeling that a little alcohol might be a good idea." When both Peggy and Fletcher declined, he took a swig himself.

"Is that everyone?" Hunter asked.

"Not quite."

"For God's sake, who else is coming?"

As if on cue, another car pulled up outside. "Sit tight, everyone," Caroline said, heading for the front door and returning moments later, the latest arrivals in tow. "I think you know almost everyone," she said.

"You gotta be kidding me," whispered Hunter.

"Well, look who's here," Steve said, setting down both his beer and his plate of food and rising to his feet.

"Do I know these people?" Mary asked.

"I don't think you've ever actually met," Caroline said. "Mother, meet Jerrod and Rain Bolton. They were with us in Mexico. I believe they'd already left by the time you arrived."

"Very nice to meet you," Jerrod said, managing to sound as if he meant it. He smiled nervously at Caroline.

"And of course you remember Peggy and Fletcher." Caroline smiled at Rain. She was wearing jeans and a mauve sweater, both of which were several sizes too small. Her hair still hung in long blond waves past her shoulders, as if she were auditioning for a part on one of those *Real Housewives* shows. But despite a face-lift that had rendered her once-lovely face almost immobile, her discomfort was obvious. There was a panic in her eyes that no amount of Botox could disguise.

"You probably don't recognize Michelle," Caroline told them.

"Oh, my God," Jerrod said. "Little Michelle."

"You're so grown up," Rain said.

"It happens," said Michelle.

"And this is Samantha."

"Samantha, my God," Jerrod said. "I watched you on TV this afternoon. Could *not* believe my eyes."

Rain released a long, deep breath, said nothing.

"I heard you two were separated," Hunter said.

"We are. Thanks, in part, to you," Jerrod acknowledged with a grin. "But when the FBI suggests a reunion, one is hard-pressed to say no. Especially when they send a car to pick you up."

"The FBI?"

"That would be me," Greg Fisher said, entering from the foyer, where he'd been waiting.

"What's he doing here?" Steve asked.

"He said he'd like to be here if we ever found out the truth about what happened the night Samantha disappeared. I thought it was only right to oblige."

"What are you talking about?" Hunter asked. "We don't know what happened."

"You remembered something?" Steve asked Samantha.

"Please, everyone," Caroline directed. "Have a seat."

Rain squeezed herself in beside Mary, Peggy, and Fletcher on the sofa, while Jerrod helped Greg pull a few chairs in from the dining room. Steve sank back into the chair in which he'd been sitting as Hunter lowered himself into its counterpart and Samantha balanced on one of its wide arms. Only Caroline and Michelle remained standing.

"I still don't understand what Jerrod and I are doing here," Rain said.

"I thought it might be helpful to re-create that night," Caroline told her.

"How can that be helpful?" Steve asked.

"I think we should start with a brief recap of that week," Caroline went on. "Just to refresh our memories. Make sure we agree on the basic facts. So that we understand exactly how it all played out."

"How *what* played out?" Fletcher asked.

"Samantha's kidnapping."

There was a moment's silence.

"This is absurd," Steve said.

"You all got to Rosarito before us," Caroline said, ignoring her brother's remark. "I remember being so surprised to see you. And a little disappointed, if I'm being honest. I'd been hoping to spend more alone time with Hunter, and I was frankly a little shocked by whom he'd chosen to invite. I could understand Peggy and Fletcher. Peggy's been my best friend since forever. But Jerrod and Rain, well, we weren't particularly close friends. Of course, I didn't realize you were sleeping with my husband at the time, Rain . . ."

"Really? Is this necessary?" Rain glanced toward Hunter, who refused to meet her gaze.

"And as for you and Becky," Caroline continued, looking at her brother, "well, as I recall, Hunter told me the whole surprise thing had been your idea, that you'd more or less invited yourselves along. But Becky and I hadn't been close in some time."

"She was always jealous of you," Mary said.

"Mother, please," Steve said. "The poor woman is dead. Can we let her rest in peace?"

"No," Caroline answered. "I don't think we can do that."

Another moment's silence.

"What are you saying?" Steve asked.

"That our mother is right. Becky *was* jealous of me. She resented my supposedly stable marriage, my ease at having children, my so-called 'perfect' life. And that when the opportunity presented itself . . ."

"You think she's the one who took Samantha?" Peggy interrupted. "How is that possible? How could she have pulled that off?"

"Think about it. I lost two keycards that week. I assumed I dropped them or left them lying around, but Becky could easily have taken at least one of them. She had plenty of opportunity. She was with us all the time. And don't forget, it was a woman who called and canceled the sitter the night Samantha disappeared."

"This is crazy," Steve protested. "These are wild suppositions. You have no proof that Becky took your keycard or canceled the sitter. Frankly, I'm astounded at your leaps in logic. You're the math teacher. Where's your proof?"

"I have absolute proof that Becky was involved," Caroline stated.

"What kind of proof could you possibly have?" Disbelieving eyes shot toward Samantha. "Are you saying you remembered something?"

"Not Samantha," Michelle said. "Me."

"You?"

"I saw Becky."

"You saw her? When? Where?"

"In our suite. In my bedroom. I saw her lift Samantha out of her crib."

There were collective gasps from around the room.

"How could you have seen anything?" Rain asked. "You were asleep."

"I wasn't."

"You were awake?" Hunter said, his voice barely audible.

"I saw everything."

"This is unconscionable," Steve protested. "It was fifteen years ago. You were a child. It was dark. Even if you *were* awake, who knows what you really saw?"

"*I* know what I saw."

"And you kept quiet about it for fifteen years?"

Michelle looked toward her grandmother. Her grandmother looked toward the floor. "I repressed it . . ."

"You repressed it? How convenient."

"Steve . . ."

"For God's sake, Caroline. To do something like that, Becky would have had to more than resent you. She'd have had to hate you. You visited her in the hospice. You saw how much she cared about you. Do you really think she was capable of doing what you're accusing her of?"

"I don't think she hated me. I *do* think she was desperate and probably more than a little afraid."

"Desperate about what? Afraid of what?"

"In the hospice, she kept apologizing," Caroline continued, ignoring Steve's questions, "telling me how sorry she was. I assumed she was talking about our estrangement, how she hadn't been there for me after Mexico. But now I realize she was talking about her part in the kidnapping."

"Her part in the . . . What are you . . . ?" Steve rose from his seat, then sat back down, throwing his hands in the air. "Will you just listen to yourself? Do you hear what you're saying?"

"I know exactly what I'm saying."

"That your former sister-in-law, my ex-wife, kidnapped your daughter. That's what you honestly believe?"

"She *knew* Samantha hadn't been taken by some pervert. She *knew* she was alive. She told me as much, said she was certain Samantha was with people who loved her . . . I thought she was just trying to give me hope. But now I know she was trying to tell me the truth."

"The truth? She had a brain tumor. She didn't know what she was saying half the time."

"And you took care of the other half, didn't you?"

Another silence. Another collective intake of breath.

"Excuse me?"

"Keeping her stoned, staying by her bedside every minute. I always thought it was so strange, your sudden turnaround when Becky came back to town. You were so miserable to each other when you were married. You didn't speak after your divorce.

When I think of the vile things you said about her . . . And then she gets a brain tumor, comes back to San Diego, and checks into Peggy's hospice. And calls *you,* of all people. Do you want to know why I think she did that?"

"By all means," Steve said. "Enlighten me."

"I think she was going to come clean about what happened and she wanted to give you fair warning. She told me she owed you that."

"Why would I need fair warning?"

"Because you were there with Becky. Because taking my daughter was your idea."

"Oh, my God," Peggy whispered into the stunned silence that followed.

"Now you're accusing *me*?" Steve jumped to his feet. "You know what? I've had enough of this crap . . ."

"Sit down," Greg Fisher told him in no uncertain terms.

"This is absurd," Mary sputtered.

"You knew," Caroline said, spinning toward her.

"What? I knew no such thing."

"Michelle told you what she saw."

"A five-year-old child told me what she *dreamt,*" Mary insisted with such vehemence Caroline almost believed her. "She was confused. She was hysterical. There was no way your brother had anything to do with what happened that night. I didn't believe it then. I certainly don't believe it now."

"It was Uncle Steve, Grandma. I saw him."

"You imagined it."

"No."

"This is preposterous. Why would he do such a thing?"

"My guess?" Caroline asked. "He needed money. Isn't that what these things usually come down to? He's a gambler. Becky had lost her job. He was strapped for cash."

"You're crazy," Steve said. "The real estate market was booming in those days. I was making a fortune in commissions."

"And losing it just as fast. What happened, Steve? You bet on the wrong horse? You owe the wrong people money? They threaten you? You offer them something in trade? Ultimately convinced Becky to go along with you or risk being the target of a mob hit?"

"A mob hit?" Steve laughed. "I think you've been watching way too much TV."

"I think you'd been planning this for quite a while, that you bided your time, waiting for the right opportunity."

"And I think you're forgetting a little something," Steve said, turning around in hapless circles, as if appealing to everyone's better judgment. "I was with you guys when Samantha was taken."

"No," Caroline said, shaking her head. "You weren't."

"Yes, he *was,*" Rain said. "We were all together. Except for Becky. She'd gone to her room with a headache."

"And then *you* left to check on the kids," Peggy said to Caroline.

"And when I came back, you were gone," Caroline said to her brother.

"I went back to our room to try to convince Becky to rejoin the party. All of you . . . you know that. It wasn't my idea to go back, but you were giving me such grief about it . . ."

"Yes, we played right into your hands, didn't we? Except you didn't go back to your room because you knew Becky wasn't there. She was waiting for you in the lobby, or wherever it was you'd arranged to meet. All you had to do was wait for me to check on the kids and leave."

"Your timeline is all wrong," Steve insisted. "You're forgetting I was with you when Hunter came back from checking the kids at nine-thirty."

"Except he didn't check on them," Caroline said.

"That's right," Jerrod concurred. "He was too busy screwing my wife."

"Do we have to keep harping on that?" Rain asked.

"You saw Hunter in the hallway," Caroline reminded her brother. "You told me so yourself. You realized then he hadn't checked on the kids."

"Which proves only that Hunter was a liar, not that I'm a kidnapper."

"Which proves you had both the time and the opportunity to kidnap Samantha."

"So you're saying that Becky and I stole Samantha from her crib and then . . . what? What exactly did we do with her?"

"You put her in some kind of carrying case," Michelle said. "A man was holding it. He'd been standing in the doorway. I couldn't see his face. He closed the bag and walked away."

"You're out of your mind."

"Everything worked exactly according to plan. Even better, actually," Caroline continued. "You thought you had half an hour to steal Samantha and spirit her out of the country. Turned out you had twice that."

"How would I know for sure you'd leave the kids alone?"

"You didn't. But you knew Hunter. You knew he'd arranged a special surprise for that night because, once again, that surprise was your idea. You knew he'd probably be able to persuade me."

"That's a whole lot of probability. Again, where's your proof?"

"Come to your Uncle Stevie," Michelle said in a tiny voice.

"What?"

"That's what you said when Aunt Becky lifted Samantha out of her crib and handed her over to you. You said, 'Come to your Uncle Stevie.' The same thing you said to her yesterday. That's when it all came back to me. That's when I knew for sure it was you."

The room fell silent.

Steve's eyes shot to Greg Fisher. "This is wild speculation. Surely you don't believe this garbage. They have nothing —"

"They have an eyewitness," Fisher said, smiling at Michelle. "She sounded pretty credible to me." He reached into his pocket for his cell phone, pressed a series of numbers, and spoke softly into it. "There are agents waiting outside," he told Steve, taking his elbow and leading him to the door. "You might want to contact an attorney."

"You're not actually going to arrest him," Mary protested, following them outside.

The rest of them remained rooted to the spot, unable to move, barely able to breathe.

"What just happened?" Jerrod asked as the front door slammed shut.

Caroline sank to the floor beside the Christmas tree. Her eyes darted from Hunter to Peggy and Fletcher, to Jerrod and Rain, their shocked faces reflecting their attempt to make sense of everything they'd just heard. Michelle and Samantha sat down on either side of her, holding tight to her hands.

"Did I tell you that Jerrod got us tickets for *Dance with the Devil*?" she heard Rain ask, her voice reaching across fifteen years, transporting Caroline back through time.

Caroline closed her eyes and watched that night unfold behind her eyelids, as if it were a movie she'd seen before. Only this time she was playing all the parts.

THIRTY-SEVEN: FIFTEEN YEARS AGO

"Did I tell you that Jerrod got us tickets for *Dance with the Devil*?"

"What's that?" Caroline snuck a glance in the direction of her suite and then at her watch. She pushed away what was left of her lobster dinner, which was most of it. She was too nervous to eat. It was almost time to check on the kids.

"They were fine when I checked on them thirty minutes ago," Hunter whispered. "They're fine now. Finish your meal."

"*Dance with the Devil?* It's only the hottest show on Broadway. It's impossible to get tickets, especially on Thanksgiving weekend. But Superman here managed to do it." Rain threw a proprietary arm across her husband's shoulders, sneaking a smile in Hunter's direction.

"So you'll be spending Thanksgiving in New York," Becky said. "Lucky you."

Rain smiled. "What are you guys up to?"

"My mother always has Thanksgiving dinner at her place," Steve said, providing Becky with the perfect opening, and wondering if she'd take it. She'd been vacillating all day, threatening not to go through with their plan.

"You can just imagine how much I'm looking forward to that," Becky said, following Steve's lead. She knew what was at stake, that the men her husband was dealing with weren't the type to look kindly on a sudden change of heart. One man was already here in Rosarito, having flown in by private plane earlier in the day, and was at this very minute waiting patiently in the lobby with the special carrying case he'd brought in which to hide Samantha.

You don't piss these people off, Steve had warned her.

Still, she wasn't sure she could go through with it. No matter how hard she tried to rationalize what they were about to do, no matter how many times she told herself she had no choice, that Steve's reckless gambling had put both their lives in jeopardy, no matter how many times she told herself that Caroline would survive the loss of her child — she still had one healthy little girl; she could always get pregnant again; Samantha was going to a loving home; Caroline's perfect, fairy-tale existence could use a cold shower of reality — she didn't know whether she was capable of inflicting such pain on a woman with whom she'd once been close.

Still, what choice did she have?

Steve glared at his wife, silently urging her to keep it simple. It was important that they start slow and build. Their spat had to sound like just another one of their endless arguments. Which should be easy. It seemed that all they did anymore was fight. "Let's not start."

"Stop looking at your watch," Hunter told Caroline. He checked his own watch, feeling a stirring in his groin at the thought of his upcoming tryst with Rain. It was accompanied almost immediately by an unwelcome stab of guilt. Not at the affair itself. He'd been having casual, meaningless flings for years. This one was no different except for the added frisson that it was taking place right under his wife's nose. But this was his anniversary, for heaven's sake. Surely he owed it to Caroline not to betray her tonight, of all nights. Still, she'd thought little of almost canceling the dinner and had spent most of the evening worrying about the kids. They were her first priority, not him.

"You know what my darling mother-in-law said to me last Thanksgiving?" Becky asked, warming to the charade. At least she got to vent. "She'd just been to a funeral and I made the mistake of asking how it had gone, and she said, and this is a direct quote: 'It was a lovely affair. Her daughter selected a beautiful coffin. Much nicer than the one you had for *your* mother.' "

Steve bristled, despite the charade. Did she really have to bring that up again? "I assure you," he protested, "she said no such thing."

"That's exactly what she said."

"You're exaggerating. As usual."

"And you're defending her. As usual."

"So, what are we all thankful for?" Peggy interrupted, trying to keep their argument from mushrooming out of control. It was her best friend's anniversary. Could Steve and Becky not manage even one evening without a fight? "Come on. Three things, not including health, family, or friends. We'll just assume you're thankful for those."

"Never assume," said Becky. *Oh, God. Can I really go through with this?*

"Oh, this is fun." Rain clapped her hands. "Can I start?"

Peggy indicated the floor was hers, suddenly grateful for Rain's presence. A normally positive person who made a concerted effort to find something admirable in everyone, Peggy had been struggling all week with her feelings for Rain, feelings that veered from mild amusement to strained impatience to active dislike. The truth was that she just didn't trust her. There was something sneaky about her, the way her compliments always carried the sting of a slap. "Kidding on the square," her mother used to call it. Still, it was nice to know you could count on Rain for something. In this case, that something was glomming onto anything that provided her with the opportunity to talk about herself.

"Well, first, obviously, I'm thankful we'll be spending Thanksgiving in New York and not at some horrid family function, no offense intended. Second, I'm thankful for the new necklace Jerrod bought me. And third, I'm thankful gray hair doesn't run in my family. Your turn." She smiled at Caroline.

"I'm thankful for this past week," Caroline said. "I'm thankful to be celebrating ten years of relative wedded bliss."

"What do you mean, *relative*?" Hunter asked. What kind of a dig was that?

"I'll drink to *relative,*" Jerrod said, raising his glass in a toast, and thinking it would be a miracle if he and Rain made it to their tenth anniversary. He suspected she was already getting restless. Hence, Thanksgiving in New York. Hence, the expensive diamond sparkler around her neck.

"Go on," Peggy said. "One more thing you're thankful for."

"I'm thankful for the ocean."

"Seriously?" Rain asked.

My sentiments exactly, Steve thought. *The ocean? That's exactly the sort of sappy thing Dad would have come up with. And what a loser he was.* "I'm thankful the San Diego real estate market is so strong." *Not fucking strong enough, mind you. Never strong enough.* "I'm thankful I was able to persuade Hunter to let us join you here in beautiful Rosarito to help you celebrate." *I can't wait to get the hell out of here.* "I'm especially thankful that my mother is such a great cook." He narrowed his eyes across the table at Becky. *The ball's in your court,* his eyes said.

"You're so full of shit," Becky said obligingly.

"Is our mother not a great cook?"

"Our mother is indeed a great cook," Caroline said. "And you are also full of shit."

Everybody laughed.

And you are so fucking smug, Steve

thought. *Let's see how smug you are later on tonight.*

Becky noted the anger that flashed through Steve's hazel eyes, like a sudden bolt of lightning. He'd always been scornful of his older sister, minimizing her accomplishments and belittling her comfortable lifestyle, but it was only lately that Becky had come to realize his enmity went far deeper than that.

He'd always been their mother's favorite, told his entire life that he was the special one, that all he had to do was smile that killer smile and the world was his for the taking. Except it hadn't quite worked out that way. His charm had carried him only so far before people started expecting more. They wanted a glimpse behind the killer smile and were inevitably disappointed to find there wasn't much there. He'd failed at everything he tried, probably because he never tried very hard. In fact, in his most recent incarnation as a real estate agent, when times were so good that all you had to do was show up in order to collect a six-figure commission, he couldn't be bothered doing even that. Soon sellers took their business to other agents; buyers went elsewhere. Commissions dwindled. What little money he made, he gambled away. His mother had always been there to bail him out, but even she couldn't help him this time. They were in debt up to their eyeballs. They owed money to everyone, people who would gladly wipe that killer smile right off his face.

And here was Caroline, his beautiful, boring sister, a high school math teacher, for God's sake, quietly going about her business, and she seemed to have all the answers. How the hell had that happened?

Becky rubbed her forehead. She was getting a headache. She'd had a lot of them lately. Probably the stress of a bad marriage combined with the more recent stress of what she was about to do. Could she really follow through with their plan? Could she really be part of something so horribly evil?

"Your turn, Becky," Rain said.

"I'm sorry, everyone. I've had this terrible headache all afternoon, and it seems to be getting worse." Tears filled Becky's eyes, and she made no move to hide them or brush them aside. She rose to her feet. "If you'll excuse me," she said, pushing back her chair and getting to her feet.

"Oh, sit down," Steve said. "You're fine. Don't be such a prima donna."

"Fuck you." Becky turned and stomped away.

Well played, Becky, Steve thought, watching her leave. He needn't have worried. Maybe they weren't so ill matched after all.

By the time she reached the lobby, Becky's eyes were dry. She stationed herself behind a large floral arrangement that afforded her a sweeping view of the area. Now all she had to do was wait.

"Shouldn't you go after her?" Fletcher asked Steve.

"What — you think I'm as crazy as she is?"

"I should go check on the kids," Caroline said.

Hunter stood to kiss her cheek. "Hurry back."

"Oh. So sweet," Rain said. *Gag me with a spoon,* she thought.

Caroline was more than happy to get away. Her anniversary celebration was proving something less than celebratory. Rain was getting on her nerves and Hunter seemed distracted. Plus she was worried not only about the girls but about her brother and Becky as well. That they thought nothing of fighting in public was obviously not a good sign. She doubted their marriage would survive the year.

She proceeded to the elevators, unaware that Becky was watching from behind one of several huge arrangements of colorful fresh flowers. She got off the elevator at the sixth floor and hurried down the hall, hearing her children's imaginary cries leaking through the walls. But when she opened the door to her suite, she heard only the reassuring hum of silence. A quick check proved the girls were sleeping soundly in their beds. *Hunter was right,* she thought. *I've been silly to worry.*

"You really think I should go after her?" Steve asked soon after his sister had left. He couldn't afford to leave the table too early. Nor could he afford to wait too long. The timing was critical if they were going to pull this off.

"I'd go, if I were you," Fletcher said.

"Remind her we're supposed to be celebrating," Peggy added.

"Just say you're sorry and get it over with," Jerrod advised. "Remember — happy wife, happy life."

"Fine." Steve pushed back his chair and stood up. "I'm doing this for you guys." He walked into the lobby, nodding first toward Becky, then toward a balding man in casual attire who was sitting unobtrusively in a large wicker chair. The man was perusing a brochure, a large carry-on bag at his feet.

What the hell is taking Caroline so long? Becky wondered as time dragged on and

Caroline still hadn't returned. All she had to do was check on the girls and leave. Unless one of the girls had awakened, and then all bets were off. What would they do then?

What the hell is she doing up there? Steve was also thinking, pretending to use the house phone while keeping an eye on the bank of elevators nearby. He could feel the balding man's eyes burning a bullet-sized hole in the back of his beige linen shirt. If she took too long, Hunter was liable to get anxious and go up there himself. And then where would that leave them?

Which was when the elevator doors opened and Caroline emerged. She looked straight ahead as she cut across the lobby to the restaurant. As soon as she was out of sight, Steve headed for the elevator, Becky and the balding man following casually after him. Becky got into the first elevator, Steve and the balding man in the one beside it. They proceeded individually down the sixth-floor corridor, Becky the first one to arrive at the suite. She pulled out the keycard she'd lifted from Caroline's purse earlier in the week and unlocked the door.

It was dark in the living room and Becky almost tripped over the coffee table. "Shit," she muttered.

"Ssh," Steve warned, bringing his fingers

to his lips for emphasis.

Ssh yourself, Becky thought, as she followed her husband into the girls' bedroom. The man with the carry-on bag waited by the bedroom door.

Becky moved quickly to the crib, relieved to note that Michelle was all but buried underneath her bedsheets, and that Samantha was sleeping peacefully on her back. She reached in and gingerly scooped the toddler into her arms, cradling her head beneath her chin. Samantha made a gurgling noise but didn't wake up. She was so soft, so sweet, Becky thought, swaying back toward the crib. It wasn't too late. She could still put the child back and no one would be the wiser.

It was at that moment she heard her husband's hoarse whisper.

"Come to your Uncle Stevie," he said, prying Samantha out of his wife's arms and carrying her quickly to the man waiting by the bedroom door. He lowered the toddler into the carry-on bag and watched as the man snapped the bag shut and hurried down the hall.

The whole enterprise took less than five minutes.

"Oh, God," Becky whispered. "What have we done?"

"Shut up," Steve told her. "It's over."

They waited a few more minutes, until they were certain the man had departed the premises, and then they left the suite, taking separate elevators down to the lobby and then returning to their room in the other wing.

"What do we do now?" Becky asked, lowering herself to her bed, her head pounding.

Steve checked his watch. Soon it would be Hunter's turn to check on the kids. Then all hell would break loose.

"I should go check on the kids before dessert gets here," Hunter was saying.

"And I need a sweater," Rain announced, patting her chest. "The girls are getting chilly."

Caroline watched her husband and Rain go their separate ways at the entrance to the restaurant.

Except, of course, they didn't go their separate ways at all. Hunter doubled back, meeting Rain at the elevators that serviced her wing of the hotel. He'd look in on the kids later, assuming he had time. If not, so be it. They'd been checking them every half hour all night. And for what? Nothing was going to happen to them. He'd already left

Samantha alone this afternoon for twenty minutes while she was napping and she'd been just fine. Not that he'd told Caroline about it. How could he, after all, when he'd been with Rain? Luckily, he'd had time to take a shower before she came back. Besides, she was being unreasonable and overprotective. If she wasn't careful, she'd turn into her mother. Which wasn't fair, he knew, even as he was thinking it. Caroline was absolutely nothing like her mother. But it made him feel better, a little less guilty, to think ill of her, to pretend that his betrayal was at least partly her fault.

"Come here, you," Rain said as the elevator doors closed. Immediately her hands were at the zipper of his pants.

"Whoa," Hunter cautioned, grateful there were no cameras in the elevators. Or anywhere in the hotel, for that matter, which made sneaking around that much easier. "We have to be careful. What if we run into Steve or Becky?" They'd thrown a definite monkey wrench into his plans with their abrupt and unscheduled departure.

"Fuck them," Rain said with a laugh. "We'll think of something. I've been waiting to get my hands on you all night. I'm not waiting any longer."

Hunter almost laughed at the urgency in

her voice, and was ashamed to find himself so excited.

She already had his jacket halfway off by the time they reached her room. "You are so damn sexy," she told him, tugging at his pants and falling to her knees.

He wished she'd shut up. That was her problem, he was thinking as she guided him toward her mouth. She talked too damn much.

"Come to Mama," she said.

And then mercifully, she was silent.

"I don't get it," Steve said, looking from his watch to the clock beside their bed. "Hunter should have discovered Samantha missing by now."

"Maybe he has."

"No. We'd have heard something. I'm going back down."

"What? No."

"I have to. It'll look weird if I don't. Are you coming?"

"Are you crazy?"

"Fine. I'll tell them I tried to get you to come back but you refused to listen to reason."

"You really are a piece of shit."

"And you're the whipped cream on top." He opened the door.

And saw Hunter hurrying down the corridor.

"Holy crap."

"What?"

"I'm pretty sure I just saw Hunter."

"What? That's impossible. What would he be doing over here?"

"I'm wondering the same thing."

"You don't think . . ."

"I think we just bought ourselves another thirty minutes."

"Look who I found in the lobby," Rain said, gathering her newly acquired shawl around her as she and Steve rejoined the others.

"I was about to send out a search party," Jerrod said.

"I forgot I'd already packed the damn thing. Had to unpack my whole suitcase to find it."

Liar, liar, pants on fire, thought Steve. He smiled at Hunter.

What the hell is he smiling about? Hunter wondered.

"Serves you right for being so organized," said Peggy. "I haven't even started packing."

"I take it you couldn't convince Becky to come back," Caroline said to her brother.

Steve shrugged as he pulled out his chair

and sat down. “Women,” he said to the men present. “Can’t live with ’em, can’t shoot ’em.”

“Nice talk,” said Caroline.

The waiters returned and began preparing the crêpes.

“Kids okay?” Steve asked Hunter.

“Kids are fine,” Hunter said.

Thirty-Eight: The Present

Okay, so maybe it hadn't happened exactly that way, Caroline thought, watching the movie play out in her head again. Maybe she would never know the precise sequence of events of that night or the inflection of each spoken word. Maybe she'd never be privy to the actual thoughts of everyone involved, or the convoluted feelings behind those thoughts. But it didn't matter. She knew enough.

"Are you all right?" Samantha asked her.

Caroline nodded, focusing on the beautiful young girl kneeling in front of her.

"Are you sure?"

Caroline looked around the now empty living room, trying to remember when everybody had left. The dishes, along with the remains of the Chinese food and the empty beer bottles, had been cleared away, although an assortment of smells remained. "What time is it?"

"Almost midnight. Even the reporters have gone home."

Caroline smiled. "Where's Michelle?"

"Getting ready for bed. You should come, too."

"I will." She sighed. "How are *you* doing?"

"Okay. It's been quite the night."

"That it has." *My own brother,* Caroline was thinking. That her sister-in-law could have done something so heinous was bad enough, but *her own brother.* Had he really hated her that much?

Or worse, had he not cared at all?

Jerrod and Rain had left almost immediately after Greg Fisher escorted Steve to the waiting police car, Mary following them to the station in Steve's Buick. "There goes our lift," Rain had remarked.

Peggy could only shake her head. "At least she's consistent. You gotta give her that." She looked over at Hunter. "You're an idiot," she said.

"No arguments there," Hunter agreed. "I'm so sorry, Caroline," he apologized again.

"It wasn't your fault," Caroline said. "Turns out that even if you hadn't been with Rain, even if you *had* checked on the girls, it was too late. Samantha was already gone."

"Thank you for that," he said, turning to the daughter he'd lost. "I don't know what to say."

"You don't have to say anything," Samantha told him.

"I hope you'll give me a chance to make it up to you."

She nodded, allowing him to take her in his arms.

He kissed her forehead. "I'll call you tomorrow."

"Okay."

Peggy and Fletcher had helped Michelle clean up before they left. "Try to get some sleep," Peggy advised. "It's going to be another media circus tomorrow."

She was right, Caroline knew. Her brother's arrest meant more questions, more headlines, more public scrutiny. That was okay. She'd had fifteen years of practice. She could handle it.

The phone rang.

"Who's calling at this hour?" Samantha asked as Caroline reached for the phone.

"Hello, Mother," she said, not even bothering to check the caller ID.

"How could you?" Mary demanded.

"How could *I*?"

"They've arrested him. Charged him with kidnapping. Did you know there is no statute of limitations on kidnapping? That it's a federal offense? He could spend the rest of his life in jail."

"Which is no less than he deserves."

"You have to go to them, convince them it's all a tragic mistake. Michelle doesn't know what she's saying. She doesn't know what she saw."

"She knows *exactly* what she's saying. She knows *exactly* what she saw."

"Even if that were true, and I'm not saying it is, it happened so long ago, darling. Fifteen years!"

"I don't care if it was *fifty* years!"

"I understand you're angry. I really do. But what do you gain by putting your brother in jail? Samantha's home. You have your child back. Please don't take mine."

Caroline could scarcely believe her ears. Even coming from her mother, this was too much. "He's not a child, Mother. He's a grown man who committed an unspeakable act —"

"He was desperate. If he *was* involved with the mob, as you yourself suggested, they would have killed him. Maybe you, too. He didn't know what else to do."

"Are you seriously suggesting he did this

to protect *me*? That he had no other option but to kidnap my baby?"

"I'm saying he didn't know what else to do. He's weak, darling. He's always been weak. Not like you. You're so strong. You've always been so sure of yourself. There's a right answer, and there's a wrong answer. That's always been your motto."

"And the right answer in this case would be to let him off the hook?"

"What happened is a tragedy, darling. There's no doubt about that. But it has a happy ending. The right thing to do now would be to put it behind us and move on."

"I don't think I can do that."

"Then think of the horrible publicity, the indignity of a trial . . ."

Caroline almost laughed. "I assure you I'm way past worrying about indignity."

"I'm begging you not to do this."

"You're asking for too much."

An angry silence, followed by her mother's low growl. "He'll never be convicted," she said. "It's Michelle's word against his. The word of a mixed-up, spiteful young woman who'll do anything for attention . . ."

"Goodbye, Mother."

"Just think about what you're doing. He's your brother, for God's sake."

"No," Caroline said. "Not anymore. But

he is definitely your son." Then she pressed the key to disconnect the call.

The all-news channels were filled with breathless reports of her brother's arrest. Caroline watched them from her bed, switching channels continuously, as if one of them might tell her something she didn't already know. Samantha finished up in the bathroom, then crawled into bed beside her, glancing at the TV image of Greg Fisher guiding Steve from the house to the waiting police car. "Do you think he'll be convicted?"

"I have no idea."

"Maybe he'll cut a deal."

"Maybe."

"Do you think Beth knew?"

"I don't know," Caroline told her honestly. "But I'm sure the FBI will want to talk to her again. At the very least, she might be able to tell us more about the men her husband was involved with." She gathered their blankets around them. "Do you want to call her?"

"No."

"It's all right if you do."

"I don't want to speak to her ever again. I hate her."

"No, you don't. You love her. And that's

all right."

"How can I love her when she lied to me for fifteen years?"

"Because you do," Caroline said simply. "Because for fifteen years, she was the only mother you knew. Because she loved you and looked after you. And whatever else she did, however much she knew or didn't know, I have to be grateful to her for that."

Samantha burrowed in against Caroline's side. "Maybe I'll call her eventually. I don't know."

"You don't have to decide anything tonight."

"It'll be strange, not spending Christmas with my brothers."

"Well, maybe they can come visit one day." Caroline looked up, saw Michelle standing in the doorway.

"Is this a private party?" Michelle asked.

"It certainly is," Caroline said with a smile. "Only mothers and daughters allowed."

Michelle approached the bed, a small paper bag in her hand. She offered it to Caroline.

"What's this?"

"It's for the tree. I bought it this morning. When I was out walking around. I tried to get a star or a giant snowflake, but all they had left were angels. Not that I believe in that stuff. It was just all they had."

"It's lovely," Caroline said, taking the glittery, white plastic angel out of the bag and laying it on the night table beside the bed. "You can put it on the tree in the morning." She turned off the TV, pulled back the covers, and beckoned Michelle in. "Come on. Sleep here tonight. There's plenty of room."

"Nah. That's all right."

"Please," Caroline and Samantha said as one.

Michelle hesitated. But only for a moment. "All right. But I'm warning you," she said, climbing into bed beside her mother, "I move around a lot."

"You can dance, for all I care."

"I just might do that." Michelle reached over and turned off the bedside lamp, burrowing her backside into the concave curve of Caroline's stomach.

"Good night, Micki," Caroline said, kissing the top of her shoulder.

"Actually, I think I prefer 'Michelle.' "

"Good night, Michelle," Samantha said without missing a beat.

"Good night, Samantha."

Caroline smiled as Samantha's hand wrapped around her waist. At some point, it would undoubtedly benefit all of them to seek family counseling, but she'd deal with that later. Right now she just wanted to enjoy the moment, lying in her bed, her daughters' heartbeats bracketing her own. Tears filled her eyes and she stifled a sob.

"You're not going to make the pillow all wet, are you?" Michelle said.

"I just might do that," Caroline said, repeating Michelle's words.

"All right, but try to keep the noise to a minimum. Okay?"

"I'll try."

"Good night, Mommy," Michelle said.

"Good night, Mommy," Samantha echoed.

Tears of gratitude ran freely down Caroline's cheeks. "Good night, my beautiful, beautiful girls."

ACKNOWLEDGMENTS

You'd think I'd get tired of saying the same thing. But I don't.

As always, a huge debt of gratitude to my great friends Larry Mirkin and Beverley Slopen, who read early drafts of all my manuscripts and offer their comments and insights, most of which make it into the final product in one way or another. I also want to thank my husband, Warren, and my daughter, Shannon, for their help in this regard. It's never easy to accept criticism from one's family, but either I'm getting mellower or they're getting better at it. At any rate, I took their comments into account and this novel is the better for it. Thanks also to my wonderful agent, Tracy Fisher, with WME Entertainment, who has been a tireless and brilliant supporter, as well as a good and reliable critic, and to her former assistant James Munro and her current one, Alli Dyer, for all their hard work on my behalf. Then there's my terrific editor, Linda Marrow, who is able to look at the material I submit and pinpoint the exact areas requiring special attention. Just as important, she's able to tell me why. A nod also to Dana Isaacson for his careful attention to detail and suggested line edits, as well as to Elana Seplow-Jolley for her patience and hard work. And to Steve Messina, the production editor, for doing such a great job.

To Lindsey Kennedy and Allison Schuster, who work in publicity and marketing — thank you for all your efforts in getting my book out there. And to Scott Biel for his wonderful cover design. You're amazing.

A special thank-you to all the people at Penguin Random House in Canada, although I really wish the newly merged company had chosen the name Random Penguin, simply because it's such a wonderful image. To Brad Martin, Kristin Cochrane, Adria Iwasutiak, Val Gow, Constance McKenzie, Martha Leonard, Amy Black, Erin Kelly, and everyone else involved in the publishing of my books, thank you for your continuing support and hard work. You had a vision for making my novels a success and it worked, and for that I'm beyond grateful. I'm also grateful to Nita Pronovost. Even though she is no longer with PRH, I felt her hand guiding mine as I pruned and trimmed the manuscript, ridding the prose of unnecessary clutter and repetition. I wish her all the best in her new position.

Heartfelt thanks to Corinne Assayag at World Exposure, the company she founded while putting herself through law school, and which grew to be such a success that she never got around to practicing law. She recently redesigned my website (joyfielding.com) to make it a more interactive and state-of-the-art experience, and I think she succeeded brilliantly. Let me know if you agree.

Again, my thanks to my various publishers around the world and their wonderful translators. Please keep doing what you've been doing all these years. However my words are being refigured and expressed, it's obviously working.

A special shout-out to Helga Mahmoud-Trainer in Germany, as well as an admonishment to stay well.

To my publishers who've only recently joined the fold, welcome aboard. I hope you'll enjoy the ride.

Thank you to Annie, Courtney, Renee, and Aurora for all the love and help you give me on a daily basis. I love you, too. And to my beautiful grandchildren, to whom I've dedicated this book, I wish for you the happiness in your lives that you've given me in mine. You're the best.

These acknowledgments would be incomplete without mentioning my very own long-deceased grandmother Mary, my father's mother and as miserable a woman as ever walked this earth. She was the inspiration for Grandma Mary, and while this novel is unquestionably a work of fiction, many of the quotes attributed to her came straight from her mouth. There are times, as Caroline observes, when "you can't make this stuff up."

ABOUT THE AUTHOR

Joy Fielding is the *New York Times* best-selling author of *Someone Is Watching, Now You See Her, Still Life, Mad River Road, See Jane Run,* and other acclaimed novels. She divides her time between Toronto and Palm Beach, Florida.

JoyFielding.com
@JoyFielding

The employees of Thorndike Press hope you have enjoyed this Large Print book. All our Thorndike, Wheeler, and Kennebec Large Print titles are designed for easy reading, and all our books are made to last. Other Thorndike Press Large Print books are available at your library, through selected bookstores, or directly from us.

For information about titles, please call:
(800) 223-1244

or visit our Web site at:
http://gale.cengage.com/thorndike

To share your comments, please write:
Publisher
Thorndike Press
10 Water St., Suite 310
Waterville, ME 04901